AUDREY D. DEBOER

Vispilio

First edition

ISBN: 979-8-9921045-0-9

Cover art by Cover Kitchen

This book was professionally typeset on Reedsy.
Find out more at reedsy.com

To everyone who encouraged me to keep writing.

Acknowledgments

A story 15 years in the making doesn't get started or finished on its own.

I don't remember which teacher assigned the short story to me. It might have been Mr. S. It might have been Mrs. V. All I know is it was in 6th grade, and that was the first time Antony came into my life. Adelaide, John, Carter, and the rest came not long after.

I want to thank Mr S. and Mrs. V., regardless. Both of you were instrumental in my growth as a writer. Mr. S., thank you for spending so much time in history on the Middle Ages. You have no idea how much that shaped me as a person.

Thank you, Mr. V., for reading some of my stories aloud in our fifth-grade class. I cringe about it now, but hearing my words told as a story to others changed me for life.

Thank you to C, E, L, and so many others who were the first readers of the printed-out (on our home printer, with a hand-drawn cover) copy of *Vispilio.* Your feedback was invaluable...even if I didn't use it all.

Thank you, Mom and Dad. I spent a lot of your money on printer paper. And notebooks. And workshops. Ask me about royalties. I won't get offended.

And I can't talk about *Vispilio* without talking about the man who inspired him—Robin Hood, whoever he was, or wasn't. Thank you to everyone who has ever told his story. I've read and watched so many versions. His story deserves to be told—a story of fighting against tyranny, of standing up when things aren't right.

Thank you to Todd for starting a virtual writers' group in that encouraged me to keep writing even when things were uncertain. Thank you to all the members of that group, past and present—Ian R., Anna, Ian G.,

Gordon, Mike, James, Perry, and Zach.

Thank you to Faith for your developmental edits on an early draft when I got serious about publishing in 2021. Your edits kicked me in the pants and got me to tell the story I really wanted to tell.

Thank you endlessly to Veronica for your thoughtful coaching and feedback. Thank you to Max at First Book Coaching for introducing me to Veronica, and being patient with me until I finally said, "I'm ready!"

Thank you so much to my beta readers. You helped me get the final draft on track and helped me understand my future readers better. I hope the book was a gift to you as well. You were certainly a gift to me.

On that note, thank you to my advance reviewers—especially Meredith, my dear friend and fellow writer and story-lover.

Thank you, Jerry. You didn't have to download your wife's manuscript into a PDF to read on your Kindle instead of reading *Eragon*, but you did. And I love you endlessly for it.

I would be remiss if I didn't acknowledge the One True Myth that all other myths are mere shadows of. I hope and pray that in some small way, this myth may point you to the only one in history that has ever been true—the true myth of creation, fall, redemption, and restoration.

Thank you, reader, for reading. For being hungry for this kind of story. There's more coming. I hope it doesn't disappoint.

Audrey D. DeBoer
August 2024

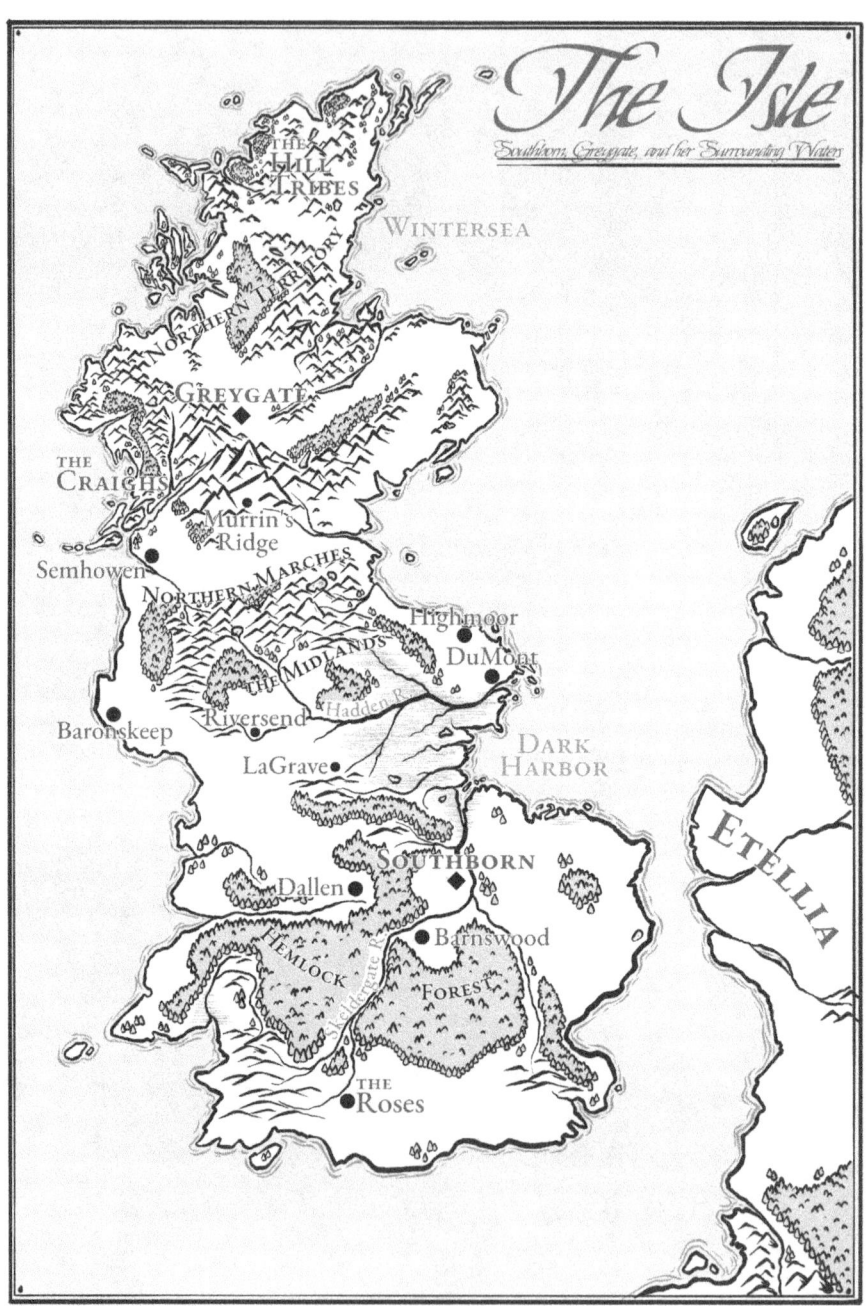

I

PROLOGUE

The Woodsman

He called his daughter's name, and the trees echoed it back.

She's done this before, he thought as the cold nagged at his thin tunic. *She knows her way home.*

But this time felt different. The Harvestmonth night felt so total around him. The girl was only ten but knew her way around the Hemlock Forest. She'd never come into contact with anything—or anyone—that could harm her in those woods.

That may have just been luck.

The woodsman chopped the trees of the forest to make his living, yet he didn't dare to step into the forest as far as she. He could understand why she loved it. Hemlock was ethereal, magical even. Great, wide oaks that seemed a thousand years old and a thousand feet tall stretched above him, their drying leaves falling in a steady rhythm to the ground. He watched his step for fear of tripping over their gigantic roots.

He wasn't a superstitious man, but he felt the coarse hairs rise on the back of his neck as though he were being watched—studied. The women of Barnswood liked to talk about how the trees of the Hemlock came alive at night and would dance under the Harvestmonth moon. The woodsman looked up at the bright silver orb resting just above the skeletal trees. On a night like this, he could almost believe the stories.

The forest was too quiet. It waited with him for something to happen. It held its breath.

He made to call his daughter's name again, but the sound stopped in his throat when he saw the body.

The woodsman's breath caught at the sight, thinking for one horrifying moment it was his girl lying there, a bundle of crumpled clothing. But then he saw the length of the body, the outstretched arm, and saw that it was a man. A long, narrow shaft jutted from the man's back. An arrow.

He scrambled to the body. His first thought was outlaws. They would be quick to kill a villager who entered their territory. The woodsman scanned the dark forest around him. Then he looked down at the body.

The man was on his stomach, his head turned to one side. A handsome face, with dark hair that glowed in the moonlight. He wore a long, luxurious cloak brightly embroidered, and the arm that extended from his body wore a velvet tunic.

"By Aug's beard," he breathed.

The man's eyes snapped open, stared at him helplessly. The eyes were unafraid.

"Your grace," said the woodsman. "Your majesty."

The pale face smiled. "No longer," he breathed.

Then, the king of Southborn died.

The woodsman remained still, kneeling beside the body of King Alfred. He'd never seen the king in the flesh before, only his likeness on tapestries and coins. He seemed so young, younger than the woodsman himself. His face was stern, yet noble, even in death. His dark eyes shone like dying embers, even as their light went out.

"May the Nine carry you to your rest," whispered the woodsman.

He jumped when he heard feet crashing through the underbrush. He darted away into the trees, his heart pounding.

There he waited, hoping to see his girl's small form appear in the clearing. But those footsteps were too loud. His daughter knew better than to crash around like that and cause a ruckus. The woodsman feared his heart thundered so hard it could be heard throughout the forest.

Two men appeared, one tall and one short. The shorter one held a long, deadly bow in his hands, but he threw it into the underbrush as they approached the body.

"Murder!" cried the taller man over his shoulder. The woodsman thought he heard a distant thrum, like hoof beats. "They've killed the king!"

The shorter man knelt beside the king and put a hand on his neck. "Dead," he said gruffly.

The taller man's shoulders heaved, as though he were breathing a heavy sigh.

"Thank you, Edwin," he murmured. The woodsman could see the outline of a sharp nose and a strong chin as the taller man looked around.

"The king is dead," said the shorter man, looking up at his companion. "Long live King Tanor."

His companion shushed him. "Soon," he said.

Another figure clambered out of the underbrush. This one was small and thin. A child, but not his daughter. A boy—a small boy.

"John," barked the bigger man. "Is it done?"

The boy, panting, turned and vomited. The bigger man scoffed.

"He's never seen death before, Lord Tanor," said the smaller man. "Look at him. He's covered in blood. Must have been worse than Innermost Hell for him."

The woodsman saw dark stains on the boy's tunic, as rich and velveteen as the king's. His stomach turned. His thoughts turned to his daughter. *Whoever these folks are,* he thought, *they can't find her.*

The bigger man's head snapped up, and for a moment it seemed as though he stared right at the woodsman in the silver light. The woodsman dipped deeper into the shadow as silently as he could. There was no way the man could see him—was there? At this hour, the Hemlock Forest was made of shadow. Men could see that which wasn't there without seeing what actually was.

The woodsman bolted from the scene. He knew how to run through the brush undetected. He'd done it before to avoid being caught chopping wood from the king's forest. A man crashed and crunched recklessly through the brush. A deer, however, bounded in quick jumps and light steps. He kept his strides long and quick—the two men wouldn't suspect a thing.

Don't forget what you've seen tonight. The thought surprised him. All he wanted was to forget what he'd just seen. He expected to hear footsteps pounding behind him. *Saint Aug, let them strike me down. Let them kill me for what I've just seen. Don't let this burden fall on me. Just let me find her.*

He stopped, out of breath. His lungs burned from the cold. For a moment, that was all he could hear, that and the blood rushing through his ears, eliminating the silence of the night.

But that blood turned cold when his breaths quieted, and he heard footsteps running behind him. *Don't let them find her,* he thought desperately.

But the footsteps were quiet—too fast and nimble to be a grown man.

A small, warm body collided with him, wrapping its small arms around his waist. His little girl buried herself in his tunic, her shoulders shaking with sobs. His heart wrenched as he lifted her in his arms, her tiny frame feather-light. She immediately dug her face into his neck.

He whispered her name and stroked her red hair, tinged with silver in the moonlight. His heart could have burst with relief.

"You're all right," he said. "You're all right."

His girl looked at him, her big eyes red and swollen, her lip trembling. She tried to catch her breath to speak to him. She nodded.

"I found Antony," she said. "I found him."

But the words didn't stop her tears.

II

Part One: The Prince that Was Lost

10 Years Later

King Tanor

He'd dreamed the same dream for the third night in a row and awakened alone as the first light of dawn crept through his window.

And as he'd done the previous nights, Tanor Behrens, King of Southborn, lay in silence and considered what the dream could mean. They all had meaning. Each one had meant something, ever since he was a boy.

In the dream, Tanor was in the woods again. Edwin was beside him, bow in hand. The former king, Alfred, lay bleeding before them, just as he had that Harvestmonth night. The memory was so vivid in his mind, burned there like a brand.

But the dream was not the memory. As he and Edwin spoke in the dream, a beast emerged from the woods—a beast that seemed to be made completely of darkness. Shaped like a man, but no man that Tanor had ever seen. It seemed to loom larger and larger every night, and every night it held a severed head in its hand. Tanor didn't know whose head it was.

Every night, it whispered something to Tanor.

You are not the only Unburied Boy.

In the dream, Edwin never heeded the monster. He always asked Tanor the same question before the king awoke—"What shall we do now, your grace?"

Light crawled further into Tanor's bedchamber, illuminating the wide wooden canopy above his bed, the thick purple rug on the floor, the huge hearth glowing with embers that had kept him warm all night. Dawn rose on the first day of Harvestmonth, and the first day in ten years that the South had not been at war.

He would officially proclaim the victory to the people of Southborn that morning, and their strife would be over. Their king had won against the treacherous North and had gained a foothold in the mountains that divided the two kingdoms.

Maybe once the celebrations began, the nightmare would stop.

It could mean anything, Tanor thought. The image of the beast still hovered in his mind. Some said that in times of war, demons were released from Innermost Hell to torment the world while blood was spilled. Perhaps the beast was a demon, reminding him he sent so many men to war yet never set foot in the North himself.

Or it was to tell him that his son, John, had died. Tanor wouldn't be surprised if he were—the little runt couldn't fight his way out of a cloth sack when he was a child. Perhaps the severed head belonged to his son.

A thought made Tanor sit up in bed. For once he was glad he awoke alone—the queen slept alone during her pregnancy and his lover had left long before midnight. Either would have thought him mad to see the wildness in his eyes.

Was someone in the woods that night?

He relived every moment in his mind: Edwin firing two arrows from a safe, undetectable distance. The sight of Alfred, unmoving, unbreathing. Calling out to the rest of the hunting party in a frenzy. John reappearing, covered in blood.

And Tanor turned and saw a shadow in the forest beyond. A man-shaped shadow. A shadow that dissolved into the surrounding darkness.

The thought set Tanor's heart racing. That night was a buried secret he had lied and killed and started a war for. *You are not the only Unburied Boy.*

"Be careful of the deeds you do in the dark," his father had once said. "They will always be brought to light."

Doddering old fool, Tanor thought as he lay back with a heavy thud. The shadow had only been a shadow. If it had been a man, it was more likely an outlaw, a vagrant who wouldn't dare speak of what he saw for fear of punishment.

His heartbeat slowed. The light crept in further, milky and pale. The palace around him would be waking up by now, preparing for the king's announcement. They would celebrate him and his victory. He would throw a ball for them, and they would love him even more. That's what being a king meant, he'd realized long ago—in a storm of being hated and criticized on every side, finding moments he could be loved.

King Tanor closed his eyes and went back to sleep as the day dawned.

Antony

Most people who picked a fight with him went down fairly easily—they threw punches as if they were throwing rotten fruit at Antony's face.

But Robert the Red, one of the biggest men in Barnswood, was a different opponent entirely.

Antony had been in a good mood—the war in the North was over. News had filtered from Southborn that the Northern men had retreated over the mountains, and the Northern queen, now a widow, had begged for mercy. King Tanor had announced it two weeks before—the South was victorious.

Bourne Tavern was busier than it had been in months, maybe years. Townsfolk brought their instruments—their lyres and hornpipes and fiddles—and the barroom became a dance hall. Antony had caught the eye of Marie, the miller's daughter, and under the influence of too many tankards of ale, had asked her to dance. In the swirl of motion, Marie had taken him back to the stable and planted a firm kiss on his lips, cupping her soft hands around his jaw.

Robert had found them, stumbling out of the tavern, looking for her. Robert wasn't much taller than Antony himself, but a good deal wider. And while Antony had the powerful arms of a bowyer, he wasn't a solid wall of flesh like Robert was.

"You want to dance, squirrel?" Robert had said, sizing him up with beady, dark eyes. "Then dance with *me*."

Robert had thrown the first punch—and missed, his knuckles connecting with the wooden post at the stable's entryway. Half-drunk men who had stepped out of the barroom to relieve themselves stayed to watch. They all knew Robert, and they all knew Antony. They seemed to think Robert had victory in hand. Antony heard them placing bets.

"Two pennies says I can hit him square in the nose," Antony said to one of them while Robert was wringing out his hand. The drunk man smirked and shook Antony's hand.

"You can't just kiss another man's lass, Antony," said the man. Antony turned to watch Robert stalk toward him.

"I didn't know Marie was anyone's lass," Antony retorted, not breaking eye contact with Robert. The man's thick red beard was matted with sweat and mead, and an oily smile spread across his face.

"All right, squirrel," he said, his voice coming from deep within his barrel-shaped chest. "Time to dance."

Antony braced himself as the big man charged toward him. For all his girth, Robert moved pretty fast. Antony's instinct was to dodge him, but he stood his ground and braced himself.

It wasn't a good idea.

His tense body felt the full impact of Robert's as they collided. Robert threw him back into the dirt, and the onlookers jeered and snarled. They backed away as Antony landed. The wind left his lungs and a throbbing pain burst across his back. He lay there for a moment, stunned, wondering if he could stand up again. Then, a blond head appeared in his line of vision, glaring down at him.

"What did you get yourself into this time, little brother?"

Two big hands grabbed Antony's arms and pulled him back to his feet. Robert had backed up heavily, waiting for Antony to stand, like a wolf circling his prey.

"I'll tell you later, Carter," Antony patted his brother's shoulder and turned back around. He heard Carter sigh behind him. Antony still felt the impact of Robert's tackle in his bones. He'd be smarter this time. The onlookers pawed at him as he returned to the makeshift circle they had created. He looked across the circle and saw Marie, who stood behind

Robert with her arms crossed. Antony gave her a slight, annoyed shake of his head. She merely shrugged and smirked.

Antony shook off the blow and balanced on the balls of his feet. He could tell Robert would charge again—he'd keep charging at him until he won, until he wore Antony down. That's what big men did. They tried to overpower without a strategy. Skill had nothing to do with it.

But Antony was ready this time. Robert charged and, just before the moment of impact, Antony skirted to the left on nimble feet, like a dancer. Robert tripped and splayed on the ground, right in front of Carter. The crowd reacted with brays of laughter. Hearing the crowd turn against him, Robert growled and scrambled back to his feet. He charged again, harder this time. This time Antony not only dodged his girth but also stuck out his foot, and Robert fell, splayed out again on the floor. A roar rose from the appreciative crowd. Robert looked up at Antony with poisonous eyes. Antony shrugged and cocked an eyebrow at him.

He could tell Robert was enraged as he heaved himself onto his feet. He backed up and stamped his feet like a wild boar.

"You can't win this, Antony," Carter warned. "Run while you still can. Robert won't quit."

"Not before I hand him his arse," Antony said.

When Robert charged again, Antony ducked down and braced himself. He felt all of Robert's bulk tumble over him and winced as one of Robert's feet caught his rib cage. Robert toppled head over heels and landed on his back. Antony quickly unfurled himself and straddled Robert's stomach, trying to keep him down. It proved a difficult task. Robert tossed about like a fussy child, flailing his arms and trying to push Antony off him by clawing at his face. One of his fingers caught on Antony's lip and tore it from the inside. Antony prayed to every one of the nine saints he could think of and punched Robert in the nose. And once more, for good measure.

Robert's head lolled to one side, and he lay motionless, his arms falling limp to the ground. The giant was felled. Antony heaved an exhausted sigh of relief. He turned to the drunk man he'd made the bet with.

"I think that will be *four* pennies," Antony said.

The drunk man scoffed. "That weren't the deal and you know't." He tossed two copper coins onto the ground and retreated inside.

"You really can't help yourself, can you?" Carter asked as the rest of the onlookers filtered back inside. Robert was still out cold. Even Marie had abandoned him. "You know he'll be twice as angry when he wakes up."

"I'll just make sure I'm not here when he wakes up," Antony said. He scooped up the pennies. "Let's get a drink."

The inside of the Bourne Tavern was just as raucous as when Marie had pulled Antony away. Carter and Antony dodged the dancers who reeled across the barroom, the tables and chairs of which were pushed aside for such an occasion. The damp heat of so many sweaty bodies and the hoppy scent of ale hit them as they entered. Dancers skirted carelessly past him and his older brother, jostling Antony's already sore body. Carter pushed through them like a determined mule toward the bar. He'd never been one for revelry.

Fred, the tavern keeper, greeted them, and Carter wordlessly held up two fingers. The merry barkeep whirled around and poured two fresh tankards from the tap. Antony sat and immediately downed half of his.

"The lads are saying you cleaned my stable with Rob the Red," Fred said over the roar of his patrons.

"Yes, sir," said Antony with a smirk. He caught Carter rolling his eyes as he took a draft of ale.

Fred chuckled, his giant belly jiggling as he wiped sweat from his broad forehead. "Can't even be cross with you on a night like tonight," he said. "One of the best nights I've had in years. Instead of men comin' in to drown their sorrows, they're here to celebrate."

Antony slurped his ale greedily, glancing over his shoulder. No sign of Robert.

"Would you like another, boyo?" asked Fred. Antony nodded.

Carter sat next to him, turning his body toward the door. He wiped froth from the ale off his chin with the back of his hand.

"You should settle down and marry, Antony, instead of kissing other men's women," he said.

Antony raised his hands in defense. "I didn't know Marie was anyone's woman."

"Shows how much you pay attention," Carter said. "Robert started courting her when he got back from the North almost two years ago, but she kept refusing, 'til one day Robert's father up and dies and leaves him the tannery."

"What's that supposed to mean?" Antony asked.

"It means," Carter said, "that Marie never set out to marry a bowmaker's apprentice, with nary a penny to his name."

"I have *two* pennies to my name," Antony replied, placing the coppers on the table. Fred swiped them up gratefully.

"All I know is *I'm* not paying for you to get drunk tonight. And I won't have to explain to Pa why you're late in the morning."

"I won't be late," Antony said. He took a sip from his new tankard. His head spun—he needed to slow down. Their father, Bron, was the village bowyer. He knew he had to meet with a potential buyer in Southborn the next day. And he knew he'd be on time with it. He certainly wouldn't miss the Commoner's Ball the following night. The ball would have plenty of other girls to kiss and ale that was leagues better than Fred's.

The merry music had petered out behind him, and the throng of villagers had hushed. He turned around, afraid he'd look straight into the eyes of Robert the Red. But he didn't.

The doors of the tavern had swung open and a rugged group of five soldiers stepped in, some of them blinking in the barroom's light. A short man led them in, his boyish face scanning the room, looking for a table. He limped, as though he had a wounded leg. His men followed him in the sudden silence, some of them glancing cautiously back and forth. They looked weather-beaten and exhausted, their cloaks tousled from travel. Antony saw their armor, the long shirts of chain mail they wore under their cloaks, the green tunics they wore that bore the silver dragon of Southborn—the sigil of the king's army. They were returning home to the capital.

16

A burly man whose face was red from drink loped up to the short man and put a heavy hand on the commander's shoulder.

"You're home," said the burly man. "It's over."

The short man smiled ruefully and covered the burly man's hand with his own. "So we are," he breathed. His face was round and ruddy—he may not have been much older than Antony's twenty-three years.

The burly man stretched one enormous arm toward the bar. "Their first round's on me, Fred!" he roared, and the din of the tavern started up again. The big man led the group of soldiers to a table shoved up in the corner.

Antony watched the group of men shuffle to the table. Something about them seemed relieved and content, but tense. He had noticed it when men had come home to Barnswood from the war, from injury or insanity, or simply because they were no longer needed. Some of them had a difficult time returning to ordinary life, of no longer being on guard at all hours of the day. These soldiers all watched warily as the burly man doled out their drinks, but then smiled warmly as he walked away. Other patrons in the tavern gathered around them as the music swelled again. They patted the men on their shoulders and shook hands. And it wasn't long into their first round of ale some women in the tavern invited them upstairs. Antony was surprised that one of those women wasn't Marie.

Antony was so preoccupied watching their table that he hadn't noticed one knight had sat down at the bar a few chairs away from him and Carter. The man hunched his broad shoulders over the bar and cupped his tankard of ale in one hand, gazing at the wall across from him. Fred had a likeness of Saint Hogarth mounted over the bar. Hogarth was the patron saint of laborers, and men like Fred believed that having his likeness in his place of business would make him prosperous.

But the man wasn't looking at that. Antony could tell that he wasn't looking at anything at all. He seemed to stare at something hundreds of yards away and only in his imagination. He had a young face with a high forehead and a dark, heavy brow that carried a haunted expression.

"You all right, mate?" Antony leaned closer to him, startling the man out of his trance. The man blinked a few times and swung his gaze toward

Antony. He had eyes the color of sea glass, a blue so pale it was almost colorless.

"Yes," said the man. His voice was deep and quiet. He took a long draft of ale.

"How long were you there?" Antony asked. "North, I mean."

"Ten years," replied the man. Dark whiskers flecked his face, which he scratched absently. "I was thirteen when I left. I went as a squire and came back as a knight."

The man was the same age as Antony, he realized. "What's it like up there?" Antony prodded. "Is it as bad as everyone says?"

The young man's face was expressionless. "Worse," he said. He took another long drink and then pushed the tankard toward Fred. He sighed. "I'll take another, please."

"A lot of boys from this village have gone up there," said Antony. "Some of them come back, some don't. They tell me grown men become so terrified at the sight of the Northern armies they piss themselves."

The man scoffed and smirked mirthlessly. His gaze locked into the middle distance once more, as if he were picturing it all over again.

Antony was going to ask him another question when he felt Carter's hand squeeze his shoulder tight.

"Brother," Carter said with warning in his voice. "Turn around."

When Antony did, he saw Robert shuffling toward him through the crowd, his face smeared with mud. The young knight took notice as well, throwing a glance over his shoulder.

Robert shoved a few patrons aside to get to Antony. "You little bastard," he snarled, spittle flying over his red beard. Dried blood still clung to the corners of his nose, and his eye was quickly swelling shut.

"I won fair and square, Robert," Antony said, his voice sounding smaller than he intended. "And I promise you, I'll never kiss Marie again."

"You cheated!" Robert spat.

A hand landed on Robert's shoulder, and Antony looked over. The knight at the bar had stood up. He was a giant, towering over everyone else in the room. Robert's gaze crawled up the man's arm and looked into his face. As he searched the man's face, a look of fear grew in his eyes.

"Johnny Behrens?" Robert sputtered. "Johnny, I haven't seen you in—"

"In a long time, I know," said the man. "Ever since we were fighting on the same front. Remember how you used to bully all the squires? Pick on boys who were smaller than you?"

Robert's one good eye darted back from Antony to the man. "He—he kissed my girl! He kissed Marie!"

The man's hand didn't relent in its grip on Robert's shoulder. The knight pushed Robert back firmly, his arm straight and muscles taut.

"Would Marie like to know about all the Northern women you took by force?"

Robert's eyes widened. "No!" Antony had never heard the big man sound so frightened. Robert looked around and quieted his voice. "No, don't tell Marie. She's a good girl, she is."

"Not really," Antony muttered into his tankard of ale.

"Get out," said the knight. "Go home to Marie. We've won the war. I'd like to say you helped us win it, but I can't help but remember when you pissed yourself at the sight of the Northern army."

The knight cast a sideways glance at Antony, one eyebrow cocked. Antony felt a wash of relief as Robert skittered back and pushed out of the tavern as fast as he could go, running into patrons as he went. A few people watched, hiding smiles behind their hands and glancing at the tall knight.

The knight sat back down as if nothing had happened, grabbing his tankard and taking a long drink.

"Thank you," Antony said. "You didn't have to do that."

"I wanted to," said the knight. "Robert's always been a bully."

"Can I repay you?" Antony asked.

The knight turned to him. "Maybe someday you can," he said. "What's your name?"

"Antony Bronson," said Antony, and stuck out his hand.

"John Behrens," said the knight. He clasped Antony's hand and pumped it once. Then he turned to Fred, fishing two large silver coins out of a pouch at his side. He placed them on the table.

"For the ale," John said. "And a room. It's too late for us to be riding the Weschurch Road."

"Of course, sir," Fred said. "My wife will show you upstairs."

John stood up and nodded once to Antony and his brother. "Until we meet again, Bronson." Antony silently lifted his almost-empty tankard to him as the knight ducked into the stairway leading up to the inn's rooms, following Fred's wife.

"I'll be damned," Carter breathed as soon as he was gone. "Johnny Behrens, the royal bastard."

Antony grimaced. "What?"

Carter leaned in. "The king's whoreson. King Tanor probably thought he'd die out there." Carter's wide face broke into a smile. "I wish I could see the look on His Royal Ass's face when his son jaunts into the castle tomorrow."

Antony was still confused. He'd never heard of him. News about the royal family only came to them when a town crier made a proclamation, or when he ventured to the capital on business. "I thought King Tanor only had one child—his son Charles, with the queen consort."

Carter hesitated. He had a strange look on his face. "You *would* think that." He slapped his younger brother on the back.

I guess I would, thought Antony absently, his brain muffled by drink. *If it happened before the fall, I guess I wouldn't have known.*

"I have to get back to the farm," Carter said. He was a day laborer for Barnswood's grain farmer, and it was harvest time. "Don't drink too much, little brother."

Antony nodded and watched his brother's broad shoulders squeeze through the dwindling crowd. He looked over at the weary knights. Two of them still sat at the table, conversing quietly with one another. What would they do now? They'd spent half their lives fighting. Would they simply forget all about the battles they fought and go on living? Antony was glad he'd never had to fight a war. And he prayed to all the Nine that he'd never have to.

John

He lay awake in the cold, dim hours of the morning. John had begun the night on the small straw cot in the room of the inn, but it was too short for him, and he'd spent the last ten years either sleeping on the ground or on a pallet as thick as a man's thumb.

The cot was too soft. The floor was better.

Still, he couldn't sleep. Crickets sang somewhere in the meadows that surrounded the village of Barnswood. He smelled the dew settling on the eaves of the inn—the smells of the South. It was still so damn hot, even after nightfall. Something he'd have to get used to again.

And he'd have to get used to the memories. The memories of hacking. The sickening thud of a sword hammering into flesh. John remembered the look in his eyes. He had never seen anyone more afraid, not even Adrian when—

John sat straight up on the floor, his heart pounding. He banged the heel of his hand against his forehead as if to shake those memories out. With all the things he'd seen in the North, it had been easy to cast those memories aside, to bury them deep.

John lay back down. He stretched his long limbs, feeling the strength pulse through them. Ten years. And the next day he would see his father again. The one who'd created this Innermost Hell for him.

He lifted the sword, his arms shaking from the weight. It glinted at him with a deadly wink. He had hoped that one simple chop would do the trick and it would be over with. But it wasn't. It took cut after cut, as though he were cutting a branch off a tree. That horrible feeling, as the blade cut through bone and flesh...

John's stomach turned. Before he'd gone to war, Lord Edwin had told him he'd never forget his first kill. And he hadn't. He lived it night after night, even after the memories of all his others had faded away.

As he finally found sleep, a final thought crossed his consciousness. He wondered if he'd ever have to kill again.

Antony

"*H*old still. Do you see it?"

Antony saw it. The dappled side of a fat doe. Her neck was bent as she rooted through the brambles for food, but Antony knew by the flicking of her ears she was keenly aware of any movement around her. His movement would have to be quick, lest it be futile. Each breath he took seemed thunderous in his ears.

In one determined fist, he held his longbow. It was shorter than his father's by nearly half, crafted just for him, and he'd spent long hours practicing to become strong enough to draw it. An arrow waited on the string, nocked and ready. He felt his father's eyes watching him.

"Focus on your target," said his father, his voice just below a whisper. Antony focused. "Only draw when you're ready. It's like taking a breath."

The autumn sun was setting fast, leaving only a fiery red glow beyond the trees behind the doe. Branches and brambles rose around her like shadowy, skeletal fingers, while a tepid moon hung in the sky, ready to take over her kingdom. In the daytime, the Hemlock Forest was beautiful, almost fairylike, even in autumn, but at night it became dark and foreboding.

Antony drew his bow, took a breath, and fired—

Antony's eyes snapped open. Groggily, he lifted his head, feeling his whole body lurch as he did so. As he blinked in the bright light of day in the tavern windows, he cursed.

"Shit," he moaned.

Outside, he could hear the sounds of a day in Barnswood—carts rattling down the main road, the lowing of a herd of cattle, the cluck of chickens.

23

Muted conversations over breakfast all around him in the inn. He caught the eye of Fred as the rotund man dragged a broom across the floor.

"Too much celebration for you, Bronson?" Fred asked with a heavy chuckle. "You've slept half the morning away. Wasn't gonna bother you."

"*Shit.*" Antony found himself fully awake. He leaped off the bar stool and pushed past Fred, but immediately regretted charging into the morning light. It pierced his eyes like an arrow. He wanted to lie down again, preferably somewhere dark and quiet. But if he did, he would be even later. He very well might have missed his appointment in Southborn already.

He staggered out of the alley and onto the main road. If he'd walked the other way down the alley, he would've walked past the brothel—a fairly modest one for a fairly modest town. That part of the village was called The Skirts for a reason—men fled there after dark to find the warm embrace of a woman. He imagined a few of the knights from the tavern had found themselves there.

Memories from the night before came back in glimpses. Marie. Robert the Red. The big knight who had saved Antony's hide from Rob the second time. His head may have smarted, but Antony hadn't seen the tavern that busy and joyous in a long time. They'd won the war. Things would be better now.

The street eventually widened as Antony neared his father's house. Here, the houses were less crowded and had clean upstream water in the river behind them. Antony could hear it gurgling, satisfied by the early autumn rains.

Antony's father had done well for himself, all things considered. He was a bowyer like his father before him and had lived his quiet life in his quiet village. He was well-loved and admired by the villagers and their lord—his weapons helped keep the savage Northerners at bay.

Antony's heart sank when he saw his father in front of the house, hitching the mule to its cart. The cart was laden with bows for the Southborn contact. Autumn was a good time to sell bows, just before deer rutted and the weather became too cold to hunt.

Bron turned to look at his son with quick brown eyes. His eyes were always keen, whether he was hunting a deer or a suspicion.

"Antony!" he called out cheerfully. Bron had a big, deep voice that on this morning grated on Antony's ears. "The wayward apprentice returns." Bron tugged on the mule's bridle. The rolled-up sleeves of his tunic revealed his sinewy forearms. They rippled as he brushed his hands on his shirt front.

Antony could tell his father was impatient with him, even behind his smile. He threw open his arms.

"Here I am," he said. He probably looked as well as his voice sounded.

"Quite the to-do at Bourne Tavern last night?" Bron asked, looking Antony up and down. Antony knew his tunic was disheveled and probably covered in mud. He felt as though his father was being loud on purpose. "I heard you made Rob the Red quite angry."

"He deserved it," Antony grumbled. He walked up to the cart and looked down at the bows laid neatly on the cart's bed. Bron pulled a leather canvas over them.

"Well, if you were merely my son and not my apprentice," Bron said, "*you'd* deserve a whipping for being so late. If you're going to run my shop when I'm dead, you'd best be up before the sun."

"You won't die for another hundred years, Pa," Antony said with a smirk. Moving his face too much made his head hurt worse.

Bron chuckled and slapped Antony on the back. It didn't help his headache. "Go in and put yourself together. Sam has been fed and watered, so he won't tarry on the road." He gently patted the old mule's neck. Sam shook his big ears gratefully.

Antony dragged his feet as he entered the house. He was three-and-twenty, far past the age of being chastised by his father, but that didn't make him above reproach. Selling bows in Southborn would make them the money they'd need to last them through the year and to pay the Harvestmonth tax.

Bron's workshop was at the front of the house, with a workbench in the corner where a freshly steamed yew bough lay. Bron used the fresh water from the river to steam young branches into bendable pieces he would string into bows.

As Antony entered the house, he saw his younger brother, Benjamin, sitting in front of the hearth, whittling at something. He tiptoed behind the boy and grabbed his shoulders.

The boy jumped, dropping his project. He turned and looked up at Antony with startled eyes.

"I could've cut myself!" he whined. He held a small piece of wood in his hand that he was carving into a figure. Ben was thirteen, a thin, reedy boy, but blond and fair like his brother Carter. They'd gotten that from their mother, not dark-eyed, dark-haired Bron. Antony had taken more after their father.

Antony laughed and ruffled Ben's hair. "Not with a knife that dull," he said. "We need to get you a good hunting knife one of these days. You're old enough for it."

"And *you're* old enough to be home in time to muck out Sam's stable," Ben said. "It's not even nine bells and I'm exhausted. I was supposed to go fishing with Mattie today, and now I smell like shit."

"The water will do you good, then." Antony knelt at a large oak chest against one wall of the room and heaved it open. He pulled a satchel out of it, then stepped over to the larder and threw in a hard piece of cheese and a small loaf of bread.

"Do you know where Pa's put the ledgers?" he called over his shoulder to Ben.

"How would I know? *I'm* not his apprentice."

Antony sighed and whirled back into the workshop. He couldn't waste any more time. He looked around Bron's workbench. Nothing there but an old pouch. Antony grabbed it. He would need something to put their money in.

He walked back outside, again dazzled by the piercing early autumn light. "Where are the ledgers, Pa?" Antony asked.

"Right here," Bron patted the seat of the cart. They were there, wrapped in leather. Antony rolled his eyes. *Of course they're already out here.*

"Have you said your prayer to Saint Hogarth yet?" Bron asked as his son clambered up onto the seat of the cart.

Antony almost rolled his eyes again, but restrained himself. He put two fingers to his forehead, then moved them to his chest, then his belly. "By Saint Hogarth, I work. Let it be so."

Bron repeated the motion—the mind, the heart, and the will. Pointing to each was an invitation for the Nine to enter them. Antony had never been much for praying, but it was important enough to Bron.

"Now, get a move on, boy, or you'll miss the market," Bron said. Antony slapped Sam's reins and the little mule lurched forward, heaving the cart behind him. Antony waved once more at Bron as the cart pulled away. His father's broad face was smiling after him.

Antony slapped the reins a little harder. The bumping of the cart across the rough road did nothing for his headache, but he stared out into the road and then further to the Hemlock Forest on the edge of the village. He was surprised to find himself humming a tune as the cart rolled along. The war was over. Business was still good, taxes be damned. And after the sale with their contact in Southborn, he had the Commoner's Ball to look forward to. With any luck, there would be pretty girls to dance with and kiss—and not ones betrothed to a behemoth redhead.

Adelaide

delaide DuMont spent the duration of the carriage ride wondering if Aunt Pauline's bodice would hold. Pauline was a generously proportioned woman, and she took great breaths before she spoke as if her lungs were bellows. A few times, Adelaide heard the whalebone in her corset creak and quickly averted her eyes in the event of the unimaginable.

Pauline took no notice. Her expansive frame took up the bench opposite Adelaide. In one fortnight's journey, Adelaide had learned everything there was to know about Aunt Pauline.

"I would trust Jacob with my *life,* as I would no one else," Pauline explained, tapping the roof of the carriage to acknowledge her driver. "I do not get into a carriage unless Jacob is driving."

Aunt Pauline had breezed into Adelaide's life unannounced only a month before, the solution to all Adelaide's woes. Pauline was a widow and lived comfortably on her husband's legacy. He had been the lord of Easthempton and had set them up well for their twilight years, which Pauline enjoyed without him. They had seven daughters, all married and "scattered about the place."

Adelaide listened with an absent mind, comfortable with the company, although she wished she were alone. She was relieved that Aunt Pauline wasn't one to ask questions, only answer them, tell long-winded stories, and prevent silence. Adelaide merely listened, occasionally touching the leather satchel at her side to make sure it was still there. The piece of sealed paper inside secured her fortune.

"The king will be favorable toward you, my dear," Pauline had said when she gave Adelaide the paper. "He may not have your father's money to count on any longer, but he has mine. I have patronized him for many years. You will find a husband at court with his help."

The morning slowly faded to afternoon, and Adelaide knew they were close to Southborn. The carriage jostled and jumped on the uneven roads.

"Such dreadful roads this far south," said Aunt Pauline, steadying herself. "We would not have stood for it in our little corner of Easthempton. Every street—cobbled. Clean. My husband made sure of that. He was a good friend of King Alfred, mind. Perhaps you do not remember that time."

"Oh, I remember," Adelaide interjected before she could think. For once, the topic excited her. King Alfred. Prince Adrian. She'd only been eleven when they'd been murdered and the war started. Had it already been ten years?

"I was a young girl when he died, and my father was on his council," Adelaide continued. "I knew the prince very well." *I was betrothed to him,* she almost said.

Miraculously, Aunt Pauline was quiet. Her muddy eyes bugged out of her head as she stared at Adelaide. She seemed shocked by the sound of Adelaide's voice. Then she scoffed quietly.

"Your father was a good diplomat, I suppose," Pauline murmured, her lips a tight line. "Landon does not seem to have that gift."

Adelaide rested a protective hand on her satchel. Her heart ached at the thought of her older brother.

"He certainly has a gift for drinking," she said quietly. Pauline scoffed again.

"He won't get a penny of my money," she said. "And none of your dowry, either. I only expect you to think of your dear Aunt Pauline and little Easthempton when you have the king's ear."

Adelaide smiled at her, closed-lipped and tense.

"Show your teeth, my dear," Pauline said. "You look so horribly pained when you smile like that. A wealthy lord loves a pretty smile."

Her smile, Pauline had told her, would be her greatest asset at court. But

29

Adelaide imagined a wealthy lord would have other things on his mind, too. She widened her grin, letting her teeth peer out from barely-parted lips. As soon as Pauline looked away, she dropped it.

"We must be getting close now," Pauline sighed, sitting back on the bench. Adelaide pulled back one of the heavy curtains across the carriage door and peered out. Through the window, she could see the Hemlock Forest rattling past them, its tall trees painting shimmering shadows across the road. The Weschurch Road was one of the larger highways in the kingdom, wide enough for two carriages to pass one another easily. But the dense forest made the road more dangerous, too, especially at night.

Nerves rose in her stomach as she realized how close they were to Southborn. She wished she were back in her father's arms, at the lodge on the shores of the sea, watching snowflakes drift across the slate sky. When she'd been warm and happy. She remembered their ritual every winter night—her father would wrap her in a fur mantle and hold her against his chest as they sat by the huge hearth at the center of their manor house. Landon, her lanky teenage brother, would sit across from them, his long legs slung over the arm of a chair. How she loved his carelessness back then, his humorous, glittering eyes.

She'd once wanted to know why the South hated the North so much. A Northman had been caught on her father's lands that day, spearing fish in the river. Rowan had let the man go, but she remembered how angry the townspeople had been. They'd wanted the man to die for being somewhere he didn't belong. Adelaide had to ask him dozens of times before he told the story.

"Power, Addie, will tear people apart," he'd said. "Fathers from sons, brothers from brothers. Power breeds bad blood. At the beginning of the world, the Great Maker blessed our Saint Augustus with two sons. The older of the two was tall and graceful, handsome and fair, a peace-loving man. The younger was a warrior, stronger than ten men, with fury in his veins and fire in his sinews. It was Augustus's desire that his sons rule the Isle together, while Augustus governed the Great Continent to the east of its shores. But power tore them apart. Strong blood ran through these young men: they were both conquerors, champions. They built this land from nothing—tamed it, subdued it. They reigned together for many years, with their father's hand to help guide them.

"But Saint Augustus was one day called to return to the bosom of the Great Maker. With their father no longer there to guide them, they fought ever more between themselves."

Adelaide had closed her eyes and imagined a huge, beautiful palace with marble walls and pearl gates and satin tapestries. She pictured Saint Augustus and his long golden hair, seated atop a golden throne, and on either side sat his heirs: the older was handsome with golden hair like his father and clad in a white robe: the younger was broad shouldered, adorned in silver armor.

"Their fighting worsened. Each man won others to their side and built armies. Brothers that once loved each other now wanted the other dead. The fighting became so bloody that in the middle of a battle, giant Saint Hogarth appeared and with a mighty bellow, his roar caused the earth to shift and crack until a range of mountains separated the two armies. That was when we became North and South—the young warrior in the North, the gentle peacemaker in the South. Hatred grew and thrived in the younger son's heart. He brooded in the northern climes of the split kingdom. He held council with wolves and other wicked creatures of the forest. He sought the guidance of heathen priests who lived in the snowy solitude of the northern mountains. In the mountains, he built a fortress with his own hands, huge and cold and terrible, a fortress of war. Greygate. He then built up his army again, an army of wild men…"

Adelaide's eyes had widened. She stared into the fire and imagined the younger son sitting on a crudely made throne, clad completely in fur. Instead of knights, gentlemen, and ladies, his court was full of wolves and bears and vultures. She huddled closer to her father's chest.

"Our kingdoms have been divided ever since by the Great Mountains that Hogarth caused to spring up from deep beneath the earth. There was no other way to end the ceaseless bloodshed." Her father took a strand of her long chestnut hair and coiled it around his fingers. "It is better that the

Northern and Southern Realm remain divided. The people of the North still cling to that bad blood, just as we do. And there are people in the kingdom who wish that the realms would be one again—but would make it so by force."

"People like who, Father?" Adelaide had asked, perking up and looking into his deep-set eyes.

Her father never answered her. He had ushered her off to bed.

Power breeds bad blood.

The memory made Adelaide's heart ache. That had happened before the Northmen betrayed King Alfred. Before the war. And before the fire.

She wished she were still by the sea. Adelaide felt trapped on land. On the day before the fire, more than a year ago, her father had taken her to the shore. It had been a cloudy, blustery day, but Adelaide embraced the waves that broke upon the shore. She waded out through the black sand and let the waves engulf her. Her father, though nearing sixty, had run in with her, catching her every time the waves swept her off her feet. She wished she could have floated there forever in the breakers. She wanted to walk across the ocean and see what was on the other side, what was below. She wanted to hear her father bellow with laughter forever.

But the fire killed her father and his laughter. Now the black sand beneath her feet was mud. And she was going back to a place she never wanted to return to. A place without her father, or King Alfred, or Prince Adrian.

Adelaide peered out the window again. The morning was bright and fine and she wouldn't let dark thoughts spoil it. *I'll make the best of things. I have to,* she thought as the fresh autumn air breathed into her face. Early Harvestmonth in the South could still be hot and muggy, even though it came at Second Summer's end. Many of the trees lining the road were already half-golden with their dying hues.

As they rode, the trees became closer, denser. Eventually, the sky seemed to darken with thick foliage. Adelaide found it peaceful. It seemed as if they rode through a grand, ornate castle with high leafy ceilings and tall wooden pillars. If only all castles could be like this, she thought, bright and airy and open, not dismal and dark. The carriage passed a massive oak tree, already riotous with fiery red leaves.

The flames licked the wood like hungry hounds, swallowing her childhood home whole. The lodge stood like a flaming beacon on the cliff, the village below watching in horror.

If only everything could be perfect and lovely…

Rowan wrapped her with his mantle to keep her warm against the chill of the sea air. "Landon," he breathed, looking around. "Where's Landon?" He looked back at the flaming house. "Landon!"

Rowan ran into the house. And he disappeared into the flames forever.

Landon hadn't even been home that night. He'd gone out in the early evening, choosing to spend the entirety of his night at the village inn. Adelaide felt resentment rise and fought to force it back down. *The fire wasn't his fault,* she reminded herself. *Father's death wasn't his fault.*

But almost losing all their money was. And Landon wasn't in the carriage with Aunt Pauline to be married off. Saints knew where Landon was. The ache returned to Adelaide's heart.

I'm not doing this for him, she thought. *I'm doing it for Father.*

"Close that curtain," Aunt Pauline snapped. "I don't like the draft."

Adelaide pursed her lips and shut the curtain. As she did, the carriage lurched to a sudden stop, and Aunt Pauline heaved forward, nearly spilling onto Adelaide's lap.

"Good *heavens,*" Pauline sputtered, collecting herself. She none-too-discreetly shoved some of her cleavage back into her corset, and Adelaide tried not to look. With a balled fist, Pauline pounded on the roof of the carriage.

"Jacob!" she called. "What on earth have you stopped for?"

A loud rapping on the door was the response, and Pauline stifled a scream. Adelaide's heart was already pounding. *Stay calmer than your aunt,* she told herself. The carriage door flew open.

"Out." said a stern voice.

Adelaide's hands trembled as she steadied herself down the carriage steps, Pauline fumbling out behind her.

There, in front of them, stood two cloaked figures, their faces concealed by thick woolen masks. The smaller of the two stood closest to them, slim and reedy, with hazel eyes that shone out from under his cloak. The other was tall and broad-shouldered. In one hand, he held the side of the carriage horse's bit, and in the other, he held a dull sword streaked with rust, long overdue for a whetting. The smaller figure held a hunting knife.

Pauline cried out wordlessly, but Adelaide put a hand on her arm to quiet her. Now was not the time to cause a scene. She glanced up at Jacob, still sitting in his seat atop the carriage. He sat pale and frozen. Adelaide wondered if he'd ever encountered outlaws before. Her mind raced, trying to remember every story her father told her about vagabonds in Hemlock Forest. Most of it was hearsay or legend, and probably unreliable.

She looked between the two men. *What would Father do?* He would be calm, she decided. He wouldn't do anything rash, and he would protect the people he was with.

"I think you know how this goes," said the taller outlaw, his voice thick and harsh.

Adelaide nodded. "We don't want any trouble," she said. She glanced sideways at Pauline. She'd never seen her aunt's eyes wider.

The outlaw chuckled. "Nobody ever does."

"We'll do what you ask," Adelaide said. She felt her voice shaking. *You can do as outlaws ask, and they'll still kill you if they want. They know you're wealthy by your clothes. They know that if they let you go, you'll be bound to tell the king's men.* She urged the thought away. They were just men, just flesh and blood. The stories weren't true.

"You," barked the bigger outlaw up to Jacob. "Throw them trunks down." Adelaide and Pauline had two large trunks that Jacob had strapped to the top of the carriage.

"I cannot throw them down, they will—"

"Throw the damn trunks down."

Jacob immediately agreed. He unfastened the trunks and heaved down each one. They crashed to the ground, much to Pauline's dismay. Adelaide had to stop her from kneeling and protecting hers like a beloved child.

They're just dresses, Adelaide told herself. She glanced into the open door of the carriage, where her satchel still lay on the seat. She prayed to all the saints that they wouldn't find the note to the king. *If they know Aunt Pauline has the king's favor, then we're hostages.*

The small outlaw flung open Adelaide's trunk and began rooting around in it, throwing dresses and underclothes onto the ground all around him. Adelaide couldn't be embarrassed. Her mind was trained on the satchel in the carriage, willing the outlaws not to turn and see it, just beyond the open door.

The small outlaw worked quickly, poking through the clothes with his blunt knife. He found Adelaide's prayer necklace—a strand of nine beads for her nightly prayer to the saints.

The outlaw slung the beads around the blade of his knife, examining them with curiosity. Adelaide knew they were made of cheap glass, dyed and blown to look ornate.

The outlaw then found a hairpin and weighed it in his hand. It was gilded metal with cheap gemstones embedded into it, an introductory gift from her aunt. He pocketed it.

"You cowards!" Pauline wailed. It struck fear into Adelaide. *Shut up. Please, shut up for once.* "Preying on those who cannot protect themselves? Can't you see we have nothing to offer you?"

The small outlaw took two steps toward Pauline, his head cocked to one side. He stood in front of Pauline, staring up at the tall woman. Adelaide could see the shadow of his face. The woolen mask was tucked just over the man's nose, but she saw his glinting eyes and stern, furrowed brow. Adelaide glanced down at the blunt knife that was still in his hand.

"Nothin' to offer us?" asked the small outlaw gruffly. Wait—was the outlaw a *woman*? The voice was rough, but not deep. The outlaw gestured all around to the scattered contents of the trunk. "You have plenty to offer us, just nothin' worth having. Unless…"

To Adelaide's horror, the outlaw had turned to look inside the carriage.

"*No—*" The word flew out of her mouth before she could stop it. The outlaw whipped around to look at her, and Adelaide now saw the

35

narrowness of her face, the delicate lashes around her eyes. A small tendril of red hair had fallen out of her hood.

Before the outlaw could say anything, a long brown streak whizzed just inches past the girl's nose.

Thock! The arrow embedded itself in the carriage door. Then another. And then another, but this one flew past the big man's head. If the arrow had flown any farther left, the man would've lost an eye.

The outlaws exchanged a glance, then the woman looked icily at Adelaide. "Thanks for your contribution," she said. Without another word, the outlaws ran back into the forest, quickly dissolving into the thick greenery.

Antony

I*t's like taking a breath.* Antony remembered what Bron had told him. An archer's bow was an extension of himself, just as a knight's sword was to its wielder. From the moment Antony notched an arrow on the string to the moment it found its target, it was a part of him.

Antony drew the arrow back, feeling that familiar tension across his shoulders. He loved the feeling—the resistance of the string as his muscles pulled back, the feeling of power and strength as his arms and the bowstring were balanced for one exhilarating moment.

Then he fired, through the trees, straight toward the carriage around the bend.

He loved the sound of the arrow hitting its target almost as much as he loved firing it. Even from his distance, he could hear the *thock* as the arrow buried itself into the open door of the carriage. He couldn't help but smile, but not before notching another arrow to the string.

This arrow landed right next to the other on the carriage door. Antony felt the rush he always felt when the arrow hit its mark. It only made him want the feeling more. He pulled out another arrow, drew, aimed, and fired in one fluid stroke. He watched in satisfaction as the arrow flew just past the bigger man's head. A warning shot. Antony never missed what he aimed for. And he had aimed for the tree just behind the man.

The two men ran off from the scene, disappearing quickly into the thick underbrush, as quickly as startled deer. The younger woman immediately reached into the carriage and took out a brown satchel, slinging it around her shoulder and looking relieved. Antony clicked his tongue, and Sam

37

loped into a slow trot toward them.

Only the young woman turned as he approached. The older one had busied herself on the ground, collecting the scattered contents of a traveling trunk. She fretted loudly, rambling about the soiled clothes and looking for tears in the dresses she neatly folded back into the trunk.

"I'm sure they have a laundry at the castle, Aunt Pauline," said the young woman sharply. Antony slowed Sam and hopped off the seat of the cart. The young woman watched him. A swath of chestnut hair was slung in one long braid down her shoulder, and flyaway tendrils framed a small, heart-shaped face and large green eyes. Her gaze was cautious, but grateful. *Pretty*, Antony thought. *No. Not pretty. Beautiful.* His cheeks heated at the thought and he forced himself to look away.

"Thank you, sir," she called out to him. Her voice was clipped and her accent stately. Judging by the gowns spilled on the road, she had more money than Antony had ever seen. He ducked down to help the older woman collect some gowns, taking them gingerly in his hands.

"Is there any way we might repay you, sir?" she asked.

Antony chuckled. "I'm no 'sir,'" he said, then quickly added, "my lady." He closed the lid of the trunk. They were heavy, but he heaved both back up onto the roof of the carriage, the driver guiding him and fastening them back into place. Antony was aware of the young woman's eyes on him. He was standing close to her now. *I hope I don't smell too bad.* He realized he hadn't answered her question.

"Well—" he started. Then he looked at the carriage door. "It should be me repaying you. I damaged your carriage." He pulled the arrow out of the door. It had bore a small hole into the wood. He would need to resharpen the iron tips before using them again.

"Oh, pay that no mind, young man," said the older woman, stepping between him and the young lady. The woman looked at him differently than her younger companion, assessing and judgmental. "A damaged door is better than two slit throats."

The young woman laughed. "I don't think they were going to kill us, Aunt Pauline," she said. "If you're sure there's no way we can repay you—"

"Your smile is payment enough," Antony said. In his mind, it had sounded more charming. Out loud, it sounded stupid. *Did you really just say that?*

The young woman raised her eyebrows and looked away from him. Her cheeks flushed a deep red. The older woman raised an eyebrow at him in warning.

"Very well then," said the older woman. "Good day."

They stepped past him into the carriage, and he closed the door behind them. The carriage rattled on. All the while, Antony watched, cursing himself. Why was his heart beating so hard?

The ladies' carriage clipped off at a much faster pace than Antony's, and he lost sight of it amidst the golden-green trees. It didn't help that Sam often wandered the side of the road and picked through the underbrush for something to eat, slowing their pace to a crawl.

Antony pulled Sam back to the center of the road. "Are you a mule or a pig?" he muttered to the gray animal, who merely shook his ears. They were still in the thick of the forest and Antony guessed it was nearing noontime. It was still cool and dark in the dense trees whose leaves were yet to fall. At this rate, they would be to Southborn by mid-afternoon. Hopefully, the contact would wait for him at the Five Oxen.

You damn fool, he thought to himself. He could still feel his father's disappointment, even though Bron had tried to hide it. Antony needed to show him he'd be capable of taking over the shop. It was that or become a farm laborer like Carter.

"And I don't like smelling like horseshit," Antony said aloud. Sam snorted, as if offended. He was determined to go no faster than a loping trot, and Antony was growing increasingly annoyed with him. Or perhaps he was annoyed by the headache that still lingered in his temples.

The Weschurch Road bent suddenly to the left. This stretch followed along the bank of the Skeldergate River for a mile or so. The river was at its narrowest here, and its fastest. It widened as it flowed closer to Southborn, feeding the canals that were dug through the city. Through the thick trees, Antony could just make out the moving water, swift and frothy.

Something about the rush of water always made him feel uncomfortable. Sometimes he could barely walk to the bank of their village's canal without blanching and turning back. Something about looking down to the bottom, barely seeing its murky depths, thinking of how cold it would feel on his skin. Thinking of how he'd fall in and gasp for air, but only inhale water. He'd tumble through the rocks, his head throbbing, his life washing away.

It was because of his fall.

Antony knew that well enough. When he was thirteen, he'd run away from home. He'd been angry with Bron. When Bron came looking for him, Antony had climbed up a tree but had fallen off its highest branch and into the river. Or at least that's what he and Bron had pieced together—the events of that day and all those before it were dimmed by the blow to his head.

The next thing Antony had known, he was in his bed, wrapped tightly in furs and drinking hot spiced wine. He remembered the horrifying moment when he looked at his father and didn't know who he was. Or Carter. Or Ben. He didn't even know his own name.

"Antony, thank the saints," Bron had said when he woke up. He held the boy tight in his big arms, and Antony had let his father embrace him, but the cloud of confusion in his mind remained.

He'd relied on his father those first few weeks to tell him who people were—that was Phil Butcher, that was Fred the tavern keeper. Since then, Antony slowly remembered. He remembered Bron taught him how to shoot a bow. That he had played in the woods often, and that was why he'd run away there.

But one thing Antony could never remember was why he had tried to run away. When he'd asked Bron, his father merely shrugged.

"You were a boy on the verge of manhood," Bron said. "You were angry. I told you to do something you didn't want to do. So you ran off. You'd done it before and you usually came back. But you didn't come home that evening."

Antony could picture it if he tried hard enough. He could remember that night—the sun had been blood-red as it set behind the trees. The

Hemlock Forest became dark and cold quickly. He remembered running, too, and how the cold air stung his lungs.

He remembered all the important things—he knew who his family was. And he knew how to shoot a bow. He didn't need to remember why he'd run away or the nightmares he had as a child. He didn't even need to remember the color of his mother's hair or the games he played with the children in Barnswood growing up. He had his family, and he had his bow. And that was enough.

His mind wandered back to the girl in the carriage. *Your smile is payment enough.* He cringed at the words. He was better at touching and kissing women than at talking to them. And the woman had rendered him nearly speechless.

"Your weakness is good ale and pretty women," Carter had once told him.

"That's not true," Antony had replied. "You're just jealous because Sally likes me more than you."

His older brother was betrothed to Sally, the miller's daughter, who was nothing to look at. He had told Carter so. Sally had buck teeth and coarse hair, like a horse's mane. And she was a little bit fat.

Carter had rolled his eyes at that. "Of course she does," he had said. "She likes every man better than she likes me." Their betrothal was one of convenience, not love. And Carter was ugly. He had a big, round nose and a freckled face that turned as red as a beet when he got angry.

There will be more girls to compliment at the Commoner's Ball, Antony thought. *But first, you need to get money. And you're later now than ever.*

John

The South was too damn hot.

John had sweated through his underclothes even before the sun had fully risen that morning. They'd left the tiny village before the cock crowed, stepping around a handful of hungover villagers as they glided through the tavern. A few of Sir Lucas's men met up with them outside—they had spent their night in an entirely different sleeping arrangement. John wasn't surprised to see one of them was Sir Markus Huston, a youth with a round face and curly blond hair. He'd only been North for two years and had spent most of those years whoring his way all along the border. He was young and small and soft, and John had no love for him.

They approached Southborn by mid afternoon, breaking through the trees of the Hemlock Forest and overlooking the hilly landscape around the city. The kingdom sprawled below them in the valley. Lush pasture and fields surrounded it, ripe for harvest—a picture of abundance. John could even see white, cloudy sheep dotting the hillside beyond. Nothing had changed. It was home, but he felt like a stranger.

I don't belong here. Not anymore.

Now that they were out of the thick forest, the sun beat down on their necks. The men had to wear layers during their journey south. They each only had a small leather saddle bag and no other way to store their clothes. John felt the heat radiating off the lathered flanks of his horse. He would've preferred a biting wind gnawing at his face than heat that clung to his skin like lice.

The castle itself stretched like a waking giant over the village, with tall towers at each of the four corners, banners flapping in the breeze. The last time he'd been to Southborn, the banners had borne the lion rampant—King Alfred's house sigil. Now they bore a dragon on a green field for Tanor's house. *That won't be the only thing that's changed.*

"I stink like a Northman's ass," Markus said. "I pray they have a hot bath waiting for me." His golden curls bounced as their horses picked their way down into the valley.

"They've got naught waiting for us, Mark," said Sir Lyman. He was older than the rest of them, with brown hair receding from his forehead and a nose that had been broken more than once. John had watched Sir Lyman take the hilt of a sword to his face in a battle. He'd never thought a nose could bleed so much.

"We'll have beds, at least," said Sir Lucas. Lucas Widlowe was small and stocky, four years John's senior, but no taller than a woman. He was built like a barrel, though, and had a deep, powerful voice. A true commander, despite his youth. "There's room in the barracks. I've sent word to make sure of that."

"Will your father give you a bed in the tower, Johnny?" asked Mark, peering over his shoulder at John with a smirk. John didn't know where the boy found his audacity. It certainly wasn't in his strength. Maybe it was from between his legs. "A feather bed and a rosewater bath for the king's bastard?"

"Mark," Lucas said sharply, turning to the young man. "Did I not teach you to treat your elders with more respect?" He turned back and looked at John apologetically. Before John had been knighted on the battlefield, Sir Lucas had been his master. The commander had knighted him after John had carried him out of the battlefield, where Lucas had been pinned under his horse and broken his leg.

Markus, for once, said nothing. He turned and rode on in front of John. The road flattened as they approached the palace, and on either side lay ripe fields in mid-harvest. John smelled the sweet, sunny smell of the cornstalks. They clattered against one another as the horsemen passed. It was Harvestmonth, and it appeared Saint Juniper had smiled on Southborn. Harvest was typically a bountiful time, and few of the villagers feared the mild winters that followed. But after the splendor of autumn, winter was gray and rainy.

They crossed the wide stone bridge over the Skeldergate River and approached the palace gates. As they grew closer, John's stomach turned. The city seemed more or less the same—even the faces of the stern sentries at the gate seemed unchanged. They ushered the horsemen in with a nod. Perhaps the cobbles were more worn, the sentries older, the banners flapping overhead more ragged, but to John, it still felt as huge and uninviting as ever.

The last time John had seen those gates was ten years ago, just before winter, and only a week before his fourteenth birthday. He left with Sir Lucas following the death of King Alfred and Prince Adrian. He remembered the large wagon full of men from across Southborn, most sent out to be foot soldiers—the first to die. At the beginning of the war, almost no man had been spared, unless they were needed for making weapons or farming.

The stink of drunken breath and vomit had surrounded him in the crowded wagon. He was squashed between Sir Lucas and an expansive, dirty man whose belly heaved every time he laughed or belched or broke wind.

"What business have *you* goin' up there? They'll eat you alive," he'd said to John, puffing his pungent breath in the boy's face.

"They'll skewer 'im and feed 'im to their children. He's too small to be a course for them!" said a surly man on the bench across from them, who had vomited earlier. "They'll wear your guts for garters, boy."

"If we don't first," rumbled the expansive man. Then he poked John in the stomach with a fat finger. When John jumped, the man howled with so much laughter that a wet cough rose from his throat.

Lucas, then only seventeen and nearly as frightened as he, had put a reassuring arm around the boy. "Pay no heed to them, John. They can't see your strength."

John *had* been convinced he would die in the North. When they arrived, it was colder than he'd ever thought possible. The other squires mocked and belittled him for his size, but Sir Lucas had been a kind and patient mentor to him. He remembered struggling to lift and swing even the awkward wooden training swords the boys used.

"Keep practicing until you can," Lucas had always told him. And John did. He would practice with Sir Lucas until the young man doubled over, catching his breath and asking for respite.

And eventually, the other squires were afraid to fight him. He grew tall and strong, and unlike their awkward teenage frames, he used his bigger body with grace and ease. While he worked and trained, the other boys would go about to the various towns, drinking and abusing their newfound freedom. Most of them grew soft and lazy during long stretches of no fighting. He surpassed them all soon enough, and it filled him with a sort of pride to look into their fearful eyes as he walked by. By sixteen, he was a giant. He'd see other squires run away from battle or even wet themselves from fright before it began. They'd lie in their beds shaking, muttering inaudibly. But John thirsted for the fight, for the feeling of his sword in his hand. He'd found a purpose on the battlefield he'd never had before.

He hadn't wanted to go back to Southborn. Ever. Every memory of the North, no matter how bloody, was sweeter than going home.

"The sooner I can get back to my mum, the better," said Sir Lyman. His mother was old and had sent word to him she was sick not long before the war ended. John had seen the deep lines of his face crease deeper throughout their trip to Southborn. His mother lived south of the capital city, in the village of Dallen.

"You'll get back to her, all right," said Sir Artemis, a round-shouldered man a few years older than Lucas. "With more gold and land than you could ever hope to see." Artemis had come North five years before to fight alongside Sir Lucas, leaving behind a daughter and a young wife who was with child. "I'll buy my little girl all the fancy dresses they're wearing at court these days."

The knights who rode with John had talked endlessly about who was waiting for them at home. For Sir Lyman, his mother. For Artemis, his wife and daughter. Sir Markus would see his betrothed again, and Lucas would return to his father and sit on the king's council. John had spent the twenty-day journey wondering who was waiting for him. His father certainly wasn't, and he had no mother to speak of.

But he might have a friend, he realized, suddenly thinking about Addie. He'd sent her letters when he was young, but she'd never responded. She had her own life, he supposed.

John honestly didn't know what his father would do when he laid eyes on him again. When he left, Tanor had given him a light embrace and sent him on his way. His father had always been a huge, towering man, at least to John. A man to be feared and obeyed. Why would he be any different now that he was king?

He got what he always wanted, said a thought at the back of John's mind.

They had already passed through the poorer quarter of the town, closest to the main gate. Villagers gave them cautious glances as they passed on their tall horses. Other noblemen walked brusquely past the ramshackle huts, their long tunics brushing the dirt. A woman and her donkey crossed the road quickly in front of them. She was probably on her way to the market in the village square, John guessed.

After a few blocks, the streets widened, and they passed the Cathedral of the Nine, standing apart from any other building. It rose tall, almost as tall as the towers of the palace beyond. Two spires stretched to the proverbial heavens, and at its front was a rose window that glittered with color in the mid-afternoon light. John had been in that cathedral before—the last time he was there, it was for King Alfred's burial. It was grand on the inside, he remembered, huge and cavernous, with marble pillars climbing upward on either side and high, vaulted stone ceilings. The mournful songs sung that day had echoed and rang through the sanctuary like a ghostly choir.

Past the cathedral was the wealthier quarter, which seemed just as active that day. John knew a feast day was fast approaching, but couldn't remember which saint. The streets here were cleaner and better kept.

Merchants were busy at their stalls, sellers of wares from all over the Western Isle and from the Mainland as well—dark-skinned men from Thess selling bolts of cloth in rich colors, men with amber eyes from Jahaar selling sweetspice. Southborn was only a few leagues from Dark Harbor, where the Skeldergate River fed into the channel.

Everything about Southborn seemed strange and foreign now, John realized. The cold season was short, so villagers built their homes for ventilation—wide doorways, paneless windows, and shutters open all summer long. Buildings in the North had almost always been boarded up against raging snow and wind. The mountains brought storms and gales that would have ripped these southern structures to bits.

They continued down the cobbled street, their horses shouldering past more people than before. The towers of the castle were looming closer, and they could almost see the gates now. John's stomach was roiling. He'd spent their journey wondering what he'd say to his father, what their meeting would be like—and he still didn't know.

The horsemen clattered through the palace gate into the courtyard. It seemed exactly as John had left it. Bustling with activity, members of the court coming and going, carts full of deliveries for the kitchens or grooms exercising horses. He looked around for any familiar face but found none. It had been too long, he thought.

"Is your father here, Luke?" asked Sir Lyman as he swung from his saddle. "He wouldn't miss a chance to see his youngest child get decorated for his valor in war."

Lucas swung down from his saddle as well, though less gracefully than Sir Lyman. Lucas had four older brothers, and would probably never inherit his father's estate. But King Tanor would find some way to repay him.

"I imagine he is," said Sir Lucas. His father was an amiable man, John remembered, though Richard Widlowe had never been much of a fighter, more a coin-pusher than a warrior.

John dismounted his horse, and a young groom took the reins from him.

"Your victory is our victory, sir," said the groom. He was just beyond boyhood, his voice breaking with adolescence. He probably dreamed of fighting a war. "Welcome home."

Home. The word still twisted John's gut. He said nothing. He just knew he stank and needed a bath. John scanned the parapet, a raised walkway lined with stone pillars. What did he expect to see there? His father? He pushed his hair back from his face and turned to follow Lucas into the barracks.

The knights stopped at the sound of commotion at the gate. A carriage, tall and grand, rattled into the courtyard, pulled by two magnificent palfreys. The carriage stopped near the stairway up to the parapet and out stepped a blonde-haired woman. The grooms who were attending to her bowed deep at the waist. She was gloriously dressed in a green gown that spilled over a swollen belly—she was with child. Her sleeves were slashed at the wrist to reveal glittering gold fabric underneath. She smiled as two other ladies, dressed much more simply, followed her out of the carriage. One of them held a small boy in her arms, a cherub-faced little thing with curly dark hair. They followed on either side of the woman as she went up the stairs into the palace.

"By all the Nine," breathed Sir Markus. "I never thought I'd see a queen in the flesh."

A queen, John thought. He knew his father had married and that his wife had given him a son. The woman he'd just watched get out of the carriage was his stepmother, Queen Claudia.

"Looks like you've been knocked down the line of succession a few pegs, Johnny," Markus remarked as they followed Lucas to the barracks, down a narrow corridor off of the courtyard.

"I've never been *in* the line of succession," John murmured.

"Your father wasn't, either," Markus said. "They just couldn't find a living relative of King Alfred. A truthful one, anyway."

Take it to your grave, John, his father had told him on that night, ten years ago. *Take what you've seen tonight into the grave, or I'll put you in one myself.*

"The Northmen do it right," said Sir Lyman, his dark brow furrowed as if he were some sage philosopher puzzling through a problem. "The king names his successor, even if it's not a blood relative. That's why his second wife now sits on the throne at Greygate."

"It's a stupid rule," said Sir Markus. "If a man can't breed sons, he shouldn't sit on the throne. King Stephen the Sick was as weak as a woman, anyway. Putting his queen on the throne was the reason they lost the war."

They came to the barracks, a long, narrow room with high, narrow windows and scant light. It was neat and clean as most soldiers' barracks were, with fresh rushes on the floor and roughspun linens on the beds, made neatly. It served as the sleeping quarters for the sentries and palace guards, with a common room off to the side for their meals. *Home*, John thought. His father was nearer to him than he'd been in ten years, with only walls instead of leagues separating them.

The war truly was over, he realized. And as much as it had changed him, it had left everything else exactly the same.

Adelaide

Their carriage continued down the Weschurch Road, and Adelaide breathed a sigh of relief when they were out of the Hemlock Forest. *They wouldn't try to attack us again...would they?* She hugged her satchel close to her.

Pauline's nerves were still obviously frayed. She kept muttering something about having to wash all of her clothes when they came to the palace, and she'd have nothing suitable to wear in front of the king and queen.

"They could have killed us," she said under her breath. "But even worse, now they've made us late."

"They weren't going to kill us, Aunt," Adelaide said. But her thoughts said otherwise. *Would they have killed us if that man hadn't shown up?*

That man. She tried not to give him much more thought. She hadn't even asked for his name. He was a man that was easy for a girl to fancy—his dark brown hair and wide brown eyes stuck in her memory, and the way his lips curled in a kind of amiable pout. He was a skilled archer, too, arms strong and muscular, shoulders broad. She'd watched him lift their trunks effortlessly over his head and on top of the carriage, the careful focus of his gentle eyes—

She shook her head as if to shake the thoughts loose. A kind commoner, she told herself. A commoner she would never see again.

The tree line had broken when the sun was at its highest point in the sky. It became hotter than a bread oven inside the carriage, and the air felt close and muffled. But anytime she tried to open the curtains for some air, her aunt stopped her.

"We're about to drive into town," Pauline said. "Someone could reach in and grab us."

Adelaide stopped herself from rolling her eyes. They were still a good mile from the city gate. "Out of a moving carriage? In front of crowds of people?"

"You never know," Pauline added. "We must be more careful now."

Does being careful really mean suffocating in my own sweat? Adelaide felt woozy from the heat.

"Are you presenting me to the king yet today?" she asked. *If I'm still conscious,* she added in her head.

"I will make a request," Pauline said. "Although I will need a clean dress, and so will you, and now I don't think we have one." She huffed and muttered to herself again.

Adelaide peered out of the curtain. They had just crossed the bridge over the Skeldergate River. Her heart beat rapidly. She was about to see King Tanor again—after ten years. What would that be like?

My life is in his hands now, she thought. *My future.*

She had no reason to dislike King Tanor. Her father had been on King Alfred's council with him before the Northmen killed the king. Her father had taken her and Landon away after Alfred died and the war came.

Would Tanor remember me? Adelaide had been a girl of eleven when they left. She remembered Tanor as being big and broad-shouldered, with long black hair. His eyes, too—she remembered his eyes. They were a light blue like sea glass, their pupils like tiny, dark pinpricks in the light. He was a pleasant enough man, but his eyes never seemed to smile.

Adelaide knew they were in town when she heard the rumble of voices around her. The carriage moved slower now. She imagined Jacob had slowed the horse's pace as the streets got more crowded. Pauline made a big show of putting a handkerchief to her nose as if they could smell the street from their close little carriage. Adelaide could only smell the sweat from Pauline's underarms. She closed her eyes and prayed that they would get to the palace soon, and that she could breathe some fresh air.

"I know, my dear," Pauline said. Adelaide's eyes snapped back open, and she saw a sympathetic look on Pauline's pinched face. "I'm nervous, too. It has been a long time since I've been to court. And court is much different from your father's little hamlet on the coast."

Adelaide smiled thinly. *I know. And I don't like it.*

After an eternity, the carriage shuddered to a halt, and the door swung open. A well-dressed groom offered a hand to Adelaide, which Pauline quickly grabbed. The large woman bustled past Adelaide, and the groom sheepishly extended his hand to Adelaide again. The air outside hit her in a rush. The day was hot, but still much cooler than it was in the carriage. Instead of her aunt's perspiration, Adelaide was greeted with the smell of horse dung, and baking bread, and warm flagstones all at once. She and Pauline looked around at the flurry of activity. Grooms were already beginning to haul the ladies' trunks off the carriage with Jacob's help.

"Where shall we take these, my lady?" asked one groom.

"The king has a suite of rooms set aside for Lady Pauline Easthempton and Adelaide DuMont," said Pauline, her chin slightly raised. She turned to Adelaide. "I must tell the king about the outlaws. He will want something done about them." She looked slightly past Adelaide, and her eyes widened. "Lord Roger!"

Adelaide turned to see a middle-aged man a few paces away from them. He had receding dark hair that fell in coarse waves down to his neck, and a large, rounded nose. He beamed at the sight of Pauline and strode toward them.

"Lady Pauline, as I live and breathe," said Lord Roger in a nasal voice. He clasped the older woman's hands and kissed them noisily, bowing at the waist. He swung his gaze toward Adelaide. She caught a whiff of wine on his breath. "And who is this?"

"This is my niece, Adelaide DuMont," Pauline said. Lord Roger completed the same ritual with Adelaide but held onto her hands longer. His were big and sweaty.

"DuMont? Rowan's daughter?" Adelaide nodded with a curtsy. "An old dodger like him made quite the beautiful daughter, didn't he?" Adelaide didn't know if he wanted an answer, so she merely laughed politely.

"We have come to find a husband for Adelaide," Pauline said. There was a strange look in her eyes. Lord Roger, still holding onto Adelaide's hands, put on a baleful grin.

"And so we shall," he said. He patted Adelaide's hand with a wet smack. Adelaide desperately wanted to pull her hands away. "My own dear Loretta died last year of the Wasting Sickness. She gave me three good sons, but a man docs get lonely, Lady Pauline."

Adelaide bit her lip, waiting for her aunt to respond. Pauline wouldn't give her away this soon, would she? *I would* not *marry this man*, Adelaide thought. *My father wouldn't want that for me...would he?*

"Lord Roger," said a clear voice coming from behind them, "have you seen my father anywhere?"

Adelaide turned and used the opportunity to slide her hands out of Roger's and surreptitiously wipe them on her traveling cloak. The ends of Roger's mouth turned upward, but he wasn't smiling. Adelaide, however, beamed.

"I've only just arrived, Sir Lucas," said Roger. "But I am glad to see you back and in good condition." The man bowed again. "Ladies." He turned and sauntered off toward the parapet.

"Lucas!" Adelaide hugged the young man around the neck. Lucas wrapped his arms around her and chuckled. Adelaide immediately felt a yank on her cloak.

"*Adelaide,*" Pauline said sharply. "Show some propriety. You'll never find a husband if you throw yourself at strange men."

Lucas let go of Adelaide and smiled at her with glittering blue eyes. "I hope I'm not a strange man." His mouth burst into a smile. She and Lucas had spent many days together as children since their fathers were both on the council. He had always protected her from the other children because he was older and bigger—at least, he had seemed big when Adelaide was young. Now she found they were nearly the same height. But he was still strong and wiry, his voice surprisingly deep.

"You have no idea how happy I am to see you," Adelaide said, wanting to embrace him again.

"Yes, it's wonderful," said Pauline. "Adelaide, we should refresh ourselves before we see the king."

"The king?" Lucas smirked. Adelaide was glad to see he still had a dimple in one cheek. "Is he going to find you a husband, Adelaide?"

"It's that or marry Lord Roger," Adelaide said quietly enough so Pauline didn't hear. Lucas snorted. Pauline looped Adelaide's arm in hers and pulled her away abruptly.

I could marry Lucas, Adelaide thought as they walked toward the parapet. *He was a hero in the North. King Tanor will probably give him land and title to repay him.*

However, Pauline snapped her out of that reverie almost immediately. "Roger is on the king's council," she said as they pushed through the din of people in the courtyard. "He was on King Alfred's before he was on Tanor's. He's a trusted man in the kingdom."

But Adelaide couldn't stop thinking about the slobbery kiss. She tried to dismiss her thoughts of Roger and Lucas. Roger was a widower with three sons already—he didn't need more heirs. And Lucas had just returned home from war, probably with very little money to his name. His father would want a more substantial dowry for his homecoming son than Adelaide could offer.

When she was a child, she knew there had been talks between her father and King Alfred that she would marry the prince. Prince Adrian had been three years older than her, a tall, handsome boy. The thought of marrying a prince had set her eleven-year-old imagination alight.

Pauline ushered Adelaide through the halls of the palace, intent on bringing her to the king's audience chamber. Her aunt spoke intermittently, but Adelaide's thoughts were elsewhere. She didn't expect the palace to feel so distant and remote, so different from how it had been. *Perhaps nothing is the same when you're grown up as it is when you're young.*

But there was something more. She had looked up at the dizzying turrets, breathed in the scent of stone in the halls, and felt as though something unseen were at play.

"Great saints, is it four bells already?" Pauline said. They both heard the chimes high above them in one of the palace's great towers. "We won't have time to change, I'm afraid, after all of our...dalliances." She cast a sideways, accusatory glance at Adelaide. "Court will adjourn soon."

As Adelaide walked with Pauline through the long, narrow halls, memories flooded every corner of her mind. Though everything seemed fairly unchanged, the absence of the people she loved left it empty.

Adrian had chased her down these halls, laughing. She remembered almost running headlong into a nobleman walking the halls but barely noticing. She had turned to see Adrian following her, his ruddy cheeks glowing with energy. If she closed her eyes even now, she could still see him chasing after her.

Is your ghost still here, Adrian? Are you following me now?

He had stolen a kiss once when they were older. Adrian had taken her down to the kitchens, and they had nipped a bit of warm pastry that had been cooling on a shelf. The fat cook had seen them and chased them out with a string of curses—Adelaide could still hear Adrian mimic the man's high-pitched voice. They ducked around a corner to hide and stood there, panting, smiling, facing each other, and then Adrian leaned in. His lips were soft and boyish and tasted like strawberry tart. Addie had never been kissed before. It made her feel warm and full, a new, fluttering feeling inside her she'd never felt. Her stomach felt sick, but in a lovely way, a dizzying way. Later that night at supper, she could barely speak two words to her father.

Adelaide didn't realize how vivid her memory had been until she stood at the doors of the king's audience chamber. Somehow, she tasted strawberries.

But as the doors opened, her legs shook. She hadn't seen Tanor before he became king. *Don't trust him, Adelaide,* said a voice in her head, a voice that sounded like her father. But the thought came and went as she steeled herself to enter.

In the room, paneled with dark wood and lined with high windows to one side, King Tanor sat on his tall wooden chair, far less grand than his seat in the throne room. A plump, apple-cheeked woman sat in the lesser chair, her hands resting on a prominent belly that she caressed from time to time. She had a small, round face and a nose that turned upward slightly. Queen Claudia, Adelaide thought.

She looked back at Tanor. He was not fair and light, like men from the South tended to be. He was dark-haired with a solid, broad build, square and erect even when seated. Even from her vantage point, she could see the intensity of his eyes, pale and blue and always focused.

Pauline elbowed Adelaide in the ribs. *Stand up straighter.* Adelaide straightened her back. She was still only wearing her simple traveling clothes, and everyone in the room—at least twenty in total—wore far greater finery. Silks from the countries across the Great Plains on the Mainland, embroidery of golden thread, crushed velvet that seemed to ripple in the light. Adelaide's blue linen seemed lacking.

The room itself was grand, even for an audience chamber. The path to the throne was lined with a thick crimson rug, stretching all the way to the foot of Tanor's chair. The high windows faced south and cast long beams of afternoon light on the flagstone floor, their latticework leaving crisscrossed shadows on the wood paneling on the far wall. Interspersed on each wall were ancient tapestries that told stories Adelaide knew by heart—the story of Cedrik the Wise and his conquest of the mountains, brave Eddo the Bold and his battle with a sea snake in Dark Harbor, Stephen the Silent surrounded by his many volumes penned in his own blood while living among the Rock Monks. The tapestries were threadbare and worn, but their stories were still rich and colorful, each flat figure on the cloth with his own part to play.

As they approached, Tanor listened to a lord wearing a purple doublet who stood in front of him. Lord Roger stood near the wall—Adelaide avoided looking straight at him. Other faces were familiar, too, though they had aged since she'd seen them last. Lucas' father, Lord Widlowe, his shock of red hair going gray, stood to one side of the king. He beamed when he caught Adelaide's eye, giving her a warm nod.

"The Harvestmonth tax is fast approaching," the man in purple was saying. "My tenants struggle to pay the tax enough as it is. With the added war debts—" The man stopped and chose his words carefully. "—with the loans my father and I have given the crown to pay for this war, we have no choice but to raise the tax unless—"

"—unless your benevolent king repays his war debts. Yes, I know." Tanor smiled amicably. He scratched at the ghost of stubble on his otherwise clean-shaven chin. He had strong angular features and a sharp jaw. His voice was clear and sonorous, one that could placate a crowd or a lover in equal measure.

"Y-yes," responded the man thinly.

"I promise you, young Colvinsate," Tanor said, "you will be repaid in full, with interest. But this war has only just ended, has it not? First, we celebrate. Then I shall send Lord Edwin with your payment."

A short man appeared at King Tanor's side. He was slim and short of stature, with gray hair plastered back from his prominent forehead. He leaned beside the king as Tanor murmured something to him. The man—Lord Edwin Darkshire—nodded curtly, turned, and left.

"Thank you, your grace," said young Colvinsate. He turned, and Adelaide saw his moon-shaped face and red-rimmed eyes. Adelaide's father had been close with old Colvinsate. The boy took after his father in his homeliness.

"The war has indeed been costly," Tanor said, raising his voice. "We've done what we had to do to protect our realm. It has taken us ten years, but the Grey Queen has finally forfeited. She will repay what is due to us, though no amount of money could bring back what her people took—our former king, Alfred."

The crowd murmured. Some put two fingers to their forehead, chest, and belly in the sign of the saints. Adelaide felt a pang once again. *It's been so long.* Tanor had been named Prince Adrian's advisor in the event that King Alfred would die before the boy came of age. After their murders, Southborn stood without a king for almost two years, as Tanor served as regent, and warded off and disproved pretenders who made a claim for the throne. He even testified in front of the court, since he was one of the last men to see Alfred alive.

"I make a vow to you all," Tanor said, "our lean days are nearly done. Our brothers and sons have returned home to us. Let us celebrate."

Lord Colvinsate was nearly back in the crowd when he turned again, a thought crossing his face.

"One more thing, your grace, if you please," he said. "What of the Men of the Lion?"

Tanor's brow furrowed. "The Men of the Lion? What of them?"

"Well, your grace," Colvinsate said. He seemed suddenly embarrassed to have brought it up. "There are men in Southborn and other villages who seem to conspire against the crown—against you, in the name of King Alfred. We have seen a strange influx of them in Colvinsate."

Tanor scoffed, but not unkindly. "We are not afraid of any conspiracies or hearsay, young Colvinsate," he said. "War can stir men up in surprising ways. Any conspiracies we face will soon be forgotten in peacetime."

Young Colvinsate said nothing more. He merely nodded, his face still red, and retreated into the crowd. Conspiracies. That didn't surprise Adelaide. Even in their small village of DuMont, commoners constantly railed against the king—no matter who the king was.

"Thank you, Lord Colvinsate," said a high, reedy voice to the young lord. A man in a long, dark robe stepped onto the dais beside the queen. He looked like a shadow. Adelaide recognized him as Godfrey, once Tanor's gentleman-in-waiting. He seemed far more aged than he should have been. Godfrey had been just over thirty when Adelaide last saw him, but he seemed like a man far older. His face looked like melted candle wax and his eyes darted about, watery and fearful. "The council will conclude if there are no further remarks."

As the king and queen stood to leave, Pauline pushed forward. *She chose quite the time to be unceremonious,* Adelaide thought. She didn't follow her aunt. The woman's large skirts nearly bowled a few noblemen over as she approached the dais.

"Your grace, if you please," Pauline said, her voice loud and piercing. She bowed low in front of the monarchs. Tanor watched her with a raised eyebrow. Adelaide imagined he had a fairly good view of Pauline's generous cleavage from that angle. She stifled a smile.

Tanor beamed when Pauline straightened herself. "My dear Lady Pauline Easthempton! What a pleasure—and a surprise!" He chuckled, dismissing her impropriety. The rest of the room rumbled with laughter as well. Adelaide was a little embarrassed for her aunt. Pauline didn't seem to find any reason to be.

"Indeed, your grace," Pauline said, straightening her skirts. "You must pardon my appearance, your grace. My niece and I were accosted by outlaws on our journey here."

The men and women in the room gasped. Pauline may as well had said a dragon had attacked them on the Weschurch Road. Adelaide looked at the queen. A small, pale hand fluttered to her mouth like a little white butterfly. Her other hand wrapped protectively around her belly.

"How awful for you," said the queen. Her voice was soft and light, almost like a child's. She turned to her husband. "My king, we must do something about them."

Tanor looked lovingly at Claudia. "Now that the war is over, my dear, I can turn more attention to matters happening in our own realm," he said. He turned to Pauline. "I make that promise to you, Lady Pauline. And I thank you for making the journey all the way from Easthempton to visit us. May I ask why you have honored us with your presence?"

"Yes, your grace," said Pauline, bowing again. "I wish to present my niece Adelaide DuMont to court."

Pauline's eyes landed on Adelaide, followed by every eye in the room. Adelaide felt her cheeks grow hot. Now that everyone was looking at her, she was aware of how dull her dress looked compared to their satin and crushed velvet. Carefully, she slid the parchment out of the satchel at her side. She stepped forward cautiously, suddenly very aware of her hands and feet, and not knowing what to do with them. She found her hands were squeezing her skirt and immediately released them. But now what would she do with them? They rested stiffly at her side as she stepped next to her aunt and curtsied low. Her knees shook.

"Your grace," she said. Her voice sounded far away. Her dirty shoes poked out from the hem of her skirt. *I probably tracked mud all the way across the floor. There's a dirt track behind me.* Her cheeks flamed hotter.

"Adelaide," Tanor said, his voice soft. He stood up from his chair and stepped down from the dais toward her. He was taller than she remembered, with broad, rounded shoulders that carried a long red mantle lined with fur. The rest of his clothing was nowhere near as ornate as some of his court. He wore a simple, rust-colored doublet belted at the waist and leather trousers that matched his boots. He was handsome, even if he wasn't as thin and fit as he'd been ten years before. His black hair, flecked with gray, was swept back from his forehead and flowed to the nape of his neck like a dark wave. He wore a small silver crown. Adelaide had seen it on King Alfred's head once. Although the crown was simple, it was the oldest in the palace's vault of jewels and was said to have been forged in the fire beneath the mountains when the line of southern kings began.

Adelaide presented him the parchment without fanfare. Tanor smiled down at it and took it, but didn't open it. Instead, he took her hand in his and kissed it. His kiss wasn't wet and slobbery like Roger's. It was dry, overly polite, his hands warm and gentle. He looked down at her face with a smile.

"What an honor it is to have the daughter of Rowan DuMont back in my court," he said, giving her hands a slight squeeze. He glanced down at the parchment. "I will let Lord Edwin bother with the paperwork. I'd much rather behold your beauty than scratchings on a parchment."

His face was warm, but his pale eyes remained unsettling, even piercing. Adelaide wondered what it was like to have such colorless, intense eyes with the power to wither people to their core.

Adelaide heard a small gasp from her aunt. "She is adequate? You will accept her to court, your grace?" she asked breathlessly.

Tanor chuckled. "She is more than adequate, Lady Pauline," he said. "And we will find a husband for her here at court. In fact, I believe my wife needs another lady-in-waiting, especially after the baby is born."

Adelaide looked at Claudia. The young queen was radiant and smiled warmly at her. Adelaide returned the smile. *We are about the same age,* Adelaide thought. Tanor was old enough to be her father. She looked at him so lovingly.

Perhaps I will find a husband I can love, Adelaide thought, *but he'll need to help us first.*

She looked back at Tanor, wondering how sincere his kindness was. *If he is inviting me to court, that is enough for now,* she thought. She curtsied again.

"It would be my honor to attend to her grace," Adelaide said. "I am in your debt, your grace, after everything you've done for my family."

A brief shadow passed over Tanor's face, but it was gone so quickly Adelaide wondered if she'd imagined it.

"I am overjoyed to hear it," Tanor said. "Welcome to my court, Lady Adelaide."

Antony

A
ntony toyed with the empty leather bag on the table at the Five
Oxen. His ale was nearly untouched. It wasn't as good as Fred's
at Bourne Tavern. A pretty barmaid came around a few times to
check on him and seemed disappointed every time that his tankard was
still full. Antony had asked her if she'd seen a wealthy gentleman there at
all that day.

"We get lots of gentlemen," she'd said, "wealthy and not. You'd have to
be more specific than that."

But he couldn't be. Antony had either missed his contact altogether, or
his contact was incredibly late. The bells had already sounded six.

Antony palmed the leather bag, weighing it in his hand as though
it would magically become heavier. He could already feel his father's
disappointment. They wouldn't have enough to pay the Harvestmonth
tax. More than that, they'd have to pay their rent to the lord of Barnswood,
which had grown since the beginning of the war. He seethed with anger
and frustration. *This isn't fair,* he thought. Then he realized, *it's your fault,
though. Why would Pa ever want to leave you in charge after this?* He squeezed
the bag in his hand.

He could see through the open door of the tavern that the sun was getting
low. Heat wafted off the cobblestones and into the nearly empty barroom.
He wondered how much it would cost to stay a night there. Probably more
than he could afford.

He noticed a small man standing in the doorway, standing strangely still.
Antony realized the man stared directly at him, squinting. He stepped into

the tavern toward Antony's table.

"Antony Bronson?" he asked casually. His voice was smooth and clear, like wine from a pitcher. He scratched at the grizzled stubble on his face. Apart from his whiskers, his hair was neatly cropped and groomed, hair that had probably once been glossy and dark but was now mostly gray.

Antony nodded, feeling a mixture of relief and rage. *I bust my arse to get here on time and he saunters in as though he has all the time in the world?*

"That's me," he said.

The man inclined his neck crisply. "Lord Edwin Darkshire," he said. "I apologize for my tardiness. The king's court went longer than expected today."

Antony's head shot up. *The king?* He almost blurted it out. This man was a member of the king's court. He quickly clambered out of his chair and stood up.

"Sir—my lord—I apologize, I didn't know—" His cheeks grew hot, but Edwin only gave him a mild smile.

"Don't trouble yourself, young man," he said. "Let's get to business, shall we?"

Observing him as he sat down, Antony realized how modestly Edwin was dressed for a member of court. He only noted oiled leather boots and a silver belt buckle that gave his wealth away.

"The bows—they're good for hunting." Antony realized he hadn't practiced what he was going to say. Bron had coached him dozens of times on how to sell to prospective buyers, but Antony had hardly listened. But he knew nobles liked to hunt—not for necessity, but for sport. "They're easier to use than longbows. The design of the bow curves back in on itself—"

"Yes, yes. I know what a bow is, young man," said Edwin. Antony's face reddened. The man lifted his chin and chewed on the side of his cheek, thinking. "His grace would like new archery equipment for his sentries. Now that the threat abroad has been vanquished, we can prevent additional threats closer to home."

This man has the ear of the king, Antony thought. *If I can convince him,*

I'll come home with more money than Pa ever bargained for. He straightened, squaring his shoulders. "My father is the best bowyer this side of the mountains," he said firmly.

"That's a high claim, young man," said Edwin, watching him with a careful eye. His eyes moved slowly in their lids. "How do they shoot?"

"A bow is only as good as the archer," Antony said. The man smirked. Then he tapped the table, inhaling sharply.

"His grace wants to ensure his investment is worthwhile. Even if your father isn't the best bowyer this side of the mountains, he certainly is the most expensive one. I will organize a demonstration tomorrow," said the man. "Nine bells in the inner ward. We will see if these are weapons worthy enough for the king's sentries."

Antony's heart nearly leaped to his throat. His words nearly spilled out of his mouth. "I—yes—thank you, sir, er, my lord—"

"Edwin," said Edwin, his voice cool as glass. "Nine bells, young man. I can't permit tardiness."

"Yes, sir," Antony said, then quickly corrected, "Edwin."

Edwin smiled, nodded, then stood up and walked away. As soon as he had arrived, he had left. When he was gone, Antony quickly made the sign of the saints and whispered a quiet thanks to Saint Hogarth. The Great Maker had smiled on him that day.

He paid a copper for Sam to be kept in their stables for the night. The animal was worth that much, at least. He asked the innkeeper if he could sleep in the straw of the stable.

"Fer an argent more," grunted the innkeeper. Antony couldn't spare that. As he rubbed Sam down, Antony's mind raced. He'd never met a king before. And he'd only brought the clothes on his back. Was he supposed to bring some sort of gift or token to King Tanor? He had two argents left, an empty leather pouch and a satchel containing hard cheese and a loaf of bread.

He looked into the large, vacant eyes of his mule. "Are you a gift fit for the king, Sam?" he asked. Sam chuffed, bumping Antony's shoulder with his muzzle. "You're right. I wouldn't be able to haul this cart home myself."

Only a few steps away from the inn was the Cathedral of the Nine, its tall spires piercing the purple twilight. Antony looked up at them and became dizzied by their height. He was used to the modest two-story cottages of Barnswood. Only great cities like Southborn and The Roses to the west had such tall structures. The cathedral had been built generations before, the first thing to be built in Soutborn. King Gilbraith the Gentle had wanted a place to worship before he built a place to rule. He was long dead before the cathedral was built, but his remains were exhumed upon its completion and were the first to be buried in the cathedral's crypt.

Antony climbed the narrow stone steps. The three huge sets of double doors were open to let in the warm evening air and invite worshipers into the coolness of the sanctuary—and entice them to drop a copper in the alms plate.

It was indeed much cooler when Antony took a few steps into the sanctuary, even amid flickering candles in every corner of the shadowy room. He scanned the pews and saw a few heads bowed in prayer, facing the altar that held the nine candles. From Antony's vantage point far back in the sanctuary, their light seemed tiny and insignificant. He imagined their light seemed even more diminished in the daytime when the windows all around were illuminated in pinks and purples and blues, color dancing across the floor with every shift of the light. With no sun to brighten it, the sanctuary felt as gloomy as a sepulcher.

"Welcome, brother." A deep voice startled Antony. He turned in the half-dark to see a large man standing over him. The man wore a brown roughspun robe, the robes novices wore in the Order of the Nine. The more seasoned brothers wore ink-black robes belted with a silver chain. This man was still in training. In fact, Antony realized he was not much more than a boy, perhaps only seventeen or so, but tall and stocky.

"Hello," Antony said. He bowed awkwardly. He wasn't entirely sure how to greet a monk. They had only a handful in Barnswood who kept a small farm behind the chapel, and Antony hardly ever saw them except during services. The novice watched him placidly, his large hands folded in front of him.

"Uh—is there any chance I can stay the night here?" Antony asked.

The boy's broad face beamed. "Of course, brother," he said. "The Cathedral of the Nine is home to any who need sanctuary. You may sleep here, in the chancel, or down in the crypt."

Antony shivered at the thought of sleeping in the crypt. The brother chuckled at his discomfort. "The dead will not bother you," he said. "They sleep more soundly than any living man."

Antony wasn't convinced. He fished in his satchel for the leather pouch. "I'm sure I have some small token I can offer the church, a copper or a—" His fingers landed on something small and metal. He pulled it out.

It wasn't a copper. It was a ring.

In the flickering candlelight, Antony made out the simple silver ring. It seemed old, tarnished, worn down after being slid on and off many a hand. On its face was the sigil of a lion, the edges of its flowing mane worried away by age, its stern eyes faded. Antony grimaced. It was a signet ring, he realized, one that important men would use to seal their mark in wax.

"I'm sorry," he said, "this must have been some trinket my father had—"

"By all the saints."

Antony looked up at the novice. The brother stared down at the ring, his mouth open in awe. Antony racked his brain to remember if any saints were represented by a lion.

"You believe, too?" breathed the novice.

"Believe what?"

"Believe he's not dead."

"Who?"

The novice laughed incredulously. "The lost prince," he said. "Prince Adrian. The one they said died on the same night as his father."

A chill raced down Antony's spine, as though a ghost had flown down from the ceilings of the sacred chapel to eavesdrop on their conversation.

"Um—" Antony began. "This is just...something my father has kept. A bit of silver to melt down if we ever need it." The lie came easily. It only made sense that Bron would keep some sort of cache. It made more sense to him than believing in a lost prince.

The novice shook his head. "Never melt this down," he said. "I was only a boy when King Alfred died. But the lion lives on." The novice smiled. "Forgive me. I'm getting ahead of myself. Keep your token, brother. And keep your alms. The house of the Nine is open to all."

The novice provided Antony with a candle as Antony tucked the ring back into the pouch, trying to push their conversation out of his mind. Why would his father have a ring like that? It must have been a trinket, something he bought from a merchant years ago—maybe even a little gift for Antony's mother that Bron could never part with. When Alfred was king, there must have been many a tinker that sold cheap baubles with the lion sigil, just as many now did with Tanor's dragon.

Bron wouldn't believe something so ridiculous as that, he thought. *Pa is too practical to believe something like that. He cares about the works of his hands, not the whispers in the street.*

"There is nothing to fear, brother," assured the novice as they approached the crypt. "The kings and queens will watch over you as you sleep. Besides, if you slept in the sanctuary, we would wake you before dawn with our morning prayers."

The air was even colder in the crypt, as though a chill crept up from the depths of the earth to shroud the dead in icy sleep. The air was stale and still, untouched by the warm breezes of the night. Each tomb stood with the carved likeness of the monarch that rested beneath. The faint candlelight flickered across their features, animating them for a moment as Antony and the novice passed.

"Rest well, brother," said the novice. "My name is David. If you need anything more, I am taking the night vigil and will be in the sanctuary."

He turned to leave, but stopped, turning back to look at Antony again. "And the ring—keep it somewhere safe. I've only ever seen those rings made of tin. That one seems to be made of silver. An outlaw or vagabond would make quick work of it."

The novice left Antony in the eerie silence of the Crypt of Kings. He stood unmoving for a long time, the flame of his candle never wavering. He looked down at the tomb he stood in front of. A gentle face slept in the stone. Its eyes were closed calmly against the world, and two broad hands were clasped across his breast over the hilt of a sword. The corners of his mouth were almost turned upward in a smile, but it may have been a trick of the shadows in Antony's eyes. The marble head rested on a pillow of stone, and beneath lay the bones of a king.

Antony lifted the candle to the inscription on the side of the sarcophagus. King Alfred the Beloved.

He sat down, leaning his head against the tomb, wondering what kind of king Alfred had been. Antony could not remember the time before King Tanor. That had been before he'd run away, before he'd fallen. Why had Alfred been beloved? He'd died in his prime, as his father Bron would say. Was he beloved merely because he didn't have a chance to become hated?

Antony's eyes became heavy. He laid his satchel on the ground as a makeshift pillow and lay down. David said the dead would not bother him. But the whole night through, they wouldn't leave him alone. And they spoke only one name that Antony forgot upon waking.

John

When John arrived in the barracks, he gratefully shrugged off his satchel and cloak on one of the low, narrow beds. Each bed had only a thin straw pallet—comfortable enough for him. He sat down, the muscles of his legs complaining loudly from so long in the saddle.

"My saddle sores are the size of a new mother's teat," complained Markus from across the hall. John could feel the blisters on his own backside rubbing against the leather of his trousers.

Markus sat on the bed across from him, and Sir Lyman behind. They prattled on with each other, but John ignored them. He knew it was only a matter of hours or even minutes before he saw his father again. He wasn't frightened. He wasn't nervous. He didn't know what he was, but he knew he wasn't excited. Facing down a legion of Northern men was easier than deciding how he would greet his father.

Lucas had disappeared for part of the afternoon, then reappeared as evening drew closer. John had quickly scrubbed his face, neck, and armpits with lye soap and pulled a dark leather tunic over his head. Its plainness would probably stick out among the court, but it was all he had. He made to belt his sword at his side, but realized he didn't need it. This was court, not war. As he straightened his tunic across his shoulders, Lucas limped into the room, beaming. He walked straight toward John.

"You'll never guess who I just saw, Johnny," he said, hardly able to talk around his toothy grin. John didn't guess. "Little Addie DuMont."

"Addie with the freckles?" Markus asked. "She always hung on the prince's every word, that little fool. Running after him like a puppy nipping at his ankles."

John said nothing. Adelaide. Markus was right. Adelaide had been devoted to Prince Adrian. There were rumors that Adelaide was betrothed to the prince before he died.

Before that night in the forest, the blood covering his tunic—

John shook the thought out of his head as quickly as it came. He focused on lacing his boots as Lucas kept talking.

"She's here to find a husband," Lucas said. "Poor girl. Her father she lost to a fire and now her brother is lost in his drink."

"D'you think you'll wed her, Luke?" asked Sir Lyman. "Is she fair?"

Lucas sat down on his bed. "Oh, fair as fair can be," he said. "It'll be the king's decision who she marries." He pressed his hands to his chest in mock humility. "It could be me, if I may be so lucky."

"We'll say a prayer for you, m'lord," Markus said with a dramatic bow. "May you have many happy years and many plump little children."

Everyone except John erupted with laughter. John tightened the laces on his boots. Adelaide had been eleven when he left. He didn't think he'd ever see her again. She had been as Markus said—small and freckled, always following the prince around. But before she belonged to the prince, she belonged to John. They had been friends before Prince Adrian ever paid any attention to her.

A sharp voice interrupted the laughter. "Sir John Behrens."

John looked up. He recognized Godfrey, his father's gentleman-in-waiting. He stood in the doorway, small and unintimidating, his dark robe hanging loosely around his thin body. His eyes met John's with a cold moment of acknowledgment. John stood up and straightened his tunic again.

"Are we all to see the king now?" asked Markus.

Godfrey gave him a sharp look. His pointed beard wagged as he shook his head. "Sir John only—it will delight him to know his son has returned safely, so I want to be sure he is introduced first. His grace will see the rest of you on the morrow for your assignments."

70

"Assignments?" Markus looked around at the other confused men.

Godfrey regarded him with disinterest. "Your duty to your crown is not yet finished. Lord Edwin Darkshire will brief you *on the morrow.*"

The others looked at each other, and John tried not to look at any of them. He stepped past them toward Godfrey, who waited with his arms neatly behind his back.

"Have fun in your gilded tower, Johnny," he heard Markus murmur as he passed. John wanted to grab the whelp by the collar and pin him against the wall. He knew his neck and face were turning red—he could feel it.

He followed Godfrey out of the barracks, through the courtyard, now quiet and dusky. The sun had dipped behind the west tower and hid in a bank of clouds, its beams glimmering in a faint glow as it continued to descend. The heat of the day still radiated off of the flagstones in the courtyard.

The inner hall past the raised parapet was much cooler, cooler even than the barracks. A few torches on sconces lit the way toward the great hall. John probably still could traverse the castle blindfolded. The small man's little legs moved surprisingly fast, like a mouse scurrying through a maze. Even with his long legs, John struggled to keep up. He didn't need Godfrey to lead him to Tanor's audience chamber, or any room, for that matter.

"I hope you are well, Sir John," Godfrey said suddenly, his high-pitched voice slightly breathless. He sounded incredibly uninterested in John's well-being. "It is *sir* now? I understand you were knighted?"

"Yes," John replied. He could still smell the stink of hot blood rising from the ground in plumes at the place where he'd knelt to take the sword. He'd only been nineteen, and he'd already killed more men than most would even meet in a lifetime.

"Very good," Godfrey said. "When you arrive in his grace's audience chamber, you will immediately kneel. I will then introduce you, but do not take it as a signal to rise. His grace will tell you when you may do so."

John ground his teeth after Godfrey made his clipped speech. *His grace.* He knew his father loved every moment of being king, of being knelt to, of noblemen who once spat on his name, bowing and scraping to him. He wouldn't even let his bastard son call him father.

So what now, Father? John thought. *I'm sorry—your grace.* What purpose did he serve Tanor now?

Godfrey swung open the door to the audience chamber. No one was there. It was half-dark, as it often was at that hour, the light gone from the high windows and only every other lamp lit. The king rarely held court or took appointments this late. Shadows danced across the coffered ceilings and the dark paneling of the walls.

John looked at Godfrey, who raised his graying eyebrows and looked pointedly into the room. He still expected John to do what they discussed, even in the king's absence. John breathed a heavy sigh and stepped into the room, approaching the tall wooden chairs on the dais. He knelt on the carpeted floor, craning his head forward in a full bow. He waited there, on one knee, for a painfully long time. Then he heard the small door behind the dais open.

"What business is this, Godfrey? I was about to sit down to my supper," said a voice, a clear, powerful voice that rang through the hall. A voice John hadn't heard in ten years, but a voice that still made his body tense.

John cautiously lifted his eyes to the dais. There stood his father, now nearly fifty years old. A decade of being king had aged him, but his features were still sharp and severe. He had deep lines around his mouth and forehead. Lines of worry and anguish. He smiled down at his son.

"Stand up, young man," said Tanor, his voice softer. "You are my son. There is no need for you to bow."

If I didn't bow, Godfrey probably would've thrown me out the window, John thought, glaring back at the small man. He stood cautiously. Tanor stepped down from the dais, the mirthless smile still on his face. Surprise flashed in Tanor's eyes as he realized that John stood taller than his father—much taller. The realization made John feel strange—his huge, intimidating father, now nothing but a man who looked up at him.

But then Tanor pulled him into a firm embrace. John tepidly received it, remaining stiff.

His father held him at arm's length for a moment. "My son has been delivered safely from war," he said. "For that, I am grateful."

You should be dead, his mirthless eyes said.

John didn't have time to respond. Another shadow appeared at the door, shorter and plumper than Tanor. His father's queen stepped into the room, wearing the same green gown John had seen her in that afternoon. Claudia. Her face lit up when she saw John, and she rushed toward him like an excited child.

"Wonders will never cease!" she exclaimed, her voice light and airy. Without invitation, she stepped down from the dais, took his face in her hands, and kissed his cheek. She had rings on almost every finger. "Do you remember me, little Johnny Behrens?"

Claudia was younger than John by almost two years—he knew that much from the way the soldiers in his regiment had talked about Tanor's young queen. She must have been a child at court when he was young, but back then she had been an inconsequential little girl—not his stepmother.

The blonde-haired woman in front of him was sensual. She wore a perfume that was thick and stifling, like ointment on a corpse, and her face was caked with white makeup. His face was still in her hands as he hunched awkwardly over her. She laughed at his discomfort and turned to her husband. Tanor was watching her the way a child might look at a plaything. It sent a chill down John's spine.

John took one of her hands off his face and gingerly kissed it. "Your grace."

She patted his face. "Call me Mother."

Absolutely not.

"Come!" she said, taking his arm. She turned to Tanor. "He shall dine with us, my king. I have decreed it."

Tanor laughed. "Indeed, he shall," he said. He did not share his wife's enthusiasm. He barely gave John another look as he led them back through the door, Godfrey trailing behind. Claudia coiled her arm around John's.

"There is much to tell you about," she said. Her thick floral perfume was making John's eyes water. "You have a little brother. Charles. He will be five years old soon, and he looks so much like your father—and like you."

She looked up at him. "He has your father's eyes, that beautiful bright blue. I can't wait for you to meet him."

John felt a strange illness rise in his stomach, and his legs felt weak and weightless as they walked. He remembered the little boy he'd seen that afternoon—his brother. And he wondered. He wondered how young Claudia was when she married Tanor. Wondered how long she had been promised to him.

"We have another heir on the way, of course," Claudia said. Her small, white hand rested on her protruding belly. "I have a feeling it's another boy. Our claim to the throne is secure. I will enter my confinement soon to prepare for the baby."

Our. John could have laughed. *Nothing belongs to her, not even her children. She must not understand that yet.*

They followed Tanor into the king's dining room. The room was long and narrow, with a table large enough to seat ten people. Now, everyone seated at the table stood as the royal family—and the bastard—entered. John scanned the faces. Four ladies—John assumed they were Claudia's ladies-in-waiting—and Lord Edwin Darkshire sat on one side of the table. Across from them sat two women, one old and matronly, the other young. He recognized Adelaide in an instant when her green eyes met his.

Adelaide immediately dipped her gaze downward. She would be twenty-one now, John guessed. She was small and slender, with a long braid of chestnut hair falling down her back. John remembered Lucas mentioning her father was dead. The woman next to her must have been her guardian.

She's here to find a husband. That was the other thing Lucas had said. John dismissed the thought.

"Sit beside Adelaide," Claudia said to him as they approached the table. John awkwardly took his place and waited for the royal couple to be seated. He noticed his father eyeing Adelaide as he sat.

"You look absolutely radiant, my dear," Tanor said. Adelaide smiled politely. "I am proud to call you a member of my court."

John felt Adelaide's eyes on him briefly as they all sat again. The feeling made his neck hot, but with what? Embarrassment?

"Sorry to keep you all waiting," Tanor continued. "My son has returned from the North." He beckoned to John, and now more eyes were on him. John gave a small nod of his head to the table. He locked eyes with the man sitting across from him—a face from his youth, an encouraging presence. Lord Edwin Darkshire. The older man smiled with tight lips, his eyes creasing as he did so.

Tanor led the table in the prayer to the Nine. John was surprised at how well he remembered the words, remembered his father praying them fervently, appealing the saints for what he thought was rightfully his. If John didn't pray hard enough, Tanor had always told him he would know the true meaning of *sorry*. And those were the nights when John learned that *sorry* had a feeling. That *sorry* felt like bruises and hot tears.

The prayer ended, and they ate. John picked absently at the roast in front of him. It was better food than he ever had in the North, but after what the day had brought, he couldn't stomach it. He eyed his father. Tanor did not act like a king. He slouched slightly in his chair, and he made conversation with the lady sitting to his left, a sumptuous woman with red hair. Maybe that was why he was so well-received—he was not as stern and commanding as King Alfred had been, at least not in private company.

"It is strange to see my son with so little appetite," Tanor said, loud enough for the table to hear. All other conversations grew quiet at the sound of his voice. "He would eat me out of house and home when he was a child. No wonder he's become such a giant."

John felt his neck grow even hotter and slouched low in his chair. He tried not to look at his father or hear the giggling from the ladies across from him. Adelaide didn't seem to heed Tanor. She continued picking absently at her plate.

"No doubt Sir John has traveled a long way," said Edwin with a warm glance toward John, "and has certainly had a long day. He hasn't been home in ten years and returns to find his home much changed. That's more than enough to dampen one's appetite."

Edwin took the silver carafe from the table and filled John's goblet, then raised his cup. "A toast to Sir John, and to all the brave men who have returned either to their homes or the arms of the Saints."

The table raised their glasses—John noticed his father cast an irritated glance at Edwin. But Edwin kept his fatherly eyes on John.

Tanor quickly called for music. Godfrey summoned a trio of court musicians who played their delicate instruments for the rest of the meal. John willed himself to eat a little before refilling his glass of wine. He wanted to speak to Adelaide but was afraid he would say something foolish. She seemed occupied in listening to whatever the queen's ladies said. She too was newly returned to the court—she was probably drinking in every word the ladies said.

"Young man," Edwin said, breaking John out of his thoughts. He had a naturally quiet voice, equal parts soothing and unsettling. "You look pale. Would you take a turn about the room with me?"

No one noticed as they rose from the table, John following Edwin's path toward the hearth, which was ablaze with a fresh fire. John didn't think he could sweat anymore, but he was wrong. He took a long draft of the cool ice wine as Edwin gazed at the fire, amused.

"Such a hot day," he said, "but Tanor still insists on a fire in every room."

"The palace can get drafty," John noted.

Edwin scoffed. "So quick to defend your father," he said. He and John walked side-by-side as the rest of the table continued in their merriment. Along one wall was a line of tall, peaked windows, all flung open and welcoming in a warm breeze that rocked the chandeliers above their heads.

"What will you do now, son?" Edwin asked. "The king's court is a different kind of war than the one you're used to."

"I don't know," John replied honestly. "I suspect I'll marry, and my father will give me land and title."

"And this is what you want?" Edwin asked. John could tell he was searching. The older man's dark eyes narrowed as he looked up at him. Edwin walked carefully, his heel never touching the ground at the same time as his toe, his upper body steady. John knew from experience that his step could be deadly—a wandering deer would never hear him coming.

"I don't know," John replied again. "I didn't want to go to war."

"You were bred by war," Edwin said. They were passing by the musicians. He raised his voice only slightly above it. "Your father didn't want to raise you, so he let the battlefield do it for him."

John was slightly surprised by how bold his old mentor was. He wondered why—and how Edwin got away with it.

"I remember when you were a boy," the older man continued, "you could hardly bear the sight of a rabbit in a trap. Once, when you were nine, we found one still alive in a trap I'd set. It was wriggling, trying to run for its life. I told you to kill it—snap its neck. You couldn't do it. Even though it would've been a mercy, you did not want to kill the innocent thing with your own hand."

John remembered. Edwin had been patient with him, but when Tanor had seen his tear-stained eyes, he'd slapped him.

"I held my hands over yours as you made your first kill—a poor little hare in a trap," Edwin recalled. "We did it together. How many men have you killed since then, I wonder?" Edwin turned to look at him, his eyes glittering, his mouth a thin smile. "I've never married, John. I've sired no children—that I know of. And I've held no title. My father's name means nothing anymore. The name Darkshire will die with me. But I have done what the Great Maker put me here to do."

He stopped talking as they passed behind Tanor's chair. John wasn't sure what Edwin was getting at. It should be John's desire to wed, have children, and own land—it *should* be. But why didn't he want it?

"I think the Great Maker formed you for a similar purpose," Edwin continued as they rounded back along the other side of the room. He looked thoughtful, chewing on the inside of his cheek. "I may yet have a purpose for you, too. Welcome back, John."

He patted John's arm gently, and they returned to their seats. As they had circled the room, one of the queen's ladies had left. She returned now with a sleepy boy swaddled in her arms and presented him to the table.

"His little grace would like to say goodnight," she announced, although the boy didn't look interested to see any of them. He was a beautiful child, with curls of chestnut hair and chubby, cherubic cheeks. He fussed in the lady's arms and hid his face in her shoulder.

"Don't be shy, Charles," said Claudia. "You'll have to greet your thousands of subjects someday, my pet! Say goodnight to Papa, at least."

When the child looked up at the sound of his mother's voice, John saw the sea-glass eyes of their father. Tanor stood up and took the boy in his arms. Charles immediately wrapped his arms around Tanor's neck and grinned.

"Dream good dreams, Charles," Tanor murmured. John's chest tightened, and it took him a moment to understand why.

Tanor kissed the boy on the forehead and set him down. Claudia's lady took Charles' little hand and led him back out of the room. The other ladies chorused a good night as the little prince beamed at them on his way out the door. Claudia stared after him adoringly.

"I believe I will retire as well, my dear," she said, turning to Tanor. She and her ladies stood up, and the men stood with them. John pulled Adelaide's chair out for her. She looked up at him and smiled softly.

"Thank you," she said. Her face was flushed from the heat of the room, creating two red blooms on her cheeks. She curtsied and followed the queen.

John realized he should have said something back to her. He wished he had. He watched her slip out the door behind Claudia. He didn't want to marry. Did he? He felt even more uncertain now than when he'd talked to Edwin. Then he glanced at his father as the king prepared to leave.

It's all up to him, John thought. *For both of us. The king will seal both of our fates.*

Adelaide

Claudia demanded a bath as soon as she and her ladies exited the hall. Adelaide followed far behind the rest, and one by one each lady was sent off for one thing or another for the bath—Lydia, prepare the tub; Rachel, fetch a servant to heat the water; Ilse, bring clean towels—until only Adelaide and one other lady remained to follow the queen to her private suite. The chief lady-in-waiting was Elanor of The Roses, a tall woman with a pile of auburn hair on top of her head. The Roses was the wealthiest town in all the South, even wealthier than Southborn. It was deep in the country, where the soil was rich and the rains were good and warm. Because of that, The Roses were known for their beautiful gardens and rich vegetation. The Lord of The Roses had only daughters, and with her dignified air and her constantly pursed lips and disapproving glances, Adelaide guessed Elanor was the oldest. She walked behind the queen with a dignified air.

"You will get accustomed to the queen's moods and attitudes," Elanor murmured to Adelaide as they walked. "Our duty is to wait upon her grace, but not *serve* her. We are not her *servants,* but her handmaidens." Adelaide noted the slight disdain in her voice. "We sit with her while she bathes. We talk with her. We brush her hair and we prepare her for bed. But we do not fetch things for her. Servants fetch things for her. Servants serve her breakfast and her wine."

"I understand," Adelaide said after Elanor paused for a long time. But she wasn't sure she did. She didn't think there was a difference between a servant and a handmaiden—but Elanor seemed to think there was. She walked as though she were a queen, with her chin tilted high and her generous bosom thrust in front of her. The tall woman looked at Adelaide with a smile.

"She likes you already, I can tell," Elanor said. "She has dismissed many ladies from her presence. Lydia and Rachel have only attended to her for a year. The pair of them are very young, not yet ready to be wed. Claudia thought they were pretty, so she wanted them. I, however—I have been with Claudia since her wedding day."

The queen opened the door to her suite. It was expansive and generous, with a bed larger than anything Adelaide had slept in, adorned with embroidered pillows and thick furs. On one wall was a wide wardrobe, and on the other was a dressing table littered with pots of perfume and paints. Sitting before the hearth was a large wooden tub, in which Lydia draped sheets to prevent the water from leaking onto the floor. Soon, Rachel appeared with a manservant carrying a heavy bucket of hot water, and Ilse with towels.

When the tub was filled, Elanor helped the queen undress. Adelaide admired Claudia as Elanor unfastened the back of her gown and under-skirts. The queen pulled her underclothes off herself. All the features of her body were soft and sloping. She was full of life—not only because she was with child, but because of her youth. Although she was Adelaide's age, she seemed so much younger. She had a kind of innocence that floated around her.

"The only people who can behold a queen's naked form are her husband and her ladies," Elanor said, directing it to Adelaide.

Claudia smiled and followed her gaze.

"You are a great teacher, Elanor," she said. "Adelaide will be a true lady-in-waiting in no time."

Elanor helped her climb into the tub and guided her as she reclined. Her belly crested out of the water, large and taut and white. Adelaide wondered what it felt like to have a baby inside her body. Claudia caressed her stomach gently, splashing water over it until it glistened like the rest of her wet skin. Elanor poured a vial of rosewater into the bath, and soon the humid room was fragrant with its scent. The other ladies sat nearby. One of them poured the queen a glass of wine from a silver pitcher.

"Did you enjoy sitting next to Sir John tonight, Adelaide?" asked the queen. She looked up at Adelaide from her relaxed position in the tub. Her plump lips curved upward in a flirtatious smile.

"We didn't talk to each other very much," Adelaide replied softly. It had been a shock to see him after so long. After ten years, she felt as though they were strangers. Even though they had spent so much time together growing up, it seemed that had been another life.

"He's very handsome," Elanor remarked. "He looks so much like Tanor."

"*His grace*," Claudia corrected. She slipped a foot out of the tub and let it hang over the edge, wiggling her toes. Elanor seemed to understand the signal and bent down before it. She began massaging it with her thumbs.

"He is handsome," Adelaide agreed.

"He took my arm when we walked into supper—such a gentleman. And so *strong*," Claudia purred. Her tone made Adelaide's cheeks flame red. "Perhaps the king will make a match of the two of you. You would be my daughter-in-law. How lovely would that be? Darling Adelaide, do you see that brush on the table? Fetch it, would you?"

Adelaide did as she was told and fetched the brush from the table across the room. She knelt and pulled the pins out of Claudia's hair, letting it tumble down the back of the tub. It seemed strange and sacred to touch the queen's hair. Her yellow hair was incredibly soft, like silk from Second Summer corn. Adelaide could have played with it for hours, twisting and sliding the soft tendrils between her fingers. Her father used to let her play with his hair when it grew long. Landon did too until he grew to be a man and was embarrassed by her. The thought of the two of them sent a pang to her heart.

"There is power in being a wife," Claudia noted. She relaxed her head back as Adelaide brushed. "We hold power in our wombs. Money doesn't make sons, neither do titles nor lands or castles or any of that sort of thing. A woman with sons is the most powerful woman in the world."

"She's telling you to have lots of babies with John," Elanor said with a wink.

Claudia flicked water at Elanor, who smiled, but Adelaide thought she saw annoyance on her face. The queen reached back and touched Adelaide's arm with her wet hand.

"I simply want you to have the joy that I have, Adelaide," she said. Claudia was speaking to her as though Adelaide were a child. "My wedding day was the happiest day of my life. I felt so beautiful."

"You *were* beautiful," said Elanor. She stood up and took the fresh towel from where it was being warmed by the fire. "You should have seen her, Adelaide. She wore a dress of the finest blue, blue as the sky, and a net of pearls in her hair."

Claudia laughed. "I will never fit into that dress again," she said, rubbing her belly. Adelaide watched her face as she brushed the queen's silky hair. The queen was beautiful—like a little pregnant porcelain doll that enjoyed being pampered and played with. Adelaide couldn't help but see an emptiness in her eyes as if her happiness truly had left her on her wedding day, and now she was merely playing a part. *Nonsense,* she chided herself. *Claudia has everything. How could she be unhappy?*

"Help me up, Adelaide," said the queen, raising her hands. Adelaide took them and helped Claudia rise. Steam rolled off the curves of her body as Elanor wrapped the towel around her shoulders. The queen turned and looked at Adelaide. Adelaide was only a little shorter than her.

"You needn't worry about anything, my dear," said Claudia. "We will find you a husband, and we will find you a good one."

Adelaide curtsied. "Thank you, your grace," she said.

"You should get some rest, Adelaide," Elanor said over the queen's shoulder. "Ilse, help the queen to bed. I will take Adelaide to her rooms."

Adelaide curtsied again and left, following Elanor. The tall woman had a quick step and a confident air, one that Adelaide already found she envied.

"You'll awaken at eight bells every morning," Elanor explained. "The queen rises at nine, usually. We usually breakfast with her and attend to her throughout the day, until she enters her confinement. There is to be some sort of archery demonstration tomorrow morning, so we will attend her at the inner ward."

Adelaide's chambers were close to the queen's. If Adelaide remembered correctly, all the rooms in that corridor had always belonged to the queen and her ladies.

Before Elanor left her, she turned to Adelaide. "I have tried for many years to find a husband at court," she said. "Being at court is one big game, Adelaide."

"I know," Adelaide said. "I was a child when—"

"And you're not a child anymore," Elanor interrupted, her voice direct but not unkind. "It's a different game. Perhaps your aunt has told you it's not what you know at court, but who you know. I would offer you this advice—it's not what you know *or* who you know. It's *what* you know about who you know."

Elanor bid her goodnight and retreated to her room. Her words echoed in Adelaide's mind. *What you know about them.* She didn't know anything about anyone at court—only who they used to be when she was a child. Lucas used to be her protector. John used to be her friend. But what were they now?

She didn't want to rest. Her muscles ached from being jostled around in the carriage all day. But she didn't want to sleep. Too much had happened that day for her mind to rest just yet. She walked along the corridor from her chambers, along the south wing of the castle. The south wing was all reserved for the royal family, with private suites for special guests that would often go untouched for months. Her father's old rooms had been in the east wing, where council members had chambers to stay in when they were in Southborn.

Instead, Adelaide climbed the steps of the north tower to the ramparts. The north tower was the smallest of the palace's four towers, with only a narrow staircase that led up to the palace's high walls. A warm breeze blasted her face as she walked onto the narrow walkway. The ramparts reminded Adelaide of the cliffs by the sea at her father's house, but instead of churning water below, there was only the glow of the town and the faint hum of activity.

Adelaide could still hear the voice of her old tutor, Mistress Elda—"And who built this palace, Lady Adelaide?" Elda had been old when Rowan selected her to teach Adelaide, and she'd been old when she'd taken ill and died. Adelaide thought Elda must've been born old.

"Great King Stephen built this palace, guided by the hands of Saint Augustus," Adelaide had replied dutifully, reciting the year and dimensions of the palace. Those were lost to her memory now. When Elda wasn't looking, she'd scramble onto the wall, leaning out until she looked straight down at the village below. She'd watch for hours. From there, she could see all the town's corners—rich and poor, bawdy and respectable. She'd sometimes watch one person at a time, a wool merchant or a blacksmith. She'd wonder who they were, what their names were. Once she'd seen a man and a woman together, embracing one another tightly on a dark street. When she'd asked her father what they were doing later, Rowan had only blushed and changed the subject.

As Adelaide paced the wall, a few sentries stood idly around, hardly noticing her. A few leaned sleepily against the wall. The village hummed below, but there was no sense of danger. The huge banners snapped in the high wind over Adelaide's head. When Adelaide looked to the west, there was only a faint orange glimmer. Dusk had fallen, warm and pleasant.

A few yards down the walkway, a tall figure stood on the wall, looking out the same direction that she was. As her eyes adjusted, she realized it was John. She looked away quickly and leaned her body against the battlement so her face was obscured from his view. *Maybe he won't notice.*

Adelaide had hugged him when he left, wondering if that was the last time she'd see him. John had held onto her for a long time, and his sea-glass eyes were red when he let go.

He'd written to her while he was away. Adelaide had never written back. Her father had implored her to write to him.

"It's all he has," Rowan had said. "My dearest, write him a letter."

But she wouldn't. *Why does it matter if he's just going to die, anyway?* That's what she thought—what she *knew*—would happen. Every day, more townsfolk in their village mourned their sons. More strangers came to

Rowan's house and told him the names of the boys who'd died. Adelaide had known some of them. Afterward, she'd heard their mothers wailing in the streets. In war, everyone died. John wouldn't come back.

It seemed Adelaide was right. A different man came back. John's dark hair no longer flopped in front of his eyes. It was pushed back from his face, his high forehead and severe features. He now seemed like a man bred for war, in his stern bearing, in the way he walked as though he were surveying a battlefield. Adelaide's heart was in her throat throughout dinner—*Does he remember that I never wrote to him? Does he remember me? Does he even care?*

She watched lights fade across the city, extinguished for slumber. There was still noise in the air, and music and smoke. Much of the city was going to sleep, but much of it would remain awake for a long while. Adelaide yawned.

"I remember how much you liked it up here."

A voice startled her away from her perch on the battlement, her heart pounding. There stood John, a small smile playing on his lips. Adelaide recovered herself, brushing the front of her dress, still the pale blue gown from traveling that day. He wore similarly plain garb, a drab leather tunic and black breeches. He stood like a soldier—shoulders back, neck straight and tall, hands crossed in front of him. Adelaide's cheeks grew strangely hot under his gaze.

"We both did," she replied. "We'd help each other look over the battlements. I'd give you a push so you could see over the edge."

"You almost *pushed* me over," he said. He still smiled, but he didn't laugh. He leaned against the battlement, looking down at the city. The pale glow illuminated the lines of his face, lines that made him look much older than three-and-twenty. A thought came unbidden to Adelaide's mind—*I wonder what he's seen.*

They stood in silence for a long time, both staring out through the battlement. *What do I say?* Adelaide wondered. *It's been ten years. We were children, and now we're not.* When they'd played together as children, Adrian was often with them. He was the one who told them what to do and where to go. He would know what to say. Adelaide wondered what Adrian would be like as a man. Would his smile still crease the corners of his eyes? Or would he be like John, stern and sullen?

"Lucas told me about the fire, and your father," John finally said. "I'm sorry."

Adelaide gazed out at the flickering lights and took a deep breath. *"Write to him, dearest." All the times I didn't listen to Father and should have. All the times I thought I had more time.* A tear pricked the corner of her eye, but she willed it away. *Not now. Not here.* She swallowed the lump in her throat.

"Thank you. Everything is so different now, but his grace has been very kind to me," she said. "He's welcomed my aunt and me to court. He will find a husband for me, eventually."

"I'm sure it won't be long," John said, then looked startled he'd said it. "I'm sorry. That was forward of me."

Adelaide shook her head. "It's all right," she said. "I *hope* it won't be long."

She looked up at him. John stood head and shoulders over her. Her brother Landon was tall too, but was growing soft and fleshy from his love of drinking. John was trim and strong, his big hands resting easily on the parapet.

"After ten years away, everything still seems the same," John said. "Ten years since…"

The fifteenth of Harvestmonth. Darkest Day. He didn't have to say it.

"Did you find that when you came back to the palace," Adelaide asked, "you felt all the same things you felt that day all over again? You were there when it happened, after all."

John's face darkened. He stared steadily down at his hands.

"I hardly remember," he said. "Adrian was there one moment, and the next he wasn't. And then we were at war, and that's been my life ever since. It's been *half* my life."

He fell silent again. John had always been quiet as a boy, but now his quietness was punctuated by something else, something almost like grief, or even guilt. Adelaide knew he'd killed people. But she wouldn't ask about it.

"I think I should go to bed," she said. The air felt heavy around them now. She shouldn't have talked about Darkest Day. John looked up from his hands, but he wasn't smiling anymore.

"It was good to see you, Jo—*Sir* John." She curtsied.

He smirked only a little, standing up from his leaning position on the wall. Before she could walk away, he caught her hand and kissed it gently.

"Lady Adelaide," he said.

Her heart was pounding. She caught her breath as she turned and walked away. The way he'd looked at her and spoken to her. *I'm sure it won't be long.* Had he been trying to charm her? John had always had a softness for her as a child. But now they were grown up, and he looked at her differently. His eyes had been so intense, fixed on her so fully. They were just as arresting—just as terrifying—as his father's.

Adelaide opened the door to her modest chambers. They consisted of a solar adorned with simple tables and comfortable chairs, and her bedchamber through another door. Her aunt had been placed in another wing of the palace—mercifully so. Adelaide wasn't sure she could take another earful from Pauline that night. Her exhaustion was setting in. A bowl of water sat on her dressing table. She splashed her face, rubbing the lukewarm water into her neck and between her fingers, running it through her hair. She would order a bath tomorrow, she decided. She slipped off her simple gown and threw it over the chair by the table. Elanor had ordered a whole new closet of dresses for her, much to Adelaide's chagrin. It seemed like too much excess after the expenses of wartime.

"Your beautiful gowns will brighten the Commoner's Ball tomorrow," Elanor had said. "It brings joy to the people to see their beauty."

I'm not sure if it does. Adelaide had almost forgotten about the Commoner's Ball. Once Elanor had told her and Pauline about it at dinner, Adelaide's aunt wouldn't stop talking about it. It was the one night in the year that townsfolk were welcome in the palace to feast and dance. A Commoner's Ball had not been held for ten years during the war, so Elanor said this one would be tenfold grander than any other ball in the kingdom.

Adelaide didn't want to think about parties. She threw herself on the bed. From the bed, she had a clear view through the window into the starry sky. The breeze whispered through the thin curtains. Adelaide's eyes grew heavy. Her pillow smelled faintly of lavender.

Her eyes fluttered open to the feeling of someone shaking her gently. Half-asleep, Adelaide turned and saw in the dim midnight light that a boy stood by her bed. As he moved, he shimmered in and out of reality in her mind's eye, and she knew somehow she was dreaming.

She knew him instantly. Adrian.

He gazed at her, wide-eyed, his face bright and alive.

"Ad*die*," he whined.

Adelaide appeased him and sat up, half awake.

It was as though she could feel his hand on her arm, shaking her awake. Warm. Alive. *Alive.*

"You slept for *so long.*"

She rubbed her eyes. He was still there.

"It doesn't feel like it," she groaned. He beckoned her to stand up.

"Adelaide, you've gotten so tall," said Adrian. He was thirteen, on the verge of growing into more manly features and limbs. But death had trapped him at the edge of boyhood, his cheeks still round, his features still smooth and ruddy. "You're taller than me now, Addie."

Why does this feel so real? She looked down at him and knew he wasn't there. But it almost seemed like she could reach down and touch his fair cheek.

"Come with me, Adelaide," he said. Her weightless legs followed him out the door.

Adelaide blinked, and she stood with Adrian in the Crypt of Kings, far below the Cathedral of the Nine. She hadn't been there since Alfred and Adrian's funeral. The place was quiet and sacred, its air heavy with history. It was vast, stretching the entire length of the cathedral itself, and lit only by torchlight in the event of a vigil or funeral.

The resting place of King Alfred was laid out like a bed, and his likeness reposed peacefully upon it. His visage was gilded in gold, as noble and handsome as it had been in life, and just as stern. The hands were crossed upon his breast over a silver-colored sword, and on his marble-carved head lay a crown of pure gold. His wife, Queen Catherine, lay beside him, and in her arms was Little Cate, the baby she'd lost along with her life. Their marriage had been one of love, not ceremony or custom. Her gentle features were worn, but her sleeping stone eyes looked as though they could open at any moment and look into Adelaide's.

Between them lay a small figure, a white lily cut in stone upon his breast. There in repose lay Adrian, his small body at peace between his parents. Adelaide thought that if she looked at his marble chest long enough, she would see it move up and down.

"I'm sleeping there," said Adrian, standing beside her. He looked with wonder down at the tomb.

"Of course you are, Adrian," said Adelaide. "They found you. They found you in the forest on that dreadful night. And your father. You were buried together."

"They didn't find me."

Adrian sounded like a petulant child. Adelaide smiled fondly and realized that voice was straight out of her memory. *That's exactly how he would have said it.* But she was confused.

"No," she said. "No, Adrian. You're here. We buried you." Her voice was firm.

"No. I'm sleeping."

She reached out to touch his shoulder, but he stepped away.

"I'm sleeping," he said again.

"Adrian, they—they cut your head off." A lump formed in her throat. "This is just a dream."

Adrian shook his head. "I'll wake up," he said. "Don't worry. I'll wake up right here."

"*Adrian.*"

Adelaide opened her eyes as she whispered his name. She hadn't dreamed about Adrian in a long time. Pale morning light crept across the ceiling of her chamber, and she had tears in her eyes. She turned her face to the pillow and let herself cry in the stillness of the morning.

Antony

His consciousness stirred at the sound of ringing bells. Though he was not fully awake, Antony's mind counted each toll. By the time the eighth one sounded, his eyes were open, and he took a moment to remember where he was. He stared up at the low ceiling of the crypt. Somewhere above him, he could faintly hear the monks chanting their morning prayers. Antony drowsily mumbled his own as he sat up, each muscle of his back complaining as he did so. He'd slept fitfully but felt rested enough.

Nine bells. I have an hour to get to the palace. He stretched his arms upward, trying to will the tension out of them. He'd be no good if he couldn't shoot a bow today. His heart was suddenly racing.

In front of the king. The *king of the South. What have I gotten myself into?*

Antony looked down at the leather pouch, remembering the ring that had fallen out. He remembered something the novice, David, had said to him. *The lion lives on.* Were there really so many people who believed that King Alfred's son was still alive? And if David believed that, did he believe Tanor was a false king?

I guess people will believe anything, Antony thought, *if they don't want to believe the truth.*

Though he remembered very little about his days after the fall, Antony did remember how angry his father had been after the death of King Alfred. Bron did not easily get angry. While Antony had rested, Bron had been sure not to upset him with the news from the capital. Antony took the entire winter to get better. Bron had sat at the side of his bed every

91

night, telling him stories to help him remember—stories about his mother, about growing up with his brothers. And Antony remembered the way a sleeper remembers his dreams upon waking. Bron helped him get strong. When the weather got warmer, he took Antony out onto the croft near Barnswood to walk in the fresh air, to ride on Sam, sometimes to shoot a bow. Antony had walked into the sun, pale and emaciated, a deep scar on his scalp, but after Second Summer of that year, he was as tan and brawny as he ever had been. He no longer had sudden aches in his head. And he could remember as far back as his mother's death. Though the other villagers in Barnswood gave him strange looks, they were happy to see him recovered.

"You've got yourself a changeling, Bron Bowyer," said Fred the innkeeper when he'd seen Antony. "I've never seen your boy look better in me life!"

Antony pondered the memory as he blinked away the brightness of the sun on that warm morning in Southborn. The clamor of the city surrounded him—goats and sheep and hens being flocked to the market, vendors selling their wares to early shoppers. The day promised to be warm already, though the sun was barely above the horizon.

Sam eyed him sleepily when Antony fetched the old mule from the Five Oxen's stable. His ears twitched in surprise as if to say *you're never up this early*. Antony let him have his fill of water and hitched him back up to the cart. They trod down the streets together, Antony pulling the mule along as streets narrowed and widened and turned. Antony didn't know the direct way to the palace, but with the way it loomed over the entire village, it wouldn't be hard to find.

The bell tolled nine when Antony arrived at the iron gate leading to the courtyard. A chill crept down Antony's spine as he approached—a chill of awe and fear. He squeezed Sam's harness to prevent his hand from shaking. *Not today. I can't be nervous today.*

A guard appeared on the other side of the gate. From the way his belly ballooned underneath his leather jerkin, Antony guessed he did a lot of sitting and not a lot of protecting. He looked down at Antony with red-rimmed eyes—maybe tired, maybe hungover. His pimpled nose was red and shiny, which made Antony suspect the latter.

"And who are you?" asked the guard. He held a spear lazily in one hand, its butt resting on the ground.

Antony cleared his throat and tried to sound as important as possible. "I'm here for Lord—uh, for Lord—" Shit, what was the man's name?

The guard grimaced. "Lord *Uh?*" he chuckled. "I don't think I know of a Lord *Uh*, boy." He laughed harder. The laugh turned into a wheeze and his wine-sour breath blasted into Antony's face.

"I have bows—I'm here to show the king," Antony explained, straightening as much as he could. His face grew hotter and hotter. "A man asked me to come today, to show the king these bows for his sentries." His words poured out of him almost nonsensically, and he withered under the laughter of the fat guard.

"Everyone's got something to show the king," said the guard. "If you don't make yourself scarce, I'll show you the tip of my spear."

Antony balled up his other fist. His embarrassment was gone. Now he was angry. The guard kept laughing. Antony wanted to spit on him.

"What's the commotion here?" said a calm voice behind the guard. The fat guard stepped back and there stood the man Antony had seen yesterday. He glided calmly toward them and smiled at Antony. "Ah, yes, the bowyer's boy. Is it that time already? You're quite punctual. Tell them to raise the gates, Russel. This young man is my guest."

Antony had never seen a man suppress his laughter faster than Russel. As soon as he'd heard the man's voice, he choked on his last chuckle. Antony even saw a tear run down his face from the strain. Russel barked hoarsely up at the guards on top of the wall, ordering them to raise the gate. Slowly, the iron gate rattled upward, leaving just enough room for Antony and Sam to pass through.

The man led Antony through the courtyard and ordered a groom to stable Sam. Antony was still searching his brain, trying to remember the man's name. He was dressed well today, in green velvet trimmed with gold, his hair once again oiled back from his forehead.

"Take a few with you, but leave the rest," the man instructed, eyeing

Antony's cart. "If the king is interested, then we'll see about the rest of your stock."

Antony nodded dutifully. The morning was muggy, and he was already sweating as he unhitched Sam once again from the cart. He surreptitiously sniffed one of his armpits. Fairly rank. Hopefully, he would stand far enough away from the king. He gave Sam a rub on the nose before the groom took the old mule away.

"Enjoy this, Sam," Antony said. "You're gonna stay in a palace stable. You'll eat like a king, with all that choice hay and clean water. Don't get too fat while I'm gone, all right?" Sam chuffed and nuzzled Antony's shoulder before the groom tugged the animal away.

Antony couldn't help but feel like a mule himself as the man guided him to the inner ward. His eyes tried to take everything in around him all at once—King Tanor's banners flying high above the courtyard on the spires of tall towers, all manner of people who filled the courtyard, whether they were squires sparring with wooden swords, a cook shooing a stray dog from the kitchen door, guards playing Blind Man's Dice when their superiors weren't looking. Antony felt out of place, a stranger—and yet half-formed memories come unbidden to his mind.

Had he been here before?

The inner ward of the palace was a long stretch of trimmed green lawn. In the middle, a fountain burbled contentedly, and a handful of children were playing in it, splashing one another and laughing. Each was dressed in velvet and silk, but the fronts of their tunics were soaking wet. Antony assumed their parents could afford to buy them new clothes often.

Shimmering at the far end of the ward was a target made of hay the height of a man, with the shape of one drawn on it. Antony could just make out the bulbous head, two arms sticking out awkwardly from its sides. *Easy,* he thought as he squinted. He felt the breeze ruffle his hair and noted its direction. His heart was still pounding. He knew it would only pound harder when the king arrived. *Just don't let your hands shake. Do this for Pa.*

Antony stuck each arrow into the ground in front of him, positioning himself a hundred yards in front of the target. As he did, the voice of a groom trumpeted, "The king!"

The children in the fountain stopped playing. Dutifully, they lined up on the ground and knelt as members of his grace's court spilled out onto the lawn. The ladies hiked up their decadent skirts in the dewy grass. Antony dropped to one knee as well, taking his cue from the children and the man standing beside him. He'd never seen so much finery in one place. The ladies had clean, white faces and sculpted bodies and hands, untouched by toil. The men were all clean-shaven, their hands manicured. It was strange how few of them seemed to even notice Antony. They simply strutted to the lawn and regarded the target, commenting on how far away it was.

Antony had only ever seen the likeness of King Tanor before, either in statue or tapestry, and that was how he always imagined the king—immobile. But to see a human in place of his image surprised him a little. The light of the low-hanging sun cast shadows into the noticeable wrinkles on the man's face and the gray slivers of hair on his dark head. The tunic he wore was a hypnotizing purple embroidered with silver. It was strange to see a face so familiar—a face stamped on coins, drawn in ink—in the flesh. A man so familiar to Antony, though Antony was entirely alien to him.

King Tanor regarded him with relative warmth. The king approached him with an easy smile and clasped the hand of the small man beside Antony.

"Edwin," he said. *That's his name. Edwin. I should've remembered.* "My good man. You've got something to show us this morning, I take it?"

"I do, your grace," Edwin said in a clipped tone. Tanor swung his gaze to Antony, his eyes glittering. They were blue and pale, like the sky above them.

"This is a better way to begin the day than sitting on my arse listening to peasants complain," he said, and Antony barked an unexpected laugh. Then he wasn't sure if he should have laughed, so he stopped. The king only laughed harder and clasped Antony's hand, putting his other hand on the boy's shoulder and giving it a firm squeeze.

"It's a pleasure, master bowyer," Tanor said.

"Antony, your grace," Antony said meekly, dipping his head.

"Bron's boy?" asked the king. Antony nodded. "You're his spitting image. Your father is one of the reasons we won the war. He provided the artillery we needed to beat the Northerners back in the mountain battles. But now let's see what you have for my sentries, shall we?"

"Of course, your grace."

As Tanor withdrew his hand, Antony noticed the large ring on the king's middle finger. It bore his signet, the seal of his family—a mighty dragon breathing fire. Suddenly Antony's heart pounded violently, and he couldn't explain why. He looked up at King Tanor.

Run.

"What was that, your grace?" Antony asked. The king grimaced in confusion.

"I said nothing, my boy, only that I look forward to your demonstration," Tanor said slowly, scanning his face.

Antony could've sworn he heard someone speak. Someone told him to run. At that same moment, he felt the ghost of something. He saw a face through warped glass and heard a muffled voice, felt something cold and heavy in his hand. He remembered something terrible that had happened, but only the feeling, not the memory.

"Are you all right, son? You look a bit pale."

Antony snapped out of whatever memory gripped him and blinked up at the king. The feeling dissipated like a dream, but his stomach still turned. Edwin looked sideways at him.

"Yes. Forgive me," Antony said. "If you'll step back, your grace, we can begin shortly."

Antony swung his gaze across the crowd again. More of the king's courtiers had joined the group. Some servants had brought out two chairs—one for the king, and one for the queen, Antony assumed. A woman with yellow hair, great with child, sat in one of them already, fanning herself with her hand. Next to her, a voluptuous red-haired woman held a squirming boy who squinted in the sun. The blonde woman must have been the queen, Antony guessed, based on the small silver circlet she wore in her hair. It matched Tanor's own silver crown. The king had turned back and sat in the chair beside her. He kissed her the hand, and she giggled.

As Antony continued to scan the group of nobles, he saw the knight from the tavern a few nights before. He stood behind his father and had been staring at Antony, but averted his eyes as soon as he was discovered. He saw the strong resemblance between him and the king.

That's right, Antony remembered. *He's the king's bastard. It's generous of his father to include him in his court.*

On the other side of the queen stood a young woman—*the* young woman Antony had met the day before. They both looked at each other in surprise, and Antony's heart took to thumping hard in his chest again. She was dressed more simply than the rest of the nobles, but the dark blue dress she wore was fetching on her figure. It was made of velvet, and its blurry sheen caught the sunlight in shimmering swaths. She smiled at him in recognition. He almost didn't realize the court was waiting rather impatiently for something to happen. Antony cleared his throat.

"I thank you all—" Their chattering didn't immediately stop. Antony felt his face burn red. He started again once they quieted.

"I thank you all for indulging me with your presence here today. Lord Edwin has given me the great fortune to demonstrate for you effective weapons for the court sentries."

Antony glanced at the young woman. She was listening intently, a small smile on her face. It was all the confidence he needed.

"I understand your sentries rely on the typical longbow for power and precision." Antony hefted a yew longbow up from the ground. "These are truly powerful weapons. They fire straight and true, but they're big—the height of the man that fires it. Not an easy weapon to fire from a great distance, and not every man is strong enough to draw one."

Antony pulled an arrow from the ground and drew it across the bow, feeling the tension across his shoulders. When he pulled the string, he always felt himself unified with his weapon—equal tension, equal force.

He drew in a breath and shot. The arrow landed just above the center of the false man's heart, embedded about halfway through.

"A good shot, but not ideal for defense," Antony continued. "Because of its size, a longbow requires immense strength and training, or else it will not be effective."

He set down the longbow and picked up the smaller one beside it. "Soldiers across the sea in the Great Plains have found a new way to improve their archery tactics in war. A small bow that is as strong as its brethren, but compact and easier to draw. The strength of a longbow, condensed by the double-curve, or re-curve, of this bow."

The bow was half the size of the other, and instead of one continuous curve, this bow curved twice from each end before meeting at the handle.

"This bow is designed to be mobile. They require a little less material to make, so they are cheaper."

The bow felt light in Antony's hand but pulsed with inner strength. He could feel its power even in the handle, the balance that Bron worked many long hours to attain. He adjusted to the new weight in his hand, getting the feel for how it would draw and shoot. Then he nocked the arrow, pulled back in a fluid motion, and shot into the target. The arrow hissed gracefully through the air and landed right below the first, buried almost as deep.

Antony was satisfied by the smattering of applause he heard from the nobles, and even more satisfied when he turned and saw a smile on Lord Edwin's face.

"An archer can fire, draw, and fire again within seconds, even while moving, with the benefit of this smaller bow," he explained. Fluidly, he took another arrow out of his quiver, drew, and shot. It landed just a few inches from the second shot. "The draw weight is lighter, yet the arrow can travel almost as far. Even a woman could handle a bow such as this."

Heart racing, he turned toward the woman and looked directly at her. She stepped back in surprise as he extended the bow toward her. The older woman beside her—the same woman traveling with her the day before—grabbed her arm protectively.

"Would a member of the court like to try it?"

Antony smiled at the woman, and it seemed to inspire her confidence.

She stepped forward and extended her hand toward the bow. Antony was a little surprised she accepted his offer, but also distracted by how her dark blue dress moved around her hips as she walked.

Her eyes lingered on him for a moment as she took the bow and pulled an arrow out of the ground.

"Would you like me to show you how?" he asked. She cast a look over her shoulder.

"You just point and shoot, right?" she asked glibly.

Antony stepped back and watched her work. She looked at the target for a few moments, then nocked an arrow on the string. Her shoulders lifted and back arched as she pulled back the string and aimed. Antony saw the tension across the lines of her neck and knew she was feeling the strength that he loved to feel when he held a bow—the oneness of man and weapon, the interplay of strength between the two forces. There was only a slight tremble in her shoulders from the weight of the draw, but it smoothed out as she breathed and focused. She was holding and aiming for a long time.

"Actually, you should draw and fire in one fluid movem—"

The young woman fired the arrow, and it landed squarely in the straw man's shoulder—a good shot, to be sure. Antony swallowed the rest of his words. The woman looked at him with her lovely green eyes and tossed her braid of hair back over her shoulder.

"Were you going to tell me something? I wasn't paying attention." She smirked.

The courtiers clapped for the lady, except for the older woman. The woman curtsied, her shyness returning, and returned the bow to Antony. Her fingers brushed the palm of his hand, sending a strange thrill down his spine.

The court disbanded, but Edwin lingered behind and spoke with the king. Antony wondered what the king's court did all day—did they stand about him looking regal and beautiful? Did they watch peasants do party tricks? The young woman did not leave immediately either. The older woman seemed displeased by that.

"What you did was unseemly," Antony could hear the woman chastising her from where he stood. Her voice was none too quiet. "We shouldn't linger here any longer. You must attend to her grace—if she will still have you serving her after your little display."

"Aunt Pauline," said the young woman calmly. "I can mind my own affairs now that we're at the palace."

"Apparently you cannot," her aunt replied. "But you're right. If you're going to tarnish your reputation, you can do that yourself." Pauline turned sharply and followed the court back inside the castle.

The woman turned and saw Antony watching. A bloom of color spread across her cheeks. It made Antony smile. She approached him with an easy gait.

"I remember you from yesterday," she said. "Antony?"

"Yes," he said, his heart pounding. "I don't think you ever gave me *your* name."

Her blush deepened. "Adelaide," she said with a mock curtsy. "Adelaide DuMont."

Adelaide with the chestnut hair. The thought came unbidden to his mind.

Behind her, the servants were taking away the queen's chair. The tall knight still lingered in the yard as well, his eyes watching Adelaide. Adelaide followed Antony's gaze to the man.

"Are you coming, my lady?" asked the man.

"I'll catch up in a moment," Adelaide replied. The man didn't seem appeased by her response. No one in the court seemed satisfied with her. The man turned on his heel and followed the servants.

"People like John aren't good for much except fighting. Sure, they're stoic and strong, and maybe even smart, but they aren't very interesting," Adelaide said when he was out of earshot. She leaned toward Antony. "Don't tell him I said that."

Antony wouldn't tell him, because he hadn't heard what she said. His mind had stopped when she came closer. She was of average height

100

and only had to look up at him slightly. "I could have spared you the demonstration by telling the king that you were the one who saved my aunt and I yesterday." Her smile widened. "Did your father teach you?"

"Yes," Antony said, almost automatically. At some point, his father had taught him. And it was a memory he had kept. Even when he couldn't remember his own name, he remembered how to properly point and shoot.

"It seems like an interesting profession," said Adelaide. "Bow-making, I mean."

"Well," Antony shrugged. He gestured around himself. "I don't live in a palace."

Adelaide raised an eyebrow at him. "It's not as interesting as you think it is," she said. "Though tonight is the Commoner's Ball. Is that why you are in Southborn? Will you be there tonight?"

Antony beamed. *So there will be beautiful girls to kiss at this ball.*

"Yes," he said.

Adelaide looked pleased. "I still haven't decided what I'm going to wear," she said. She tossed a look over her shoulder, toward the tall doors that lead into the palace. "I suppose her grace will choose for me."

"Whatever you wear, I know you'll look beautiful," Antony said, and immediately regretted it. But it made Adelaide's smile widen across her face, so it was worth it.

"Speaking of, I *am* the queen's lady, so I should probably go find her," she said. "I'll see you tonight, Antony." She inclined her head slightly toward him.

"I'll see you too," Antony said. His thoughts suddenly felt thick and clumsy, as did his tongue. He wanted to say something else, to keep her there, but he couldn't. She turned and walked toward the palace doors.

Antony watched her, wondering what her lips felt like. He'd kissed many girls in Barnswood and enjoyed them in their own way, but he wondered especially what it would be like to kiss her. Maybe it was the way she was looking at him like she wanted to ask a question.

"She is a charming young lady, isn't she?"

Antony had forgotten that Edwin had been standing close by the whole time, leaving his side only once to converse with the king. The older man looked knowingly at him as he picked up the longbow from the grass. Antony knew his cheeks were red. He pulled the remaining arrows out of the lawn in front of him.

"She has recently returned to court from DuMont manor," Edwin continued. "You may have heard about the fire."

Antony shook his head, and Edwin pursed his lips, as though just remembering Antony was a commoner and not a courtier.

"It killed her father," said Edwin. "She is under her aunt's protection now, and the king is going to help her find a suitable husband."

Antony's heart sank inexplicably. Marrying Adelaide hadn't even crossed his mind, but he still felt disappointed somehow. *I just want to kiss her. Maybe I'll get the chance tonight.*

"Come," Edwin said. "His grace was very impressed by the craftsmanship of your bows. He would like some for his sentries. Would you like to come with me to negotiate the sale?"

Antony's brain snapped back from thinking about Adelaide. "Yes," he said. He could imagine the look on his father's face when he brought home the king's own gold.

Edwin smiled, squinting into the bright sun at Antony. He wasn't a tall man, but he seemed wiry and well-built. He didn't have the same jowly cheeks or protruding belly that other noblemen his age had. He was straight and slim like the shaft of an arrow, his frame a continuous straight line from feet to shoulders.

"Follow me," he said. Antony followed close behind him but didn't keep pace. He didn't know if it was rude to walk in step with a nobleman. In fact, he knew nothing about the etiquette of being in a palace. The sheer size of the castle was already overwhelming.

When Edwin brought him back through the gate to the courtyard, he led Antony up to the parapet, then through two tall oaken doors. Guards in plain chain-mail stood on either side of the doors. Antony followed Edwin down a long, cavernous hallway that reminded him of the Cathedral of the Nine and its high ceilings.

They climbed a set of stairs to a small room within the outer wall of the palace. It was set up like an office, with a long, low table stacked high with parchment and ledgers. The rest of the room was tidier—other ledgers and leather-bound books lined a shelf that filled an entire wall, and a padded chair faced the window looking out over the city. The shutters of the window were open and the fresh morning breeze blew in.

"I hear you are attending the Commoner's Ball this evening," Edwin said as he walked around the table and turned the chair around, taking a seat.

"Yes," Antony said.

"It is sure to be quite the event," Edwin said, thumbing through the open ledger on the table. He squinted as he searched the pages, each covered from top to bottom with a neat, straight script. "You're probably too young to remember a Commoner's Ball. We haven't had one since before the war." His eyes flicked up briefly from the page at Antony. "We are certainly sparing no expense."

"I'm looking forward to it," Antony said. He looked down at his plain, drab-colored tunic and black breeches. "I'm afraid I have nothing better to wear."

Edwin's mouth twitched in a slight smirk. "You won't be alone," he said. He was still poring through his ledger. "You'll be among many other unwashed bodies." Antony wasn't sure if he should be offended. "We encourage the villagers to spend the evening out in the inner ward. The Great Hall gets too crowded otherwise."

Antony imagined the nobles did more than *encourage* peasants to stay far away from them, but he would say nothing about it. Edwin finally flipped to a page and smoothed the paper. He was silent as he picked up a feather quill, dipped it in a pot of ink, and scratched a series of figures across the page. Antony stood awkwardly in front of him, waiting for further instruction.

"His grace would like fifty of your bows for fifty argents," Edwin finally said. He set down his pen and flicked through a pile of papers by his elbow before he found a fresh sheet.

"Now, will you sign? A simple scribble will suffice, right here."

Edwin had turned the parchment, so the ledger faced Antony. Antony's eyes scanned the neat, straight handwriting.

"This isn't right," Antony said as he read the bill. "I thought you said fifty argents. This reads fifty bows for forty argents."

"Does it now?" Edwin grimaced. He turned the paper back and read it. His eyebrows shot up. "Well, look at that. It's a good thing you caught my mistake. Who taught you to read?"

"My father," Antony said. *Did he just try to cheat me because he thought I couldn't read?* Edwin looked up at him with a strange light in his eyes as he ripped up the paper and found a fresh one. He presented the new bill to Antony with a flourish.

"How does that look?" he asked. Antony scanned the bill and nodded. Edwin lifted the quill. "I suppose you can write as well?"

Antony leaned down and took the pen, writing his name in the neatest scrawl he could at the bottom of the page. His hands still shook from the events of the morning. He wanted to leave this strange man's presence— leave and clean up so he didn't stink for the Commoner's Ball. Edwin produced a bag of coins.

"Oh, I have a bag of my own," Antony rummaged through his satchel and produced the leather pouch. In his trembling hands, it toppled out of his grasp and onto the desk.

Edwin's eyes were like that of a cat that had just spotted a mouse.

"Where did you get that?"

Antony followed his gaze. The ring had fallen out of the pouch.

"My father had it," Antony said. The note in Edwin's voice unsettled him. "He gave it to me."

"Did he?" Without invitation, Edwin grabbed the ring and brought it closer to his face. "Interesting…this one doesn't seem to be made of tin. Most of them are."

"Most of what?"

"These rings." Edwin tapped the face of the ring. "They're all over the village. These rings can be considered an open act of treason against the king, son."

Antony's stomach dropped. He looked down at the lion rampant design and suddenly felt ashamed.

"I didn't know," he said, his mouth dry. "Really—I didn't. It was in that pouch and—and I took it from my Pa to collect the money. I didn't know it was in there—I don't even know what it is."

Edwin lifted a placating hand. Antony's face must have been a mask of fear, and a believable one.

"It's my business to know about threats against the king. You don't strike me as one," he said. "Melt it down into coin. It's made of good silver."

Never melt this down, the novice had said, a bright ember of hope in his eyes.

"Thank you," Antony said. He dropped the ring back into the pouch and poured the money in—fifty argents for fifty bows.

"Now," Edwin said, "I can smell you from across the table, so I'd recommend finding a place to wash up before the Commoner's Ball."

Antony walked out quickly, thinking about what Edwin had said. No, that ring wasn't made of tin. It was tarnished, but not rusted. It was more than a cheap bauble. But where did his father get it?

His thoughts returned to the Commoner's Ball as he stepped into the courtyard. Edwin was right—he desperately needed a wash. But he needed something else, too. Something to help him look less like a commoner and more like a noble. Because he certainly wouldn't be spending his evening in the outer ward.

As he walked to the stable, he fished an argent out of the pouch at his side. *I'm sorry, Pa.* They'd have more than enough for the Harvestmonth tax, even with just an argent missing.

A blond-haired groom watched him enter the stable and look around. Antony assumed he was a groom—he wore a velvet emerald-colored tunic and wasn't busying himself mucking out a stall or feeding the horses. He leaned lazily against the wall as Antony entered.

"You looking for your horse?"

Antony shook his head and lifted the argent in his hand. "No," he said.

"But I'll trade you this for your shirt."

John

He watched Prince Charles from across the great hall. The busyness of the ball had scared the boy for a while, and he'd clung to Lady Elanor's skirts and whimpered, but soon enough he was wandering around and babbling to anyone who would listen. The ladies bent down and cooed at him, the lords ruffled his hair fondly between sips of wine.

King Tanor sat at the head table at one end of the room, watching his younger son bound from one end of the hall to the other as guests mingled. The night was early, so drunkenness had not reached its peak. The drunkest person John had seen so far was Lord Roger, who was in a perpetual state of inebriation. But the spirit in the room was high—the war was over, after all. A band of strings, lutes, hornpipes, hand drums, and hurdy-gurdys played joyous music as guests dined and drank and laughed.

While it was called the Commoner's Ball, the only people John saw in the Great Hall were nobles. Edwin told him that most of the commoners were shown to the inner ward, feasting on pigeon pie and ale instead of roast veal and summer wine. The less they knew of the Great Hall, the better, Edwin had said. The more ale they drank, the less they would care, anyway.

John was intent on getting as drunk as possible. He took another long draft of wine, letting the tang of the Second Summer white sting the back of his throat. He hadn't been there long, but he already wanted to leave. He felt obligated to be there and to stay, or Sir Markus would tease him about being afraid of women or not strong enough to hold his drink. John finished his goblet and motioned for a servant to fill it again. The room was swimming slightly in his eyes now, just enough for him to care a little less about being there. Other partygoers whisked past him as if he were part of the furniture. His hand had already been wrung a few too many times by a few too many noblemen and then continued on to their evening. No one wanted to think too much about the war that night. They just wanted to celebrate the fact that they didn't have to think about it anymore.

As he beckoned the servant, John noticed Sir Lyman standing in the far corner of the room, the farthest away he could be from the huge table of food, the raucous minstrels, and the chatty revelers. He stood stock-still with a silver goblet in hand, and his face was white as milk.

John strode through the throng of people toward him. When Lyman met his eye, the man's entire body relaxed, but only slightly. Something like relief crossed his face. Now that he stood closer, John could see that Lyman's hand was trembling as he held his goblet. Beads of sweat clung to his forehead. John had never seen the broad-shouldered knight look so afraid, even on the battlefield.

"Are you all right?" John asked.

Lyman looked again around the room, his eyes landing on each person as though he were counting them.

"Remember how the green lads used to shit themselves the first time they saw the Northern armies?" he asked, his voice a quaver. "Never seen war before, never seen a group of men bent on killing 'em. I never shit myself, but I sure as hell thought I was going to when I walked into this room." He barked an awkward laugh before his face became grave again.

John followed his gaze around the room. The crowd, the noise, the heat—it wasn't at all unlike a battlefield.

"You're in no danger here, Lyman," he said.

"That's what I keep telling myself," Lyman replied shakily. "But I—I just can't—"

John laid a gentle hand on the broad man's shoulder. "You don't need to stay," he said quietly. "If Markus tries to make a jape about it, he'll answer to my fist. See how the women like him without any teeth."

Lyman tried to chuckle, but seemed relieved that he was free to go. He walked as patiently as he could toward the door, abandoning his goblet on a table. He struggled to walk any slower than a fast clip. A memory came unbidden to John's mind of boys, boys as young as thirteen, running away from the battlefield. How Sir Lucas and his men had to make examples of them. How they left their bodies hanging in the Northern trees for the crows...

John shook away the thought as quickly as it came. He took another long draft of wine from his cup and breathed deeply. When he looked up at the room, he made dead eye contact with his father. He quickly averted his eyes.

I could just walk quickly with my head down, like Lyman—he'd never notice. The thought crossed his mind. But Tanor *would* notice. He always noticed. And it didn't help that John was a head taller than almost everyone in the room. Better to stay and remain uncomfortable than run and cause a scene.

As he brooded, Claudia's sumptuous figure broke through the crowd with her eyes on him. Her face broke into a smile at the sight of him. She wore a long red gown that showed off her generous bosom and huge belly. When she approached him, she immediately looped her arm around his and pulled him along as she walked.

"Take a stroll with your stepmother, John," she said, her high, breathy voice commanding. "I need a change of company after talking so long with armies of flighty women."

John said nothing, but didn't decline. He couldn't help but notice people watching them as they passed. *The queen and her bastard stepson. How generous of her to allow him into her presence.*

"It's a wonder you have asked none of these women to dance, John," she said, raising her voice above the din of the room. "I've seen several making eyes at you all night. See that one over there?" Claudia pointed none-too-conspicuously at a young, well-proportioned woman with long blonde hair, who looked away when she saw the queen pointing. "Her name is Meredeth. She's the daughter of one of your father's council members. It would make her night if you danced with her."

Couples danced on the far side of the room. John had done his best to avoid it so far. "Is she one of the flighty women you've been enthralled with this evening?" he asked.

Claudia laughed and leaned up against him. The swell of her belly pressed into his hip. She smelled obnoxiously of roses.

"Any woman can be enthralling, John, flighty or no," she said. "It just has to be the right woman. Meredeth doesn't enthrall you?" John said nothing. "You must have your eye on *someone*."

He still didn't answer. Claudia remained pressed against him as they walked. "I thought you might be a good match with Lady Adelaide," she said. Blood inflamed John's cheeks. To his consternation, Claudia seemed to notice. "She's beautiful, and smart—precocious too. You could do much worse, you know."

"Is she here tonight?" John heard himself asking. He immediately regretted it.

"She is," Claudia replied. A small smile played on her lips. She looked around. "I don't know where, though—oh."

She halted her slow step through the room when a tall, rotund man stepped in their path. He held a goblet in fingers shaped like sausages, and his big red nose had more carbuncles than John could count.

"Your grace," he said, in a thick, fat voice. He bowed as best as his broad belly would allow him.

"Regenald Riversate," Claudia said. "I'm glad you could make the journey!" John could tell her excitement was feigned by the high tone of her voice, but Regenald seemed ingratiated by it.

"Anything for your grace. And his grace," Regenald said, gesturing vaguely behind him toward the king's seat. His eyes, set deep within fat cheeks, swung up to meet John's. "And this must be young Johnny Behrens! You were no higher than my waist when last I saw you. Now you return to us a hero of the northern battlefields."

John managed to smile. "Thank you, my lord."

"You return to us too late, however," Regenald said with a wink. "My only daughter, Doloris, was just wed two months ago. You and she would've made a fine match."

Yes. The perfect match for a royal bastard, since you have four older sons who can carry on your name, wealth, and title.

John remembered Doloris. He remembered she stood the height of a boy when she was young and had broad shoulders and big hands. She had once broken some of Lucas' ribs while they played in the courtyard. Lucas said she'd been trying to kiss him. John had not arrived too late at all. Doloris was probably the size of a mountain by now.

"What a pity," he said.

"Is Doloris here tonight, Regenald?" Claudia asked.

Regenald shook his head, but there was a glitter in his eye. "She is not, because she is carrying my grandchild and is powerful ill." He nodded toward the queen's swollen belly. "Begging your grace's pardon."

"I remember the early months well enough, Regenald," Claudia said. "I spent most of my days bent over a chamber pot. Send Doloris my regards. Tell her to chew on mint leaves—it helps ease the sickness."

A beam spread across Regenald's moon-shaped face. "I will, your grace. May the Nine bless you." He bowed and continued shouldering his way past them.

"That poor man has tried to pass his daughter off to any man with breath in his lungs," Claudia said when he'd left, just loud enough for John to hear. "The second son of some lord finally claimed her. Needed her dowry for drinking money."

John had stopped listening. Straight ahead of them, across the sea of people dancing and drinking, he saw Adelaide speaking with Elanor of The Roses, one of Claudia's other ladies. Adelaide's hair had been braided and coiled around her head like a chestnut crown. She watched Elanor talk with an uninterested air, running her finger over the rim of her wine goblet.

"Oh, there she is!" Claudia said, pointing at Adelaide. "I must go attend

111

to my husband. Good evening, Sir John." She squeezed his arm knowingly, smirking as she left his side.

John had drunk just enough of the Second Summer wine to fearlessly stride across the room toward Adelaide without a second thought. Because of his size, people moved out of his way quickly—and Adelaide saw him as he crossed the room. She smiled at him and Elanor stopped talking, watching him with a raised eyebrow.

"I'm surprised to see you here, Sir John," Elanor was the first to speak after both ladies curtsied and John bowed. "You don't seem like one who would enjoy these kinds of things."

"I don't," John replied. "But sometimes the company is favorable."

Elanor snorted and looked at Adelaide suggestively. "And whose company might that be?" Elanor said. Adelaide laughed a little.

"Do you dance, Lady Adelaide?" John was doing his best to ignore Elanor, who seemed to have had several goblets of wine herself. Adelaide's cheeks blushed pink. She wore a velvet green dress inlaid with golden embroidery. It fit her perfectly, unlike any of the clothes John had found for himself in the livery so far. He felt like an overgrown squire in all of them, the trousers all too short and the tunics all too tight.

"*I* do," Elanor said, pursing her full, red lips. Her bosom heaved out of the bodice of her dress. "But only with a willing partner."

Both John and Adelaide shot her a look. "I am by no means a good dancer," John continued, "but I'm willing if Lady Adelaide is."

That made Adelaide blush even more, and she curtsied. John extended his hand, head swimming. If he weren't slightly drunk, he knew this wouldn't be happening. But Adelaide seemed willing enough.

The musicians played a slower tune as John led Adelaide to the floor, joining the other dancers. Adelaide finally spoke as the music began.

"I'm afraid you would've found a more talented dancer in Elanor than in me," she said, her voice barely audible over the music. She gazed steadily down at the floor, watching her feet as they stepped.

Look at me, John found himself thinking. *Look at me, please.*

"I think for this dance, we take two steps forward and two back," John said.

"For how long?"

"...until the other dancers stop, I suppose."

That made Adelaide smile. She glanced up at him. Her right hand was lying gently on top of his left as they both faced forward.

"Have you been enjoying yourself this evening?" John wanted to keep talking to her.

Adelaide took a moment to respond. "Not really," she admitted. "It's been so long since I've been to a Commoner's Ball, and...well, I suppose it was fun when we were children. Now I see that it's just an excuse for lords and ladies to dress in their finest and talk about everyone's fine clothes and fine lives and nothing else. I would honestly much rather be in the outer ward with the real commoners. They don't need to put on fine airs to enjoy themselves."

The music changed slightly, and John faced Adelaide, following the other men in the dance. His hand landed on her waist. It fit there perfectly— his thumb brushed her ribcage, his little finger touched her hip. He'd never touched a woman there before. He'd never really touched a woman *anywhere* other than her hand. Her hand rested on his arm, and he'd never felt stronger.

"I agree," John said, but he didn't. He would've much rather been alone than been in the Great Hall or the inner ward. But he didn't want to disagree with Adelaide, not when she was so close...

I want to be alone with her, he realized. As they faced forward again, John could still feel the curve of her waist in his palm. He wanted to hold her again and hold her closer. He wanted *her.*

The realization hit him like a rock cracking his skull. *If my father wants me to marry, it won't be anyone else but her. It can't be.*

"Has my father been successful in finding you a husband?" he asked. His heart was pounding so hard it was a wonder Adelaide couldn't feel it coursing through his hand.

"Not yet," she replied. She looked over her shoulder at the door. "I suppose he's using this evening to find one for me. He's been talking to a lot of young lords—well, and old ones, too. I am sure he's tried to parade several eligible young ladies in front of you this evening."

"There's only one I would want to be paraded in front of me." John was just drunk enough to say it. Adelaide didn't seem to catch his implication. She glanced behind them again, and this time, her eyes lingered longer.

The song ended, and Adelaide broke away from John quickly.

"Pardon me," she said and began walking toward the door. John turned and saw why.

There in the doorway stood the man from the tavern in Barnswood. The archer from that morning. Antony Bronson.

Antony

The emerald tunic fit him passing well. The groom had been of a height with Antony but more narrowly built, so the velvet stretched a little uncomfortably across his broad shoulders. He felt stiff as he entered the hall, hands folded carefully in front of him, trying to look as noble as possible so he wouldn't be kicked out. He prayed to all the Nine that he didn't look as ridiculous as he felt—in a tunic too small for him, unkempt hair wetted just enough to push back from his face, the makings of a beard scattered across his chin.

But he realized upon entering the hall that he didn't look half as ridiculous as other guests, some of whom were already far past drunk. While some more sensible men wore leather boots and fitted shirts, others wore mere slippers bedecked in jewels and fine silk tunics that reached their knees. If any of them took one step through the streets of Barnswood, their slippers would be reduced to muddy rags before they made it to the manor house.

The ladies seemed equally ridiculous. Antony noticed the older woman who had stood beside Adelaide that afternoon. Her skirt was twice as wide as her hips, and as she moved across the room, other guests had to give her a wide berth for fear of stepping on her hem. Antony didn't know how such a tight bodice could contain the woman's bosom, either. *Can she breathe? Can any of them breathe?*

Antony stood and beheld the sight of the *Commoner's* Ball. In the ward, the true commoners had already rolled out another round of ale barrels and danced on the plain wooden tables set out for them. When Antony had left them, a fiddler had started playing a Midlands reel, and everyone had taken to clapping and singing along with the folk tune. Though the wealthy guests seemed just as drunk, the music remained constrained, as did the attitudes of the men and women there.

He caught Edwin's eye across the room. The lord stood beside the king's chair, and only briefly regarded Antony with a raised eyebrow before turning back to Tanor. The king took no notice.

Edwin knows I'm not supposed to be here, in the Great Hall, Antony thought. *He doesn't seem to care. He needs to not care for a bit longer, just until I find...*

He found her. As Antony turned his gaze back toward the sea of couples dancing, he saw Adelaide crossing the room toward him. She wore a green dress that flattered her slim figure, and her long neck, and her small breasts—Antony's heart pounded.

When she reached him, she curtsied and looked up at him expectantly until he realized he needed to bow. He did so, feeling the velvet of his tunic stretch precariously against his back.

"You look very dashing," she said. "I'm glad you could be here."

"You look very..." Antony panicked suddenly, trying to find the right word.

"Beautiful? Attractive? Alluring?" Adelaide said with a smirk. "You have such a way with words."

Antony blushed at her flirtation. "Any of those would do," he said.

"Do you need a drink?"

"Always."

Adelaide snaked her arm through his and brought him into the room. The closeness of her body to his made his throat suddenly dry. He walked stiffly next to her. *They all know I'm not supposed to be here,* he told himself. The pressure of Adelaide's arm in his comforted him, and the jealous gazes of other men in the room gave him confidence. As they approached the long, wide table full of food and drink, a short, broad-shouldered man stepped in front of them, his cheeks red from heat and drink and merriment.

"Adelaide!" he exclaimed. He held a silver goblet in his hand, and

Antony could tell he'd had more than a few of those already. "Is this groom escorting you to the queen?"

Adelaide shook her head and glanced at Antony's tunic. "I suppose you are wearing the color of a groom." She looked down at her dress. "But then again, so am I, in a fashion."

"But it looks so much better on you," said the short man with a wink.

"Lucas!" Adelaide exclaimed. "You'd best not let the wine get the better of your tongue. Don't let your father hear you say such wanton things to any of your prospective brides."

"Any?" Lucas replied. "You're talking as though there are any to begin with. Although—" The man turned and looked over his shoulder at the crowd of dancers. "Lady Elanor has been casting glances my way all evening. I may ask for a dance before the night is over."

Adelaide smiled. "Then Elanor is a very lucky woman," she said. "Lucas, this is Antony."

"My lord," Antony bowed immediately. The action made Lucas bark with laughter.

"My friend, I am not a lord," he said. "And nor, I gather, are you."

Antony didn't know what to say. He prepared to turn around and leave until Lucas broke out into another peal of laughter. "Don't look so scared!" he exclaimed. "I won't report you to Lady Pauline, I promise."

"Lady Pauline?"

Adelaide rolled her eyes. "My aunt. She's so busy looking for a husband for me tonight that she's paid no mind to me all evening. And I prefer it that way. Come, let's get a drink."

Adelaide poured them both a cup of blood-red wine from a carafe on the table, reaching over a sea of cheeses that ripened the entire corner of the room. Beyond that were cuts of every kind of meat Antony could name, piles of Second Summer fruits, and tiered cakes that seemed to reach the ceiling. Antony took a blackberry from the fruit and popped it in his mouth quickly, as though he had stolen it. It exploded with juicy sweetness, a taste he didn't know summer berries could produce.

"They're delicious, aren't they?" Adelaide asked. Antony reddened when he realized she'd seen him. "I think there's blackberry brandy around here somewhere, too. It's from The Roses."

The wine she'd served him was sweet and cool and went to his head almost immediately. He drank deeply, the taste of it calming his nerves. Once he'd finished his cup, he felt the tunic fit him just fine, the guests didn't care who he was, and Edwin would never kick him out of the party. He poured himself another cup.

"That's the queen," Adelaide said as they stood together by the table. She nibbled on a small piece of cake and pointed to the blonde woman from that morning. The queen sailed around the room with a hand on her great belly. She was very young, Antony realized, younger even than Adelaide. And she was beautiful, with a jubilant face and cheeks as round as apples.

"She wanted to attend the ball before her confinement," Adelaide explained, "though the court physician, Magg, advised her not to. And that's Charles, the prince, in Elanor's arms."

Elanor was the red-haired woman trailing behind the queen. She held a sleepy, brown-haired boy.

"He's a lovely child," Adelaide continued. "Claudia hopes she will give Tanor another son."

"Tanor *has* another son, doesn't he?" Antony looked around, and no sooner had he spoken than he saw the tall, dark-haired figure across the great hall, staring directly at him. Antony's blood turned to ice and he immediately averted his gaze, turning to face Adelaide and finishing his second goblet of wine. He knew what jealous men looked like, and he saw that dangerous look in John's eye. It made Antony swell a little, knowing Adelaide preferred his company over another man's—a man who seemed to also crave her attention.

"He does," Adelaide said, "but not one that can inherit the throne." She leaned in closer to Antony. She smelled like lavender. "No one knows who John's mother is. Tanor's never told anyone. The only thing he's ever said of her is that she's dead."

Antony could still feel John's stare glowering across the room at him, burning into the back of his skull. He felt something disconcerting in that gaze, something almost beyond jealousy.

"I met him when he and his men came through our village from the North," Antony said, remembering how John had shaken up Robert.

"He's been gone for ten years," Adelaide said. "He left after King Alfred died."

"King Alfred and...Queen Catherine, is that right?" Antony said slowly. Adelaide nodded. "Yes."

"It's amazing that you live in this world of kings and queens," Antony said, looking around at the splendor of the room. "They know you by name. I just met the king today, and I could bet he wouldn't remember me."

"Oh, come," Adelaide laughed. It made Antony want to hear her laugh more. "Barnswood must be more cultured than that."

"Not by much."

"Do you dance?"

Antony smirked. "None of the refined dances of courts like this. But I've done my fair share of jigs and reels in taverns."

Suddenly, Adelaide's hand was in his, soft and warm. She set down her cup on the table. "I think this party could use a reel. It is a Commoner's Ball, after all."

She led him as they snaked through the crowd toward the other dancers. He looked around as a new dance began, fascinated by the spinning couples who seemed to move as deftly as if they were breaths of wind.

"Just follow my steps." Adelaide turned so that her right hand clasped his. "First, we turn in a circle, like this. One, two, three, four." For each count, she took a step. He followed her with awkward confidence. It made her smile. "And then, you step in, then out again." They stepped together and then stepped back. "You do that twice."

As they did it the second time, Antony's steps became more confident. He looked Adelaide in the eye, his gaze steady and strong. She gazed back. Her green eyes sparkled in the light. *Adelaide with the chestnut hair and the bright green eyes.*

"Then you link arms and do the same thing." She secured her arm in his.

They stood closer now, almost nose-to-nose. Adelaide's face softened.

"It *is* simple," he said wistfully.

Looking down at her, a strange sense of familiarity overtook him. She was *familiar* to him. Had he dreamed her? Dreamed of chasing her down these halls—of kissing her lips and tasting strawberries?

"Are you all right?" Adelaide's voice was distant. "Has the wine gone to your head already?"

"I've done this before," he said, almost unaware he was saying it. "Danced with you, I mean."

She regarded him, a tentative smile on her lips. Lips that tasted like strawberries. "You say that to all the girls you dance with," she said, but her eyes remained curious, staring into his.

A pane of warped glass fell between him and Adelaide, and the memories disappeared, just out of his reach. Before he could say anything else, he felt a firm hand on his shoulder and was pushed aside. From behind him appeared Adelaide's aunt, a stormy look in her eyes.

"Aunt Pauline—" Adelaide began, trying to collect her flustered disposition. Pauline heard nothing of it.

"*Niece,*" she said in a voice as composed as she could muster. She hooked Adelaide's arm in her own. "I did not bring you to court for you to make a spectacle of yourself."

Antony's eyes slid upward, and he locked eyes with the king from across the room. All that morning, Tanor had treated Antony with kindness and respect far above his station. But the way the king looked at him now turned Antony's blood to ice, just as John's gaze had.

"Let me be, Aunt Pauline," Adelaide said, her voice quivering a bit. She shot a brief look at Antony. "It's a Commoner's Ball, isn't it? Antony's a commoner."

"*Antony?*" Pauline turned incredulously to him. She was a tall, broad woman, almost of a height with him. "You are on first-name terms with the boy, are you? Of course, you would be, since he holds no title. It's a wonder he hasn't been thrown out of the Great Hall." Her eyes took him in and sized him up in an instant. "You don't belong here. Leave before I fetch someone to show you the way out."

Antony glanced up at the king again. Tanor's eyes were still steadily on him.

He looked apologetically at Adelaide and bowed to both her and Pauline. The song hadn't finished, but he turned and waded through the other dancers toward the door. He wanted desperately to look back, even to *run* back, to catch Adelaide in his arms and dance with her again.

His heart pounded, filling his ears as he traversed the quiet halls. The corridor stood in stark difference to the noise and heat of the room Antony had just left. It was cool and quiet, but his mind thundered. As he walked toward the inner ward, he tried to remember every detail of his dance with Adelaide—he never wanted to forget it. He had been so engrossed in her it was as if he had been somewhere else entirely. In a different time, even as an entirely different person...

The inner ward was even louder than the Great Hall. The sight was a world away from how it had looked that morning. The fountain still burbled, but no well-dressed children played by it. Instead, two unwashed boys splashed in the basin, and across from them a man deep in his cups playfully splashed a large-breasted woman. Others helped themselves to huge casks of ale, brown bread, and venison stew. A much merrier band of minstrels played a reel, with the drone of the hurdy-gurdy filling the humid night air. Above the stink of sweat, ale, and unbathed bodies, Antony could smell the beginnings of a storm in the overcast sky.

Since he had left the inner ward earlier, someone had erected a low stage on the north side of the lawn for a mummer's show. Antony rolled his eyes. He hated mummers. They didn't serve any purpose other than to tell stories everyone already knew—and yet, everyone seemed surprised and delighted to hear them again. The mummers who came to Barnswood almost always told stories of the saints, stories that Antony's father recounted daily, and stories he heard from the priests in the chapel. The mummers presented them garishly, their faces painted in bold colors, their clothes outrageous, their voices too high and too loud.

A small, timid man on the stage was trying to get the rowdy crowd's attention. Antony couldn't hear him even from a few hundred yards away. A barrel-chested, red-faced man joined him on the stage and pushed him easily aside. He boomed:

"My common folk, one and all! You who have danced in the Commoner's Ball! A tale we will tell, and without delay—my common folk, 'tis time for our play!"

That was the other thing Antony hated about mummers. They tried so hard to rhyme and speak in verse. He pulled himself a draft of ale from a barrel near him. He watched the stage as a line of men in dark robes holding torches mounted the boards and stood facing the crowd. Their faces were painted with dour frowns. Nine of them—the nine saints.

"Nine saints there have been, are, and shall be," they chanted together. "But ten there once was—one fallen, one free."

A tenth figure joined them on the stage, dressed instead in a green tunic and hose. A full mask concealed his face. Two bright eyes shone through like obsidian in the firelight, an impish smile painted across the face in permanent glee.

"The tenth was a thief of life, a stealer of breath," continued the nine figures, "he was the *Vispilio*, the bringer of death."

The crowd gasped, and Antony rolled his eyes again. Everyone knew the story of the *Vispilio*, the fallen saint who had been favored by the Great Maker. It was a legend told for generations, sometimes told as a ghost story, other times to warn children to behave—*Get in your bed, or the* Vispilio *will get you.*

Another man appeared. He wore all white, and his face was painted gray with a stern, frowning mouth and pointed beard. One eyebrow was cocked higher than the other.

"Favored by the Maker, closer than a son," said the chorus, "he crossed the sea with the saints when their work was begun."

The green-clad player bowed in front of the man in white—the Maker—who put his hand on the player's head in blessing. Antony took another long draft of ale, telling the story to himself in his head as the players continued.

The Vispilio *was the most favored of the Great Maker, the one who advised him and sat at his right side, for the Maker bore no mortal children of his own. But the* Vispilio, *when he walked out among the people of the wild land, saw the corruption and evil that could grow in men's hearts. He saw what the Maker could not see sitting on his great throne of gold.*

New players danced in front of the green-clad player—players dressed in motley rags, fighting one another, stealing bags of prop coins made of tin. The green-clad player reacted garishly, throwing his hands up to the sky in agony.

Without the Maker's knowing, the Vispilio *helped those who were downtrodden by evil men, who suffered under the hands of corrupt kings. His search for justice ended when he slew a corrupt lord along a wooded highway.*

Another motley player crossed the stage, his belt laden with fake gold and strings of pearls dangling from his neck. He chuckled villainously to himself until the green-clad player jumped out in front of him with a wooden dagger and feigned a slash at him. The motley player turned toward the audience as a red ribbon flew from his collar like a long burst of blood. The crowd gasped and giggled in delight as the man fell to a grotesque death.

The Vispilio *was damned to Innermost Hell after the Maker found out. It was for the Maker to judge the evils of men. The name* Vispilio *became a name spoken in darkness, the name of death. It is said that he walks in the forest in the dead of night. It is Saint Odette who leads men to their rest, but it is the* Vispilio *who finds them afterward to torture their souls in a never-ending nightmare, as payment for whatever ills they committed in life.*

"Let they who judge the living be warned," the players chanted, "that they will be judged by whom they've scorned."

Antony's tankard was empty by the time the players filed off the stage and merry music began. The crowd hummed again, beginning with a murmur before returning to its full volume.

"A strange play for a party," Antony muttered under his breath. Beside him, a man with receding red hair took a long draft from his tankard and nodded with enthusiasm.

"Those damn rings have the king spooked," he said. *Rings.* Antony's mind wandered to Sam's saddle bag, where he'd put the leather pouch.

"I've never understood what they meant," Antony replied. *You believe too?* That was what the novice at the church had asked him the night before.

"A bunch of hogwash, is what they mean," grunted the man. "Some folk have gotten it into their heads that Prince Adrian is still alive—" The man moved in closer. "—that Tanor is a false king. Try to prove it by sayin' since the boy's head was cut off, nobody could know if it was the prince or no. Could've been anybody, they say."

Antony shrugged. "What's the harm if they believe that?"

"Trying to resurrect ghosts isn't going to put bread on their table," grunted the man. "They want someone to make their lives better. Truth is, our lives have always been shit, no matter whose ass is on the big chair."

Antony thought of the ring again. The real, silver ring. Why did his father have one? Is that what he believed, too? Bron was always a temperate citizen, never complaining about the price of wheat—and certainly not conspiring to overthrow a king. He wasn't always happy about the king, but he was never a traitor.

The man chuckled and wiped the froth from the ale off his beard. "They haven't found him yet," he said. "Because he doesn't exist. But I wouldn't put it past 'em to find a pretender and start another bloody war. A bloody war we can't afford."

Antony watched the man walk away, his step swaying slightly from the drink. After the somber play, guests danced again, even as spatters of rain fell on their heads. The air outside was still close and warm. Antony downed his cup, set it on one of the trestle tables, and walked back inside the castle.

He knew he couldn't return to the great hall, no matter how much he wanted to. But since everyone was at the party, no one was around to tell Antony where he couldn't go. He wandered. The stillness of the palace was such that Antony could hear thunder growing louder outside as the storm came on. It occurred to him that eventually, he'd have to find somewhere to sleep for the night, or else ride through the night back to Barnswood.

Antony turned a corner and came to a long corridor with tall windows to one side and sconces with lit torches on the other. These windows were paned with warped glass—a luxury the palace could afford. Rain tapped rhythmically against them, growing steadier with every passing moment.

Just as he had felt dancing with Adelaide, an inexplicable sense of familiarity made his knees weak. He knew this place. He turned his attention to the end of the hall and two huge oak doors.

As he approached, he felt the ache of something missing, something forgotten, but how could that be?

Why did he see shapes in front of him, in the empty corridor? Why was the silhouette of a tall, stately man walking ahead of him, turning around to make sure he was following?

The doors were closed but unguarded. When Antony tried them, they were heavy, but no bolt kept them shut. He braced against both of them and pushed them open.

He stood in the throne room, silent and empty and huge.

Adelaide

It can't be.

It had been a full half an hour before the anger and embarrassment of being dragged from the dance by her aunt dissipated. Aunt Pauline had not budged from her side since, vetting every young man that so much as glanced Adelaide's way. Adelaide hardly acknowledged any of them.

At one moment, she was dancing with Antony, the handsome commoner she'd met the day before. And at the next, she was in the arms of Prince Adrian, his strong, confident hand in hers. And in that moment, she wanted to ask, *Where have you been?*

She barely heard when Pauline spoke to her again after a long stretch of icy silence.

"I take you into my care," the older woman said quietly, "I provide you with every comfort, I bring you here to find a suitable match—and you dance with a common boy?"

Adelaide felt anger rise in her throat, but she forced it down. She was surprised when she felt tears pricking at the corner of her eyes. What she had done might have been foolish. But when she'd danced with Antony, she hadn't cared about any of that. And the thought that she might never see him again twisted her stomach in knots.

"I'm sorry, Aunt Pauline," she said. Her voice felt thick in her throat. Pauline walked her toward the rest of the queen's ladies, and as they did, Adelaide caught John's eye. He stood a few yards away, towering over the crowd. His eyes were fixed on her. Adelaide turned away with a cringe.

He saw all of that. John had been a horrible dancer. His hand on her waist had felt big and awkward, and he held her too tightly. *He means well, but he's better off fighting than dancing.*

Elanor met them with a smile when they came to the table. Rachel, Lydia, and Ilse all sat at the table, having just finished a round of dances judging by their flushed faces, but Elanor leaned against the table with a seductive air. She looked beautiful in her crushed velvet dress, her bosom spilling out and her curves accentuated.

"So many men, so little time!" Elanor said decadently. "I wish this ball would go on all night." She stood up straight and faltered a bit. A drop of wine flew out of her cup and landed on Pauline's bodice. Pauline gasped.

"Wanton behavior is not prudent at events such as these, my lady," she said stiffly. "Respectable men don't find that appealing in young women."

Elanor snorted. "I didn't say I was after a respectable man, *my lady*," she said. She put her wine cup down and used her thumb to smudge out the blot of wine from Pauline's dress. Pauline immediately shirked back from both her and Adelaide. She shot Adelaide a look and retreated to another part of the room.

"I'm sorry she's your aunt," Elanor said. Adelaide could hear a slight slur in her voice. "We're at court. We can get in trouble if we want to. And we *should.* Now, I'm going to go dance with the king."

Elanor walked away from Adelaide on unsteady feet. Adelaide hadn't seen Tanor dance much that evening—he had taken Claudia out on the floor for one modest, stately dance, one with little movement for the sake of his wife's condition. Claudia was now seated at the table, fanning herself and sipping Second Summer wine. She watched with slight amusement as Elanor stumbled up to the king and bowed ungraciously. Tanor took her hand with a flourish, and the crowd of dancers parted for them. Tanor and Elanor walked through a sea of fawning glances. Adelaide couldn't help but notice her aunt looking on with disdain. She hadn't seen Pauline take a drop that entire night, and she was the guest who probably needed it most.

The dance was a quick step, but not a reel. There were quick hops and short spins to a bright melody played on a pan flute. Adelaide liked the tune, and she found herself enraptured with Tanor and Elanor, as the rest of the room seemed to be. Elanor was sumptuously beautiful, and still confident in herself, even in her drunkenness. Adelaide admitted Tanor was handsome and charming. Elanor's long, graceful form was nearly of a height with his. Her eyes sparkled looking up into Tanor's face. Adelaide supposed one would feel that way when dancing with a king.

That was how she'd felt when dancing with Antony. Why couldn't she shake that moment? His arms had felt familiar. She couldn't help but remember all the times she had danced with Adrian at balls such as these or begged him for one when she was too young to heed her manners. The way she had felt the last time they'd danced, a feeling that she'd never felt before in her girlhood, a feeling her father said would come with time—of wanting to be close to Adrian, to feel his strong arms around her, the feeling of his heart beating through his chest, his warm breath on her cheek. She remembered how dizzy she felt after that dance, how red her father said her cheeks were.

Adelaide felt dizzy now. Dizzy and confused and certain that something was wrong. That Antony should still be in the great hall with her, that they should still be dancing. That it should be them garnering the attention of the crowd, not Tanor and Elanor.

Then Elanor vomited across the front of Tanor's tunic.

The music halted. The crowd watched in horror as she heaved, and the spatter of all she had eaten that evening landed on the king and ran down the front of her dress. Tanor took a step back—he couldn't hide his disgust. Neither could Adelaide. She felt bile rising in her own throat. Vomit had always had that effect on her.

Elanor stumbled back as Edwin and Godfrey came to the king's aid, using whatever cloth they could find to wipe the mess off him. Elanor gagged again, causing Tanor to back up even farther. Her face contorted in embarrassment, turning redder as she wiped vomit from her chin. Godfrey shot her a poisonous look as he and Edwin guided Tanor out of the prying eyes all around them. Tears sparkled in Elanor's eyes as she fell back onto the floor.

No one moved to help her. Adelaide took a halfhearted step forward, but before she could make another move, Lucas barreled through the crowd like a bull. He looked around at the gawking crowd with his jaw set. Adelaide could see a vein popping in his temple.

"It's all right, my lady," he said to Elanor. He promptly scooped her into his arms with ease. Elanor was sobbing pitifully now, her face as red as her dress. Tanor had disappeared. As he pushed back through the crowd, Lucas' eyes met Adelaide's. She followed him in his wake. At least it was an excuse to leave the party.

Elanor's sobs got louder in the hall. She was an absolute mess, Adelaide saw, and drunk on top of that.

"I'm sorry," she blubbered. "I'm so sorry."

"Nothing to be sorry about, my lady," Lucas replied. He turned to Adelaide. "Was no one going to help her?" Adelaide didn't respond. "Let's take her to her room. You can clean her up."

Adelaide led Lucas up the stairs toward the ladies' chambers. When they arrived at Elanor's, Lucas laid her on the bed. He looked down at her, not with pity or embarrassment, but with kindness.

"I'm sorry this happened to you, my lady," he said. Then he shrugged and added with a smile, "We all have a bit too much sometimes."

Elanor smiled at this, followed by a fresh wave of tears. She took Lucas' hand before he turned away. "Thank you," she said. He squeezed her hand and left.

"Let's get you out of these clothes, Elanor," Adelaide said. She prompted the woman to sit up and started unfastening the back of her dress. Elanor was still trembling wildly. "Do you think you will be sick again?"

Elanor shook her head. Her red hair bounced around her shoulders with every shake. She smelled sour. Adelaide pulled the dress down to her ankles. Elanor stepped out of it.

"It wasn't that," she said. "It wasn't the drink."

Adelaide found a bowl of cool water and a towel on the nightstand. She wiped Elanor's mouth as though she were a child. The woman looked down at her with glassy eyes. She looked so young in the dimness of the chamber, not the refined woman Adelaide had met the day before.

"You don't understand, Adelaide." Elanor swiped her hands away. "I love him."

Adelaide didn't respond. She dipped the cloth in the water again and wiped the rest of the vomit off Elanor's chin. Did she mean Lucas? They had both been stealing glances at each other the entire night. Elanor swayed slightly as she sat on the edge of the bed. She was still pretty drunk.

"Let's get this off you," Adelaide said as she unfastened the front of Elanor's corset. She would breathe much easier now. She let the garment fall to the floor. "Now lay back. You'll be alright."

"I do more for him than that bitch ever could," Elanor slurred as she laid her head on the pillow. She was only in her underclothes now, a long white slip. "She's putting that child's life in danger, not being in confinement yet."

She's just drunk, Adelaide thought. *She'll sleep whatever this is off and be fine in the morning. Well, maybe not completely fine.*

Adelaide stood up. "I can take some of your morning duties if you'd like to rest tomorrow," she said. She turned and put the bowl and rag back on the nightstand. "You'll probably have a heada—"

She turned back to the bed and saw Elanor lying there, cradling something that her corset had concealed—and had probably concealed for many months. Her hand rested on the pronounced hump of her belly, and fresh tears came.

"I didn't mean for it to happen," she whispered. "But with her condition, she is not permitted to—so he's invited me into his bed. More than once."

Adelaide swallowed. Her throat was suddenly dry.

"Who?" she asked, but she already knew the answer.

Elanor's eyes flicked to her. They looked suddenly sunken and tired.

"The king," she said. "He should've married me. But my father didn't have the men and arms he wanted. Instead, he settled for a whore who batted her eyes at every rich man in the kingdom—until they landed on the king."

Adelaide's heart was pounding. She knew she was hearing things she was never meant to hear. This secret felt like a death sentence. She thought about Claudia and her baby, her son—and the king, with Elanor in his bed.

"He loves me," Elanor said, her voice sharp. "I know he does. He just can't show it." Her face was slick with tears. "He says if she dies birthing the child, he'll wed me. I'll be his queen."

Adelaide took another step back.

"I have to," Elanor continued. "I have to, or else—or else she'll turn me out, and then I'll just be another disgraced woman, and my child will be another bastard."

Her voice got fainter until it was barely a whisper, and she sobbed again. Adelaide looked her over—her swollen face and belly, her hair now a tangled mess on top of her head. Adelaide floated near the door, feeling her exhaustion settling in. Elanor wasn't so different from her, she realized. Facing a wholly unknown future.

"She won't turn you out," Adelaide said as confidently as she could. "You shouldn't worry about that right now. You should get some rest."

"Please don't tell anyone, Adelaide," Elanor pleaded.

It's not what you know or who you know, but what you know about who you know. Elanor's own words whispered in Adelaide's mind. Adelaide now knew dangerous information. Information that could ruin someone. It made her sick.

"I won't."

Elanor's head lolled back on the pillow, and she took a deep breath. She still had a hand on her belly. *Tanor's child,* Adelaide thought. Thinking about it turned her stomach even more. It was not uncommon for kings to keep mistresses, but his own wife's lady-in-waiting? And he had seemed so wholly devoted to Claudia and Charles, and their child yet to be born. While Elanor was bathing and preening the pregnant queen, she was growing the king's baby in her own body.

Elanor's breath had become deep and even, and Adelaide realized she was asleep. Adelaide was relieved. The room still smelled of the tang of vomit, and she was grateful to leave it.

131

Coming out of the chamber and into the corridor, she heard voices coming from the stairs. Claudia appeared at the top, giggling with Rachel on her arm.

"Adelaide!" Claudia called. Adelaide shut the door behind her as quietly as she could. "Have you left Elanor to sleep it off?"

"She'll be all right," Adelaide said, keeping her voice low. She prayed to every saint she could think of that Claudia would not decide to check in on her lady-in-waiting. Thankfully, Claudia and Rachel breezed past the door toward the queen's chambers.

"Would you like help getting ready for bed, your grace?" Adelaide asked.

Claudia shook her head. "Take care of yourself, Adelaide," she said. "I'll see you in the morning."

Adelaide curtsied and walked away from them, feeling guilty. How would Claudia feel if she knew the truth behind Elanor's door? She seemed possessive of Tanor and the happy life she had at court. Elanor's secret had the potential to destroy all of that.

Not what or who you know, but what you know about who you know.

She felt weary deep in her bones, but her mind was racing too quickly to rest. She was nervous about what would happen if she slept. Would the queen go into labor? Would Elanor stumble drunkenly to Tanor's bed? Would Antony come back to the ball and miss her?

Adelaide couldn't think about it. She climbed down the steps back toward the Great Hall, but walked past the double doors. She passed the inner ward, where rain poured on the remaining commoners who came for the ball. Even though the storm drenched them, they seemed to be having a much better time than she had. Lightning flickered across their faces, giving them brief, macabre masks. She kept walking.

She arrived in the long corridor that led to the throne room. Adelaide had always loved the way the rain tapped on the tall, warped windows in the hall. That night, it rattled across the panes in full force, filling her senses with its sound. It was as though she were in another world, as though she were back at her father's manor, and he was holding her close to his chest, and a winter storm off the sea was battering at the shutters.

132

Adelaide was so distracted by the memory that she almost didn't notice that the doors to the throne room were open.

No one should be on this side of the palace at this time of night, she thought. *Unless a commoner got curious.* Usually, there were guards posted in this hall, but they might have been allowed to enjoy some of the leftover revelries of the party.

Although the guards weren't there, someone else was. Past the lit torches of the hall, the throne room was gloomy. But by the scant light of the windows, she could see a shape moving in the room. What would someone be doing in there at that hour?

She approached the doors and peered inside.

The empty throne room felt strange. Normally, Adelaide had seen it full of people and brilliantly lit. When it was vacant and dark, it seemed to take on an entirely different feeling—a haunted one. When the living weren't there, the dead seemed to dance along the walls.

There was one living person there, however.

A man stood on the dais facing the throne. Adelaide watched quietly, her heart pounding. She knew who he was, even with his back turned—the straight, broad shoulders, the brown hair. She wanted to call out to Antony and tell him to stop before he got in trouble, but her voice stopped in her throat.

It's impossible, she thought. Even after Antony left the party, and after she took care of Elanor, the thought hadn't left her mind. No matter how much she dismissed it, it came back.

It's wholly impossible. He's dead. They brought his body back to the palace.

Antony was face-to-face with the throne. Adelaide couldn't tell what his expression was. His hands hung neutral at his sides, and he looked the chair up and down.

As if controlled by some unseen force, Antony turned stiffly and sat on the throne. As though he had done it a thousand times before.

The image filled Adelaide with a deluge of warmth—of peace. What she saw was right. What she saw was how it should have always been.

"Adrian," she breathed. And the tension rose in her again—the impossi-

133

bility of what she was seeing. She was seeing a young man, the age that Adrian would have been if he were alive. A young man with dark hair that flopped over his forehead, dark eyes like the dead coals of a fire.

Yet the body of Prince Adrian was buried in the Crypt of Kings.

Adelaide's peace was shattered when a large figure jostled past her.

"What are you doing?" asked the man. "Get away from there!"

Adelaide watched in horror as Adrian sat frozen while John barreled toward him, as though he were stuck in his own reverie. He seemed to snap out of it just as John reached for his collar and threw him off the throne. Adrian tumbled down the dais, landing on his side.

"You shouldn't be here," John growled. Adrian didn't respond. John grabbed his collar again and punched him in the face. And he kept punching until Adelaide saw sprays of blood flying out of Antony's mouth.

"*Stop!*" Adelaide screamed. She ran into the room. "Leave him be! He didn't mean any harm."

John's head snapped up, his eyes bewildered, as though he just realized Adelaide was watching. He dropped Antony, who flopped onto the ground and coughed up more blood.

"Leave him alone," Adelaide said. "Don't you recognize him?"

John

He could've sworn that when he'd looked at the throne, he'd seen Adrian there.

Looking down at the bloody face and body he had pinned to the carpet, he saw only Antony. The commoner. Antony held his hands to his face, cowering from John's blows.

John stumbled back. Rage had crackled through him like lightning, sudden and unexplained. It could've been anyone else sitting there and John wouldn't have cared. It was his father's throne. It would never be his own.

He stood up, his fist pulsing with pain. Adelaide's voice snapped him out of his rage for only a moment.

"Don't you recognize him?"

John looked down at Antony, wondering why he'd been so certain it was Adrian. Adrian was dead. He *was.* This was just a man. A commoner.

Adelaide stared at him, her eyes wide and urgent. *Who does she see?*

"Get out of here," John growled at no one in particular. If he stayed, he was going to strangle Antony. He rushed out quickly, not looking at Adelaide as he did so. If he weren't so angry, he would've been embarrassed.

In his mind, he was back in the Hemlock Forest, covered in blood, the weight of guilt heavy in his gut. The sour taste of vomit crept up the back of his throat. He remembered the cruel light in his father's eyes. They seemed blank and emotionless, although he'd just allowed his closest friend to die.

His father had called it the Great Maker's providence, all part of his grand plan for Tanor to take the throne. No mistakes.

One mistake. Take it to your grave, John.

John reached the barracks and lay back on his cot, his heart still pounding, his hand pulsing. He could've hit Antony a hundred more times and wouldn't have stopped until his brains were on the carpet. His blood was up—he knew the feeling well. It was how he had felt after every battle, like he could've kept fighting for days. Some knights would satiate that feeling with a woman. John never had. Lucas had sent a woman to his tent as a jest once—a small thing with limp yellow hair and dark circles under her eyes. She'd pulled down her dress to show John her breasts. The big, black bruises that covered both of her arms killed what little desire he might have left. He told her to go away.

He stood up again, feeling frantic. He desperately wanted another drink, but the party was all but over after Elanor had made a spectacle of herself. The dizzy feeling from the wine had faded with his rage. Now he was alone with his thoughts, with the knowledge. With the memories.

It had been an accident on his part—John's involvement in the plan. He brought supper to his father's chamber as he often did, but that night he stopped at the door when he heard voices. Edwin was in the room, conversing with Tanor. And the more John had listened, the less he'd been able to walk away. He'd never heard his father talk with that much hatred for King Alfred before.

"He is not the perfect man they'd make him out to be." John didn't remember all that was said, but he remembered that. "He'd let our enemies run roughshod over us—surrendering the borderlands to the sickly king of Greygate? Merely because Stephen the Sick claims they are ancestral lands? Something else must be afoot—what was that?"

The tray in John's arms was becoming too heavy the longer he stood there. He was found out. He remembered seeing that strange light in his father's eyes for the first time that night. Edwin had looked down at him warmly, taking the tray from his hands.

"I can't kill him for what he's heard," Tanor said, regret in his voice. "But we can't let him go, either."

They'd made him complicit. Involved him in a way to ensure his silence. A threat made clear and emphasized by his father, sealed with a beating. John still had the scar on his cheek. A shiny pink divot, roughly the size of a gemstone, near his left ear. The soft flesh of his young face had bled a lot. His knuckles bled now. He'd forgotten that the worst place to punch someone was in the face. His fingers got the brunt of it when they cracked Antony's nose. It would be a few days before he'd wield his sword again, John supposed.

When Lucas and Markus came into the barracks, John pretended to be asleep. If he laid eyes on Markus right then, he may very well have thrown him across the room. He heard their footsteps stumble across the flagstones. One of them, probably Markus, slurred an off-key tune. He often sang nonsense when he was drunk. John wondered for a moment where Sir Lyman had gone. Probably somewhere with fresh air, or a quiet place to enjoy more ale.

"*There's* the big man," Markus blustered from across the room. John didn't move. "Out cold already." The young man snorted. "Dances with one girl and runs off scared."

"Shut up, Mark," Lucas replied. He sounded only slightly less drunk than Markus. "A fortnight ago we were hanging Northmen who refused to surrender. That can put a fellow out of the mood."

John remembered. His last glimpse of the North. One clan in the foothills had defied the queen's surrender and was put to the sword for it. Lucas' men had strung up their bodies as a warning. The body John had hung was just a boy, the age John himself was when he began fighting. Still blue eyes stared forward into nothing, past John and into the sky.

"Let him be miserable, then," Markus grunted. "That just means more for me."

They talked for a little while longer in voices too low for John to hear. Eventually, their voices quieted, and they drifted off to sleep—John could tell by their snores. He lay there, listening. It was a familiar sound to him. He had never slept well at the front, but Markus was almost always the first to nod off. And there was no way John would rest easily tonight. His hand throbbed, and his heart still pounded. Behind his eyelids floated Antony's prone body, his face bloodied and bruised. But was it the man in the throne room floating before him, or the prince in the forest?

He heard the door to the barracks open again, and soft, measured footsteps entered. A hand touched his shoulder. John opened his eyes, already knowing who he'd see.

"Your father would like a word with you," Godfrey said.

Antony

"You need to get out of here."

John was gone—probably. Antony wasn't quite sure. His left eye was quickly swelling shut and the rest of his face throbbed with pain. John's fists had been like rocks descending on his head. He heard Adelaide, and that was enough. He felt her hand on his arm.

"Come on," she said. Her hand helped him up. "Quickly."

With her arm around his, Adelaide guided him back through the corridor. Through his one good eye, Antony watched the flicker of lightning guide their way. He struggled to keep up with Adelaide as his vision swam.

"I like you, Antony," Adelaide was saying, "but you seem to enjoy getting into trouble, don't you?"

"You like me?" Antony slurred. Adelaide didn't respond, but he saw the ghost of a smile on her lips.

Rain drove across the courtyard in sheets. Drenched figures ran to fetch horses from the stables or climb into carriages. The party was over, it seemed.

"This is as far as I dare go without garnering further attention," Adelaide said. She faced him now, and all Antony could think was how beautiful she looked, with her hair falling out of her braids and her green eyes wide and concerned. Involuntarily, he lifted a hand and touched her face. Her cheek was warm, flushed, soft...

Adelaide stepped away. "Ride safely. This storm doesn't seem to be letting up. Just be quick about it."

With that, she was gone, and Antony's heart sank. *At least I got my dance.*

I never got that kiss.

When he stepped into the courtyard, rain pelted his face. Since leaving the party, Antony had lost all sense of time. It was surely well past midnight now. Before he got to the stables, his shirt and trousers were already soaked through. He wasn't alone. Grooms bustled around him, wet to the skin.

"You're lucky," Antony said to Sam as he led the mule out of his dry stall. The animal snorted when the rain tickled his nose. "Oi, at least you didn't get punched in the face."

Antony was grateful to sit in the cart once Sam was hitched to it, but once they started moving, the jostling made Antony's head hurt all the more. It was a long ride back to Barnswood, so he gritted his teeth and wiped the blood from his nose.

He had wanted to know what it was like, was all. Did a throne feel different from any other chair? It didn't, not to Antony. Even when he tried to imagine a crown on his head and the room filled with people. It was just a chair. An old, somewhat uncomfortable one. Before John had come in, he was about to stand up and leave.

What was it that Adelaide had said? The events of the evening were already fading as the cart clattered on.

Don't you recognize him?

Of course, John would've recognized him. They'd met before, in the tavern. Why would Adelaide ask that?

A thought, dizzy and undefined, took root in Antony's addled brain. John would've known Prince Adrian too. And what Edwin had said about the lion signet ring…had John thought he was a traitor?

Maybe it was the sound of the rushing water of the Skeldergate River that churned under the bridge Antony now crossed, or maybe it was the pounding rain scourging him to the bone, but he found himself in a trance. The rain and river mingled together like a cascade, a deep current that threatened to pull him under. His forehead ached.

Images swam through his head. A flurry of movement, flailing arms and legs, the taste of dirt and blood in his mouth as he realized the ground was no longer under his feet, but falling away from him.

"You had a bad fall, Antony," Bron had told him. "It's alright if you don't remember much. The townsfolk might look at you funny. You took a long time to heal—they didn't see you for months. They thought you were dead. So did I."

The tears in his father's eyes. Antony had heard him weeping one night, and praying. The choking sobs had almost made Antony cry. Bron was big and strong and merry. But he'd sobbed that night.

"Saints, let me protect this boy," he heard. "Let no further harm come to him. Let me Keep him safe... and teach me how to love him. To love him as I loved my Antony..."

The memory surprised Antony. Had Bron said that? Antony had learned not to trust his memories after the fall. He had to rely on his father and brothers for what came before.

Of course, he might have said that, Antony reasoned. I was never the same after the fall. I know that. Carter treated me differently. I changed. I fell.

The cascade caught him again. A small boy stood in front of him.

"I hate you." The boy mouthed the words. A boy with dark hair and sea-glass eyes. "I've always hated you." The boy charged toward him, then disappeared.

I can't trust my memories, Antony reminded himself. The apothecary had told Bron that a fall muddled the temperament of the brain. It disturbed the flow of thought, so his son might never remember anything before the fall.

"But he's still a damn good shot," Bron said with a smile, dropping a heavy, reassuring hand on Antony's shoulder.

Antony swam in and out of time. Sam rattled on. The rain stopped. Was the sky becoming lighter in the east? *That was a mighty blow to my head...*

His eyelids hung heavy, his head pulsed. His body felt weightless as his sight darkened...

The fall from the cart felt slow, and Antony didn't feel the impact of the muddy ground. He felt suddenly warm and safe. But it didn't last as he came around. The ground below him was wet, like the bank of a river. Through half-opened eyes, he watched a rivulet of blood travel through the river's current like a plume of red smoke. Antony opened his eyes and realized that the vision wasn't real.

"Antony, is that you?" asked a distant voice. A kind, bearded face looked down at him first with hope, then disappointment. "We need to get him warm."

Antony opened his eyes again. He was in the village, lying in the middle of the street.

"Alright brother, what's this then?" said a much nearer voice. "You look like shit."

Carter knelt and hefted Antony's prostrate body over his shoulder. "Pa's been wondering where you were," he said. His voice rumbled through Antony's body. "I suppose you'll have some explaining to do. What with Sam's empty cart and the bruises."

Bron cupped Antony's face in his hands. Tears glistened in the corners of his eyes.

"My boy," he said. His voice weakened. "My son. I love you."

"I love you," Antony said.

"Er—I love you too. Let's get you home." Carter hefted Antony's weight more evenly on his shoulders. "You need to be warm and dry."

Antony slipped into darkness and remembered no more.

Tanor

"You are certain of what you saw?"

Lord Edwin nodded. His neat, small body was tucked in the corner of the great wooden chair in front of Tanor's hearth. Edwin's keen eyes studied the flames. Tanor had known and trusted those eyes for nearly thirty years. He shouldn't doubt them now. But he needed Edwin to be certain.

"I saw the ring," Edwin said, turning those eyes to meet Tanor's. "This one was made of silver. It must have been. It bore the lion signet. The boy was scared shitless, though. I don't think he knew what it meant. That, or he was a good playactor."

Tanor spun his own signet ring around his finger. He thought back to the demonstration, the young man in the inner ward—the way he walked and held his head. The way he handled the bow. Even the way he clasped Tanor's hand. So bold for a Man of the Lion to enter Tanor's gates, to drink his wine, to dance at his ball.

But Antony Bronson seemed like a bold one.

The rain pattered on outside. Godfrey had found Tanor a clean tunic and quickly did away with the soiled one. But Tanor still had the tang of vomit in his nostrils. Elanor was a woman who could quickly lose all her inhibitions. Tanor knew that well enough. He much preferred the sweet, rosy aroma of her hair.

Tanor swirled the wine in his goblet, watching the deep red hue reflect the glow of the fire. The guests were gone. His pregnant wife was safely in bed, his son fast asleep.

"I should have arrested him then and there," Edwin said. "The war is over, your grace. It's time to address the threat at home. He sat on your throne, by Aug's beard. If he hadn't run, I would've cut his balls off."

Edwin remained calmly folded in the chair as he made the threat. He hunted like a cat—quietly, slowly, until the right time to strike.

Word had gotten to Tanor fairly quickly about the incident in the throne room. Tanor wasn't upset by it. The throne was just a chair, no different from the one he sat in by the fire, though the chair in his chamber was exceedingly more comfortable. That throne had once been Alfred's birthright. Now it wasn't. His bloodline had been weak. That was simply how the saints operated. They winnowed away the weakest links. Alfred's line died with him.

The memory from his boyhood that should've been long forgotten clung to his mind like ivy on a wall. He was ten when the Wasting Sickness came to his father's village. His father had tried to calm the villagers, tell them to stay in their homes—but bodies rotted on the streets, abandoned and unburied, only days after the first fever. Old John had told Tanor not to go outside, not even to sit by a window in the manor house. But the disease found a way.

Tanor had a raging fever for five days. Most died within three. When he finally awoke, his father told him that the undertaker had already dug a plot for him in the churchyard—one right next to his half-sister, who had died just a few days before. The plague waned, and the village healed. But Tanor told his father about his strange dream—he'd had it first when struck with fever, then had it every night since. In the dream, he sat on a tall throne with a crown too big for his head. At his feet was a gored lion, and standing at his side was the likeness of Saint Augustus that he knew from books, his face downcast and obscured as it always was in depictions. The dream terrified him. Then the dream stopped, and Tanor forgot about it until he met King Alfred for the first time, saw the lion on his banner...

The bastard entered as Tanor mused, announced sheepishly by Godfrey. The little man had drunk too much wine that evening—his face was red, his eyes glassy. He stumbled away quickly, back into the shadows of the corridor. Edwin rose at the sound of his old pupil's footsteps. John entered the pool of firelight. Edwin looked comically small next to the huge man that John had become. Tanor regarded them both quietly as Edwin bowed at the waist to him and left.

Tanor looked him over. The firstborn he never wanted. Undoubtedly his, though. He'd known as soon as he'd seen the boy's sea-glass eyes that John was his. His mother had come to the door of his manor, big-bellied and wailing. John was whelped on the kitchen floor. Tanor was twenty-six and had never seen a newborn. John was born screaming that Wintermonth and didn't stop until Second Summer was over.

He stood quiet as a tomb now. How different children are when they grow to adulthood—and yet, they carry so many things with them from youth. John still avoided Tanor's gaze, staring steadily at the ground.

"Sit down," Tanor said, nodding to the chair across from his. John did so, sitting ramrod straight against the back of the chair. His posture made Tanor keenly aware of his own, slouched with long legs crossed at the ankle. Tanor had never been a soldier. John always had been.

"What happened in the throne room?" Tanor asked. A long silence. Tanor could've laughed. His bastard son had slain hundreds of men, but couldn't look his father in the face. Cowards come in many colors.

"Nothing," John mumbled. "A man, some vagrant, he—"

"Don't lie to me," Tanor said. He saw John's jaw working, knowing he'd been caught. "You should know better."

John took a deep breath that shuddered through his body. "I thought—I could've sworn he was Adrian for a moment," he said. Then words flowed out of him like blood from a wound. "I didn't realize it until I saw him there—"

"Adrian is dead, John," Tanor said simply. John's jaw worked again. "*Adrian is dead.* Isn't he?"

John said nothing, but he finally looked at Tanor. Those pale eyes, reflecting the firelight as an icicle refracts the sunrise.

"Yes," he finally said. "Adrian is dead."

"There are fools who believe he's alive. You may not have heard of them while you were in the North—though I should've sent the traitors there to die."

That gave John pause. The boy had always been soft. He hadn't even been able to kill a rabbit when he was young.

"They call themselves the Men of the Lion. Edwin found a silver signet ring in Antony's belongings. He's one of them. What should we do to these rebels?"

John was quiet again. His silence sometimes enraged Tanor. If he were still a child, Tanor would've smacked him for ignoring his question.

"What should we do to them, son?" he asked. He scanned John's face, how pale it was. *He's still terrified of me,* Tanor thought. His eyes rested on John's hands. His knuckles were red and bloodied. *He could easily use those on me. But he won't. He wouldn't dare.*

"They believe a lie," Tanor said, "don't they?"

Realizing it wasn't a rhetorical question, John nodded.

"It's time those believers were punished for their rebellion," Tanor said. "I was lenient with them during the war. All of us grieve in different ways. They have become bolder. Antony is one of the bold ones."

His idiotic son stared back at him. *I chose the stupidest bastard to keep. If only he had died as he was supposed to... at least now I have his muscle. I don't need his brain.*

"Men like you and Edwin can help me," Tanor said. "Help me put the fear of the dragon in the Men of the Lion. A dragon doesn't bow to the king of beasts—it strikes. And we will strike. You will strike."

"That will only strengthen their anger," John said.

"Don't speak about things you don't understand," Tanor said. "I'm not afraid of enraged peasants. They should fear me. And they will."

"What about Antony?"

"What *about* Antony?"

"He's a dissenter. He sat on your throne."

Tanor drained his cup. The dregs in the goblet were briny and sour.

"That was a foolish mistake," Tanor said. "Antony Bronson will no doubt make another one."

146

Antony

The strange visions did not disrupt Antony again. He awoke in his bed on the upper level of Bron's cottage, and the visions felt far away. All that remained was the dull throb of his bruises and the remembrance of how he got them. He could open his left eye, but barely.

I'm such a fool, was his first waking thought. He cringed at every action he'd taken at the palace—making a spectacle of himself at every turn. And it was long past time for him to get up and help his father.

His head still complained, but he sat up from the pallet and pulled off the soiled green tunic, another reminder of his foolish actions. He found the cleanest tunic he had. Antony would do his utmost to please his father that morning.

The satchel was by the side of his bed, the leather purse still in it. He reached in and found the ring. He wanted to ask Bron about it—if it was truly made of silver, they could melt it down. Then no one, not even Lord Edwin, could accuse them of being dissenters.

He found Bron in the shop, stooped on a stool, adding fletching to an arrow. A pile of finished ones lay at his elbow on the workbench. *Never my favorite part of the work*, Antony thought. It was mundane, repetitive.

A cool breeze blew in from the open door, playing with the strands of brown hair that fell out of Bron's ponytail. He wore his hair long—Mother had always liked it that way. Bron told Antony she would braid it down his back when they were young. Now, it often hung ragged and unwashed.

He looked up when he heard Antony's footsteps, his brow still creased in deep concentration. He managed a smile, but Antony could tell something troubled him. His smile didn't reach his eyes—wrinkles didn't spring from his temples as they often did when Bron was truly merry.

"There you are," he said. He pulled a stool beside his own. "Come, help me with these."

Antony sat down, feeling uneasy. He picked up a long, smooth shaft, freshly hewn and smelling of the forest it was cut from. The shop always smelled of new timber, a clean scent that made Antony feel renewed himself.

"Odd tunic you were wearing when Carter brought you in," Bron said after Antony was quiet for several moments. Bron had already trimmed and notched the shafts, varnishing them top to bottom with pine pitch. He'd been hard at work all morning, it seemed.

"I went to the Commoner's Ball last night," Antony said. "I found a better tunic to wear."

"Found. Found it with the forty argents you made in Southborn?"

"Pa, I sold the bows for fifty."

"Did you count the money?"

Antony's heart collapsed into his stomach. He ground his teeth. *Idiot.* He'd been so preoccupied with the ring, with Adelaide, with the throne. He forgot the most important step of the purchase—count the damn money, because anyone could be a cheat. Bron had faith in his fellow man, but not when it came to providing for his family.

Bron's deep-set eyes looked downcast. "The King has plenty of gold in his coffers to pay you—pay us—what we're owed. But Lord Edwin manages the coin and isn't so honest about it, especially with commoners like us." Antony could see Bron working his jaw. Then he sighed and smiled gently at Antony. "You did nothing wrong. You didn't know."

But I did. Antony seethed. Edwin's reaction to the ring had been so unsettling, so frightening, he had forgotten. He all but gave away his father's livelihood, hours and hours of work in that very shop, for less than they were owed.

"It will still be enough to pay the Harvestmonth tax," Antony said.

Bron nodded slowly, but the money didn't seem to be what bothered him. He gestured to the work in front of him.

"These are for Philip Butcher and his son. We'd best get busy with them."

But Antony's failure wouldn't leave him alone, even as he and Bron continued to work. Antony was about to take a bundle of wild turkey feathers from the bench and cut the quills, but his eyes landed on the pouch lying on his father's bench. Without another thought, he grabbed it, sifting through the coins to find the ring.

"I could sell this," Antony said. He pulled it out of the pouch to show Bron. "Folks in Southborn like them, and this one is made of something finer than tin."

Bron glanced at it casually, then something changed in his face and he looked at it again. He stared at it, mouth hung slightly open, recollecting.

"That's not necessary, son," he said. His voice was oddly quiet. "It's just a bauble, really. When the taxman comes, we will be ready with what we owe."

Antony wasn't satisfied. Bron seemed to notice his consternation.

"They play a different game than we do, one that is miles above us," he said. "You could do your utmost to get the money we're owed, but all you would do is wear Sam out on a long journey to Southborn, only to wait a day and a night for an audience with Edwin. He will feign busyness and dismiss you. And his dismissal is final."

"It sounds as though you've tried."

"I have. I even petitioned the king."

"Did Tanor give you the money?"

"No. *Alfred* didn't."

Antony leaned back in surprise. From what he remembered, he knew Alfred had been well-loved. It seemed to him a well-loved king would've been honest.

Bron seemed dismissive of it. "That was a long time ago. A king is a king is a king. They have no time for the troubles of simple folk."

Antony was quiet for a long time. He set the ring on Bron's workbench. He would try to sell it, he decided. He owed his father that much and more.

As he worked alongside Bron into the afternoon, as the shop became hot and muggy, he thought he recollected going to the palace to petition for the money. He remembered Bron, standing in the throne room before King Alfred, who seemed to listen intently. Had Edwin been there too? He couldn't remember.

Throughout the afternoon, Bron talked about what had happened while Antony was gone. Antony knew his father was trying to make him feel better, but Bron still seemed tense and troubled.

Harvestmonth was just days away. It would be difficult to get the money they needed in time. The sun hung low and the breeze that blew into the shop was warm and dusty by the time they finished their task. The shop smelled of rank hide glue, underscored by the milder scent of pitch. Bron wiped his brow and bundled the shafts together.

Antony stepped out into the evening to deliver the bundle to the butcher. His thoughts still weighed heavily on his mind—half-remembered memories, his foolishness, his pride. Before he left the shop, he'd tucked the signet ring into a pouch at his side.

I'll make this right.

His task done with Phil Butcher, he went to the tavern, knowing this time of night Carter would be there. And he was—sitting alone with his broad shoulders hunched over the bar. When Antony sat next to him, Carter looked at him with a raised eyebrow.

"Ah! He lives!" Carter exclaimed. "You're lucky I found you on my way to the field this morning."

"Thanks for that," Antony said.

"You drinking anything?"

"No."

Carter took a slurp of his ale. "Suit yourself," he said. "Pa told me about how those pigs in Southborn shorted you."

Antony bit his lip. "I know."

"Pa won't say it, but I will," Carter said. "You've put him in a bind that'll be hard for him to get out of. Because you didn't *think*. You almost never do, not til you're done acting."

"I—" Antony started to defend himself, but knew Carter would just find something to refute him. Because he was right. "Well, I'm going to make it right. I'm going to sell this." He produced the ring from his belt. "It's made of silver."

Carter glanced down at it without a hint of emotion—but maybe a hint of recognition—on his face.

"I'd melt it down," Carter said. "There's enough silver there to cover half of your Harvestmonth tax."

"Do you know where it came from?"

"No idea."

Antony considered it, running his thumb along the shape of the lion. He didn't *want* to melt it down. It was beautiful and intricate, a thing that seemed to hold memories and secrets beyond his own. Melting it down would feel like erasing something, especially after what the novice said to him. But Carter was right, as usual. Melting it would be easier than trying to sell it—and potentially getting in trouble by selling it to the wrong party.

"Does Pa know you have that?" Carter asked suddenly.

"Yes. Why?"

Carter shrugged. "He's kept it hid away for a long time," he said.

Antony fumbled with the ring for a bit. "Is he..." he began. He remembered the excited look in the novice's eye when he saw the ring. "Does Pa think the prince is still alive? Is that why he has this?"

Carter immediately shook his head. His brows were heavy and stern over his eyes. "No, and never tell Pa you asked that," he said. "Don't tell anyone, in fact. I have it on good authority that Fat Tanor isn't going to take kindly to that sort of thing anymore. The other laborers have all been talking about it."

Antony remembered. Edwin had called it treason. He felt a sudden chill. Then why did Pa have it?

"It's strange," Antony said, "that people want so badly for the prince to be alive."

Carter shrugged again. "If he were, we'd never have fought the war," he said. "People believe in things that make them feel better, that they're living for something that's not pointless."

He toyed with his mug, then took another swig. Antony hadn't seen Carter come to chapel since he moved out of Bron's house. His older brother had always seemed skeptical of the saints and the Great Maker. Antony could even see the slight disdain in his brother's eye when he looked at the carved likeness of Saint Hogarth above the bar. Carter believed in what he could feel and see—the work he did with his hands. He didn't need a saint to remind him his life was unimportant and menial.

"Well, I'm off," Carter said, draining the last of his ale. "I'd tell you to stay out of trouble, but I know you'll just do the opposite." Carter put a copper on the bar next to his empty mug. "But at least keep Pa out of trouble." He looked down at Antony, his dark blue eyes surprisingly earnest. "Make it up to him, even if he doesn't ask you for it."

"I will," Antony said as confidently as he could.

A muggy heat still lingered in the air when Antony walked out of the tavern, but a wind from the north threatened to change that, and soon. Until then, the villagers enjoyed the sunny evening. Most shops that Antony passed were closed for the day, with only a few shopkeepers working on as the sun dipped to the treeline of the Hemlock Forest, glowing like a great orange eye. Ever since the war ended, everyone in Barnswood seemed more lighthearted. Even now, as Antony passed the town square, he saw a crowd gathered around a band of minstrels playing a merry tune. Antony couldn't remember the last time he'd seen anything like that. The grief and toil had washed away from the faces of people he knew and was replaced by mirth and joy. They were no longer afraid of the Northmen invading their land, burning down their homes, and taking their livelihoods—as they had been warned would happen for the last ten years.

Why don't I feel the same? Antony wondered. Other villagers pushed past him to take part in the fun. Ale flowed freely from makeshift taps, and the smell of savory meat pies and sweetbreads wafted through the air. This was a *true* commoner's ball. But Antony wanted nothing to do with it.

He kept walking past when something caught his eye—or rather, some*one*. A small, slim figure in a cloak wove between the growing throng of people. The person probably wanted to stay discreet by wearing a hood over his face, but it only made him stand out among the bare faces on that warm night. But no one seemed to regard him or care what he was doing—Antony almost hadn't noticed what he was doing until he stopped to look. He saw it happen once, then again, and knew he wasn't wrong.

The man was cutting purses.

Moving smoothly between members of the crowd like water around stones, the figure slid behind and around the villagers, always with a glance downward. If he found the unlucky owner of an exposed purse, the opening of his cloak would flick ever so slightly. Antony caught a glint of silver as the knife found its mark, and when the figure moved away, the purse was either gone or slapping emptily on its owner's thigh.

"*Hey!*" Antony yelled.

The man's head immediately shot up and two green eyes stared right at him. A red braid flew out from under the cloak—a woman. She ducked down again as heads started turning toward her and Antony. She snaked away from the crowd, moving in the opposite direction. Antony followed much less graciously, pushing past the other villagers and shoving them out of his way.

"Stop!" he yelled, feeling gall rise in his throat. He thought about the villagers in the square, trying to make merry, only to go home at the end of the night and find themselves penniless. The small woman's head bobbed in and out of his sight line between villagers until the road cleared. But she was still faster than Antony. The hood of her cloak flew off and her braid wagged behind her as she dodged into an alley. Antony skidded against the cobblestones and followed her.

The alley was narrow. The woman's slim form slid through easily, but Antony had to turn sideways to clear it, moving at a much slower pace. On the other side was a much quieter street, and the woman was already a few dozen yards out of his reach. Antony broke into a run again.

Where is she going? Antony knew almost everyone in Barnswood. He'd never seen this woman before. She ran for the Barnswood Bridge toward

Hemlock Forest, away from town.

Before Antony could follow her any further, he felt a force at his back, and the ground came up to meet him. His knees slammed against the ground as he caught himself on his elbows, but not before two heavy hands forced his face into the ground. Someone had him pinned down.

"Let me go!" Antony grunted into the dirt. From the corner of his eye, he could see the woman disappearing around the corner.

"Let *her* go," growled a voice above him. The hands gripped his shoulders tighter. Antony struggled under the man's strength.

"She can't do that!" he yelled. "She's an—"

"An outlaw? I know."

Antony squirmed so he could make out the face above him. Underneath a hood was a gruff-looking face with deep-set brown eyes.

"But you can't steal from these people!"

"Who died and made you king?"

The man flipped Antony onto his back and hit him in the face. Antony's head rang. He floundered as the man got off him, grabbing at the outlaw's sleeve. The man slid easily out of his grasp and ran away. Dazed, Antony heard his slapping footsteps retreating from him.

He stared up at the dusky purple sky. Somewhere, the music still played. He could still smell the meat pies. His jaw hurt. *I must have a punchable face.*

After a few moments, he slowly lifted himself from the ground and dusted off his tunic. Looking around, he saw no sign of the outlaws. They were gone, probably back into the depths of the forest.

Antony thought about the people in the square, celebrating and making merry. Who knows how much of their livelihoods they carried in their purses. Most people didn't like to keep their money at home when they weren't there—some people may have lost their entire livelihoods that night.

He patted the pouch at his side. A slit, ever so small, had been cut at the bottom.

The pouch was empty.

The ring was gone.

Adelaide

When Adelaide opened her eyes, the morning was later than she expected. Full sun washed the stone floor of her chamber in almost blinding light. She sat up with a start, realizing she was probably late for her duties of taking care of the queen.

Why did no one wake me? Adelaide swung her feet off the bed and onto the floor. A tray sat on the table by her bedside holding bread, jam, and a cup of tea quickly growing cold. She'd been sleeping so deeply that a servant had come in with breakfast and didn't even wake her. She sighed heavily and undressed from her nightclothes.

Memories from the night before drifted to the forefront of her mind as she took a borrowed dress from her wardrobe, a simple one of faded pink. As she stumbled into it, there was a knock at the door.

"Just a moment—" But it was too late. Ilse, one of Claudia's maids, traipsed in, leaving the door wide open. Adelaide's face flushed.

"*Now* you're awake!" cried the small girl. Ilse could not have been more than sixteen. She had a wide, plain face and hair the color of a sparrow's wing. Adelaide had only known her for a few days but already knew more about Ilse than she ever needed to—the small village she was from in the Midlands, the name of the cook that she fancied down in the kitchens, even how sick she got during her monthly bleeding—in great detail. The girl now sat on Adelaide's bed, swinging her short legs.

Adelaide's arms were twisted behind her back, attempting to pull the strings of her bodice. Ilse made no move to help.

"Why did no one come to wake me?" Adelaide asked.

"I brought in your breakfast, but I didn't think you'd awaken even if the palace was coming down around your ears," Ilse said. "Besides, her grace has begun her confinement today. She has canceled all appointments until the babe is born. She is in bed now, and hasn't much need of us, not until she begins to labor."

"Have you been to see her? Is she in good spirits?"

Ilse nodded. "She said the cramping has begun. The babe could be here even today." She laid back on Adelaide's messy bed. "Can you imagine what trying to push out a baby will be like? My monthly cramping is already so miserable. For five days straight I always—"

"All right," Adelaide said quickly. She smoothed her skirt and ran her fingers through her hair. "Does her grace need anything?"

Ilse shook her head. "Elanor is with her now, and I will take over in the afternoon. She may need you in the evening."

Elanor. How could Adelaide have forgotten? The woman must have felt miserable that morning.

"I wonder if Elanor will tell her about the baby," Ilse said absently.

Adelaide's heart plummeted to her stomach. She turned to look at Ilse, who still lay innocently on the bed, feet swinging. She saw the question on Adelaide's face. "I stopped by her room last night after she—well, after *that.* But I heard you were already in the chamber with her. But before I left, I heard her say something about a baby in her belly." She sat up, her head cocked. "Did she tell you who the father is?"

Adelaide could've breathed a sigh of relief. *So she didn't hear everything.*

"No," Adelaide said curtly. Then she added, as warmly as she could muster, "Do we have somewhere we need to be, Ilse?"

Ilse lifted her eyes heavenward. "No...except her grace wanted me to find Magg. To make sure the cramping is nothing to worry about. Actually, Adelaide...would you want to go find her? I need to go down to the kitchens." Her face grew into a wicked smile. "Stephen wanted me to taste the new blackberry brandy he's made."

Adelaide rolled her eyes. Stephen—of course. The cook. "I'll find Magg," Adelaide said, praying hopelessly that Ilse wouldn't waggle her tongue in the kitchens too much. And Adelaide was fond of the court physician. She hadn't seen Magg since she returned to the palace. Magg had mended every scrape and soothed every fever when Adelaide visited Southborn as a child. She still had a scar on her knee from when she slipped in Miller's Pond. She had nearly drowned that day, but Prince Adrian had saved her and carried her back to the palace. She remembered his thin arms quivering under her weight, and that was the first time she'd felt her heart beating in a strange, excited way.

Ilse reluctantly left her position on the bed and bounded toward the door. When she left, Adelaide took a few bites of the dry bread and sipped the cold tea. It was sweetened with honey and would've been much better hot. *That's what I get for sleeping in.* That, and a task passed down to her from Ilse.

Adelaide knew where she would find Magg. She would be in her rooms, preparing a tincture or reading from her huge collection of annals. Magg preferred the company of books over people when they weren't ill or dying. She was always useful, as a rule.

Magg's rooms were in the east wing of the palace by the infirmary. Adelaide stepped in through the slightly open door and into the blinding morning rays that flooded the room. Through her squinted eyes, she saw Magg's long, low workbench, the shelves that were lined with herbs, poultices, and frightening-looking instruments. She shielded her face with her hand, and the room became clearer.

Adelaide took the short set of flagstone steps into Magg's room, vaguely remembering all the times she'd been there in the past. The sting of a poultice on a skinned knee. The poke of tweezers as Magg had removed a splinter. The bitter taste of medicine on a throat that was already sore and swollen. Each shelf around the workbench was piled messily with scrolls, leather-bound books—all of Magg's cures and concoctions recorded over the years.

She found Magg tucked in a corner, her long, graceful body leaned over a table, reading from a scroll. Magg was a tall woman, probably now around forty, with a sensible beauty about her. Her long neck craned out of a high-collared gray dress, a style she often wore. Adelaide had never seen her with a hair—or truly anything—out of place.

Magg turned at the sound of Adelaide's footsteps and immediately beamed. She was exactly the same—perhaps more gray in her hair, perhaps more wrinkles around her eyes, but still Magg.

"Adelaide DuMont, as I live and breathe!" she exclaimed. Her hazel eyes flashed with delight. She nearly dropped the scroll in her hands. "I heard you were here. I just didn't think I'd have the pleasure of seeing you."

"Well, I've had the unexpected pleasure of coming to find you," Adelaide said. "What are you reading?"

Magg's brow furrowed, as though she were actively trying to puzzle something out. She weighed the scroll in her hand.

"I'm looking for anything the ancient physicians may have written about the bone structure of the body. How to properly set breaks, and so forth." Magg looked knowingly at Adelaide, a small smile on her lips. "Prince Charles does not like to hold still. I've seen him climbing places he shouldn't. It won't be long before something gets broken."

Adelaide laughed. "If anyone can be trusted with scrapes and bruises, it's you. I still have the scar on my knee from Miller's Pond."

"Oh, *that* little thing," Magg said. She obviously remembered—Adelaide wouldn't be surprised if she remembered every scrape, cut, and ailment she ever treated. "I remember you were so brave that day. You did your best not to cry in front of the prince."

Adelaide shook off the memory, remembering why she came down. "Ilse sent me looking for you. Her grace is having labor cramps and is concerned."

Magg shrugged. "Cramping at this stage is normal," she said. "Her waters have not yet broken, so I'm not concerned."

"What should we do to keep her comfortable?"

Magg smiled. "She is laboring. Comfort is all but impossible," she said. She re-rolled the scroll she held and placed it among the others. "I should check on her, though. Enough about bones."

They walked together toward the door, through the shower of dust particles that glittered in the sun around them.

The ghost of a question lurked in Adelaide's mind. It would be dangerous to ask, she knew, no matter how much she loved Magg. *But would I rather be afraid, or know more than I know now?*

"Magg," Adelaide said slowly, keeping pace with the tall woman's long strides. "You saw Prince Adrian's body when he died."

"And since, yes," Magg said, her face neutral.

"Since?" That caught Adelaide off guard.

Magg looked down at her with a raised eyebrow. "My study of bones," she said, "has included the examination of bodies in the Crypt of Kings—with his grace's permission, of course. Examining physical defects in royal lines, and so forth."

"And?"

"And what?"

"What have you seen? In the bones?"

Magg considered it for a moment. "Well, in the line of King Alfred, I've seen evidence of a disease that degenerates the bones, which if Alfred lived longer might have—"

"Actually, I was wondering more about Prince Adrian."

Magg stopped walking. Her face was no longer neutral. It was something else. Not sad. Not angry. Frightened, maybe. Then she kept walking at a quick pace. Adelaide followed. For a long time, it appeared Magg had ignored her question. Then, Magg stopped and turned to Adelaide, her deep-set hazel eyes intent.

"Well, I discovered something quite extraordinary, actually."

Adelaide held her breath.

"When a bone is broken, I have found, be it arm, leg, foot—it grows back stronger," she said. "The bones inside us are alive. When tested, they strengthen, like a muscle, or a brain, or a will."

"That's very interesting," Adelaide said. Magg thought long and deeply about things, so she spoke long and deeply about them when asked.

"Prince Adrian's was an interesting case when I examined his bones," Magg said, her voice softer. Her gaze became distant. She chuckled softly.

"His medical history was exciting, to say the least. I pulled him out of his mother's womb feet first because he was too stubborn to turn around. I nursed a fever that almost killed him at only a few months of age. When he lost his first tooth, he came screaming to me because he thought the rest of him was falling apart. I tended to that boy's every injury, illness, ailment. Seeing his bones—good saints, I can't explain to you how strange that was."

How strange what *was?* Adelaide wanted to ask. But Magg had pursed her lips and started walking even faster. She didn't want to talk about it. Perhaps she simply didn't want to talk about the dead.

"I see," Adelaide replied after a long pause. "That is quite...fascinating."

Adelaide was quiet as they continued to walk, disappointed by Magg's revelation. She found herself more disturbed at the thought of Adrian's bones moldering in the crypt. She'd cried almost uncontrollably when Adrian had died, when she'd only seen his body wrapped in a sheet before he was entombed. The thought, the realization that nothing was left of him but his bones, made her stomach turn. *Perhaps that's what was strange about it. To see all that's left of someone after so long.*

It occupied her mind as they walked together to Claudia's chamber. She thought about the dream she'd had a few nights prior, of Adrian standing in the crypt. *I'm not there.* She rolled her eyes at herself. It had been a *dream*, something her mind had made up. Being back in the palace, the memories of Adrian had caused the dream.

The thoughts continued to plague her mind as they arrived in Claudia's chamber. An army of pillows propped the queen up on her massive bed. Pieces of her yellow hair clung to her forehead, and to Adelaide, she looked much older. The labor pains probably started late in the night or early in the morning, as Adelaide could tell from the heavy circles under Claudia's eyes. She wore nothing but a white dressing gown, spread like a huge white sheet over her protruding belly.

Ilse sat on a stool near one end of the bed, whilst Elanor wetted a piece of cloth in a bowl nearby. Her own belly was tucked neatly away in a sea of corsets and skirts, but Adelaide saw her face was peaked and her eyes still swollen from crying.

"Magg, thank all the saints," Claudia said as they entered. "I think the baby may be very near."

"Have your waters broken?"

Claudia shook her head.

"Then I'm afraid we may have a long time to go, your grace."

The queen rested her head back in exhaustion on the pillows. "I'd rather not labor for as long as I did with Charles," she groaned. Then she sighed and put a hand on her stomach. "That means it's another good, strong son, doesn't it, Magg?"

Magg sat down on the edge of the bed and put her hands on the top and bottom of Claudia's belly, pressing gently.

"There is no way to know while the child is still inside the womb, your grace," she said. "But you are carrying low, and that sometimes indicates a boy."

"We shall name him after Tanor," Claudia said gleefully. Then she shifted in discomfort. "As soon as he is delivered."

Elanor turned quickly away.

"The child is full term, to be sure, so the labor pains are not premature," Magg said. "And it is in the right position. Now we simply have to wait for your waters to break."

Claudia sighed, her great belly heaving. Ilse leaned forward and patted her hand.

"If you want, I can have Stephen send up some blackberry brandy," she said. Adelaide couldn't help but notice Ilse's words were a bit slurred. "It would help with the pain. The headache I had this morning is all but gone."

Magg shot Ilse a warning glance. Claudia was looking at Elanor.

"Why, Elanor, what's wrong?" she asked. "You have tears in your eyes."

It was true. Even from across the bed, Adelaide could see wet tracks along Elanor's face. She quickly wiped them away with the back of her hand. Her corset was fastened tight, and her skirts were wide. She looked stout, but not pregnant.

"It's nothing, your grace," she said, her voice thick. "I'm fine."

162

"Perhaps it is her own baby that's bothering her." Ilse had probably meant to whisper it to Adelaide, but the blackberry brandy made her voice careless.

Claudia's eyes immediately snapped to Elanor. Elanor's face went paler than it already was and she stared down at Ilse with coin-sized eyes. Adelaide felt as though her stomach had fallen into her bowels.

"Is this true, Elanor?" Claudia asked. Her voice was surprisingly calm.

Elanor's lower lip quivered as her face turned crimson red. She nodded ever so slightly, but not before shooting Ilse a look that could've killed her.

"My dearest, why didn't you tell me?" Claudia asked, reaching for Elanor's hand. "There is no condemnation here. A baby is a wonderful thing. Come, sit here next to me. Talk to me. It will take my mind off these labor pains."

Elanor looked timider than Adelaide had ever seen her as she sat on the very edge of the bed. Claudia smiled and reached out to touch Elanor's belly.

"How exciting," she said. "Two babies in the palace. They will be the best of friends!"

Elanor still said nothing. She only nodded. Adelaide saw tears brimming her eyes again. All Adelaide felt was the dread that this would not end well.

"Now," Claudia took Elanor's hand, "I ask this delicately since you are unmarried—as far as I know, though it seems you are keeping secrets from me!—what will you do? I take it you are not far along, but after a time it will become awfully hard to hide. Believe me." She gestured to her own enormous belly.

Elanor heaved a shaking sigh. She looked helplessly up at Adelaide.

"Sir Lucas seemed quite taken with you last night, Elanor." Adelaide didn't have to speak—Ilse did for her. "You could marry him. He is single and eligible. Unless, is he the father? Surely not. He just came back."

"Silly girl!" Claudia laughed. She patted Elanor's hand. "Ilse doesn't understand now babies work."

"Yes, I do! A man puts his—"

Before Ilse could say another word, Elanor burst into tears. She covered her face with her hands and wept.

"I don't want to marry Lucas," she said between shallow breaths. "I want to—I want to—"

She stood up and ran out of the room.

A long silence spread out across the chamber until Claudia looked at Magg. "Did you know anything about this?"

Magg looked askance. "No, your grace, I didn't."

"Tell the truth, now, Magg." Claudia said. The warmth she exuded with Elanor was gone. Her voice was prodding, searching, desperate. "There are few things that happen in the palace without your knowing. Especially things of...that nature."

Adelaide looked at Magg. The poor woman looked scared. Adelaide's heart felt as though it would burst from her chest. Magg drew in a shaking breath.

"Elanor is five months along," Magg said. "She came to me early on after she missed a monthly bleeding. I confirmed what she suspected. That is all she told me."

Claudia's mouth was a thin, hard line. "Are you sure? She didn't tell you who the father is?" For all the pain she was in, her gaze was focused and intense. "Someone in the palace? She hasn't traveled much lately, not even back home."

A thought struck Adelaide. Did Claudia suspect the truth? Is that why she seemed so contemptuous of Elanor? The light in Claudia's eyes was something Addie hadn't seen in her before.

"What about you, Adelaide?"

The question from Claudia froze Adelaide's heart. The answer was probably written all over her face. Her father had always told her she wore her feelings like a mummer wears a mask.

"Tell the truth now, dearest," Claudia said, her voice urgent.

"I—I don't know, your grace."

Claudia's countenance suddenly became stormy. "You must. You helped her last night. Surely she could not have kept it hidden from you in her state."

Adelaide swallowed hard. Claudia and Magg stared at her. So did Ilse from across the bed, probably desperate to hear the gossip.

"Adelaide," Claudia's voice became flint. For the first time since they'd met, Adelaide was afraid of her. "As queen and as Elanor's mistress, I have a right to know my ladies' business. Tell me what you know, or I will reconsider your position in my court."

Adelaide's blood froze. To not tell Claudia the horrible secret she knew, to protect Elanor, would mean to forfeit her position at court? That was a cruel prospect from the queen. It would mean risking her marriage prospects, her family's reputation. She swallowed and found her throat dry.

This is what Elanor meant, Adelaide thought ruefully. *It's not what or who I know. It's what I know about who I know. Saints save me.*

"According to Elanor, the father is...well, it's his grace," she said slowly. Her heartbeat hammered in her ears.

Claudia said nothing, but her face confirmed it all. The face of a queen who had everything anyone could have dreamed of, but nothing she wanted. And the face of a woman who suspected something for so long but didn't want to hear the truth, for the truth spoken is the truth known.

"Very well, then." Claudia's voice was resigned, but she maintained her strange calmness. "I should like to be alone with Magg, please. Ilse, Adelaide...please go."

They did as they were told. Adelaide was relieved to be out of that room, but once they were, Ilse turned toward her.

"It's *really* the king, Adelaide?"

"It doesn't matter, Ilse."

Ilse walked close to her elbow. "I can't *believe* it. *Elanor* having a baby? The king's baby?"

Adelaide shushed her. "Not so loud. Don't tell anyone. Let's go to court until her grace needs us again. If anyone at court asks about the queen, even his grace, we'll tell them the labor is progressing and all is well."

"But—"

"Let's go, Ilse."

Ilse begrudgingly followed Adelaide to the great hall where the king held court, which was already well underway that morning. Adelaide saw no sign of her aunt—she was probably elsewhere, scheming about who would be the most lucrative husband for Adelaide, and perhaps still fuming about the night before. *No one seems to care half so much as she*, Adelaide thought, *and she treats it like the scandal of the year.*

But she is trying to protect you, said a smaller, gentler voice in her mind—a voice that sounded like her father. *Protect you from further scandal or shame.*

Ilse immediately slipped away from Adelaide as soon as they entered, melting into the clusters of people in the room. There were more men than women that day, and as Adelaide entered, Tanor was opening new business on the Harvestmonth Tax, proposed by one of the many lords present.

"Thank you, Lord Riversate," he said above the low murmur of the room. "Unfortunately, there will be no reprieve from the Harvestmonth Tax even with the war's end. The treasury has called in every debt owed to the crown, and still, our coffers are left wanting. The crown has its own debts incurred from the war."

"And from lavish parties," muttered a voice close to Adelaide. She realized the voice belonged to Sir Lucas, who stood very near to her. She inched closer to him and he noticed. He shrugged at her.

"It's the truth, isn't it?" he added in a whisper. Adelaide shrugged back. He smiled a small, crooked smile. Being near him felt safe, reassuring.

"I'm sure his grace wouldn't want me saying this, but my father told me the situation in Widlowe is dire," he continued. "The village has nothing left to give. They've given Tanor their men, their weapons, their money... now there are no men to work, no tools to work with, and no money to pay them. It's as though Tanor thinks money comes from thin air."

"For him, it does," Adelaide said.

"Families wonder if they'd need to surrender their homes, send their children to serve a lord or even the crown... just to pay the Harvestmonth Tax."

And here I am, with my greatest worry being whom I will marry, Adelaide thought guiltily, *and enjoying lavish parties thrown at great expense.*

As if he read her mind, Lucas said, "I heard about that business in the throne room last night. You had danced with that man, hadn't you?" His blue eyes weren't accusatory. In fact, they were playful.

Adelaide nodded. "I'm as surprised as anyone," she said, then added cautiously, "I shouldn't have let him get away."

"He's harmless," Lucas chuckled. "And I doubt he'll come back with the way John cleaned the cobbles with him."

Adelaide thought of John. He had been terrifying—the light in his eyes was like nothing she'd ever seen. If he'd kept beating Antony that way, John could've killed him.

Lucas must have noticed her change in attitude. "You mustn't be upset with what John did. I know you fancied that lad, but—"

"What?" Adelaide said. A few heads turned their direction, and she felt her face redden. She added more quietly, "No I didn't."

"Are you sure? Addie, I've only ever seen that look in your eye once before, and it was when—"

Adelaide held up her hands to stop him. She knew what he was going to say.

"All right," she said. "I enjoyed my evening with him. And yes, John didn't need to be so... thorough in his beating. I'm sure Antony knew what he did was wrong without getting his skull nearly caved in."

"First-name terms, eh?" Lucas winked. Adelaide blushed deeper, then rolled her eyes.

"He's just a commoner," she said. The words felt sour in her mouth. "Even if I did fancy him, I know I could never marry him."

"All I mean to say is," Lucas continued, "John is, first and foremost, a soldier. But he's also a good man. A good man who got dealt a bad hand. By all the saints, I wouldn't be here if it weren't for him. And," he turned to look at Adelaide, "I think something happened to him the night King Alfred and the prince died. He never wanted to talk about it, but he was there. And both of you knew the prince better than anyone."

It was true, Adelaide conceded.

"I suppose you're right," Adelaide said. "Do you know where John is now?"

"I think he's in the livery," Lucas replied. "He said something this morning about a uniform." He leaned in closer, his voice just above a whisper. "The King and Lord Darkshire are going to crack down on the Men of the Lion."

Adelaide had heard only a few things about the Men of the Lion—from some nobles in Aunt Pauline's circles, they were called radicals who lived quiet lives but secretly conspired every night to slaughter any lord or lady they met. Men who took the law into their own hands, Aunt Pauline believed, who didn't fear the consequences, and were thus men to be feared.

But from others like those in her father's village, they were people who missed the days of peace, who yearned for a life, for a past, that was gone. Or, as Aunt Pauline had said, those who deluded themselves to believe that the present was far worse than anything they'd experienced.

"They want so badly for things to be as they were when things, as they were, are no better or worse," she'd said with disdain when one of her servants was found with a lion trinket and dismissed. "The past is never what we paint it, Adelaide. You long for the days when your father was alive, and all was right with the world, but nothing was right then, either."

Lucas' voice anchored Adelaide back in the present. "Edwin told me the lad from last night might have been a Man of the Lion. He had one of the rings. No weapons or anything, but I guess it rattled the King enough to do something about it."

Of course it did, Adelaide thought. Antony's face floated in front of her, handsome and smiling. The thought made her heart ache. *I thought he was you, Adrian. I really did.*

"Shouldn't you be with the queen?" Lucas asked. Adelaide was relieved at the change of subject.

"She needed time alone with Magg." Adelaide explained. That situation still gnawed at her, too—any time she looked up at the king holding court, she thought about it. The thought of him and Elanor, of him and whoever else…. and he was the one who would find a husband for her. She didn't realize how tightly she'd held her fists until just then. She relaxed her hands at her sides.

Lucas' father beckoned him from the other side of the room. Lord Widlowe was a stern, serious man, very unlike his youngest son. Lucas gave Adelaide an apologetic look and slid through the crowd to his father's side. When he left, she felt unmoored with nothing to cling to.

We are all slaves to what our elders want from us, Adelaide thought. Lord Widlowe was a slave to Tanor too, as a member of his council. Despite how his village suffered, he could take no action that the king did not approve of.

"I will send men with every tax collector to ensure taxes are paid and there's no trouble," Tanor was saying. "These men have recently come back from the war. They will remind Southern folk what we fought for and what we sacrificed. When they complain about the tax, show them the scars those men bear. None of them could ever pay a higher price than that."

Adelaide saw many in the room solemnly shaking their heads. *It means nothing to them,* she thought. *They sacrificed nothing. The war cost them nothing.* When Tanor had welcomed her to court just days before, she'd thought he was so warm and kind. Now, everything about him seemed false.

Her mind kept going back to the night before, seeing Antony on the throne. The feeling she had seeing him there…how right it looked.

She clenched her teeth at her own stupidity. *That's not real,* she thought. This *is real—Claudia, and Elanor, and the child about to be born.*

She glanced around the crowd gathered again and was surprised to make eye contact with Aunt Pauline. Her heart jumped at the sight of her, remembering how foolish she'd felt when her aunt had cornered her at the ball. Beside her stood her driver, Jacob—gray hair stuck out from every direction on his head, and his pale green eyes rolled around in his sockets, as though detached from anything else in his head. Adelaide wondered why she was there—if Jacob was with her, maybe she was going to leave soon.

Godfrey approached Tanor's chair and whispered in his ear, his eyes darting toward the door. Tanor nodded, one eyebrow raised. Then he smiled.

"I have nearly forgotten that today is Saint Myra's Day," Tanor said. "Not a holy day for feasting, as we all know, but a day of honoring the dead through almsgiving. I expect many of you have made plans to pray at the Cathedral today, but if you have not, a young novice has arrived from the brotherhood to lead us in a prayer for the dead."

Adelaide saw him—a young man wearing the roughspun brown robe of a novice shouldering his way awkwardly through the court finery, standing out like a mud stain amidst the crushed velvet and satin. Under Tanor's smile, Adelaide saw irritation.

The young novice was probably only seventeen, maybe eighteen, but tall and powerfully built. His habit was too small for him—the sleeves hardly reached his wrists. He had a wide, homely face, with a big nose and a heavy forehead. His whole figure was bulky, as though he were made of cinder blocks crudely put together. But he smiled earnestly and bowed to the king. In his hands, he held a deep wooden bowl.

He faced the court. Adelaide saw his hands trembling. Most novices were required to complete menial tasks like prayer and almsgiving before taking their final vows. The boy in front of her probably started as a novice when he was eleven or twelve, and probably wouldn't enter the true brotherhood for another five years. The Order of the Nine had many requirements for young novices—probably so the monks didn't have to get their hands dirty among the people.

"Let us pray," he said. The prayer was long and rehearsed, and Adelaide hardly listened to the words. She instead prayed her own prayer, one for her father. She hoped against hope that when she opened her eyes, she'd see him standing next to her.

"The brotherhood accepts your alms on behalf of the dead on this Saint Myra's Day," said the young man.

Tanor's smile hadn't moved. It remained stiff on his cheeks. "Court is adjourned for the day," he said. "As you depart, leave your alms with this kind novice—what is your name, son?"

The boy's tanned cheeks flushed when the king addressed him. "David, your grace,"

Members of court filed out. Lord Widlowe dropped a coin into David's bowl, but scarcely no one else—Adelaide wasn't surprised to see Aunt Pauline leave without giving her alms. She couldn't help but notice David's face looked downcast as even the king rose and left the audience chamber without providing a single coin.

Adelaide had no money on her. She had a few coins in her satchel upstairs—if she was fast enough, she could go upstairs and fetch some before the novice left.

She bolted out the door, momentarily lost in the sea of crushed velvet, and began darting down the hall toward her chamber when a metallic voice stopped her.

"Where do you think *you're* going, my dear?"

Adelaide didn't need to turn to know who the voice belonged to. She heard the quick step of footsteps behind her before Pauline grabbed her arm and spun her around. Over Pauline's shoulder, Adelaide saw a few curious glances from courtiers. Her cheeks flamed with heat.

"You are not a little girl anymore, my dear," Pauline said in a none-too-quiet voice. "You can't simply go darting down the palace halls whenever you feel like it. Besides, you should be tending to the queen. From what I understand, her labor has begun."

"She wanted to be alone," Adelaide explained. Pauline's mouth remained a rigid line. Her grip tightened on Adelaide's arm.

"You merely need to be careful, my dear." Her voice was quieter now. Almost, Adelaide thought, a bit gentle. "You are new to court and there is much that you don't understand."

Adelaide nodded absently. Jacob had appeared at Pauline's side, as though waiting for her.

"Are you going somewhere?" she asked.

"Back to Easthempton," Pauline said with a sniff, "to collect your dowry."

Adelaide's stomach dropped. "My dowry?" she asked. "So the king has found...?"

Pauline responded with a simple nod, one that nearly made Adelaide tremble. Over the course of only a few days, her future had been decided. She should've been happy, but something in her core felt deeply disturbed.

"Who is it?" she asked.

Pauline ignored her. "I will be gone for a day or two," she continued. "I won't be here to protect you. You need to be careful."

Adelaide could've rolled her eyes. *Protect me.* But a softer voice inside her reminded her—*you know nothing. Pauline protects you more than you know.*

"Have a safe journey, aunt," Adelaide said with a curtsy.

The presentation seemed to please Pauline. She inclined her head slightly. Then with a whirl of her voluminous skirts, she and Jacob had turned the corner toward the courtyard.

The young novice appeared at the door of the audience chamber, looking crestfallen, almost embarrassed. She approached him, and when he looked up from his bowl to meet her gaze, he seemed surprised.

"M-my lady—" he stammered with a flush crossing his face. He bowed awkwardly.

"I'm afraid I have nothing on hand at the moment," Adelaide said, "and I may not be able to come to vespers tonight. Her grace is in labor and will soon have her child."

"You are her lady?" David asked. "I will pray for a safe delivery for her grace's child. You needn't worry yourself with it, but I will be at morning prayers tomorrow collecting alms, and two days hence I plan to deliver whatever I have earned to the surrounding villages."

"Surrounding villages? Like Barnswood, perchance?" The question bubbled out of Adelaide before she could stop it. *Antony.*

"Yes, Barnswood has been especially affected by the war, with so many farmers taken from their land. Why do you ask, my lady?"

It was Adelaide's turn to blush. "Oh, no reason," she said. "A good friend

172

of mine lives in Barnswood."

David didn't seem suspicious that a lady would have a friend in so common of a town as Barnswood. "And what is your friend's name?"

"Antony."

David beamed. "If I cross paths with Antony, I will tell him his friend, Lady...er—?"

"Adelaide."

"That Lady Adelaide said hello."

Adelaide smiled genuinely for the first time that day. The boy's kindness and zeal were infectious. His life was a simple one—without the gossip and machinations of court. *Perhaps I should have become a Sister of Saint Aethel.* Sisters lived a cloistered life similar to the brothers, and were often midwives or gardeners, tending to growing things all the year round.

Adelaide bid David farewell and walked along the corridor with a quick step. The thought of Antony had brightened her so much, she'd forgotten the news Aunt Pauline had told her. She was to be married. It shouldn't have surprised her—it was her sole purpose for being at court. But it seemed so *soon*, so sudden. Pauline hadn't told her who it was.

Someone who is regularly at court so that I can continue my position as lady-in-waiting, she thought, though it made her stomach sour. She remembered the look of betrayal on Elanor's face. But if she'd lost her position at court, if Claudia had turned her out for refusing to tell the truth, no member of court would want to marry her.

"The truth spoken is the truth known," her father had told her once. A simple phrase, but a meaningful one. It had been tied to some sort of story or parable he'd told her as a child—she couldn't remember which one.

She went straight to her chambers, finding her bed freshly made by one of the servants. If Magg or the queen needed her, they'd be sure to look in her chambers first. Adelaide wasn't tired, but she knew it would doubtless be a late night, so she lay down on the bed and closed her eyes.

When her eyes snapped back open, the light in her room had shifted. A late afternoon sun shone hazily through her windows, bringing with it a warm, sleepy breeze. Adelaide blinked off her daze, trying to wake her mind up. She didn't even remember falling asleep. Now that she was awake, she felt bleary-eyed and foggy-headed.

And then she realized why she woke up so suddenly. Someone was knocking on her door.

"Come in," she groaned, propping herself on her elbows.

Ilse, the last person she wanted to see, entered the room. Her cheeks were flushed and her hair was tumbling out of the braid that fell down her back.

"Adelaide, I've been knocking for nearly five minutes!" Ilse exclaimed. "Her grace needs you. The baby will come soon, and Elanor is with her, and—and it's not good."

Adelaide immediately felt a surge of energy as she sat up on the bed and smoothed her hair. Ilse was already halfway out the door before Adelaide could stand up and follow her.

She heard Claudia's distress before she entered the room. A few pale-faced servants walked by and glanced at the queen's door at the sound of her cries. Adelaide glared at them and followed Ilse inside.

The queen lay where Adelaide had left her earlier, but now her night-gown was drenched in sweat and her knees were bent on the bed. Claudia's head lay flat against the pillow, her face red with strain, its color a stark contrast to her yellow hair, which lay in wet tendrils around her. She panted in exhaustion while Magg bathed her forehead.

"We are nearly there, your grace," Magg was saying wearily. She turned and saw Adelaide and Ilse in the doorway. "Oh, thank all the saints."

Floating in a dim corner of the room was Elanor, looking terrified. She seemed to cower away from the queen. As Claudia collected herself, she glared at Elanor, her eyes sending daggers across the room.

"She is *not* allowed to leave," Claudia said, her voice deep and strained. "I want her to witness what she will become. A whore begging for mercy on a birthing bed."

Elanor blanched and turned away. Adelaide rushed toward the bed and knelt beside Claudia, who barely seemed to notice she had entered.

"Elanor returned not long ago, and it sent her grace into a fit," Magg

174

said in Adelaide's ear. "She's been laboring for quite a while now, with no progress." She turned back to the queen and said in a consoling tone, "Very good, your grace. You can rest now."

Claudia's eyes fluttered closed. When she opened them, she was looking at Adelaide.

"How long did you know, Addie?" Despite her furrowed brow, her voice was surprisingly calm.

"Your grace, I don't know what you—"

"You know exactly what I mean!"

The queen's demeanor changed in a flash. She sat up with a wince of pain, rage alight in her eyes. She immediately fell back and cried out.

"Please stay still, your grace," Magg said quietly.

Claudia slowed her breathing and looked back up at Adelaide, anger still floating behind her eyes.

"How long did you know about the harlot in my husband's bed?" She didn't even look at Elanor. Adelaide did and saw how afraid the woman looked. She had her arms crossed protectively over her chest as she huddled against the wall.

"Your grace, it makes no difference," Adelaide said. "You must focus your energy now. You're tiring yourself."

"It makes a difference to me," Claudia said with a sob. "It makes a difference that you didn't tell me." She glared at Magg. "No one did."

"Your grace, I need you to push soon," Magg said. Adelaide could tell she was trying not to let the queen sting her. "Ilse, get me some more cool water."

Claudia's eyes trained on Elanor now, simmering with something close to hatred. "He'll forget about you," she said. A shudder of pain washed through her. "Once I've given him another son, I'll take his bed again, and you'll be crawling out the palace gates and onto the streets where you belong."

"He loves me," Elanor said between clenched teeth, her voice shaking. "He's told me so. He never wants to share your bed again."

"Liar!" Claudia roared, then another labor pain overtook her. Magg

175

urged her to push. The queen forgot her anger for a moment as she gritted her teeth and bore down.

"You must calm yourself, your grace," Magg said. The pain subsided for a moment, and Claudia lay back again.

"He loves me," Elanor said, taking a few steps away from the wall. "You're just a doll, a pretty plaything he could marry and breed with."

"I am your queen, you whore!"

Claudia cried out in pain. Elanor's mouth twisted in disgust, and she turned away again.

Claudia sobbed, a mixture of sadness and exhaustion. Adelaide helped Magg by bathing the queen's forehead, slick with sweat.

"Why didn't you tell me, Adelaide?" Claudia asked. Her voice was soft and pitiful, a reminder of the beautiful, innocent queen Adelaide had met only a few days before.

Adelaide didn't have a good answer. Elanor had told her not to tell, but that wouldn't be good enough for the queen.

"I don't know," she replied.

"Were you worried it would—" Claudia swallowed back a wave of pain. "It would affect your marriage prospects? To serve alongside the king's mistress?" Claudia suddenly clutched Adelaide's hand, fierce and strong. "I would have ensured you were above reproach, Adelaide. So long as you didn't leave my side. But you...but you *kept* her secret from me. You betrayed me."

Adelaide's throat felt thick. *Betrayed.* The worst thing someone could do, her father had told her, was to betray someone else. To speak good tidings to their face and speak ill of them in the dark. It didn't matter that she'd told the truth. She would be cast out anyway.

Claudia's labor continued as the afternoon turned to evening, and evening turned to night. The lines on Magg's face became more pronounced as the hours passed and the baby still didn't come.

Finally, Claudia erupted in a wave of pain, and with her last ounce of strength she pushed through it, and a purple, slippery thing was delivered into Magg's hands. Adelaide still knelt by Claudia's head, pushing sweaty hair from her face. Claudia fell back into her pillow with one choking sob. Elanor watched from across the room, her eyes glazed and exhausted.

"Thank all the saints," she said. "Magg, let me see him."

But Magg didn't look relieved, and Adelaide realized why. The baby hadn't cried. The physician unwrapped something from the neck before severing the baby from its mother.

"I'm sorry, your grace," Magg said, her voice barely audible. "She is dead."

Claudia stared blankly at Magg for a moment. Her mouth tried to form words, but only small stutters came out. She looked at the bundle in Magg's arms—gray, silent, unmoving. Everything a newborn baby shouldn't be.

"The cord connecting you to her was around her neck," Magg explained, "and with every push, she—"

"*No*," Claudia said. "*No*." She turned her head away from the bundle. She shoved her head into her pillow, her body convulsing with sobs. She moaned in a way that Adelaide had never heard from a human. She looked across the room at Elanor. She almost thought she saw tears dancing in the woman's eyes.

Claudia lifted her head, her face a mess of tears. She whipped around to look at Elanor, pointing a cruel finger at her.

"You did this!" she roared. "You caused my child harm. *You killed her!*"

Magg put a hand on Claudia's arm. "Your grace, please. Rest. You've been under immense stress."

"Because of her," Claudia burbled. Her finger didn't move. "Because of *her*." Claudia turned her face slowly toward Adelaide. The look in her eyes made Adelaide's blood turn to ice.

"And because of you," Claudia said, her voice disturbingly quiet. "If you'd told me sooner, if you'd told me when you *knew...*"

Exhaustion took Claudia, and she lay back, but her eyes didn't leave Adelaide's.

The afterbirth came, and Claudia could finally rest after Magg made her comfortable. She said nothing more. She lay in the bed with a fresh blanket around her, staring into space. Magg beckoned Adelaide over to her table of instruments. The baby was also placed there, looking so strange and still bundled in a cloth. Her face was so small, frozen in contortion, as if at any moment, she would take in a huge breath and cry.

"I'll stay with her grace the rest of the night," Magg said, "and make sure there are no further complications. I'll send for someone to take the child and inform the king. Tomorrow will be a day of mourning for the little princess. You should rest if you can."

Adelaide wasn't even sure if she was tired. She felt the ache of her body, but her mind felt awake and crackling with so many things. She turned and looked back at Claudia, who still lay staring at nothing.

"Adelaide," Magg said, touching her arm. "This was nobody's fault. There is no way to know when a child in the womb is in such distress." She looked squarely into Adelaide's eyes and said again, "This was *nobody's* fault."

Adelaide felt tears behind her eyes. She bit her lip angrily. "I've spoiled it," she said. "I've spoiled everything. I'll be dismissed, I'm certain of it."

Magg squeezed her arm. "There's nothing to be certain of yet. Your fate is still yours," she said. "Go get some rest. Attend her grace tomorrow. She will need you."

Adelaide's mind didn't stop racing as she left the room. She wondered what she would do if she were dismissed. Her marriage prospect would disappear as quickly as it had been decided on. She would have to go back to DuMont, to the village surrounding the ruins of their father's estate, to the little destitute room her brother kept above the town inn. The lord's son drinking himself to death and the daughter who was a failure at court, under the same roof once more.

And who was she to marry, anyway? The question remained unanswered. It had been brusquely dismissed by Pauline. Her dismissal made Adelaide fear the worst—perhaps it was Lord Roger. She remembered how delighted Pauline had been to see him when they first arrived.

Exhaustion settled on her like a stifling wool cloak and thoughts of marriage dissipated. It should be the least of her worries, she realized. The queen had lost a child that night. Adelaide had never seen a baby so still. The most innocent among them had died that night.

Adelaide tried to shake off the memory. She still smelled the tang of blood and afterbirth in her nostrils. She needed air. The doors to the king's chambers came up on her left. As Adelaide whisked by, she stopped abruptly when the door opened a crack and Elanor slid in cautiously. The room was dark on the other side. As Elanor closed the door, she locked eyes with Adelaide and gasped, quickly shutting it behind her.

Adelaide immediately turned away and kept walking. All of her fear and exhaustion turned to rage, an anger so deep it felt like sadness.

Why do I even want to be here anyway? She thought. She finally admitted it to herself. *I hate it here. It's not...it's not the same.*

Adelaide turned and kept walking, tightening her fists to prevent them from shaking. A thought flashed through her head.

This is how John must have felt. She could've easily beaten somebody senseless in that moment if she had John's strength. Elanor knew what she was doing, and that it broke Claudia's heart. She did it anyway. Adelaide could have screamed.

She stood outside on the parapet overlooking the quiet courtyard. The day had long been over, and only a few torches burned along the parapet and surrounding the courtyard. She sat on the balustrade and leaned against a pillar. She realized how tired and aching her body felt. It was so quiet she could hear her heart thrumming in her ears.

The queen doesn't trust me anymore. I don't trust Elanor, and surely not Ilse. Magg is kind, but there's nothing she can do for me, nor I for her. Who do I have to turn to now?

The air blew crisply in her face, and on it, Adelaide could smell the promise of true autumn, of drying hay and sun-washed leaves. The moon hung low and silver and full, like a heavy fruit on a celestial branch. The courtyard was washed in pale, shadowy light.

"Adelaide?"

Adelaide jumped a little and turned. To her surprise, John stood in front of the double doors. He gave her a small, conciliatory smile.

"You certainly have a way of sneaking up on people," she said.

"Sorry if I'm intruding," he said. "I can leave if you want."

Adelaide shook her head. "No," she said. She could use the company, regardless of who it was. She still regarded him coolly as he crossed the parapet toward her. He had a bottle with a long, narrow neck in his hands. He was so calm now, strolling casually to join her at the parapet, so unlike his countenance the night before, the rage alight in his eyes as he beat Antony bloody. The big hands holding the bottle had bruised knuckles.

"I heard what happened," John said. He stood across from her, leaning against the other pillar across from her own. He gestured to the door with his head. "Almost everyone in the palace has by now."

I'm sure you didn't hear about the king's whore, she thought. She didn't have the heart to tell him. His mother had been Tanor's whore, too.

"I'm sorry about last night," John said after a pause. "I know I upset you."

Adelaide was too tired to be angry with him. She cringed at her own foolish thoughts from the night before. But Antony's hands had been so strong and sure, his face so gentle…she shook the images away.

Love makes us do unnatural things, like cling to someone who has died, or run to a king's bed while his queen is with child, she thought. And it was true, she realized. After all these years, the child within her still loved the prince who had died. Still missed him deeply.

"He wasn't where he was supposed to be," she said, her throat suddenly full. "It was an insulting thing for him to do—just waltz into the throne room and have a seat."

John nodded. He looked out into the courtyard, and the moonlight caught his eyes. In the pale light, they were milky, almost colorless. Then he seemed to remember the bottle in his hand. He lifted it. Adelaide thought she saw his hands trembling.

"Blackberry brandy," he said. "I found some in the kitchens—well, stole it."

Adelaide smiled despite herself. A hundred memories came back to her.

"It's been years," she said. "I got sick on it once when my father wasn't paying attention. I drank far too much at one of King Alfred's feasts. Remember?"

"I do," John said with a small laugh. He didn't laugh as easily as he used to. He pinched the cork and pulled it out. Adelaide watched the muscles of his forearms tighten. He handed the open bottle to her. "You first."

Adelaide took the bottle from him and tipped it against her lips. The thick, sweet liquid flooded her mouth, then burned as she swallowed it, warming her all the way down.

"It still tastes just as good." She handed the bottle back to him. He took a long draft.

"You asked me something last night," he said, "in the throne room. You asked me if I recognized that man."

"Yes?" Adelaide was cautious, but strangely optimistic. *Did* John recognize him? Is that why he was so apologetic?

"I met him in a village when we were on our way back," John said. "A small village north of here, somewhere past the Hemlock Forest. An old soldier I knew was giving him trouble."

Adelaide's heart sank. So she was insane for thinking it, for trying to believe it.

"Why did you ask?" John asked. "Does he remind *you* of someone?" He took another swig of the brandy.

She knew she had to be careful. But if John suspected nothing, why would it hurt?

"He sort of reminded me of Adrian," she said. "What he would be like now."

She held her breath as John considered it. Then he shrugged and handed the bottle to her.

"Maybe," he said.

"I know it's impossible that it *would* be him," she said. She took a long drink. The brandy was making her mind hum pleasantly. The world softened around her. "But...I don't know. Being back at the palace...it brings back a lot of memories. We were all such good friends."

A dark shadow crossed John's face.

"We weren't friends," he said.

"What?"

John toyed with the neck of the bottle. "Don't you remember? Adrian hated me. And I hated him. That was why you and I always went up to the wall, remember? To get away from him."

Adelaide sifted back through her memory, trying to think of what John was talking about. He always had bruises when he met her on the wall. He always told her it was the older boys who hit him. But Adrian liked to pick fights.

Maybe she never connected the two. Or didn't want to.

"I guess I'd forgotten," she admitted. She took another sip. The bottle felt much lighter than before.

"He pinned me to the ground once," John said, "In the middle of the courtyard. No one stopped him. He called me a worthless bastard. I knew what that word meant from the time I could talk, but I was surprised *he* knew it."

A darkness spread over his eyes, something dangerous and sudden, like the black cloud of a summer storm. Even the moonlight couldn't touch it. The same look from the night before.

Then it was gone. John's gaze was gentle again. "That was years ago," he said. "I don't want to speak ill of the dead."

"He wasn't perfect," Adelaide said. It was all she could think to say. *Was Adrian really as bad as that, and I simply don't want to remember him that way?*

"Maybe so," John said. He drew a breath, one that seemed shallow, almost nervous.

"Are you all right?" Adelaide asked.

He looked startled, then nodded. "I suppose your aunt didn't tell you, then."

Adelaide thought for a moment, then her heart raced. "She told me she'd found a husband for me—she and his grace."

"She did," said John.

She wondered how John knew, but only for a moment.

"You," she said.

John said nothing.

Adelaide's mouth went dry, and she had to look away. She didn't know why—perhaps it was to hide the disappointment she felt. She liked John, but—but what else had she been hoping for? *Love?*

And why did it feel like she was losing something?

She thought about Elanor, skulking out of Tanor's rooms, his next bastard in her belly. About Antony and how he'd reached for her before he left. About Pauline's anger and haughtiness, the way she'd grabbed her arm like a hawk that afternoon. And about how every day since she'd arrived, she'd wished her father was there to help her.

She cried.

The tears came and didn't stop. They deepened with every sob, tightening her chest like a vice. She slid off the balustrade and onto the ground. The moonlight was gone. Anything that happened that night vanished. She had nothing but memories, and memories gave her nothing.

It took Adelaide a moment to realize there were arms around her. They were wrapped loosely on her shoulders, unassuming, until Adelaide leaned into John's chest and hid her face in his tunic. *Warm. Safe,* she thought fleetingly. He squeezed her tighter. She hadn't been embraced that warmly in a long time. She lingered there, her tears flowing beyond her control.

He will be your safety, your surety, said the kind voice in her head. *You may learn to love him in time. Let him be the one you need.*

Her tears waned into shaking breaths and her senses returned to her. She looked up at him. His face was unreadable as he helped her back to her feet.

"I'm sorry," she said. "I'm grateful. I am. I've just—I've had a long day."

"Grateful?" John asked. A small smile played on his lips. "I'm not marrying you as a favor. It's my honor and privilege to have your hand."

The words warmed her slightly. He held her hand in his, gently but confidently. *Let him be the one you need.*

"Let me take you back to your chamber. You need rest."

After he was gone and Adelaide was in her chamber, she collapsed into her bed once more. Sleep enveloped her almost instantly.

John

The brandy, though it dulled his senses, did nothing to calm his mind. John had known Adelaide since they were children, and a warm embrace was as familiar to them as a curtsy or handshake. But the closeness of her had sent his head reeling.

She had wept when he told her she would be his wife. She'd said it was because she was tired, but John wasn't sure. He knew how deeply she clung to the past, as though it was all she had. In a way, it was. Adrian's death had broken her to pieces.

The thought of that day kept him awake all night, as it often did. But the thoughts had been worse since he'd seen Antony on the throne. He had that same carefree ease, the charm that drew Adelaide to him, as Adrian once had.

He'd seen Antony sitting on the throne, and all he could hear was Adrian's voice.

You worthless bastard. Go back to the gutters and leave me alone.

King Alfred had been infuriated when Prince Adrian had punched John in the middle of the courtyard for all to see. It was all because John had beat him in a spar. Edwin had taught him a maneuver that twisted the clumsy wooden sword out of Adrian's hands.

He remembered the warm swell of pride in his chest followed by sheer terror when Adrian had come barreling toward him, tackling him, punching him, and uttering the words that rang in John's head every day since. Adrian was punished with extra lessons from Father Maleus on the virtues of the saints. John was punished by being throttled by Tanor within an inch of his life. He had to wear high-collared tunics in Second Summer to hide the bruises. Sometimes he wished Tanor had killed him then.

Tanor never hurt him on his face, except for the night Alfred died. Then he couldn't contain his rage. John had the small, pink scar where stubble didn't grow to prove it.

No one can know, he reminded himself. He remembered the blood soaking his velvet tunic, how he'd vomited before he could tell his father anything. *Take the secret to your grave, or he'll put you in one.*

His thoughts were tangled in the web of the past until morning. John was used to sleepless nights, followed by long days. Somehow, he always felt relieved when he saw the first fingers of light. From his narrow bed in the barracks, he could see it creep through the high windows, casting faint, square beams across the other sleeping men. Daylight meant he could cast aside his dark thoughts, bury his unanswered questions, and do his duty instead.

John rose with the others when the gray light turned yellow and the cocks that wandered the courtyard crowed.

John, Lyman, Artemis, and Markus put their new uniforms on. Lucas shaved his youthful face in a basin nearby.

"Her grace lost her babe in childbirth last night," he said softly. "A little girl, a princess. The king and queen won't make any appearances in court today."

"Damn," Markus said quietly. "Well, at least it wasn't a boy, was it? She's young. She'll have more."

Lyman glared at him, then turned to Lucas. "Did they give the lass a name?"

"No. I don't think so."

"Pity. They should have. I'd like to think she'd been named after her Ma."

Lucas put down his razor and turned to Lyman. "Ly, I thought you were to go home to your mother. The king has you putting on a uniform."

"Aye," Lyman replied, a little coldly. "I serve at his majesty's—and Lord

Edwin's—behest."

"There it is," Markus said with a snort. "Seems Edwin has his fingers in all the King's pies." He looked lewdly at John. "Maybe the queen's, too."

"Shut up, Mark," Lucas said before pulling a tunic over his head.

"What?" Markus threw his skinny arms open. John wanted to crack them in half like twigs. "I ain't stupid. I know how it is in court. My father has a bastard or two of his own, and more on the way, I'm sure. I'll have some before I'm through, anyway."

"If you sow anything worth planting," Lucas muttered. Lyman stifled a snort. Even John cracked a smile. Markus took notice of it and spoke red-faced to John.

"You of all people should know, Johnny," he said. "You're one of the king's. How many others does he have running about?"

Plenty, John answered silently. He was unlucky enough to actually be acknowledged by his father. But in all his years without a wife, Tanor made good use of his freedom. John didn't doubt marriage stopped him, either.

"And here you are, no better than a monk," Markus continued when John didn't answer. "It's past time you've made bastards of your own. Hell, you're older than me and I've got a running start on you."

John ignored him and walked out of the barracks. If he was going to ride alongside Markus for days on end—again—he couldn't spend all his patience at once. He went to saddle his horse instead, tugging the sleeves of his shirt as he did. No shirt ever seemed to have long enough sleeves for him, and this uniform was no different. It was tight across the shoulders, too. As far as material, it was just refined enough for members of a royal guard, but didn't empty the coffers. The uniform was a simple green tunic with Tanor's dragon sigil emblazoned on the front, inlaid with leather. No armor, no weapons other than small daggers better suited for hunting. If they were to journey to the surrounding villages to help collect the Harvestmonth Tax, Edwin did not wish to do so in an antagonizing way. That would attract the wrong attention and undoubtedly scare off Men of the Lion.

Edwin was already in the stable. When John arrived, he found his horse already saddled. The stallion he'd rode for the years leading to his return had been sent to pasture. This was a quarter horse, tall and lean and ready for a long journey, but not nearly as muscular and unruly as John's warhorse had been.

"We might as well ride donkeys," John muttered. The horse was half the size he was used to. He almost looked it in the eye.

"Now that's a sight I'd like to see," Edwin said with a grin. "We're not marching into battle. Not yet. Not unless it comes to that. First, we must show them his grace is serious. That insurrection won't be tolerated."

John knew what he meant by *them*. Men of the Lion. Anyone who held the belief that either Alfred or his son were still alive, that Tanor had a false claim to the throne.

Tell no one. Take it to your grave.

"Lyman and Artemis should be home with their families," John said. "And Markus has served his time, too. Why are we doing this?"

Edwin tightened the girths around his pony's belly. "They serve at the pleasure of their king." His eyes flicked upward, dark and dangerous, to meet John's. "Do you have something you'd rather be doing? Wooing a woman, perhaps? I heard the happy news from his grace."

John didn't answer. He thought of Adelaide, how she'd cried.

"Good," Edwin continued. "We'll start by going north to the surrounding territories. Barnswood, to start."

Barnswood. Of course it would be Barnswood. He could get no respite from that place. He sighed and rolled his shoulders.

Edwin smiled, creases forming near his eyes, and despite the mirth on his face, John couldn't help but be terrified by his smile. Edwin's flinty eyes remained cold, their centers like obsidian, reflecting the light but not exuding it.

The tax collectors they were to ride with were called Till and Midge. Though he was told they weren't twins, to John, they looked remarkably similar. It might have been their long black robes cinched at the waist with a belt and black skullcaps clinging to their heads, but even their faces had similar shapes. Rigid, cold, used to staring at numbers and not people. They didn't ride horses with Edwin and his men. They tucked themselves into the covered wagon that would soon brim with the commoners' money. John didn't mind seeing less of them on their journey. He felt more comfortable riding in the company of his own men, Markus excluded. Except Lucas wouldn't join them because of his injury and the pain that travel caused.

John looked over at Lyman. His mother awaited him in Dallen if she was still alive. The worry lines on Lyman's face told the truth—he knew she might not be. John was pleased to see the color in his face again after the Commoner's Ball. He'd never seen the man look so haunted. He was wearing a uniform again—maybe this was what he truly wanted, was truly born for. Like John.

He scanned Artemis' face. John hadn't given Artemis much thought since they'd returned. He'd never talked much to him. Artemis had often gone out with Markus after dark, searching for a local village to go whoring in. That usually left John, Lyman, and Lucas sitting around the fire, drinking weak, mulled wine to keep their insides warm. Three men around a fire are more like to bond than in any other place.

They set out while the sun still hung near the horizon. John had noticed the light change even in the last few days. Shadows had deepened. The bright beam of the sun had become a golden yellow. Autumn was upon them. The darkness and cold that John was used to would come in time.

The company first passed through the well-to-do quarter of the city, much of which was still quiet. Such folk did not have to rise early to earn their keep. Their keep was already earned and continued to be earned while they slept.

"Do you think any of 'em are Men of the Lion?" Markus asked as they passed the tall houses with steepled roofs.

"Doubtful," said Edwin. "They have their money to put their faith in, no matter who sits on the throne."

The poorer quarters already teemed with activity. John saw Markus screw up his nose as they drew closer. The smell was ranker, with so many more bodies in close quarters, sharing tenements, even sharing rooms. The streets were kept less clean, and bathing was harder to come by. When John looked into the faces of those they passed, however, he saw faces no different from those he saw in the palace. Some fair, some ugly. Some old, some young. Some with deep lines of worry on their faces, some oblivious to their troubles.

People watched them warily as they journeyed slowly through the crowds, pushing past those walking on foot. John heard plenty of mutterings all around him.

"Come to squeeze us dry."

"Here comes the Harvestmonth man."

"Is the king planning another Commoner's Ball?"

Edwin, who rode beside John, leaned closer to him. "Look at their hands," he said. "Look for rings made of tin. Some will wear them brashly, others will keep them well-hid."

John started glancing at hands as best he could. Most were bare, dirty, calloused. The work these people did with their hands didn't benefit from wearing rings. For many of them, it would hamper it. Perhaps they were wrong—perhaps none of the commoners were so bold as to wear a ring proudly on their fingers.

Then Markus pointed. "There," he said, his voice clear. "That man."

John followed his finger to a man he guessed was near his own age. He carried a basket on one shoulder full of bread, and the left hand that steadied the basket bore a simple, silver-colored ring. The man looked up in alarm when he noticed Markus staring at him. Markus steered his horse out of step with the company and charged through the crowd toward the man. The townspeople had to run out of the way to not get trampled by his horse.

"You!" Markus yelled and grabbed hold of the man's arm before he could run away. The basket tipped, and its contents scattered onto the dirty road. A few opportunistic passersby swiped up the bread before it could be further trampled.

Markus held the man's arm aloft, obviously causing the man pain. With his other hand, Markus yanked off the ring and examined it.

"Just as I thought," he said. He looked at Edwin. "He's one of them."

"Back in line, soldier," Edwin said sternly. "Unhand that man."

Surprised, Markus dropped the young man's arm. Rolling his shoulder, the man scrambled to pick up whatever was left of the bread on the ground—his livelihood, John guessed. Most of it was spoiled now. Markus' horse had stepped on the basket and flattened it.

"Though he is a Man of the Lion," Edwin said, loud enough for those around to hear, "the king will show him mercy if he turns from his ways and swears fealty to Tanor. If not, then—"

"Tanor ain't no king!" cried the man. He had stood up once again and held his battered bread in his arms. "Long live the lion."

With that, he slid through the crowd before Markus could grab hold of him again. Markus fell back in line with the company, his face red and fuming.

"Men like him will get their reward in due time," Edwin said. "Today, we sent a message, as we will continue to do on our journey."

Markus continued to seethe. John could feel the anger coming off him in waves as the younger man rode astride him. John couldn't help but understand his anger. After all, why else were they traveling with the tax collectors other than to frighten the villagers? Edwin telling them the king would show mercy meant nothing. If anything, it emboldened them.

Is that what Edwin wants? John wondered. *To embolden them so they come out of the woodwork?*

They continued through the village without incident. Those who lived in the poorest quarter of the city didn't dare go near them. They gazed at the company from their corners, eyes haggard. It wouldn't matter if they were Men of the Lion or not. They had no money even to buy a tin ring. Their beliefs would only ever lie in their hearts.

The rest of the day continued on its journey to night as the company to Barnswood. John spent the day letting his mind wander, thinking back to the times he and Markus and Lyman had trekked all day together in very different terrain: on ponies through narrow mountain passes, across flat moorlands on foot, where the wind whipped their faces ceaselessly. They had spent more time in the North traveling than anything else, going wherever their commanders bid. Now, they still went where they were commanded. Perhaps that would never change.

The company arrived in Barnswood as afternoon turned to evening. The days were growing increasingly gloomy, and as they arrived at the gate, thick, flat clouds blanketed the sky, draining the color out of the town. John kept his eyes straight ahead as they rode toward the manor house at the end of the main road. He didn't need to see Antony or his bruised face by accident. Although he fixed his gaze forward, he couldn't help but feel suspicion in the air, even hostility. The lord of Barnswood probably didn't even want them there. He had to pay his fair share of taxes as well.

They waited outside the manor while Edwin got an audience with its lord, ensuring they could stay the night. Edwin was diplomatic, so John knew he would get what he wanted. They waited in the yard, their horses stamping impatiently, hoping as much as their riders for warm lodging and hearty food.

"Oi, you see that fine one over there?" Markus said, leaning over in his saddle to John. John followed his gaze to a small young woman across the yard from them, shooing a small flock of chickens away from what John presumed was a kitchen door. She had the pretty, round face that John knew Markus was fond of, and bright red hair tucked into a cloth cap on her head. She barely gave them any notice, but Markus needed little encouragement.

"Bet she's a sweet one," Markus said. John sensed something like hunger in his voice. He remembered what Markus had said earlier that day about having bastards. Seemed he wanted another one on a poor serving girl.

Not long after he went in, Edwin returned with a few grooms who helped escort the horses away and secure the wagon. Edwin said that the lord was more than happy to host the king's men that evening. John wondered if the lord believed his hospitality would save him a few coins off his tax. Regardless, it would still mean a warm meal and a night spent under a roof.

The inside of the manor was immaculately clean, despite it being nowhere near as grand as the palace, or even as some of the larger estates in the south. It was made mostly of timber and mortar, with a foundation made of fieldstones. It had probably stood for at least a few hundred years already, and if it stayed within the lord of the manor's family, it could stand for hundreds of years longer.

Lord Barthow was there to greet them in the foyer. He was youthful-looking, slightly overweight, and round of face, with a full head of golden hair. His daughter, a girl of probably seventeen, stood beside him, matching him in figure but not in hair—hers was long and chestnut-brown. John knew Lord Barthow was a widower and had been since John was a boy. He had three other children whom John had met at the occasional state dinner or ball, but they were all older than John. Hatty was the youngest and had never played with the older children at court. John wasn't surprised to see Markus' eye wander to her as well.

Artemis seemed to notice, too. "Don't you have a girl at home, Markus?" he asked softly as they followed Lord Barthow to the great hall.

"Yeah, and what of it?" he snorted. "She'll still be there when I get back."

Artemis shook his head in disbelief. "Suit yourself, boy. A woman can smell dalliance from a league away." He leaned toward John and added, "I learned that the hard way. Suppose he will, too."

John couldn't help but think of Adelaide. Hatty was pretty, but Adelaide was prettier. He remembered the way her green eyes looked in the moonlight the night before, clear yet clouded with memory. *My wife,* he remembered, and felt strangely sick.

Supper was as elaborate as a petty lord could muster, but the stew and fresh bread were warm and filling. Lord Barthow found no suitable wine in his cellar, but offered First Summer ale to help fill their bellies. Markus glanced up at Hatty often, and she seemed to enjoy the attention. His gaze shifted, however, when the red-haired serving girl from the courtyard entered to refill their mugs. She was a tiny thing who reminded John of an elf from a storybook. She hefted the decanter of ale, and John noticed she made a point to brush Markus' arm as she bent to fill his cup. He needed no further invitation.

"What's your name, then?" he asked in the middle of polite conversation.

Edwin blanched. "Sir Markus, it is exceedingly inappropriate to—"

"Actually," Lord Barthow interjected, turning to the young woman, "I don't believe I know your name either, child. I make it a point to know the names of the servants in my employ."

The girl curtsied to Barthow. John noticed she wobbled a bit.

"Ellena, m'lord," she responded in a clear, high voice. She wore a leather thong around her neck that John got a better look at when she turned away. The rest of the necklace was hidden under her shapeless dress.

Markus watched her as she left the room. Hatty fumed across the table from him, her smile fading and her face growing suddenly cold. The rest of the meal continued in quiet conversation until Markus, Lyman, and Artemis excused themselves to retire for the evening. John remained for another cup of ale and listened to the idle talk from Edwin and Barthow about the lord's lands and harvests.

John retired up the stairs not long after, passing the other men's chambers on the way to his own. The door to Markus' room was wide open, and there he sat on his bed, Ellena on his knee. He was running his fingers along her leather necklace, trying to sneak further down her bodice.

"What's this, then?" he asked, snaking his hand under the high collar of her dress. She smacked his hand away playfully.

"Let a girl have her secrets, m'lord," she said.

"M'lord!" Markus exclaimed. "So I'm a lord now. Well, m'lady..." He leaned in as if to kiss her, but his eye caught John's. He turned slowly to him, seemingly unashamed of the spectacle.

"Want to join, big man?" he asked. He leaned toward Ellena. "He's a virgin, you know."

Ellena feigned surprise, then gently took Markus' hand off her neck. "I really shouldn't be here," she said, suddenly bashful. "I'm needed in the kitchens before I go home."

Markus was about to protest, but Ellena slid off his lap and skirted out the door, but not before looking up at John. Her eyes were a muddy hazel.

"Careful with that one," she said. "He don't care who he gets into trouble." Then she disappeared down the dark corridor.

John dismissed Markus and went to his own room. Barnswood manor was much more spacious than he thought. His quarters were wide across but with a low-slung ceiling, so much so that he had to be careful not to hit his head on the beams. A fire roared in a great stone hearth, and the shutters of the window were closed against the coming cold. John went to the window and opened it against the stuffy heat of the fire.

Outside, a strong north wind sang through the trees beyond the town. Soon, the trees would be robbed of their music, with only their bare bones bracing against the cold. Heavy gray clouds had descended as night fell, and only a few lanterns lit the main road below. John had a clear view of the courtyard, which was populated with a few torches. In the empty courtyard moved a small figure, bundled in a cloak two sizes too big for it. Even in the gloom, John recognized the cap on the figure's head. She pulled it off, and a mass of red hair fell down her back before she pulled up the hood of her cloak. Then, she went not to the kitchen, but right out the courtyard gate. John watched her as long as he could, darting down the main road like a fish in a stream, quickly dodging anything in her way until she was out of sight.

He dismissed it and washed his face and forearms in the basin by the bed. To his surprise, a mirror was propped on the table. Mirrors were rare in the houses of petty lords. Only the finest craftsmen knew how to make them, and there were very few in or around Southborn. The mirror was old, speckled with age around the edges, but John could still see his face fairly clearly.

He looked old. Older than his years. His face was set in a hard frown, and the skin around his mouth wore wrinkles that showed it was familiar with that expression. His thick brows grimaced over his eyes like thunderclouds. The light of the fire caught the pink scar on his cheek. He backed away so he could see more of himself, the curve of his neck and the thick lines of his shoulders. He was strong. That was what he had. There were few burdens he couldn't lift. He remembered lifting Lucas from the battlefield, how his commander had fainted from the pain of his broken leg. The bone had jutted out of Lucas' trousers, splintered as easily as a tree struck by lightning. John had hefted him on his shoulders and walked a mile back to their camp. By the time he'd returned, he'd forgotten he was carrying someone.

John looked out the window again. The darkness was more complete. A stray light from a tavern here, the lantern of a late-night traveler there. A sharp, cold gust blew into his face.

It's too heavy, he thought suddenly, thinking about where he was and what he was doing. Secrets were harder to keep at home. Southborn was steeped in memory, with the ghosts of both the living and the dead. The ghosts of strangers and friends.

Being a soldier was easier than this.

Antony

He awoke the next morning with a sinking feeling in his stomach. He'd seen the soldiers the day before on their way to Lord Barthow's manor. He'd seen the wagon. The tax collectors were in Barnswood, and he and Bron had just enough to give them.

Lines of worry etched Bron's face that morning when they sat down to a simple breakfast of day-old bread and hard cheese. And that worried Antony more. His father was never one to show his concern.

"Chill in the air today, isn't there?" Bron said after a bite of bread. "There's no doubt it's Harvestmonth now."

Another bad sign. Bron wasn't one for small talk.

"Pa," Antony finally said. His heart raced.

"Son?"

"I lost the ring."

Bron grimaced, trying to remember. Then his face softened.

"Ah, that ring," he said. "Well, that's a shame. It was a pretty thing, wasn't it?"

His eyes wandered across the wall behind Antony. There was something Bron wasn't telling him. Was that pain in his father's eyes? He toyed with the blunt knife on his plate.

"There's naught to be done about it," Bron replied, the pain dissipating from his face. "Now, I need to be in the shop all day today. You can go up to the big house with Carter for the tax. I want to show Ben how to fletch an arrow today. He's been learning well."

"And what am I to do about the money, Pa?" Antony asked. "What if we don't have enough?"

There was the worry again. Bron shrugged to hide it, setting down the knife. "It's not worth wondering *what if.* But, if we don't, we may offer them something else."

"Something else?"

"Well, Ben could go to Southborn and be, say, his grace's cupbearer for a season. He or any of us could serve to pay our debt—"

Anger flared in Antony's chest with sudden power. "So you'd sell our family to slavery to pay this debt? A debt that's hardly ours to pay—"

"Antony, we owe a debt to the crown for our lands, our home, our *livelihood.*"

Antony stood up noisily. There his father sat defending a crown that had cheated him twice. "So fat Tanor can use our money to pay for more parties, more wars, and never pay us what we're owed?"

"Do not speak of your king in that way." Bron stood as well, squaring his broad shoulders. The neck of his tunic was unfastened, and the thick, bearlike hair of his chest spilled out of it. "I've worked hard this year knowing the Harvestmonth tax would be heavy. And I cannot say the same of you, son. You seem not to care about the livelihood of this family until we're in trouble, so you can come and save the day. But before that, you're nowhere to be found. If you want to run my shop someday—if you want to amount to *anything,* you'll need to try harder."

Antony was quiet. Bron's words stung, and Antony saw on his father's face that he regretted saying them. But they needed to be said, Antony realized. He slunk back down into his chair, trying to find words to refute him.

His father softened. "I love you, son. Really, I do," he said. "Could be the work just doesn't suit you. And that's no fault of your own. You—" He stopped, gathered his thoughts, then said again, "No fault of your own."

Antony felt like his chest was open and exposed. He took a shaking breath. "I should go," he said quietly. "The lodge will be busy today. Better get a head start."

Bron managed a smile. "Good lad," he said. "Take care of yourself, y'hear?"

Antony emerged into the gloomy morning with the small purse of coins clutched in his hand. His thoughts were all sour and continued to darken as he approached the lodge.

Carter jogged up beside him and fell in step, saying nothing. They made a gloomy pair as they strode down the main road to the manor house.

Could be the work doesn't suit you. Bron's words rang in Antony's ears. He loved the work well; he loved the feeling of a completed bow, taut with power, ready to be drawn, to be useful. When he tried to be useful, he never seemed to be useful in the right way.

A chill wind blasted their faces. The weather had turned quickly.

Antony's heart pounded. *If we must work off our debt, it should be me. It will be me. I owe my father that much.*

He braced himself as they entered the manor house and servants dismissively led them to the great hall. Compared to what Antony had seen at the palace, the manor seemed so simple now, the Great Hall so bare.

To Antony's surprise, Edwin stood behind the collector's table. His worry turned to hope. *He'll know me. He'll know he owes me—us.*

Confidence rose in his chest and he stood straighter. *He'll listen to me. I'll make him listen to me.*

He scanned the faces of the other men at the collector's table and was surprised to see Sir John there too, wearing the same green-colored uniform as the other men. None of them wore a sword at their side. It was strange that so many men had come with the tax collectors—especially with no arms.

"You look like you're about to shit yourself," Carter muttered in his ear. In any other circumstance, that might have made Antony laugh, but it only made him angrier.

Antony held the pouch firmly in his hands as they approached the table. The man in front of them was finishing his business with the tax collectors. Antony knew him to be Phillip Butcher, his rounded shoulders slumped in defeat over the table as the tax collector with the upturned nose looked at him as though he were repulsed. Phillip surrendered three gold coins to the man. Those weren't common argents—they were arums. Arums were close to priceless for people like Phillip, something he'd probably kept locked in a box for years. The tax collector pinched each delicately between his fingers, as though he'd be contaminated by Phillip's touch. Seeing that much money—money that Philip owed—made Antony's stomach turn as he realized how light his leather purse was.

When Phillip turned around, his face was ashen. He was older than Antony's father, with gray streaks shot through his dusty brown hair. He seemed even more stooped than usual. Carter clapped him on the shoulder as he passed.

"Phil," he murmured. "You all right?"

Phillip shook his head and cast a disdainful look over his shoulder.

"None of us will be after today."

His words sent a chill through Antony's spine. He knew Phillip was right. The war was over in the North, but their struggle at home was just beginning.

Antony approached the tax collectors as Carter lingered behind, speaking a bit longer with Phillip. He suddenly felt awkward as six pairs of eyes watched him approach in the otherwise empty hall. The tax collectors looked like copies of one another—both old, both stern, with red, angry rims around their eyes. They watched Antony haughtily.

"Name," drawled one of the tax collectors, a pen outstretched over a long list of names.

"The household of Bronwell Bowyer," Antony said. His mouth felt dry.

A long silence dragged on as the tax collector dragged his finger down the parchment, then across it. "The Bowyer household owes one hundred argents to the crown for the annum."

"That's double last annum's," Antony said. He'd stood in that same spot the year before and paid with a bag of coins. "And what about Phil Butcher over there? How does a butcher in a small town owe the crown three arums? That's a large sum even for the lord of this manor."

Words tumbled out of him in an angry torrent as the fire in his belly rose. His conversation with his father that morning had started a fire in him that hadn't seemed to burn out. He clamped his mouth shut as tight as he could when he saw the green men fidget.

"Wars cost money," said one of the men in green. He was young and slender, with wavy locks of hair falling over a delicate, almost effeminate face. "Did you serve your time in the North as we did?"

"We were needed here," Antony replied. "There were weapons to be made. Land to be farmed."

"And there were Northerners to be killed, and men to be paid for killing them," said the young man. "Else you want them plowing your fields…and your women."

"Sir Markus," said the commanding voice of Edwin from the other side of the table.

"Regardless of how you feel," said the tax collector with disinterest, "payment is still due."

Antony presented the pouch on the table. The tiny amount looked pathetic now, and he felt his face go hot. The tax collectors looked as though Antony had placed a piece of rotten fruit on the table.

"This is the money given to me by Lord Edwin Darkshire two days ago. I'll have you know Lord Edwin did not pay me—did not pay my father—the money that was owed."

"You didn't think to count it? Well, maybe you can't count," said the blond man with a bark of laughter, then stared at Antony blankly. "You're not serious, are you?"

One of the tax collectors scoffed at Antony. "This is not enough."

"Lord Edwin," Antony looked at the older man. "You cheated my father out of ten argents."

Edwin leaned over the table, eyebrows raised. He gave his short beard a quick swipe, then shook his head.

"I don't recall any business transaction with you, young man."

The heat bubbled from Antony's stomach into his throat. "He's lying," he snapped at the tax collector. "He knows he's lying!"

Edwin dropped his chin and looked at Antony with condescension. "And can you prove it before you accuse me of being anything else? Shall I call a court of the king's bench for you to plead your case?"

Antony's mouth hung open. He couldn't. All he had was forty argents.

"Antony." He felt a warm hand on his shoulder and turned to see Carter standing over him. "Let it go. Pa will find a way to—"

"No, *I'll* find a way," Antony said. "I'll join his grace's service if need be. I'll fight for him—"

The tax collector chuckled. "There's no need for fighting now, son. I'm afraid you're too late for that," he said. "We'll expect payment one way or another. Your father may have goods he's willing to part with, or property. A collector will be back in two days to collect what is due."

"We have nothing to give," Antony said desperately. His anger was quickly turning to tears welling behind his eyes. He blinked them back.

"Your father is a bowyer, yes?" asked the tax collector. "Then he has a lucrative business to provide to the crown and one that his grace would be happy to have at his disposal."

Antony ground his teeth so hard he thought they'd turn to sand. Carter squeezed his shoulder.

"Antony," he said. "Not here. Now's not the time."

Antony's eyes flicked around the room, at each person standing in front of him. Sir John stood back, expressionless, his eyes on the floor. The man Edwin had called Markus looked incredibly smug. Antony wanted to pull his smirking mouth clean off his face.

"Apologies, Lord Edwin," Antony said. His voice trembled. "We will pay the debt."

A smile crawled across the tax collector's lips. "Excellent," he said. He scribbled something next to Bron's name. "Next."

Antony stood back as Carter provided payment for his tax. His sum was smaller than Bron's, but he still could not pay it. He had to promise his wages for the next three months. Carter remained surprisingly calm through the transaction, but Antony could see a fire behind his blue eyes. Carter knew his place too well to do anything, as much as he wanted to. His docility made Antony fume with even more rage—taking on the burden without hesitation, like the stupid, blue-eyed mule he was.

As Antony waited, a serving girl slunk into the hall from a back door, carrying a tray of mugs. She was small, with a tiny, pretty face wreathed by a halo of red hair piled on her head, covered with a loose-fitting cap. She moved quickly and deftly, like someone else Antony had seen only days before.

That's the thief. He remembered the moment the red braid flicked out of the hood of her cloak. And the man she had been with…

She caught his eye as she crossed the room. One of her eyebrows shot up, and a smirk played at the corner of her mouth. Then, her face returned to the neutral, dutiful expression of a servant as she delivered the mugs of ale to the men at the table.

Carter finished his business and made to leave. Antony continued to watch the girl. Markus seemed to take particular interest in her, and her with him. She brushed delicately against him as she passed, and he made a reach for her rear end before she sidled out of the way.

"Are you finished makin' eyes?" Carter asked as he brushed past Antony toward the door, startling him out of his fixation. Antony turned away quickly and caught up with Carter at the door. His rage had abated for a moment, but it returned as soon as they left the lodge.

"That girl in there—she's the one who stole the ring," Antony said.

Before Carter could respond, the doors to the lodge opened again, and out burst the girl in a streak of speed. After her came Markus, who pushed between Carter and Antony, his face red against his yellow hair.

"That bitch stole my coin!" he sputtered. The girl had already gained a lot of ground between them. Markus darted after her on quick, slim legs.

"I told you," Antony muttered to Carter. Markus continued to shout down the street, but the girl had disappeared from view.

He jogged after them. If he helped the knight get his money back, maybe Edwin would take a little pity on him. And if the girl still had his ring, it would be dually important to catch her.

Markus doggedly followed the girl's trail, cutting behind a row of houses into an alleyway where Antony had last seen her. But when Antony rounded the corner behind him, Markus was nowhere to be found. A thin mist blew from the sky, coating Antony's hair and clothes in a damp sheen. He trotted a few more paces, looking along the street on the other side of the alley. No sign.

Then he heard a sharp scream. A woman's scream, somewhere from where the alley continued across the road. Antony bolted toward the sound, narrowly missing an oxcart clattering on the muddy path.

When he came to the next alley, he looked around. He heard movement nearby, around the corner behind Bourne Tavern. Then he heard the voice of Sir Markus, sounding ragged and strained.

"You seemed more than willing last night, my dear," he was saying. "Why not now?"

Antony turned the corner. There he found Markus, pinning the small body of the girl under the eaves of the tavern's roof. The man's hand was hastily hiking up the girl's skirts while she squirmed under his weight. She had dropped the bag of coins, and it lay on the muddy street by Markus's feet.

"Let go of her!" Antony yelled. Markus whipped around to look at him, but didn't surrender his position. His face was flushed, his eyes wild.

"What's that? You want a turn?" he asked. Then he laughed. "I don't think you can afford her."

Antony jumped at him, grabbing Markus's shoulders. He wasn't a big man, and Antony had the powerful arms of an archer. He peeled the man easily off of the girl, and Markus went stumbling back into an empty ale barrel. Antony turned to the girl.

"Where is the ring?" he asked. The girl looked mortified and ready to run away the minute Antony got out of her way.

"I don't—" she began, then suddenly she elbowed Antony out of the way. Antony turned around and saw her charging at Markus, who had collected himself from his fall. She slapped him squarely across the face. It nearly sent him reeling.

"You bitch," he spat, holding his cheek. "And you—" He rounded on Antony. "Mind your manners, lest you want to get thrown into a cell."

"*You* should be thrown in a cell," Antony said. He turned to the girl. "And you should get out of here."

"Not so fast," Markus said. "Neither of you has learned your lesson yet." He rolled up the sleeves of his green tunic and drew a dagger from his belt.

Antony grabbed the girl by the arm and ran. She yanked herself from his grip but continued to follow him.

"You and I could've taken him, you know," she said. "He's very small. In more ways than one."

"Where's the ring?" Antony asked over his shoulder. Markus followed them a few paces behind.

"What ring?" asked the girl, panting. They rounded a corner and nearly barreled into the corner of a house.

"The ring you stole from me."

"Listen, I steal a lot of things. I don't really keep track of who they're off of. And why are *you* leading the way? Follow me."

The girl sprinted ahead of him and led him quickly through a labyrinth of side streets and alleys, many of which Antony was familiar with. His boots were nearly soaked through with water and mud by then. The girl's path took them to Saint Hogarth's Row, close to where Bron lived.

"We're almost there," said the girl.

"Where?"

"The woods. That's the only place to hide until they leave town."

Antony thought of several other places to hide while the girl guided him past Saint Hogarth's Row and around a corner behind the blacksmith's shop. They found Markus waiting for them, the front of his tunic covered with a spatter of blood, and his blonde hair pasted to his cherry-red face. He held his knife out, ready to strike. The girl slid to a stop and Antony jostled into her.

"Don't touch her," he said to Markus as the knight stalked closer. The blacksmith had a barrel of broken scraps of metal behind his shop, within reach for repurposing. He and Markus were the same distance away from it. A sickle, slightly crooked and with a broken handle, lay on the ground near the barrel. Antony tried not to look at it for too long, in case Markus followed his gaze.

"Why should you care what happens to that bitch?" Markus asked. "There's already a patron saint of virgins, and she's not even that."

"You got your money," Antony said. "Leave her be."

"She still stole it," Markus said. "There's a debt to be paid."

"Then I'll pay it."

Markus barked a short laugh. "*You* don't have what I want. In fact, you have *nothing*. You have less than nothing. The crown owns you and everything you love."

Antony didn't move. He and Markus were fixated on one another. Markus took a few slow steps toward Antony.

"The only thing you have left to offer is your blood."

They both lunged, Antony reaching for the sickle. Antony grabbed the broken handle, but Markus fell on top of him, trying to wrestle it out of his hands. Antony pushed him off and grabbed it, swinging it in front of him.

In the blur of movement, the sickle caught something and tore through it. Something else splashed onto Antony's face and hands, something warm and thick.

He stumbled back with the movement of the sickle and looked down at the blade. The crooked metal was no longer a rusty gray. It was red.

Then he looked up at Markus. The man's face had gone pale.

Antony had seen the inside of an animal before, but never a man. He'd watched Phillip Butcher dress pigs, deer, even a cow. He'd never realized the inside of a man would look so similar.

Markus tumbled to the ground, and his bloody hands fell away from his middle. From his stomach spilled his insides, collapsing out of him like huge, fat worms. Markus coughed a spray of blood.

From Markus's mouth came an unholy yowl that pierced Antony's ears and caused the girl to run away. Antony found he couldn't move. He couldn't look away from what he'd done, even as Markus's yelling attracted people to the scene. Blood poured from his wounds and mixed with the mud at Antony's feet. It would run along the slope of the alley and into the street soon, Antony realized numbly.

Markus stopped screaming. His horrified eyes were frozen, staring directly into Antony's. He didn't move.

Edwin and John appeared at the far end of the alleyway.

"Murderer!" Edwin yelled. "Seize that man!"

Antony turned and bolted. He couldn't feel his legs move, but he ran all the same. He felt as though he were running through water, each movement thick and slow. The sky above had become dark. A storm was coming. Gales of wind blasted through the alleyways of the town where he ran, and fat, cold drops of rain pelted his face. The only thought he had was he wanted to go home. He wanted desperately to go home.

When he no longer heard voices behind him, he ducked into an empty shed. He was almost across town, and close to his father's house. But he felt like he was about to collapse. He leaned against the wall of the shed. The smell still lingered in his nostrils, that horrible smell of death. The body of Markus still lay in front of him, torn open.

I didn't mean to. It was an accident, was all he could think.

Antony wiped his face with the front of his tunic before looking down and realizing he was spattered with blood—his chest, his hands. *I killed someone. I killed a man. A* boy. Markus looked like he was younger than Antony. Dizziness swam in his head.

He held his breath when he heard voices and wet boots slapping against the mud outside. Someone, probably Edwin, was barking orders. Another voice asked if someone had seen anything.

"Nothin', sir," replied the voice of a villager. "I was up at the lodge when the commotion started."

"We're looking for Antony Bronson," said another voice. "It's quite urgent."

"Bron's boy? Nah, I ain't seen the foundling," replied the villager. The voice was gruff and growling. Antony realized it was Rob the Red talking. He hadn't seen Rob since the night in Bourne Tavern. The big man still sounded angry.

"Foundli—what do you mean, foundling?"

The villager lowered his voice and spoke again. "The boy's not Bron's."

"Is that so?"

"'Tis. He's a foundling. Bron went off one day looking for his own lost boy and brought a different one home. We all told him his *real* Antony had turnt changeling, and this boy weren't his real Antony at all."

The voices continued to speak, but grew quieter as they retreated from Antony's hiding place. As soon as they left, Antony's stomach got the better of him, and he promptly turned and vomited.

He took a few moments to regain whatever composure he had left. Hands still trembling, he cautiously looked out onto the street. The harsh wind had driven everyone inside, and the clouds had made the sky almost as black as night. They scudded over the rooftops like deep bruises on pale flesh.

Antony ran into the wind and along the buildings to his right, looking for his father's house in the gloom. The wind blasted into his face, bringing tears to his eyes.

He turned the corner and found his home, but the feeling of safety was gone. In the gloom, John's tall figure ducked out of the door and turned his hood up against the gale. Antony pressed himself against the wall of a house. John walked on in the opposite direction, his cloak flapping like a banner behind him.

When he was gone, Antony charged through the storm toward Bron's house. He was drenched now, but blood still stained his hands. He couldn't go to Bron looking like this—especially not after John had just spoken to him.

He took a left before reaching the front door and instead walked alongside the house, back toward the stable. *I'll hide there until the soldiers are gone,* he thought. Then it occurred to him that the soldiers might not leave until they found him.

Between the eaves of the houses, Antony found more protection from the rain and wind. A few drops fell from Bron's roof, but Antony pressed himself against the wall to avoid them. He stood there for a while, catching his breath. Bron had the shutters closed against the sudden storm. But

Antony could hear something through them—and it sounded like crying.

He leaned his ear against the shutter, listening between a crack in the wood. He felt the warmth from inside Bron's house on his face and relished it. But the feeling disappeared when he realized it was Bron who was crying. Antony had never heard him cry, not like that. These were sobs from deep within his chest.

"Good Saint Aethel, I've loved the children you've given me," said Bron, his voice weak and thick. "Even the one that didn't come from my wife's womb." He continued to sob for some time. "I thought loving him would keep Antony alive...my Antony. My little lost boy."

Bron's voice disappeared in an ocean of sobs. Antony didn't stay to hear anything more. Tears pricked his eyes, and not from the wind. *The one that didn't come from my wife's womb.* He hadn't wanted it to be true all along. He'd barely believed it when the villager had said it only moments before.

When his father said it—when Bron said it, it became true. And the truth thundered in his chest.

Antony ran past the stable and didn't stop until he was deep in the Hemlock Forest.

Bron

He held the note in his hands. The lettering was crude, the spelling horrible. Bron himself could only read enough to get by, but he and his brother used a shorthand that few others would understand, anyway. He read the words again and pondered them.

He is no longer safe.

The day wore on, and Antony didn't come home. Bron had helped Benjamin muck the stables, but Ben had run off in the early afternoon to go play with Matty, the miller's boy. Ben was the child Bron was least worried about—he was even-tempered, unlike Carter, and reliable, unlike Antony. Ben also looked the most like his mother: soft-featured, hair as golden as First Summer sun, and gentle blue eyes with long lashes.

It was Antony he worried about most, he admitted. Bron was alone in front of a crackling fire, worries clouding his mind.

The boy is late for everything, Bron reminded himself as he set down the message and continued idly whittling at a small piece of wood in his hands. A chill had settled on the village that day, and he had a fire roaring in the hearth to keep it at bay. Then he chuckled to himself. *Boy. He's no longer a boy and you know it, Bron. He is of a height with you and matches your strength in most things. What he doesn't have is the patience to do the work set before him.*

And maybe he never will.

Bron's thoughts had been dark that morning after Antony left. He continued to think about what he'd said to Antony that morning. *He's getting too close to the truth now,* he thought. *I can't conceal it from him forever, nor should I.*

But there never seemed to be a right time or a right place. How was he supposed to tell his son that he was *not* his son? And how was he supposed to tell him how he came to live with them?

I will. Soon, Bron resolved. *It would be spiteful to keep it from him forever. And what he does with what he's learned will be his burden to bear, just as it was mine these last ten years.*

He thought of Antony. *His* Antony. The child who'd wanted nothing to do with him as he grew older. *Oh, how similar the two of them are. How similar my Antony would be if he'd grown to see the age of three-and-twenty.*

The tears threatened to spill, welling up behind his eyes as they always did when he thought of the boy he lost. A hand clenched tightly around his heart. Before he could return to his whittling, there was another knock at his door. As Bron opened it, he was greeted by a sharp blast of wind that rattled his entire house.

The man at the door was large and broad-shouldered, but still very much a boy in Bron's eyes. Probably of an age with Antony, with dark hair tousled by the weather.

"Come in from that blasted wind, sir," Bron said loudly over the din of the storm. Outside, he could see sheets of rain beginning to pelt the ground, and anything not fastened down was rolling down the street.

The young man ducked inside gratefully, and Bron closed the door against the cold blast. The man stood dripping and panting for a moment, pushing the wet hair from his face. Underneath his soaked cloak, Bron saw that the man wore a green tunic with the sigil of King Tanor. He was one of the taxmen.

"I suppose you've come to collect a debt," Bron said. "I understand. It's not an easy task, but I will pay what I owe, one way or the other—"

"Actually, sir," said the man, catching his breath. "I'm not here for a debt."

Of course he's not, Bron thought. *I should've known. Something more serious is going on.* The man's face was pale. He was breathing heavily as though he'd been running. His pupils were like pinpricks in his bright blue eyes.

"You are the father of Antony Bronson, sir?" continued the man.

"Yes, but no need to call me *sir,* for I'm not one," Bron replied, becoming more uneasy. "I'm simply Bron."

"Bron," said the man awkwardly. He was obviously raised to address his elders with respect, but rarely addressed someone of Bron's station. "Do you know where your son is?"

He's probably in some kind of trouble again, based on your questions, sir. Bron sat down at his bench to continue whittling, to look unbothered and unworried. The boy was about to tell him Antony showed up drunk to the lodge, or refused to pay any tax and is in a cell somewhere, or punched one of the other taxmen. He would attend to it after he got his work done for the day, he decided with a sigh.

"Last I saw him, he was on his way to the lodge," Bron replied. "That was before this storm blew in. I suppose you're here to tell me that something's happened to him? Whatever it is, I'll see to it later."

"Well, sir—Bron—" said the young man. "It's a bit more serious than that."

"And how serious is it?"

"Your son has killed a man."

Bron froze. He thought he'd known how that day would end—Antony would come home huffing about the tax, about the debt and how they'd pay it. Bron would talk to him, calm him by the fire, safe from the wind. Ben whittling, his fair brow bent in concentration. Perhaps Carter would visit and drink his father's ale and complain. If Bron could get Antony in a better mood, the boy might sing an off-color ditty to keep the cold and wind at bay. Their family. Peace.

That day was long a fantasy now. Now there was only a cold emptiness that had filled Bron's chest, one that had replaced the warm normalcy that dwelt there.

When the young man spoke again, his voice sounded distant.

"We wondered if he returned here or has run off. We've sent out searches throughout the village and into the forest. I am to join them after I speak with you—unless you know where he's gone."

Bron shook his head. "No, I don't," he said. His voice felt hollow. "Nine times out of ten, I never know where that boy is."

"I see," said the man. "I'm sorry to have bothered you, s—Bron. I will return when we find him. Unless you wanted to join the search?"

"No, no," he said. "I'm afraid I wouldn't be of much help in this storm. And I've another son to look after."

"You understand that if we find him, he will have to be…punished."

Bron wordlessly nodded his head. *He is no longer safe.* That was what his woodsman brother had written to him. And he was right.

The man stood awkwardly by the door for a few more moments. Drops of water fell from his leather cloak and onto the floor, creating a wet halo on the ground around him.

"Who did he kill, young man?" Bron asked, surprised he could still find words to speak.

"He was one of the king's men, as am I," replied the man. "A knight. It seems there was an altercation between the two of them in an alleyway, and—"

"And how old was this knight?"

"A little older than eighteen."

Antony. My son, yet no son of mine. Why? He didn't know if he should feel angry, or horrified, or saddened by what Antony had done. *And if he were my true-born son, would I feel differently? If he were Carter or Benjamin? Or my own Antony, who hated me?*

"Thank you, sir," Bron said. "I doubt he will return home, but if he does, I will inform your men immediately."

"Thank you, Bron."

Bron stood up and saw the young man out, back into the gale. After he'd gone, the room seemed eerily still, despite the howling wind outside, despite the crackling fire. Bron slumped back into his chair, suddenly exhausted. The oil lantern on his work table flickered as the wind crept through the cracks and crevices of Bron's house—the house his father had built when Bron was but a quickening in his mother's belly. The house was the same as it had always been. The lantern flickered as before. But everything within Bron had changed.

"Good Saint Aethel, I've loved the children you've given me," he said. The words sprang out of his mouth without him thinking about them. Tears threatened again, more urgently this time. The image that danced in the flame before him was his own Antony, the second-born of his children. The one who ran away and came back an entirely different boy.

"Even the one that didn't come from my wife's womb. I thought loving him would keep Antony alive...my Antony. My little lost boy."

Carter had been angry with him that night. He thought Bron should have looked harder for his brother, instead of bringing a different boy home. *We help those that we can,* Bron had told him. Whenever Antony had run away, he'd always come home. He knew the forest well enough to know where to go and where not to go. Bron knew there was no point in trying to find him, but Carter hadn't understood at that age.

Bron had only grieved in private. He had a strange boy to take care of, and another son who was barely out of smallclothes, and yet another who was growing into a surly young man. When his children were in bed, he'd wept. Wept for the son he knew would never come home.

Now, the tears finally sprung from his eyes and didn't stop.

He will resent me forever because I never told him. And now I'll never have the chance to. Another angry son has run away.

"Aethel, you gave me a prince to raise," he whispered. "And I have failed in that task."

Antony

Hunger gnawed at his insides. In the middle of the Hemlock Forest, there was nothing to eat. And his feet kept telling him to run.

Antony was well and truly lost now. Night had fallen, and the storm had continued. Even in the forest, harsh blasts of wind blew into his face and blinded him.

A thought consumed his mind. *I didn't mean to.* He saw the scene again and again in front of him. When he swung, and when the swing caught the soft flesh of the boy's belly. The image made him dizzy all over again.

And another thought trailed behind it, a thought he didn't want to recognize. *I am not my father's son. I am someone else. I was someone else. And he never told me.*

Good Saint Aethel, I've loved the children you've given me...

My Antony. My little lost boy.

Somewhere in that forest, the corpse of a boy with Antony's name rotted away. A boy who fell from a tree and wasn't found by his father. He found a different boy.

Somewhere in the gloom of the forest and the pelting of the rain, Antony heard the burbling of the Skeldergate River. Its cold rush was like blood through a vein, a constant roar between the trees.

I didn't fall out of a tree, Antony thought. *I fell in the river.*

An image flashed in his mind. A small boy stood in front of him with a rock in his hand.

"I hate you," said the boy. He hurtled the rock into Antony's skull.

214

Antony touched the scar at his hairline. *I didn't hit my head. I* was *hit.*

His feet told him to run, so he did. Away from the sound of the river that filled his head.

He could still feel the smack of pain at the front of his skull.

Who was the boy?

The boy had wanted to kill him; he knew that. He had chased him up to the ridge after...

After he saw his father, skewered with arrows in a moonlit forest. His father, dying. His father, the king.

It wasn't his legs telling him to run. It was his own father. Amid the bare trees, dying, Alfred whispered a word.

"*Run.*"

Antony ran, the stormy night dark and close around him. He ran until the ground disappeared underneath him, and he fell, just as he'd fallen ten years before. He fell with his face buried in the dirt, thick with the warm and oaky rot of fallen autumn leaves. The cool earth, sweet with death. It surrounded him, and he fell into a deep, hungry sleep.

Herne

"They should have been here by now."

Rain drove down on Herne and his daughter, crouched beside the Weschurch Road in a ditch that hid them from view. Ellena was impatient, as she always was. In the gloom of the night, Herne could see her small figure coiled and ready to spring.

"Not after what happened, Da," she said, her murmur barely audible above the rushing rain. The drops smacked the surrounding underbrush, enveloping them in sound.

Ellena had told him. A man in the tax convoy—not much more than a boy, really—had been killed. They'd gotten into a scrap in the town. Ellena hadn't said why.

"I think we should just go, Da," she said. "I don't think they'll be coming tonight."

Herne remembered being Ellena's age. She was twenty and lived her life with a sense of urgency. And with the sort of life they lived, it served her well—until she was forced to wait. Even now, she was poised against the embankment that led to the highway. She was quieter than normal, though. Something bothered her.

"A few moments longer," Herne said. He felt bitter words rise in his throat. "They hold money far above human life, even the life of one of their own."

"Which is why it's only fair we take a bit from them." Ellena finally smiled for the first time that evening.

Herne chuckled to himself. *I've taught her well.*

They both heard it at the same time. Not from the Weschurch Road, but somewhere behind them in the depths of the forest. Footsteps crashing noisily through the underbrush. Herne and Ellena knew the sounds of the forest—this wasn't the quick skitter of a squirrel or the careful, small steps of a deer. Besides, it was well past dark, and not much moved on a stormy night. This was the heavy, clumsy step of a man who didn't know how to keep himself unseen.

Herne didn't need to tell Ellena to be quiet. Through the rain, they listened. The sound was coming closer to where they stood. Herne nodded to his daughter, and they made their way down the embankment. They knew how to move with the rhythms of the forest. Their steps were nearly silent.

Neither of them could see much in the moonless gloom of the forest. Rain kept tumbling from Herne's thick eyebrows into his face. He pulled his hand down his face and through his beard, wringing it out and pulling the hood of his cloak further over his head. Rainwater slid easily off the slicked leather as it rolled off the rattling leaves above them.

Ellena had much better ears than he. Herne let her lead, following closely behind her shadow. He couldn't help but be proud of her. This was never the life he intended for her—she wasn't even his natural child. Herne's wife had been a midwife and had helped Ellena's mother with the birthing. Marga had saved Ellena, but not her mother. Wasting Sickness took Marga a few years later, and Herne had been left with a red-headed daughter who wasn't his.

I've done my best, my love, he thought. *I hope you can look down from the stars and forgive my shortcomings.*

Ahead of them in the gloom, a lone figure plodding through the depths of the forest. An obvious fool, Herne knew. No one went off the beaten path in the Hemlock Forest. Especially not at night, in the pouring rain.

And with no clue that outlaws were stalking him.

Herne saw Ellena's head move and knew she was looking at him, waiting for a nod. They were within yards of the man now, hiding the sound of their movement in his loud, crashing footsteps. Herne almost laughed at the man's stupidity, but he had to concentrate. Ellena waited for his signal.

Wait. He said to her without words—a shorthand they'd both learned to understand. They continued to stalk their prey for a few more steps, trying to get as close as possible. *Wait.*

Now!

Ellena took off like a lightning flash, her small body low to the ground. Before the man knew what was happening, Ellena dove into the underbrush and grabbed his legs. The surprise and the impact caused him to trip and land on his face in the dirt.

Herne sprung into action. He pulled his hunting knife out of the sheaf at his side and kicked the man in the side to roll him onto his back. Herne straddled the man's chest, putting the knife to his throat. The man fought against him, but Herne was strong. He pinned the man's shoulder down with his other hand.

"You shouldn't travel out in the dark alone," Herne said, "unless you're not afraid of what's out here. Wolves, bears...all manner of things."

Herne twisted the knife slowly, so the blade scraped across the man's clean-shaven throat. The man tensed.

"Let me be on my way," said the man, his voice husky. "I mean you no harm."

Herne barked a laugh. "Course you don't. If you did, you wouldn't be staring down this blade, would you?" He twisted the blade a little more.

"Da," said Ellena, who crouched next to him. "He's from the big house. He's one of them. I recognize him."

"Do you?"

"Look at his tunic. The same one those tax men wore."

She was right. The dragon sigil. He and Ellena had watched the taxmen make their way down the Weschurch Road the day before. And Ellena had seen them in the big house.

"You were much nicer than the yellow-haired one," said Ellena to the man.

"You're one of them, are you?" Herne asked. He couldn't help but feel real anger looking down at the man, knowing what men like him had put him through in the past. "Soft old crooks, sitting on their fat arses whilst others break their backs to put food on your table—"

The man sprang without warning. In a swirl of motion, he twisted the knife away from his hand and jumped up, shoving Herne off of him. Herne tried to gain his composure, but Ellena was quicker than him. She had her own knife out now and held it to the man's middle, backing him into a tree.

"Make one move and I'll drive this into your guts," she snarled. The man towered over her small body, but she stood her ground.

"What are you doing out here?" Herne asked. "Why aren't you in Barnswood?"

"I don't have to tell you anything," said the man, his voice hardly louder than the pouring rain.

"I think you do," Herne said. He put his knife back up against the man's throat. "Perhaps you'll kindly tell us why you aren't in Barnswood. Wasn't one of your own killed today?"

"Your daughter can tell you about that, too," said the man. "She was there. She saw it. It was she who stole from Markus and caused it all in the first place."

"You rat *bastard*—" Ellena growled. If Herne hadn't known better, he would've thought Ellena would've punched a hole through the man with her knife then and there.

"I'm looking for the man who killed Markus," said the man. "Antony Bronson."

"Never heard of him," said Herne. He flicked a glance over at Ellena. She was quiet, her mouth a firm line.

Herne hoped and prayed that his brother had received his message, that he'd found it where Herne always left it. And he prayed Antony was somewhere this man couldn't find him.

"If you find him, there's a high reward," said the man. "Five hundred argents, dead or alive."

"You think we're no more than thieves," Herne chuckled. "Money-grubbing chiggers like you. I doubt you'll find him. The Hemlock Forest is big, the night is dark, and this storm is fierce. He's probably fallen into the river by now. Beyond finding."

Ellena twisted her knife and the man grunted. "C'mon, Da, what are we going to do with him?"

Herne looked the big man up and down. Herne was tall, but didn't quite meet the man's eye. This man was younger, broader. Too many advantages should it come to violence.

"We're going to let him go," he said. "We'll point him toward the Weschurch Road and be on our way."

"And you think I'll let you just walk away?" asked the man.

"Yes," said Herne.

Herne took hold of the man's shoulders while Ellena dropped her knife and grabbed the man's cloak. In one fluid motion, she flung the cloak over his head, leaving him tangled in it.

Herne and Ellena stepped quietly away as the rain poured around them. Once the man recovered himself, he wouldn't be able to track them.

"You didn't tell me," Herne said when they were well enough away.

"Tell you what?"

"That you were there. That you stole that boy's purse."

Ellena shrugged. "He won't miss it now."

"Were you there when he was killed?"

Ellena said nothing.

"Ellena?"

Ellena stopped. She stood there in the pouring rain.

"Antony didn't mean to, Da," she said softly. Her voice sounded thick. "He was trying to help me. That boy was going to—do something to me. He was going to—"

She didn't finish. But Herne knew well enough what boys liked to do to girls like his daughter. And in that moment, he hated a boy he never knew, and was almost happy he was dead.

And why shouldn't I be? One less of him in this world. One less of him to step on us.

They arrived back at their encampment at the bottom of a steep ridge.

A tree grew on top of it, its roots growing out of the embankment and hanging above the entrance to the cave they called their home. It was difficult to spot if someone was walking from the direction of the Weschurch Road. On a dark night like that, it would be just as easy to miss it and tumble into thin air.

That was on Herne's mind when he kicked something that groaned.

"Hell," he muttered in surprise. It set his heart beating fast. He didn't believe in ghosts or things that haunted the night, but this was the last thing he expected to find. Sprawled out in front of the cave entrance was the body of a man—presumably alive—lying face-down in the wet earth.

Herne nudged him with his boot. Then he used his foot to push the man onto his back. Ellena came up behind him and saw what he was staring at.

"By Aug's beard," Ellena said. "It's him. Da, it's Antony."

Adelaide

She let the cold blasts and icy rain pelt her. It reminded Adelaide of the sea. All that was missing was the salt on the air and the crash of the waves somewhere far beyond. She closed her eyes and imagined the rain as spray, tried to taste it on her lips.

When she opened her eyes, all she saw was the dreary courtyard.

All that day, she'd had nothing better to do than wander about and wait to be summoned by the queen. She hadn't seen Claudia since the night before, and the palace had been quiet with the mourning of the little princess. Magg had sent the baby to be embalmed by the monks before a private burial in the Crypt of Kings. Adelaide kept thinking about the small, silent thing that slid out of her mother's womb already dead. She was perfectly beautiful, from her tiny nose to her eyes pinched shut. Adelaide hoped they carved her face as beautifully into the stone of her crypt.

The babe would be buried without a name. Claudia refused to name her.

"She will be named by the saints when she enters the heavens," Magg said that morning with sadness in her eyes. "I'd like to think they'd name her Celeste, for she never knew the toil of this world. She was born into the stars."

With that on her mind, Adelaide resolved to see Claudia. She'd gone too long without seeing her. Whether the queen knew it or not, she needed company. And if her dismissal was imminent, Adelaide needed to know.

You didn't betray Claudia, Adelaide reassured herself. *It's not your fault the baby died.* But she couldn't bring herself to believe it.

She knocked softly on the door to the queen's chamber. No one answered on the other side. Adelaide pushed it open, peering inside. The room had a total stillness about it, even with the storm blowing outside.

Adelaide found Claudia at the window, sitting in a high-backed chair and looking out with disinterested eyes. Her face was still pale and drawn, her hair still tumbled about her shoulders. She was dressed though, wearing a green gown hastily thrown on. Ilse might have helped her dress that morning—Adelaide had never been summoned. The poor queen's belly was still distended, but now empty of life. Everything about her was void of it.

"Your grace," Adelaide murmured. Claudia's only response was a slow blink. Adelaide knelt by her chair. She could see now the deep circles under the queen's eyes, the red tracks on her cheeks where tears had been chased away.

"How are you feeling?" Adelaide asked, though she believed she already knew the answer.

The queen didn't respond. She continued to stare out the window as gusts of wind brought rain pelting onto the glass. Her gaze seemed distant, unseeing.

"I saw Prince Charles this morning," Adelaide said to fill the silence. "He looked hale and healthy as ever. He was chattering on to the governess about—"

"I never saw her eyes," Claudia interrupted her suddenly. "I wonder if they would've been like his. Charles's were from the moment he was born."

"I don't know, your grace." Adelaide tried to take Claudia's hand, but the queen moved it away and folded it with the other neatly in her lap.

"I wonder if *her* child's eyes will be blue like his," she continued. Adelaide saw her lips tighten bitterly.

"Elanor's?" Adelaide asked.

A flash of hatred crossed Claudia's face. "Yes." she replied. Then she was quiet again. The silence fell around them once again.

"Do you need anything, your grace?" Adelaide asked. "I wanted to make sure you were settled before I went to supper—"

"I'd like to go downstairs," Claudia said suddenly. "To supper."

Adelaide was surprised. The queen didn't look in any state to go anywhere. But she was the queen.

"Of course, your grace," Adelaide replied, and helped Claudia out of her chair. Claudia's legs trembled with the effort. She still seemed so weak.

"Are you sure?" Adelaide asked when Claudia leaned heavily on her arm. She bent slightly over her still-swollen belly.

"Yes," Claudia breathed, straightening herself. Adelaide adjusted a coil of the queen's hair behind her ear. "The court needs its queen, no matter what."

Adelaide took Claudia down to the dining room with slow progress. Despite her weakness, the queen seemed determined, and Adelaide thought she knew why. She would show her husband her strength, her determination to be by his side. The court needs its queen, and so does a king. She wouldn't soon be locked away.

Adelaide opened the door for Claudia, and the noise and light from the room hit them at once. It was exactly like Adelaide's first night, with all the gaiety and laughter. But it stopped as soon as Claudia entered the room. Everyone at the table stood. Except for one.

Elanor remained in her chair. The chair on the King's right hand. The one usually occupied by the queen. The red-haired woman took a long draft of wine, glaring over her cup at the queen.

Adelaide saw something dark pass across Tanor's face before he smiled at his wife. "My dear," he said. "And Lady Adelaide! My soon-to-be daughter-in-law, as I understand it. I do believe congratulations are in order."

"Thank you, your grace," Adelaide said mildly.

A small, annoyed smile played on Tanor's lips. "We didn't know you'd be joining us this evening, my dear. Are you quite well?"

"Quite," Claudia replied. Her face had gone white at the sight of Elanor. "And it seems there is no seat for me."

"There is not," said Elanor. She'd remained seated, her back straight; her

224

manner prim. "You should be resting. You lost the king's child two days ago. Perhaps you should not have danced at the Commoner's Ball so close to your confinement."

Claudia balked at that. Adelaide squeezed her arm.

"Your presence here has given me a shock," Elanor said firmly. She stood up. She was no longer trying to hide her pregnancy. Her belly jutted from her high-waisted dress, and she put a protective hand on it. "It's not good for my child. I must eat and take care of it better than you took care of yours."

Hatred flashed in her eyes. She looked at Tanor, then back at Claudia. The king remained expressionless.

"It was as though you hadn't a care for your king at all, to let his child die inside you."

Claudia let out a little cry that broke Adelaide's heart. Tears glistened in the queen's eyes.

"Your grace," Adelaide said to her in a low voice. She felt Claudia's body tense, like she was ready to spring. "Do not confront her. She is trying to hurt you." But Adelaide struggled to swallow the bile rising in her own throat as well.

She watched Claudia decide. She didn't lash out as she did a few nights before. Instead, she straightened, letting one tear fall down her face. The rest of the table looked on her with pity, while Elanor's face remained unchanging. Tanor's face frightened Adelaide the most—it carried no expression whatsoever.

"Very well." Claudia said. She looked at Ilse, who stood beside Elanor at her place at the table. "Ilse, would you bring a plate up to my chambers later this evening?"

"I have given Ilse the evening off," Elanor replied. "Perhaps dear Addie can do that for you."

Claudia bit her lip until it turned white. "She will," she said, leaning a bit more on Adelaide. "Good evening."

As soon as they left the hall, Claudia burst into tears, falling into Adelaide's shoulder. Adelaide did her best to steady her. It took even longer to return Claudia to her room, and her tears continued during the entire journey.

When they returned to Claudia's chambers, Adelaide sat her down on the bed. The queen immediately lay down and buried her face in a pillow as her sobs waned. When she looked up at Adelaide, her eyes were bloodshot and swollen, and her lips were twisted into a grimace.

"What has my life become, Adelaide?" she asked. "How did it change so quickly?"

Adelaide didn't answer. She got up and brought a carafe of wine from the table over to the queen's bedside and poured them both a cup. She encouraged the queen to drink it. After a cautious sip, Claudia laid back, gaining her composure.

"This place is a poison," she said. Her eyes became distant again. "It has poisoned my husband against me, poisoned my favored lady-in-waiting. It poisoned the very child that was in my belly. And now, it's poisoned me."

Adelaide took her hand. *She needs you more than ever,* she thought. She remembered what Elanor told her on her first night there. *Not what you know or who you know, but what you know about who you know.* It was nonsense, she realized. Claudia was more than that—she was a woman whose heart was broken by the truth. And what good had it served?

"I'm sorry," Adelaide said. "I'm sorry I didn't tell you sooner. I should have. Elanor is an ambitious woman. She will do and say whatever she needs to get what she wants."

Claudia blinked. "She'll ruin herself in the end," she said emptily. "Every woman who tries to climb the ladder of court usually does. We are meant for what we are meant for, and nothing else." She cast her empty eyes on Adelaide. "And you are marrying his son. I had hoped better for you, Adelaide. But the king was convinced it was a good match."

"John isn't a bad man," Adelaide said. "I don't love him, but he has always been a good friend to me."

Claudia's eyes darkened slightly. "He still shares blood with Tanor," she said. "You'd best be careful."

The words chilled Adelaide to the bone.

"I'll let you rest now, your grace," Adelaide said, before she could be tempted to say anything else. She could see Claudia's eyelids drooping with sleep. "Would you like anything from the kitchens?"

"No, Adelaide. I'm afraid I'm not hungry at the moment."

Adelaide nodded. "Of course, your grace. Good night."

"Good night, Adelaide."

She made the brief journey to her own bedchamber, feeling exhaustion seep into her bones once again. The storm outside had seemed to calm itself after blustering on for nearly an entire day. She took her time undoing her hair, slipping out of her gown and into her nightclothes.

She winced as she sat down at her dressing table to braid her hair. Her blood had come in that day and had made everything even more miserable. She absently wondered if Magg would have something for the pain. The cook at DuMont manor had given her raspberry leaf tea, if she'd had any on hand. It was too late to ask Magg, she supposed. She'd have to deal with it for the night.

Adelaide supposed she'd soon have to ask Magg about other things, too. A date had not yet been set for her wedding, but she figured it would be soon. And there was much Adelaide didn't know, having had only a brother and a father to guide her. Magg had helped her when she'd had her first blood—the sight of it had alarmed Adelaide so much she'd nearly fainted.

She lay in bed, pressing a pillow to her stomach and closing her eyes. She remembered what Magg had said about Adrian's bones in the crypt. Maybe she was down there in the Crypt of Kings now, examining the bones. Adelaide wondered how it could be that a bone could grow back stronger after being broken. How did the body know how to do that? The same way her body knew to bleed every month, she supposed. Her thoughts became muddled as sleep played on the edges of her mind. Landon had broken a bone once, she thought absently, in his hand whilst playing with a wooden sword. She wondered if the bones of his hands were stronger because of it—

The more her mind wandered from memory to memory, everything became clear—as clear as it could have been. Landon had broken his hand. She remembered his wrist in a cast made by Magg to keep him from moving it. It took weeks to heal, and it still ached from time to time.

But she was fairly certain Adrian had never broken a bone.

She didn't know how long she'd been lying in bed before the thought had shaken her awake. But her mind was alert now, and the pain of her bleeding had only become greater. There was no way she would go back to sleep. She needed something—*anything* else to do to distract her from the deepening pit in her stomach.

He'd never broken a bone—I don't think he had, anyway, Adelaide thought. It was all she could think about. *But the bones in the crypt had been broken before.*

Which means it's not Adrian in the crypt.

No one was in the kitchen when she arrived, and when she searched some cupboards for tea, she came up empty. As she searched, Adelaide heard voices in the room adjoining—the small dining room where many of the guards and servants took their meals. The kitchen shared a wall with the barracks, and both rooms connected to the common hall.

On her way out of the kitchen, she peered in. By the light of a candle on the table closest to the door, Adelaide was surprised to see the shapes of Lucas and John hunched over goblets of wine. A few bottles accompanied them on the table.

Have they collected all the taxes already? Adelaide wondered. Perhaps the storm had brought John and the rest of the men back early.

Lucas caught her eye, and the shadowy lines of his face brightened a little.

"Adelaide?" he said. John also turned at the sound of her name, and they both stood up. "Come in! What are you doing here?"

"I couldn't sleep," she replied, trying to keep the shakiness out of her voice. She took a step into the room. It was cold. The drafty shutters rattled against the wind outside. Based on the way both men swayed while they stood, John and Lucas seemed to have been in their cups for a while.

"I could ask the same of you both," Adelaide continued. "You're back awfully early from tax collection."

John didn't respond. He sunk back into his chair. Lucas answered for him.

"Well, it's bad news, I'm afraid," he said. His voice was strained. "We lost one of our men in Barnswood. Not entirely sure what happened—none of them are. Edwin said it was an angry commoner who killed Sir Markus. Said his name, too—I don't remember what it was. Do you, John?"

John didn't hesitate. He looked up at Adelaide, his bright eyes sunken in his face.

"Antony," he said. "It was Antony Bronson who killed him."

The air flew out of Adelaide's lungs. She reached out to a chair to steady herself. *It's not Adrian's bones in the crypt.* The thought still plagued her mind.

"Oh," she said, trying not to let her emotions show. "That's dreadful. I—I remember him from the Commoner's Ball."

"That fellow?" Lucas said. "I didn't realize. Well, I can understand why you're shocked, Adelaide." He sighed. "The common folk are angry. But he took his anger out on the wrong person."

A murderer. She remembered the way Antony had held her, the way it had been so easy to talk to him. He had to have a good reason—hadn't he?

Lucas clutched his stomach suddenly, leaning his weight against the chair.

"Oh, I beg your pardon," he said, belching as modestly as he could. "The drink has caught up to me quicker than I thought." He limped out of the common hall and through the door into the barracks.

Adelaide was left with her ears ringing. Her brain buzzed with thoughts, most of them afraid. She sank down into a chair at the table.

You've known Antony for all of how many days? Three? And you believe you know everything about him, about his character?

She took Lucas' cup from across the table and emptied what was left of one of the bottles into it. Maybe that would help the pain, she thought absently. The wine was sour, probably weeded out of the king's cellar for

229

the staff to swill on. But the warmth of it shuddered through Adelaide's body, taking the edge off her fear.

"He didn't deserve to die," John said. Adelaide had almost forgotten he was there. He was slouched back in his chair, his eyes heavy. Unshaven stubble shadowed his face, making him look years older.

"Markus wasn't a good man, but he didn't deserve to die," he continued. "He was younger than me. And if he were to die, it should've been on the battlefield. Not on the street like a dog."

Adelaide tried to read the vacant look in his eyes. "Are you sure it was Antony?" she asked. John's eyes fixed on her intensely, and it was all the answer she needed. "He just—he didn't seem like someone who would kill—"

"Everyone is capable of killing, Adelaide," John said, his voice suddenly sober. "I've seen it. In another life, Markus would've been a soft lord who would never know battle." He looked away from her, his eyes becoming distant again. "I was only thirteen when I first killed."

"You were too young," Adelaide said. "It was all you knew, but that doesn't mean everyone is—"

"I shouldn't have come back," John said. Adelaide realized they weren't talking about Antony anymore. He took another long drink from his goblet. "My father sent me there to die."

"There's no way you could know that."

John chuckled bitterly. "My own father didn't want me alive. He *never* wanted me alive." He stood up suddenly. He kept a hand on the table for support. "I should be dead, Addie. I should be dead a thousand times over."

"What you should be is in bed, John," Adelaide said. She stood up and walked around the table toward him.

"The things I saw that no man should ever see," John said, standing up to his full height with sudden rigor. "The things I did. I don't deserve to be alive. It's as though I'm alive in sheer spite of *him.*"

Adelaide put her hands on his arms, worried he would fall. He stared steadily at the ground, as if unaware that she was even there.

"You've done nothing to deserve that," she said. "You don't deserve your father's hatred."

He looked at her with bloodshot eyes, his mouth hanging open as though in awe of her. Only then was she aware of how close she was to him. She could feel his heat through the tunic he wore, the strength that pulsed in his arms. *Your husband,* she thought.

Before she knew what was happening, he was kissing her gently, his lips hardly moving. They were briny and tasted like stale grapes. When she recovered from the shock, she immediately pulled away. John's hands were cradling her neck, just below her jaw. They slid down to her shoulders.

"I don't know why I came back here," he said. "Maybe it was to find you again."

Adelaide took a step away from him. John's hands fell to his sides, and his whole body drooped.

"I'm sorry," he said, folding back into his chair. "I'm making a fool of myself."

"You should get some rest, John," Adelaide said. She turned to leave.

"None of this would've happened if I'd just killed him."

Adelaide stopped. "What do you mean?" she asked slowly.

"I was supposed to do it," John said.

"Do what?"

"Kill Adrian."

It's not his bones in the crypt.

Adelaide's heart sank into her bowels. As she tried walking closer to the door, her legs felt heavy. John looked suddenly grim, suddenly an entirely different person she'd never met. *On that night, he was* supposed *to kill Adrian? When he was only...?*

"Why?" She didn't know how the word came out of her mouth. She felt as though she'd never move again.

John scoffed. "My father asked it of me. But even then, I wanted to."

"*Why?*" It seemed to be the only word she knew how to say.

"Don't you know?" John asked, his eyes bleary and red-rimmed. "You of all people *would* know. *We* would know. We were his friends. Some friend he was to me. I saw the way he looked at you when we were young and

231

the way you looked back." He looked up at her balefully. "I looked at you, too."

His words made the wine in Adelaide's stomach turn to vinegar. All this time, something had felt wrong, and she'd wondered why. Now, she wished she'd never known—she wished she'd ignored any suspicion, any thought. Because that meant John had never been a friend. And he was even less of one now. She wiped her mouth.

The truth spoken is the truth known. She wished she'd never known.

Supposed to. But he hadn't done it. *The bones in the crypt didn't belong to Adrian.* Her body suddenly pulsed with electrifying energy that set her heart pounding.

John's red eyes just raked across her body. *My husband,* she thought again, but the thought felt worse this time.

"It's difficult to cut off a head with a sword, you know," John said. "Harder than you might think…" His face had gone pale, and his head leaned heavily against the back of the chair. His eyes closed, and his breathing became rhythmic.

I should cut his throat right now, Adelaide thought with a surge of emotion. She took a deep, trembling breath and walked out, praying to all the saints that John wouldn't remember their conversation in the morning.

He won't. But I will. And I'll never forget it.

John

A throbbing sensation pounded his mind awake. When John opened his heavy eyelids, he saw the bottles of wine strewn across the table in the mess hall. His stomach turned when he remembered how much he'd drunk the night before. He wasn't one to overindulge—he couldn't remember the last time he'd drank that much. But circumstances had made it almost necessary.

Death on the battlefield was something else entirely, in John's mind. It was the nature of things, for men to die in combat. He'd seen thousands of horrors that could've struck any man dumb or driven him insane. But for John, death belonged on the battlefield. Seeing death there didn't frighten him.

But seeing Markus strewn on the cobblestone road of a common town, his blood forming cobwebs of red across the ground—John's bowels had turned to water when he'd seen it. Markus was young and stupid, but that didn't mean he needed to die. He needed a good whipping, but he didn't deserve for his entrails to be poured out because of a peasant's dispute. He'd somehow survived the battlefield. He deserved to die after many long years, surrounded by his wife and his children and his bastards and grand-bastards.

They'd brought his body back the next day. The men had been quiet. Whatever had ailed Sir Lyman at the Commoner's Ball struck him again. John and Artemis had to hold him back after they'd found Markus' body. He had a crazed look in his eyes, as though he were facing down the enemy all over again. Lyman was ready to kill the next man who so much as

233

looked at him. On the ride back to Southborn, he was quiet and pale.

So was John. He didn't tell the other men about the outlaws—that he'd seen the servant girl Ellena in the forest. Evidently, she was no servant girl, but that didn't seem to matter anymore. He'd seen no sign of Antony.

John's head throbbed as he bent down and washed his face in a basin of cold water. Lucas came into the barracks, looking oddly upright for a man who was smaller than John but had drunk nearly as much. John ran a wet hand through his hair. He felt as though he still reeked of wine.

"Good morning," Lucas said. "You look like shit. His grace wants you at the council meeting. It's in an hour."

John's stomach sank low. Of course. Tanor would want a report of what happened. And he would want that report from John. Because he lived to torture his bastard son. In front of his council, Tanor would speak sweet words about John—how brave he was, how selfless he was to continue to serve the crown even after winning the war.

"We are burying Markus today," Lucas added quietly, "and sending word to his family. Lyman will tell them." He shook his head. He looked older than his twenty-seven years. "Hell. I wish I'd been there. You don't know how much I wish I'd been there."

"I understand." John put a hand on his shoulder. As a commander, Lucas had already seen enough men die. And no matter their flaws or foibles, Lucas loved all of his men as though they were all brothers.

"You'd best start getting ready."

"What about the taxes?"

Lucas shrugged. "Edwin told me he is...re-evaluating his grace's strategy on tax collection. Till and Midge will go about their collection without the presence of you lot. For now."

John washed his face one more time and checked for stubble. He decided the grayish shadow across his face would have to do. His green tunic was still damp from the rain and dirty from his fight in the forest. He found a rust-red tunic in the livery that fit him passing well. The barracks didn't have a mirror—he'd have to trust he didn't look like a complete vagabond.

He walked to the council hall, hoping his headache would subside as he walked. It only seemed to worsen the closer he got. He should've eaten breakfast, he realized—although he barely knew what time it was.

Tanor sat at the head of the table, crown affixed neatly on his head, a great fur mantle draped around his shoulders against the cold. Edwin was at his elbow, leaning over the table at a pile of parchments. This was what Tanor always wanted, John thought—to have complete control over everything and everyone, even if it meant doing menial tasks like council meetings.

He examined his father more closely. Tanor's eyes were sunken. He and Edwin had goblets of wine and a carafe sitting in front of them, while a servant set cups at each of the other twelve places at the table. John waited awkwardly at one end of the table, waiting for the king to address him.

"What happened?" Tanor's voice cut through the dingy silence. He didn't look up from his papers. He lifted his goblet to his lips. Edwin's eyes flicked up at him before returning to the papers.

John found his heart pounding. "Markus was trying to…take advantage of a village girl. Another villager intervened and—"

Tanor slammed his goblet on the table. The sound cracked through the hall like a peal of thunder. It shot an arrow through John's aching head. Edwin didn't flinch. John did.

"*What. Happened?*"

He'd asked John that before. After Adrian fell over the ridge. After John couldn't find his body. After he'd—

"Markus was attacked," John said, "by a villager in Barnswood."

"By *who?*"

Another breath. "Antony Bronson."

Tanor sighed heavily. He set down the papers and shuffled them into a neat pile. "And *you* couldn't find him?"

A familiar fear was growing deep in John's core. A fear he hadn't felt since he was a child. It was the edge in his father's voice that fostered it. The edge started quietly and rose to a near scream before blows rained down on John's head. Tanor's chair scraped back against the flagstones and he stood up, taking one more swallow of wine. He swung his gaze to

John.

"Where is he now?" He stalked toward John as though he were approaching prey. John had the inclination to back away, but he stood his ground, though his knees shook. His head pulsed. His stomach roiled.

John searched for an answer. He lowered his eyes, watching his father's footsteps toward him. Suddenly, he felt a sharp pain on his cheek and a flash of light in his eyes. He toppled onto the floor, his skin stinging from where Tanor had slapped him. When the light left his vision, he saw his father standing over him. A stern hand landed on his arm and squeezed.

"*Where is he?* And why isn't he dead?" Tanor seethed. All of John's strength seemed to leave him. He knew he could fight back—he wasn't a child anymore. But he couldn't. He felt as weak and defenseless as he had ten years before.

"I can make this right," he said, his voice small. "I'll leave tonight, and he'll be dead by morning."

"Why should I trust you now?" Tanor growled.

"You can trust me," John said. His own pleading voice made him sick.

"I can trust you to tell the council today exactly what I want you to tell them," Tanor continued.

"What do you want me to tell them?" John asked. His cheeks still burned. The pit in his stomach grew.

Tanor paused, looking back at Edwin, who gave him a solemn nod. "That Antony Bronson is a pretender. He thinks he's Prince Adrian, come back to life. He's trying to stir up sympathizers of Men of the Lion and start a revolution."

Does he know? A fear deeper than John had ever felt settled into his core. If his father knew, he would be worse than dead.

"It could start a war," John murmured. "A revolution."

"And so what if it does?" Tanor said. "If a few peasants die, the other peasants will have more to eat. They'll thank me."

Tanor's tense body relaxed, but he still glared down at his prone son. He lifted his arm again. John flinched. Then he realized his father was only straightening his mantel across his broad shoulders. But it was too late—Tanor had seen John's fear.

"It's good to see nothing's changed."

John barely had time to recover before other members of the council began streaming in. Godfrey had opened the doors from the outside. While there were twelve seats at the table, John only counted ten council members who walked in. Richard Widlowe, Lucas' father, was the first to enter. He was a tall, portly man, nowhere near as fit as his son. Richard had never been a knight, but he had always been very wealthy. Probably why Tanor kept him on his council. He gave John a glimmer of a smile, but was businesslike as he found his seat.

Lord Roger Brockhempton followed soon after and took a seat next to Richard. He looked as though he could be drunk already—hair disheveled and cheeks ruddy.

To John's surprise, the next people to walk in were Queen Claudia and two of her ladies-in-waiting, including Adelaide. John glanced at his father—his face reflected the shock of his own.

Adelaide looked stunning in a red dress that offset the gold of the queen's, and a headpiece that encircled her hair like a halo. Elegant ceremonial garb for an official event. John hadn't seen Claudia since the Commoner's Ball. She'd lost her newborn daughter since then, only a few days before. John could see that her belly was still a little swollen, and her face had lost its color. Her keen blue eyes were dull, as was her normally lustrous yellow hair. But she walked proudly as she entered the hall and took her seat at the end of the table opposite Tanor.

John tried to make eye contact with Adelaide. She seemed determined not to look at him. In his vague memories from the night before, he remembered speaking to her—but not what he said.

Nothing stupid, I hope, he thought.

Other lords came in behind the queen that John remembered from his youth—Edward of Tench, Martin Sudbury—each of them looking older now. John gave each of them a small nod of recognition. It had been ten years—maybe they didn't remember him. John marked as well the absence of Lord Rowan DuMont, Adelaide's father. It seemed the position had not been given to her brother Landon.

John sat down as the lords entered, feeling eyes on him. Not just the burning eyes of his father, but curious glances from the council members. They made him feel even more out of place.

When everyone was seated, Godfrey seemed to appear from among them and banged his hand on the table, calling the council to order with his high, reedy voice. A smile spread across Tanor's face like honey on a bear's maw.

"Gentlemen," he said, "not only do I have the privilege of welcoming you to this council meeting, but I also have the distinct honor of welcoming you to our first council meeting in a time of peace in ten years."

The council members rapped the table with appreciation. Lord Roger shouted, "Here, here!"

"It was the tireless work of this council, in part, that brought the war to a close," Tanor continued. "From this room, we made key decisions that determined the tide of battle. And because of that, more men came home."

He cast a meaningful look at John that many council members followed. John's neck felt hot. *You didn't have to make the decision to run back into the fight to rescue your commander,* he thought. He bit his lip hard.

In a flash, Tanor's demeanor changed as he swung his gaze to Claudia, who sat patiently on the far side of the table, flanked by her ladies. The lines around his mouth tightened, and his eyes stopped smiling.

"It seems I also have the privilege of welcoming my wife, her grace Queen Claudia, to today's meeting," he said. "Although, my darling, you really should be resting. You've suffered quite the ordeal these past few days."

"I certainly have," Claudia replied glibly. Despite her obvious exhaustion, her wit was still strong. "I've survived both a childbirth and a slight on my character in a matter of days."

A rumble traveled across the table. John was confused. The young council member sitting next to him seemed to notice his confusion.

"Her grace has recently discovered that his majesty has a lover," he whispered with a chuckle. "As though it's a surprise the king beds women other than his wife."

That didn't surprise John, either.

"I thought Lady Elanor would be present," Claudia continued. "She seems much more involved in...matters of state, as of late."

Some around the table could barely stifle their laughter at her implication. Tanor's jowls were turning red. John knew the look well—his father could contain his anger to a point before it spilled out onto his face. His mouth was still a firm, placid line, but his blue eyes blazed at his wife.

"She will go nowhere in her delicate condition," he responded.

"Except to supper."

Another rumble. John had known none of this. He glanced at Adelaide. She had a deep pallor on her face.

"Anything else you'd like to contribute before we continue our meeting, my dear?" Tanor asked. His voice only had the slightest growl to it, but John knew that was dangerous enough. Claudia said nothing.

"Very well," Tanor continued. "Before we continue with our regular agenda, I would be remiss if I didn't address the unfortunate incident that happened in the village of Barnswood. I'm sure you are all aware by now that a young man—a man who served in the North—was slaughtered by a commoner whilst trying to do his duty to his crown."

Tanor's voice caught in his throat—theatrical emotion. John dug his fingernails into his palms. His heart was pounding. He knew what was about to happen. He glanced at Adelaide. Her face had gone beyond ashen.

The king's gaze swung toward John. "This brave soldier was in Barnswood and witnessed the attack. And we have learned something truly disturbing about the killer, something that must be addressed immediately."

The council rumbled again. Some exchanged concerned glances or toyed with the neck of their goblet. They had just fought a war—what else could be so disturbing?

"Sir John?" Tanor said coolly. All eyes turned to him, and he stood up, his chair scraping harshly against the stone. He felt like a stone statue amid delicate glass goblets—out of place and awkward. He felt Adelaide's eyes on him more than the rest. They burned into him. *What did I say to her last night?*

And then, in a sudden, sober flash, he remembered. *I kissed her.*

"Sir John, would you like to tell the council what happened in Barnswood two days ago?" asked the king.

"Sir Markus Huston was brutally murdered by a commoner named Antony Bronson, a bowyer's son living in Barnswood." John said. His voice didn't feel like his own. "A man who, we have since found out, makes a profanity of the dead Prince Adrian's name by claiming to be him."

The air in the room tightened and hummed. Everyone knew about the Men of the Lion and the conspiracies they whispered. But they couldn't have imagined a real pretender claiming to be Adrian.

A member of the council spoke up, a young man with a round, youthful face who sat near the king.

"How did you learn this, Sir John?" he asked. "How did you learn the identity of this pretender?"

"I spoke to his father," John said. *All saints, forgive me for slandering that poor man.* "The man knows that his son is mad. He is not culpable for Antony's actions." He drew in a breath. "When Antony killed Markus, he said it would be the first of many of the king's men to die before he takes the throne from his grace."

The young council member's mouth hung open. Tanor looked mildly impressed by his lie. After a rumble of whispers, another council member spoke. It was Lucas' father, Lord Richard.

"And you were there when Markus was killed, Sir John?" he asked. "You witnessed the murder?"

"Yes."

It shouldn't be this easy to lie.

Then the young council member spoke. "We must do something about this…traitor. This murderer."

"And we will," Tanor said. "The man is currently on the run, but I am going to send a message out to all the villages that there is a price on his head. Five hundred argents to the man who captures Antony Bronson."

The council seemed in favor of his proposal. John sat down and barely listened to the rest of the meeting. His mind teemed with unbidden thoughts. In the midst of them all was the feeling of Adelaide's lips. The most trivial thing that could be on his mind, and one that he was ashamed to think about. He had kissed her alone and unchaperoned. He was no longer surprised by her cold regard for him that day.

His thoughts continued in that way until Godfrey adjourned the council meeting, and its members began shuffling slowly out of the room, making scant conversation with one another as they did. Claudia, flanked by her ladies, had gone up to the king and was speaking in a low voice to him. Her face looked distraught. Tanor's looked strangely loving. He caught John's eye and beckoned him over. As John approached, Tanor dismissed his wife.

"I will come to you tonight, my dear," he heard Tanor murmur as Claudia walked away. "Adelaide, might I speak with you and John for a moment before you attend to my wife?"

Adelaide visibly bristled. She turned back to the king, her eyes remaining downcast. She didn't look at John.

"This Antony Bronson fellow," Tanor said. "You've both had some dealings with him. I understand he found himself at the Commoner's Ball a few days ago."

Adelaide's green eyes flicked to John until she realized the remark had been pointed at her.

"Yes, your grace," she said quietly.

"And he also found his way into the throne room."

"Yes, your grace."

Tanor lifted his chin. "Did he…say anything to you? About his affiliations?"

John was in awe of how strong Adelaide remained under Tanor's intense gaze. She said without hesitation, "No, your grace. We merely danced."

Tanor looked up at John. Something else was in his eyes, beneath their icy surface. He had the look of a man who was trying to regain control of the threads of his life unraveling. John felt it had more to do with the queen than with him or Adelaide—even so, he grasped at power wherever he could take it.

Adelaide excused herself to return to the queen, leaving John standing alone with his father. Tanor's sea-glass eyes met John's. They were full of a thousand threats and biting words, but he said none of them. He turned away dismissively, reshuffling the stack of parchments in front of his seat.

"If Antony Bronson is not dead by the time the year is out," Tanor said under his breath, "you will be."

Tanor

His rage bubbled closer to the surface with every step he took toward his wife's chambers. Tanor could handle many things—the weight of the crown, the distrust of his council, even the debts he owed—

But he would not tolerate being made to look a fool.

Claudia had seemed placated to hear that he would visit her. Her anger toward him came from desperation to win his affection again. Tanor knew how to use that. He should've known from the moment he married her that Claudia would be a jealous woman. Young women always were.

The remembrance came unbidden to his mind. The woman with milky eyes who had come to his father's village, who had stared right at him and pointed.

"The Unburied Boy," she'd said. "Buried yet still alive."

Tanor had just recovered from his nearly fatal illness, the one that had killed his stepsister. The woman saw this. Perhaps she'd perceived it from his thin frame and sunken cheeks. Or perhaps she saw beyond that.

"Each woman you lie with will bear you only one child," she'd said. "Yet, only three seeds will take root. One cursed, one loved, one forgotten."

The memory stuck in his mind as he opened the door to Claudia's chamber. She was there, standing by the window. How she had changed in just a matter of days—her once vibrant yellow hair hanging limply around her face, her arms wrapped around her still-swollen belly, her breasts taut, full of milk for a dead child. A dead daughter. Not a son. Easily forgotten.

She turned to him as he entered. Her eyes were tired, even spiteful. Her ready smile was gone. Only twenty-one, yet looking so much older. The mother of two children, one already sent to the grave.

"My darling," he said. His voice was calm, floating just above his rage. The rage would wait. Rage would not gain her trust.

"I'm surprised to see you in my chambers," she said bitterly. "I cannot be a conquest of yours. Not so soon after birthing your child."

"I'm not here for that," Tanor said. "I'm here for your forgiveness."

She softened a little. Her shoulders remained tense and high, near the delicate line of her jaw. As a girl, she'd been tall and gawky, but as a young woman, she'd grown into her grace.

He stepped toward her. In the light of early evening, tears glistened at the corners of her eyes. *She protects herself with anger,* he thought. *But she really is just the silly, vain girl she's always been.*

"Come here," he said. She came to him, and as he wrapped his arms around her, she sobbed into his shoulder. Blubbering like a child.

"What has she given you that I can't?" she said, barely audible in her tears. "That I *couldn't* give?"

"You have given me everything, my darling," Tanor said softly. He told her what he told them all. "And I'm immensely grateful. Elanor fills a need for me that all men require, but Elanor does not have my heart."

She looked up at him, her face red and blotchy, her eyes swollen, bloodshot. Ugly. A hideous little girl. "And I want to give you more," she said. Her hands slid down his arms. She pulled him toward the bed. "I can make myself ready for you."

"My dear, no," he said. He knew this was what she was going to do. "Not so soon after you've given birth to your child."

She fell back on the bed, a strange smile on her face. A smile that looked out of place on a face stained with tears. "I desire you," she said. "I have given you one living child. I can give you more. So many more. To continue our legacy, to grow our royal line."

Leaning over her on the bed, something angry bubbled within Tanor. Something that his anger before couldn't even touch. Claudia was unlacing the front of her gown, and her white breasts were spilling out eagerly, so pale and swollen he could see the criss-crossed blue veins of her lifeblood. A girl. A poppet. His means to continue his line. *His* royal line.

"*My* royal line," he found himself saying, barely above a whisper. Claudia stopped undressing.

"What was that, my dear?" she murmured.

Claudia, the preening slut. That was what Elanor had called the queen once when she and Tanor were abed. *She only wed you so she could be the mother of kings. Her father sold her to you, remember? I'm here willingly.*

"*My* royal line," Tanor repeated. He slid his hands down her body, along her waist, across her breasts. He squeezed them. It thrilled him for a moment as his hands climbed to her neck. She moaned, opening herself to him, her mouth ready to be kissed.

He didn't kiss. He squeezed.

Tanor squeezed and kept squeezing. That tiny, delicate little neck. The neck of a preening slut. He felt the pulse flutter under his fingers, the muscles and tendons panicking when Claudia realized he wasn't in a fit of passion—he was in a fit of rage. Her throat tried to cry out, but all that came out was a crackle. A gasp. Another crackle. He squeezed harder. It stopped. Her breath was stuck.

Tanor squeezed and kept squeezing. The preening slut. *Our* royal line. As though Claudia had known the half of what Tanor had to suffer—what he had to *do*—to get that royal line.

He squeezed even when he knew it was long over. When the fluttering pulse stopped, the muscles relaxed. He looked up at her face. Her face was close to purple, her eyes flooded red. Her mouth hung open, half in shock, but half still ready to be kissed at any moment. Her eyes showed no emotion, as though death were just another part of lovemaking.

Preening slut.

Tanor pulled the sheets from her bed and wound them until they created a rope.

* * *

Elanor was waiting for him when he returned to his chamber. He took her immediately. His blood was up—he knew the feeling. He'd felt it after he killed Alfred. He could've had any woman in that moment and been satisfied. It had been a serving girl the night of the murders. He hadn't known who she was and hadn't cared.

But tonight, it was Elanor who surrounded him. He wordlessly took her, more passionately than he ever had before. Her body sang beneath him, the swell of her belly pressed against him, invigorating him more. He finished without a word, and she left before the sun went down.

Edwin came to tell him without fanfare that the queen was dead—she had hanged herself using her own bedsheets.

Tanor was asleep not long after. For a while, the sleep was deep and dreamless, but then, he dreamed of dragons and blood. He dreamed of John's mother, her face lost to him in the past. *One cursed. One loved. One forgotten.*

He awakened and never fell back asleep. He lay in the echoing stillness of his spacious bedchamber.

Their love had been true at the beginning, he thought as he stared unseeing into the dark. Claudia had been sixteen on their wedding day, and blossoming into womanhood. Tanor's bastard son was gone from his life and he realized his need for a legitimate heir as soon as he succeeded to the throne. He was captivated by Claudia, her youthful flirtatiousness, the soft curves of her body, the plumpness of her lips.

Their wedding day may have been the only truly happy day of his life. He had loved the way her eyes glowed like warm honey in the candlelight that night, the way her dress slid so easily off her pale, unbroken skin. He cherished any opportunity they had to make love, and she seemed to do the same. No other woman seemed to matter.

Tanor remembered being overjoyed when he saw the gentle swell of his wife's womb. His heir. She was pampered endlessly by physicians and ladies-in-waiting, cloistered in a separate room to rest while servants prepared the nursery.

On a stormy Harvestmonth night, Prince Charles Tanor Behrens I was born. Tanor had only seen glimpses of Claudia during the last months of her pregnancy. They finally shared a bed again, and Tanor thought the joy of her embrace would wash over him again. But she seemed less eager, more tired. The supple lines of her body wilted, like a flower that had been toyed with too many times by a child's hands.

We were never supposed to lie together again, thought Tanor, his thoughts returning to his dark room, his empty bed. *Our daughter should never have been conceived. She was doomed to die.* He saw the woman with milky eyes floating in front of him. *One cursed. One loved. One forgotten.*

Tanor's chamber door creaked open, and he startled, wondering if it was Elanor again. He looked up at the vague silhouette in the doorway. He recognized the figure immediately as Charles. Tanor could hear faint sniffles.

"Papa," said the small voice. "Papa."

Tanor sat up. "Come here, my boy."

Charles immediately ran into the room without shutting the door behind him. He leaped onto Tanor's bed and clung to his father's side.

"I had a bad dream, Papa," Charles said.

Tanor wrapped an arm around him and held him close to his chest. "It can't hurt you, Charles," he whispered. "You're safe."

"There was…a dragon," Charles continued. He had always implored Tanor or one of the servants to take him down to the library and look at the illuminations in all the books. His favorites were the intricate dragons and monsters sometimes drawn alongside the stories.

"We should stop reading scary stories," said Tanor. "Let's not read about dragons anymore."

Charles whined. "But I *like* dragons." He leaned his curly head of hair against Tanor's shoulder. "Papa, where's Mama? Is Mama in here with you? I don't see her." He whimpered. "I dreamed a dragon ate her."

An icy hand clutched Tanor's heart. "Your mother has gone away," he said. "She had to go be with your little sister."

"But why?" asked Charles. Tears entered the boy's voice. "I want Mama. I miss her." He sobbed the small, pitiful sobs of a child. In the dark, Tanor couldn't tell the difference between his sobs and Claudia's earlier that day. Tanor held him closer. He stroked Charles' hair, trying to console him. The boy continued to cry into Tanor's nightshirt until his tears formed a small, wet blot on the cotton.

Finally, Charles' small cries turned into deep, even breaths. Tanor eased his small body, so he lay across the bed and gently pulled the quilt up to the boy's chin. Wet tracks snaked across Charles' face. He had been crying for a long time before he'd come to his father. Tanor settled back into the bed beside his son, continuing to gently stroke his hair. The boy slept peacefully—no more nightmares. Tanor stared at him for a long time. Charles looked more like his mother than like Tanor: his hair was soft and chestnut brown with flecks of yellow, unlike the coarse black hair of his father.

My royal line, was Tanor's last coherent thought before sleep took him again.

Antony

As he stirred, Antony became aware of a warm, close smell around him. Earthy. As though he were in a grave. For a moment, he believed he was. It was all over. His true life. His false life. The lies he'd been told. The life he'd taken. Now, he simply waited to be taken to the stars to be weighed on Saint Odette's great scales.

But then his eyes opened. He was only in a cave. His back was on a hard, earthen ground. He was covered with a greasy deer pelt that offered little warmth. But the cave itself was warm.

Every memory flooded back to him. First, it was the murder. It was Markus, dead at his feet, giant worms crawling from his middle. Then, it was his father's own words.

Good Saint Aethel, I've loved the children you've given me...

Antony looked around the cave. In front of him was a bend, and from there he could see light. But no one was around. No sounds of life. A few items were scattered on the floor. Antony could make out their shadows. A clay cup. Another pelt haphazardly folded. A rotting basket. Someone lived here. Someone had taken him in here, put a pelt over him...

He heard footsteps at the mouth of the cave, and a small figure appeared. She stopped short, staring at him.

"Oh—Antony," was all she said. "Er. You're awake."

Antony said nothing back. He realized who she was. In the dim light of the cave, he saw the girl from the village. Her eyes stared widely down at him, and her mass of red hair was piled on top of her head. She held something in her hands—something that smelled cooked, but cooked badly.

"I didn't—" she continued. "I didn't think you'd wake up for a while."

"Where am I?" asked Antony.

The girl looked around. "You're in our house, mate," she said. "We found you last night. You must have fallen in the dark. After everything that happened...well, I'm glad you got away."

"I didn't mean to," was all Antony could say. Markus was dead. Antony killed him. That thought remained rooted in the back of his mind, a dark shadow cast over all his other thoughts.

"Well, I'm glad you did," said the girl suddenly, strongly. She set down the pan she was holding. "This is liver. It's what we had left. I think it's from...a deer?"

The smell was revolting. But Antony's stomach was gnawing itself apart from hunger. The mass on the pan was half burnt, half raw. A hot, slimy piece of it fell apart in Antony's mouth unpleasantly.

The girl just stared at him as he ate, now sitting cross-legged across the pan from him. He felt her gaze burning into him and stopped chewing.

"You know my name," Antony said. "What's yours?"

"Ellena," said the girl.

"You...live here?" he asked, wanting to think about anything other than Markus.

Ellena nodded. "Sometimes we do. We find places here and there. Wherever it's safest. I worked at the big house for a little...but that was spying more than it was working. And stealing. Probably can't get away with that anymore. When we're in Southborn, people will take us in sometimes. But we always seem to find ourselves back here."

Antony pieced together what she was saying with his groggy mind. "So you're..." He hesitated to say it. Not because it wasn't true, but because of what it meant. Meant for him.

"We're outlaws," Ellena said matter-of-factly. "My Da wasn't repaid what he was owed. He took it for himself. They didn't like that very much."

They. Antony didn't have to ask who she meant. He saw their pinched faces in his mind. The tax collectors. Edwin. The ones who owned Bron and everything he'd ever earned.

He chewed thoughtfully on another piece of the grimy flesh. The thought of Markus came unbidden to his mind, and suddenly the meat was even more unpleasant. He swallowed it and ate no more.

"Are you…" Ellena began. She was young, Antony realized. About twenty, probably. She shook her head, as though she were embarrassed. "Sorry. But who are you?"

"What do you mean?"

"Well, you sure as hell aren't Antony Bronson. 'Cause I knew Antony."

Antony was taken aback. The words of Bron's prayer still rang in his ear. With every passing moment, his father seemed to become more of a stranger. His memories—the ones he thought he knew—became all the more shadowed. Who was saying anything about who he was? Bron had said who he wasn't.

"Because my Da thinks you're—" Ellena looked uncomfortable. Her small, round face was puckered, looking for the right words. "Well, maybe I shouldn't say that. But…" She took a breath and began again. "First, I should tell you there's a price on your head. For what you did in Barnswood."

Antony nodded numbly. It seemed so trivial. Unsurprising. He was an outlaw, too. Markus's stink was still in his nostrils.

"Now the king says you're a pretender. Announced it this morning. Says you claim to be Prince Adrian. The dead one."

Antony scoffed, but he felt something deep in his chest. If he wasn't Bron's boy, who was he? All along, there had been a suspicion, but any memory he had flew away in an instant. The frosted glass between him and his life before Bron remained.

"I haven't claimed anything," Antony said.

"I was in the woods that night, you know," Ellena said. "The night he died."

"The night the prince died?"

"The night Antony died."

Antony reached up and touched the scar, running his finger on the first

251

bump, then the second. It had a strange shape, like the bare branches of an autumn tree. When he was bored or absentminded, he'd trace his finger along it, but it always stayed hidden under his forelocks. It was too high on his forehead for anyone to notice.

He hadn't fallen. He'd been *pushed.*

"How did…he die?" Antony asked. Bron's real son. His thoughts were confused—he felt alive and dead, trapped between what had been and what he currently was.

"A boy killed him," Ellena said simply. Her face wasn't sad, only matter-of-fact. "A black-haired boy. He seemed panicked when he did it. Then he cut off Antony's head."

A shuddering realization. A black-haired boy—*John.* John had been the one who pushed him. The body of the prince had been found without a head. He didn't want to think about it anymore, but his mind was drawn to it. Because it was real. Because it was the truth.

"What else do they say about the prince?" he asked. "The people who think he's alive. The Men of the Lion."

Ellena shrugged, as though Antony's entire life didn't hinge on what she knew. "Well, a lot of them say different things. All across the kingdom. It's become a bit of a legend, really. You either believe Prince Adrian died on the same day his father did…or you believe he didn't. Everything else is just details. But what a lot of them say is—I mean, not that I believe them—is that it wasn't the Northmen who killed them. It was King Tanor. It sounds like something a villain in a storybook would do, so I dunno if I believe it."

Run. Antony remembered that word whispered to him. A snatch of a memory came back—a man dying, bathed in moonlight, his hand to Antony. Antony gripped it, then the hand slid lifelessly out of his. The memory was gone as soon as it came.

"There's not many of them in Barnswood," he noted. "Or maybe they just never talked to me."

Ellena shook her head. "There's not. Most of 'em live in Southborn. Da meets with them sometimes. There's some here and there in the villages.

They meet up together sometimes. Others just keep quiet, keep living their lives. But some want a revolution."

The thought sent a chill down Antony's spine. A revolution sounded unpleasant, especially after ten years of war. Everyone was already weary. Their kingdom had just celebrated a victory. It was time to rest.

But if it's true...then there would have to be, wouldn't there? If it was true. If his whole life was a lie. Antony didn't want to think about who he truly was—who he could be.

"The ring." He remembered suddenly. Ellena grimaced at him. "Where is it? The one you took from me. The lion ring."

Ellena put up her hands in defense. "I don't have it no more," she said. "I sold it. Someone paid a handsome sum for it."

"Who?"

"My friend David. He's a novice at the cathedral. I think he used church money to buy it off me. He seemed guilty about it. I didn't care."

Antony remembered the priest he met at the cathedral. The young novice. A friend. A Man of the Lion.

"I have to go to Southborn," he said. He stood up, his body feeling sore and rickety. "Do you have a cloak I can borrow?"

Ellena stumbled to her feet, obviously confused. "We have...pieces of cloaks. And I can't promise they're not full of fleas. But why are you going there? You're a wanted man. They could kill you."

"You said yourself there are more Men of the Lion in Southborn," Antony said. "Maybe if I talk to them, they can help me—"

They can help me remember. He didn't say it. Ellena handed him a cloak that was more holes than fabric, but it had a hood so he could hide his face. But she was right. He was putting his own life in danger.

He saw them near the entrance to the cave. A short bow, a leather pouch full of arrows. He scooped them up as he walked out.

"Uh—those are mine—" Ellena said, trailing behind him.

He shot her a look over his shoulder. "These are for the ring."

Antony turned, blinking into the bright autumn day. The trees were changing quickly, and the forest floor was a golden hue of dappled sunlight.

He stopped his determined march when he saw a figure standing in front of him, a doe slung across his shoulders.

The man was tall and broad shoulders with cautious eyes hooded by thick, black brows. There was something oddly crow-like about him, but not in a frightening way—in a roughshod, inquisitive, and filthy sort of way. The man's long, stringy hair receded sharply from his forehead, making his face stick out like a dome. A hooked nose hung over an unkempt beard. Antony could smell him from six feet away, and the smell wasn't pleasant.

"Leaving so soon?" The man's voice had gravel. "Can't say I'll miss you, but we've had worse company."

"Thank you for—" Antony didn't know *what* to thank him for. "—for not killing me."

The man looked him up and down. Antony saw the ghost of a smile under his scraggly beard. There was something familiar about the man, yet so foreign and unknown.

"Is that what you expected us to do?" he asked. "Well, tell your friends in the town we very well might have saved your life. It's often not blood we want from the common folk. It's kindness."

Antony saw something like pity on the man's face. He'd seen the worst of what people could do, Antony realized. He'd seen what true injustice was.

"What is your name?" Antony asked.

"Herne. Once Herne the Woodsman, but they took that from me too. They took the honest living away from me. They made me a killer instead. They made you one, too."

They. Antony saw something deep and sad in Herne's eyes. They were large and black and glittered like obsidian.

Herne cast a glance over his shoulder. "You won't find your way back to the Weschurch Way on your own," he said. "Ellena, help the boy find his way. I think he trusts you more than he trusts me. For now."

"Yes, Da. I'll take him to David," said Ellena. She breezed past Antony and her father, and Antony followed.

"And Antony," Herne said sternly. The note in his voice made Antony

254

turn around.

"Yes?"

"You'll find the world will be a lot less kind to you from here on out. There is a place for you here if you need it. But our ways are different from yours—and your Pa's."

Pa. Herne's words were chilling. Antony felt a sudden, deep sorrow in his chest—he could never go home. He might never see Bron again.

Antony followed Ellena, getting one last rank whiff of Herne before they continued into the forest, climbing up the steep ridge that housed their cave.

Ellena was short and spry, only the height of Antony's shoulder. Her tattered dress skirted around her ankles as she walked, and underneath she wore deerskin boots—practical, not fashionable.

"How do you find your way from here?" Antony asked, huffing as he climbed the ridge behind her. His calves burned as his feet found purchase on the steep ground.

"We've carved the symbols of the saints in twelve trees that lead to the Weschurch," Ellena said. "I don't need 'em no more, though. I know the way by heart now."

If Antony's mind hadn't been plagued by dark memories, it would've been a beautiful day. A clear blue sky winked out from beyond the tall trees. The leaves were tinged with their golden autumn splendor, as they often were toward the beginning of Harvestmonth. The air smelled dry and sweet and ancient.

"Your father said he's killed," Antony said, still thinking about Herne's words. He tried to keep pace with Ellena once they were at the top of the ridge. "Who did he kill?"

"People who deserved it," Ellena said without hesitation. She stared straight ahead as she walked. "People who wanted to take me away from him and lock him up. Lock him up for stealing so we wouldn't starve."

Antony was amazed by how quiet her steps were—all the while he tramped through the underbrush like a drunken deer. Ellena swung her gaze up to meet Antony's.

"That boy deserved it, too, you know," she said, her eyes completely serious. "You shouldn't feel sorry for him. I don't."

But guilt still clawed inside Antony's gut. "But he was just—"

"He was just what?" Ellena stopped and rounded on him. "About to tear off my clothes and have his way? Does a man like that deserve to live?"

"It wasn't—" Antony stopped. A part of him felt like she was right. But something else was missing. "It wasn't for me to decide that."

He thought he saw Ellena roll her eyes as she continued on a few paces ahead of him. "So I'll take you to David," she said, her voice light again. "What are you going to do then?"

"What I can," said Antony. "If I can just explain what happened, someone will understand."

Ellena snorted a laugh. The sound filled Antony with anger. "What?" he asked.

"No one's gonna understand," she said. "Except, well, me, because I was there. But they think you're a murderer now—which you are—and your word won't change that. Don't try to prove yourself right to 'em. It won't work. Da tried. It only made 'em angrier."

She's wrong, Antony thought. But a small voice reminded him that Bron had been cheated by those same men. And that *he* had been cheated, too.

But someone *will listen,* he thought, thinking of the Men of the Lion. Of Adelaide.

Ellena kept stealing glances at him as they walked. "What?" he asked.

"Nothing. You do look like him. If I squint my eyes the right way."

"Like who?"

"Like Antony."

Neither of them spoke. The name hung between them—Antony's name. His stolen name.

"If he'd grown up," Ellena's voice was softer now, "I think maybe he'd look a bit like you now. If he'd grown up." She seemed to shake the thought away. "Do you remember anything? From before that night?"

A boy with brown hair, brown eyes. Unremarkable. Antony thought of the memory of standing with Bron in the palace, urging the king for payment for his wares. That story didn't make sense now either. But he could *see* it in his mind. Bron had truly convinced him he was someone he wasn't.

"No," he said truthfully. Everything Bron had told him, the memories he'd planted, weren't his own now. "I really don't."

"I try to remember my mum sometimes," Ellena said. "The mum who took me in, I mean. She died when I was small. But sometimes if I think really hard, and focus just on what her face would look like, I can see her. She was a midwife and helped my real mum give birth to me."

"I've never tried to remember, really. Things just…come back sometimes," Antony said. The past remained behind a pane of warped glass. Bron had always said his mother was a big woman, with long yellow hair. Antony tried to remember. In the recesses of his mind, he thought he saw someone tall and slender, with a long brown braid down her back…

"It doesn't always work," Ellena said. "But at least I'm thinking about her."

The day continued as they walked. A chill had settled into the air after the storm. Antony realized it was almost the twelfth day of Harvestmonth— the day he fell. The day Bron said he ran away.

The real *Antony ran away. And a false Antony was found.*

But the memory remained, clearer than the others. He and Bron in the palace, appealing to King Alfred. He saw it in his mind's eye, with every detail there. Bron wore his threadbare brown cloak, looking plain in the grandeur of the throne room. It was late, and there were shadows across his face from the candlelight. He was younger then, but still wore his age.

But in the memory, Antony wasn't standing beside him, looking at the king. He looked *down* at Bron from the dais. On one side of Bron was Carter, long locks of yellow hair over his eyes, and on the other was a brown-haired, brown-eyed boy.

Wasn't that me? Didn't I go with Pa that day?

No, said an inner voice that nearly turned his bowels to water. Your father the king wanted you to learn that day.

King Alfred had brought Adrian to listen to the appeal of this commoner from Barnswood. Afterward, his father told him that when he was king someday, he would have to make hard decisions for the benefit of the realm.

And a few weeks later, King Alfred would be dead.

The warped glass was gone. This memory was clear as a spring stream flowing through Antony's mind. He had a perfect sense of who he was.

With no way to prove it.

"We'll be there by midday, I think," Ellena said, and the warped glass came crashing down around Antony's thoughts again. The clarity was gone, as though it were a dream and he was waking up. The fragments blew away and scattered like the leaves around his feet. They stood on the Weschurch Road.

Ellena pointed in front of them. "We'll take this as long as it goes. You know that, though. You've been to Southborn before, yeah?" She looked earnestly up at him. "Just remember to watch your back when we get there. Don't think someone's your friend just cos they're nice to you."

"You've been nice to me," Antony said. "Are you my friend?"

"Ha!" Ellena laughed and winked. "Never." But her smile said otherwise.

Adelaide

"Adelaide, you are going to look lovely for your betrothed."

Elanor pampered her as though she were a doll. Adelaide imagined it had something to do with getting her mind off any guilt she felt.

Claudia would be laid to rest with her daughter that day.

Adelaide stared into the mirror in Elanor's chambers at the stranger's face in front of her. The blank, hollow eyes. The mouth turned downward. A pale, haggard face, one that was *not* lovely. People had always called her beautiful. Not today.

"My dress fits you passing well, does it not?" Elanor asked. It didn't. The black gown had to be cinched tightly around Adelaide's waist and the bust pinned around her small breasts. She looked like she was wrapped in a black shroud, not an elegant gown. "You're such a slip of a thing, Addie."

"It's not my aim to be beautiful today," Adelaide said. Her voice didn't sound like her own.

"Oh, but John will be there," Elanor said. "And he will see you. Don't you want to please him?"

No.

Elanor pursed her lips. "I do hope there are no hard feelings between us, Addie," she said, toying absently with Adelaide's hair. "There are certainly none on my part. You did what you had to do, after all, when you told the queen about my condition. And now the situation seemed to have righted itself on its own."

Adelaide clenched her teeth. *By the very convenient death of the queen.*

Elanor was in high spirits again because she got what she wanted—Claudia was out of the way now. Adelaide's betrayal didn't matter to her. And Adelaide was sure Elanor would never tell her a secret again.

Even before Claudia's death, Adelaide's mind had been crammed with dark thoughts. It was John who attempted to kill Adrian all those years ago. He was part of the plot.

But who had been buried in Adrian's stead? Who had John actually killed?

Elanor's belly swelled under her dress. She wore a silver headpiece in her hair—not at all unlike a crown—and a lovely silver necklace Adelaide could have sworn belonged to Claudia. According to Elanor, she would be made the queen now that Claudia was dead. She was gathering ideas for her wedding to King Tanor. Claudia had been dead for two days.

"You will make a lovely bride, Adelaide," Elanor continued. She stood Adelaide on her feet and cupped her chin in her hands. She tilted Adelaide's face to look up at her. "Once this business is all over, I will dedicate every moment to your wedding."

Her wedding. The idea turned Adelaide's stomach. When she was a girl, she often playacted her wedding. Sometimes she would rope her father into the charade, making him walk her the length of the great hall to her makeshift altar. Sometimes her groom was the son of a visiting lord, sometimes he was a mere sack of flour. But what she remembered most was her father's beaming face, his eyes laughing down at her.

"Now, young man, you'd better take good care of my daughter," he would say to the boy or the sack of flour. "She's the most beautiful and perfect girl in the world, and you are ill-suited for such an angel."

Suddenly, Adelaide felt tears spring to her eyes. The memory of her father caught her by surprise. He would never see her marry. He wouldn't walk with her in the chapel. Tanor had sent a letter to her brother, Landon, to inquire about her dowry. Landon would walk with her—maybe. If he was sober.

I've let you down, Father, she thought. *I have come to Southborn and left only death in my wake.*

"Tanor told me he is going to gift Sir John with a tract of land by the sea," Elanor continued. "You love the sea, don't you, Addie? The poor lord of Highmoor is sick and dying, and he never got around to making an heir. Always the bookish sort, he was. It's a fair estate, with several tenants already. The village people are of good stock, so I've heard. I will miss you, though." Elanor added her last words dispassionately.

The sea might be a comfort, Adelaide thought. *But not today.*

Her aunt met her in the hall. Pauline looked stately in her voluminous black gown. She even had a thin black veil over her eyes, though her face was still pinched and proper, showing no signs of sadness. She curtsied stiffly to Elanor as she passed, then she took Adelaide's arm in hers. Adelaide felt a slow rage building in her gut—her aunt, who had cursed her to a marriage with a murderer.

But when Pauline looked at her today, Adelaide saw a strange gentleness in her eyes, something almost like pity.

"Don't become her pet, my dear," she said in a low voice. "That woman is a harpy and a witch. I've known many like her in my time, and they are not worth knowing."

Adelaide said nothing. She hadn't spoken to her aunt since Pauline told her about the engagement. Her cheeks flared red just thinking about it.

"You are angry with me," Pauline said stiffly. They didn't look at each other as they walked down the hall toward the courtyard. The funeral procession would begin soon. "I have five daughters. I know an angry girl when I see one. I've arranged five marriages—well, six now."

She paused. "When I stood at your father's grave, I told him I would protect you." Her voice was suddenly strained. Adelaide looked up at her. A tear danced in the corner of Pauline's eye. "People were talking about you and that peasant boy after the Commoner's Ball. I even had to quash a few rumors. Rumors that are not appropriate for civilized ears."

That peasant boy. Pauline seemed to forget that Antony had saved them. But, Adelaide realized, Antony was a murderer now, too.

"Believe me, Adelaide, you do not want to be a woman of shame at court. You do *not* want to be Elanor of the Roses. As loved as she is by the king today, she will not be tomorrow."

I am not a woman of shame, Adelaide wanted to scream. *Everyone around us is lying, don't you see that?*

And yet, the look in Pauline's eyes made her soften. Her aunt was merely doing her best for her—just as Adelaide was trying to do for herself. Aunt Pauline was doing right by Rowan.

"Hold your head high, my dear," Pauline said, her voice quieter. "Mourn today. But lift your head. Marry Sir John. He's an angry man, but not a man who will harm you. I think he truly loves you, and a man who truly loves you is one you can control."

Adelaide didn't want to think about John. They would be married in Wintermonth, just before John's twenty-fourth birthday. They would live in Highmoor and probably visit court only a few times a year. Perhaps Aunt Pauline would live with them and give her estates to one of her daughters. Strangely enough, the thought gladdened Adelaide ever so slightly.

Hold your head high. She clung closer to Pauline.

The day was far too beautiful for a funeral. The sun pierced the cloudless blue sky, warming the chill in the air. Sparrows fluttered around the turrets of the palace, squawking merrily as they flitted to and fro from their nests between the stones. The courtyard was strangely quiet for how many people waited for the procession. A covered carriage bore Claudia's body, shrouded by dark silk. Servants watched the preparations and whispered to one another. Adelaide caught the eye of Magg, who gave her a solemn nod.

Magg, she thought. *I need to talk to her. I need to talk to her about the bones.*

She tried not to look at John. Adelaide saw him as she and Pauline came down from the dais. She could feel his eyes on her now.

Elanor arrived in the courtyard on the arm of King Tanor, who was swathed in a black velvet tunic and cape. Adelaide heard her aunt audibly scoff as she watched them descend from the dais. Ilse followed in tow, holding Prince Charles in her arms. The boy didn't understand what was happening. His face was vacant and naïve.

A long line of carriages waited in the courtyard to bring members of the court to the Cathedral of the Nine. A sea of black dresses and surcoats boarded them, while less important members of the court mounted horses to follow behind. Lucas was among the men on horseback. His handsome face looked out across the courtyard, as though he were a commander once again, leading well-dressed soldiers into a battle with grief.

Pauline and Adelaide slid into Jacob's carriage toward the back of the processional. Adelaide didn't miss the warm closeness of the carriage. It seemed like only yesterday she and Pauline had taken the long journey from Easthempton to Southborn. Adelaide tried to open one of the curtains, but Pauline gently smacked her hand away.

"We don't need to be a spectacle for the common folk, on today of all days," she murmured. Adelaide breathed in the thick air and nodded.

Adelaide was surprised when the carriage door opened again. She was even more surprised when John ducked in.

"There you are," Pauline said. "I suspected you wouldn't be riding with your father."

John's cheeks flamed red as he pushed himself into the carriage. Pauline humphed loudly when he stepped on her wide skirts and positioned himself on the bench across from them, his long legs awkwardly entangled with theirs. He looked plain and out of place, wearing a simple roughspun black tunic. His eyes looked tired, and his face was marked with unkempt stubble. He didn't look at Adelaide. He hunched his large frame into the seat and stared at his hands.

Adelaide's heart was pounding. She looked at his hands, too. Big, like the rest of him, with strong blue veins coursing through them. Dirt under his fingernails. Those hands had killed more people than Adelaide knew. And had tried to kill Adrian. And had killed whoever was in the crypt in Adrian's stead.

He's known this entire time, she thought. She remembered when they talked on the castle wall, and how good it felt to have a friend beside her again. John had known then. She thought about when he comforted her. John had known then. Even when they were children, and he'd said goodbye to her before going North. John had known then. He'd always known, and he didn't love her enough to tell her.

Pauline rested her hand on Adelaide's. Her touch was simple—the warm, papery hand of an older woman. She merely rested it here.

At the church, Pauline and Adelaide joined the line of mourners after they disembarked from the carriage. John loomed quietly behind them. Adelaide steeled herself for what she was about to walk into. She was grateful to have her aunt's arm to lean on.

The cathedral was filled with light that day, its stained glass windows bursting with color. It seemed more fitting for a celebration. Adelaide looked around at the statues of the nine saints that surrounded the sanctuary, with Saint Augustus at the chancel, his head bowed and hands extended downward. It was strictly forbidden to carve the likeness of Saint Augustus—his face was to always be obscured. Adelaide didn't know why— she vaguely remembered a tutor telling her that a council had decided how the saints were to be depicted thousands of years ago, based on ancient texts from the first Rock Monks.

She liked Saint Odette's statue most of all—she always had. Despite leading men to their deaths, her likeness was always warm, her face kind. She stood on the north side of the nave nearest to Augustus. Her stone-carved eyes stared upward, her hands lifted to the heavens as she lifted souls into the stars.

Adelaide stared at her so she wouldn't have to look to the front of the church, but once she did, she couldn't look away. There lay Claudia's lifeless body with her daughter at her breast. She was dressed in a high-collared blue gown to hide the marks on her neck. She was just as beautiful, even in death. Her belly had not fully flattened. It still held room for her dead child.

As monks chanted the Song of Saint Odette, Adelaide sat in a pew with her aunt, and John flanked her other side. She wished he hadn't. She wanted him far away from her that day—she was too surrounded by death already.

A priest stood and recited the prayer of Saint Myra over Claudia's body.

Adelaide listened halfheartedly. Saint Myra's prayer was one of deep grief, something Adelaide already felt. She'd heard it at her father's burial and at King Alfred's, and at Prince Adrian's.

And may the tears that are shed today water the seeds of our hope to meet again in the stars.

Adelaide mechanically touched her head, her heart, and her belly with the rest of the mourners.

The monks sang more chants, and the priest spoke more words, but Adelaide hardly listened. Her mind wandered as her eyes landed on Tanor and Elanor in the front pew. Elanor held her head high. Adelaide's eyes slid to Magg.

I need to ask her. I need to ask her about the bones.

The service continued on for what seemed like an eternity, with Adelaide trapped in her own mind. Then, two novices appeared and covered Claudia's casket. One novice was a tall, broad-shouldered boy. Adelaide recognized him—it was David, the one from Tanor's council meeting.

The novices lifted Claudia's casket and brought it down the aisle back to its carriage. She would return to her countryside home and be buried in the catacombs of the church she was given to as a baby. It had been her widowed father's wish.

As the novices solemnly brought the casket through the sanctuary, Adelaide tried to catch Magg's eye from across the room. But her gaze was downcast. Adelaide's heart sank.

After the casket departed, many of the mourners filed out of the church. Pauline fidgeted in the pew beside Adelaide. Adelaide stood and let her pass. John had already left. *Good,* Adelaide thought. When Pauline was gone, she knelt at the pew as the baleful chanting receded into the bowels of the cathedral and monks continued their daily duties. Adelaide remained.

Even though Claudia's body was gone from the church, Adelaide wasn't finished mourning. Her heart was too heavy to allow her to stand. She closed her eyes but didn't pray. She merely thought about how it had all happened. How the saints were cruel. How Saint Odette had taken so many people she loved. How Adelaide couldn't make a friend without losing them soon after.

Highmoor is by the sea, she thought, remembering what Elanor had told her. She missed the sea, the feeling of black sand between her toes, of swimming out as far as she could until the cold water stung her skin. The shallows were warmer, but she preferred swimming where her feet no longer touched the sand. That was when she felt truly free, unfettered by the ground. She would gaze out to the horizon, at the water that changed so much it seemed unchanging. She would wonder what went on in the quiet depths while the rest of the world fought with itself. She wondered what secrets the water kept.

Then, she'd return home with her father, the dune grass scraping her bare legs, sand clinging to her wet skin. Her father wouldn't be there when she returned to the sea. Would it be the same? Would John watch her from the shore and walk her home? Would she watch their children play in the shallows?

Is that what's in store for me, Great Maker? Adelaide prayed. She wasn't supposed to pray to the Great Maker, but to the saints who would intercede for her. She didn't care. She needed to know. *Is this the vision you've given me? I came to Southborn to determine my fate—is this it?*

Until a few days before, Adelaide hadn't known her future. Knowing it now was too disappointing to bear.

She opened her eyes, her gaze landing on the statue of Saint Augustus. She followed his downward-stretched arms—and it appeared he was pointing directly to Magg, who lit one candle among many at the base of the sculpture. Adelaide nearly leaped to her feet, then remembered she was surrounded by mourners and monks.

Magg made her way down the nave, her head still lowered. From what Adelaide saw in her face, Magg looked deeply pained.

I need to tell her.

Adelaide took a deep breath, rose, and followed Magg out the door. To her surprise, Magg didn't exit the cathedral. Instead, she turned, making her way to the Crypt of Kings.

"Magg," Adelaide said when they'd left the sanctuary. Her voice still felt too loud in the sacred space.

Magg stopped and turned. Her eyes were red and her face drawn, but she managed a small smile. Adelaide struggled to return it.

"My lady," Magg dipped her head. "Are you coming to the Crypt as well?"

Adelaide caught up with her. "Yes," she lied. *Only to speak with you.* They fell in step together as they descended the stairs into the bowels of the cathedral. The steps were shallow and the ceiling low, and around them was an even more all-encompassing silence than in the sanctuary.

"I'm sorry, Magg," said Adelaide. "I know she was a loss for you as much as anyone."

"I helped her deliver Charles." Magg's voice broke. "His birth was so… easy. Her pregnancy had been, as well. This pregnancy had been fairly easy on her, too. I don't…I don't know what happened."

"You couldn't have done anything different, Magg."

"But I *could* have. There is much study on childbirth, on why a cord might wrap around a child's neck at delivery…I should have scoured the Annals for anything I could find on the subject. But I was too preoccupied by my study of bones."

My study of bones. Adelaide bit her lip.

They arrived in the Crypt. The only light came from small lanterns suspended from the ceiling, shuttered to only give a scant glow. Magg walked with a determined step, her eyes scanning each sarcophagus as if searching for one.

"Magg, I need to tell you something," Adelaide said. Her heart raced. "Something I think you should know."

"What is it?" Magg didn't look at her. Her intent eyes continued scanning as they walked, and she whispered the names of each royal under her breath as they walked.

"It's about Prince Adrian."

Magg paused. Her face didn't change. She still didn't look at Adelaide, but she cocked her head to one side, as if interested. "What about him?"

Before she knew what she was doing, Adelaide grabbed Magg's arm. The older woman turned at the touch, looking down at Adelaide with a furrowed brow. The sadness in her eyes was so deep, so total. Adelaide saw the guilt there—the guilt that her knowledge could not save the queen.

"You said that the bones in Prince Adrian's crypt had been broken," Adelaide said. "The other night, I remembered something. He'd never broken a bone. Ever."

Magg's eyes widened slightly, but she said nothing. Adelaide waited for the physician's face to tell her something—confusion, surprise… confirmation. But her face remained neutral, her lips pursed.

"And there's something else, too. Sir John—"

"You must be mistaken, Adelaide."

Magg's interruption startled Adelaide. Her voice was cold, expression-less. Adelaide had expected the frantic excitement Magg always had when she solved a problem.

"But—but I remember," Adelaide said. "It was after my brother broke his hand, remember? Adrian told me then that he'd never broken a bone. I even remember that he talked about losing his first tooth—how he thought the rest of him would fall apart. Just as you'd said."

Magg's throat bobbed. "Yes, he did say that," she said. "But I think you're misremembering."

"But—"

"*I think you're misremembering.*"

The note of Magg's voice changed. It was sharper, but no less kind. She looked down at Adelaide earnestly.

"Adelaide." Her voice was quieter. "To imply that the body in Prince Adrian's crypt is…not the body of the prince is to imply *many* things. Things that…should not be implied."

Adelaide saw it. Magg was *scared. She knows,* Adelaide's mind screamed. *She knows.* "But if it's *not* Adrian, where is he? Who *is* in his crypt? Don't you want to know?"

"No," Magg said firmly. "No, I don't. I did my duty in embalming the child—and his father. And yes, their bones offered me an opportunity for great study. But it seems I should have had my attention turned elsewhere."

Adelaide felt a lump in her throat. Magg straightened a little before continuing. Her voice was barely above a whisper this time.

"I have worked hard to achieve the position I have in this court," Magg said. "I have made a name for myself. I have foregone marrying or having children—all for the pursuit of health and medicine, to care for the royal family with the utmost consideration. I failed in that task when I lost Queen Claudia's child."

She blinked hard, as though willing tears away from her eyes. "I was not born into wealth like you, Adelaide," she said, "nor am I wealthy now. If I were to say something that—that compromised my position, I would lose everything. I would lose the trust of those I care for. And I care for the *living*. I cannot care for the dead."

She looked meaningfully at Adelaide, who swallowed back so many emotions. Hot tears pricked at her eyes and she realized she was shaking. Magg wouldn't help her.

"The truth spoken is the truth known," said Adelaide without thinking.

"And this truth, however grave, should not be spoken. It will put too many people in danger. Good afternoon, Adelaide."

She stepped away from her quickly, retreating up the stairs.

Magg wouldn't help her. And Adelaide could hardly blame her. Magg was not of noble birth. She was a woman who had fought for what she had. And she was too afraid to surrender it for the truth.

If in fact, it was the truth at all. Perhaps she *had* misremembered.

It wasn't long before she found herself in front of King Alfred's crypt. There lay Alfred, and Queen Catherine, and Prince Adrian.

I'm not here. She remembered her dream. She had seen Adrian. The sight of him made her heart ache, as though no time had passed since she last saw him alive.

A shadow moved in the darkness beyond King Alfred's crypt.

Adelaide nearly stumbled back in fright. Her initial visceral thought was *ghost.* Until she heard boots shuffling on the stone ground. The gasp of someone in the darkness. A man.

He stumbled into the light. And he shocked Adelaide more than a ghost. Before her stood Antony.

Antony

He knew he looked a sight—he was hungry, tired, and had itchy stubble growing on his chin. He could easily have been mistaken for a ghost hiding there in the crypt. He'd arrived at the city gates and moved through the crowds with his head lowered, finally ducking into the cathedral only to find a funeral going on.

Luckily, he'd found David, and David had helped him. He still had the ring he'd bought from Ellena—and he sheepishly gave it to Antony without hesitation. It was on his finger now. He didn't care who saw it.

"Go to the Five Oxen tonight at seven bells," was all David had told him before leaving him in the crypt with a stale crust of bread from the brothers' larder. Antony hadn't been able to ask him any other questions—the young man had disappeared hurriedly back up the stairs.

Antony was happy to see Adelaide. She looked far less vibrant than the last time he saw her. Her face was drawn and pale, stark against her black dress. But she was still beautiful, and her small figure remained prim and contained despite her obvious surprise.

"Adelaide," he said quietly. Adelaide wasn't looking at him the same way she had at the Commoner's Ball.

She knows what I did, he thought guiltily. *Everyone does.*

She didn't move as he came from around the crypt toward her. But as he came closer, she took one cautious step back.

She knows, he thought again.

"Who are you?" she asked. Her voice wasn't accusatory. It broke Antony's heart to realize that she truly wondered who he was. Markus' snide face flashed through his mind.

"I didn't mean to do it," he began. Those words had run through his head over and over. "I was just trying to—"

"Who are you?" Adelaide asked again, more firmly this time.

A thought occurred to Antony. "You called me something at the Commoner's Ball. A name. What was it?"

"I didn't know you then," Adelaide said. Her voice was cold. Her face was expressionless. "Now I realize I don't know you at all."

She turned away. Her chestnut hair tumbled around her shoulders, soft and glowing in the low light. Antony had the sudden urge to reach out and touch it.

"So I'll ask you again. Who are you?" She didn't look at him.

"I don't know," Antony said. The reality of those words hit him. He wasn't his father's son. Every story told to him about his mother, his brothers, his childhood—was all a lie. His memories had been created, painted in his mind by his father—by Bron. His mind was a castle of false stone, ready to crumble.

Adelaide turned slightly to him. "How can you not know? Who are you? A killer? A prince? A commoner?"

"I'm not a killer."

"Markus Huston's family would say differently."

"I didn't mean to do it."

Adelaide turned to him, her eyes flashing. "But you did. You killed him. You didn't have to. You could have let justice be served for whatever he did wrong."

It was Antony's turn to be angry. "You don't understand," he said. "He—"
He deserved it. That was what he wanted to say. *But if he deserved it, then don't I deserve this?*

"I do understand," Adelaide replied. "I understand that I made you out to be someone you're not."

Antony tried to bite back his words, but he couldn't. He saw Markus' body in front of him again, felt the terror of what he'd done rise in his blood.

"You know as well as I do that this kingdom isn't just anymore," he said. "Maybe you can't see it because you're too busy living in a castle, having every care tended for you."

Antony hated the look in her eyes. For a moment, he wondered if she hated him now. He almost wanted her to. It would make forgetting her easier.

A tear fell down Adelaide's cheek. She was so close to him. Antony lifted his hand out of instinct. He could've lifted a finger and wiped her tears away. And he wanted to.

Adelaide caught sight of his hand—the ring on his finger.

"Does that belong to you?" Adelaide asked.

Antony nodded. The ring felt so solid and real, more real than anything else.

"How did you get it?" Adelaide asked.

"I don't know," Antony said.

"You *have* to know," Adelaide's voice shook with frustration. "How can you not know?"

Antony felt more anger rising in his chest. She was on his side only a few days ago. If only she understood what had happened, she wouldn't be so upset.

"I don't know anything," he said. "About myself. My fa—the man who said he was my father found me in the forest. He told me later that I'd fallen from a tree. I have some memories, but…I don't know which ones are true."

Adelaide paused. She looked him up and down. Fresh tears sprung to her eyes. "It's truly uncanny how much you look like him," she said. "How much you…remind me of him."

"Who?"

"Him."

She looked down at the crypt in front of them. The boy. The prince. Antony looked down at his face. The stone masons had carved a look of peaceful repose on the young boy's face, a shoot cut down before its prime. Beside him lay his father and mother. An entire royal line extinguished.

272

"Have you ever broken a bone?"

The question surprised Antony. It rang for a moment in the silence of the crypt, in the stale, tepid air. He thought for a moment, then looked at Adelaide. She stood closer to him now, looking up at him with gentler eyes rimmed with red.

Then she grimaced. "You probably don't know, do you?" She turned away again, almost disappointed. "How could you know?"

"I don't—" Antony stopped. It was true. He couldn't remember, and that was never a story Bron had told him.

"Surely you'd remember something like that," she said. Now it seemed like she was pressing him, urging him.

"I suppose," Antony said. "But…trying to remember is like looking through a foggy pane of glass. I can only see shapes of things. Sometimes I'll think of something, but any memory will be gone as soon as it comes. And Bron told me so many things, trying to make me believe I was his son."

"Why?"

Antony realized he didn't know that, either. What had Bron known about him? If he ever saw the man again, Antony didn't know how he would speak to him. A ball of anger rose in his throat when he thought about the man he'd called father.

They stood in silence, looking down at the grave of the lost prince. Antony almost wished he was buried there now. That boy had probably never known the true pain of life, not until his final moments, at least. A boy didn't deserve to be murdered. And Antony had murdered one. Would he still be taken to the stars by the saints? Or would Odette bury him so deep he would never be touched by light again?

"I want to believe it's you," Adelaide finally said. She still looked at the crypt, as though speaking to the body that lay beneath it. "I don't know how to prove it, or if I can prove it. But I want to believe it. And maybe I'm a fool for believing it."

"For believing what?"

"That you might somehow be the prince that was lost. Prince Adrian."

The words seemed to pain her. *Adrian.* That was the name she'd called him, and the name he'd heard so many times echo in his dreams. *Adrian.* He wouldn't forget it now.

"Is the funeral over?" Antony asked, before realizing how insensitive the question was. Adelaide had lost a friend that day.

"Yes," Adelaide said, seemingly unoffended.

Antony relaxed a little. "I need to get out of here for a bit," he said. "And I need a drink like a fish needs water."

A smile tugged at Adelaide's lips. Antony had an urge to make her smile, to make her laugh.

"Anytime I go to a tavern, I usually end up getting in trouble," he said. "It's a wonder I still have all my teeth."

That made Adelaide smile. It was radiant to see her smile after her tears. He wanted to make her keep smiling. A thought came to his mind, one that had felt foolish to him for years. *And it's a wonder I remember it.*

"You know, there is something I do remember—quite well, actually," he said. "When I was young and lost my first tooth, I ran to someone—my mother, it might have been—and I was screaming because I thought I was falling apart. I thought the rest of me would shake loose and break off, too."

Adelaide's smile faded, and her mouth dropped. Suddenly, she was looking up at him with something like awe—on the verge of confusion.

"What is it?" Antony asked. She was quiet for a while, the silence of the crypt enveloping them. Then, she looked back down at the boy's crypt and spoke.

"The truth spoken is the truth known. And everyone will know the truth soon."

John

Lucas had called it a celebration. But John saw their foray out into the town for what it really was—a patrol.

They wore their green garb but covered the color with heavy wool cloaks—partially for the chill, and partially to stay inconspicuous.

Edwin pushed through the narrow street in front of them—John, Lucas, Lyman, and Artemis trailed behind as crowds thronged in the Ale District of town. The tower had just rung six bells, which for many meant time for ending their working and starting their drinking. For Edwin, it also meant it was time to go hunting.

"But not without a drink, first," Lucas had said. "A marriage to a woman like Adelaide is cause for celebration enough." He'd had a twinkle in his eye. After what had happened in the previous days, he sought happiness wherever he could find it.

John was hunched beside him against the stiff wind now, keeping pace with his limping strides while Edwin charged ahead. Edwin had agreed to the drink, but he seemed dead-set on getting one as quickly as possible. He didn't seem to care if people knew who he was—his hair was perfectly coiffed back from his temples and his boots were freshly oiled. The rest of them hadn't made nearly as much effort.

Edwin led them into a tavern that looked slightly more respectable than the rest in the quarter. The immediate cobblestone street around it didn't smell like vomit, and it seemed like the sign was freshly painted. John wasn't surprised by Edwin's choice. Had any of the other men chosen, they would've been in a watering hole with the unwashed of Southborn.

The inside was tastefully lit, every surface polished wood, the smell of burning wax and briny ale buried deep in the floorboards. Edwin shepherded them to a table in the middle of the floor, shouldering past well-dressed commoners who barely gave them a second look. Somewhere on the second level of the tavern, a minstrel played a lute. John heard a few quiet notes float over them in between the rumble of chatter around them.

"Lucas, fetch the barkeep, will you?" Edwin said tersely as they sat. "We cannot stay here long. There's work to be done." He shot a steely look at John, as though he was the one who came up with the idea.

Lucas slid away toward the bar. Soon, they had tankards of dark beer in front of them, froth seething over the rims.

"To John and Adelaide," Lucas said with a glimmer in his eye. Then, with sudden somberness, "and of course, to Markus."

They drank. The ale was thick and nutty. John felt his cheeks flush from its warmth.

"Did it really happen the way you said, Johnny?" Lucas asked with a sort of grim fascination. "It was a…a pretender who killed Markus? Someone who claims to be Prince Adrian?"

John nodded, taking another draft. "It seemed to be," he said.

"I've gotten word that the young man may be in the village tonight," Edwin said. He hadn't touched his drink. His keen eyes darted across the room as he spoke.

Lucas chortled. "I don't think you'll find him here, sir," he said. "How is it you know?"

"In order to stop a revolution, we need eyes everywhere," Edwin said, "and I have them."

Lucas and the other men shifted uncomfortably. Artemis hid his face in his tankard.

"But we can pause to celebrate our groom, of course." A brief smile flashed across Edwin's mouth as he put a hand on John's wrist. "And the new lord of Highmoor. You'll be leaving our ranks soon. What will you do as a lord, with nothing at all to do?"

"*You're* a lord, my lord," Lyman said mildly. He had looked uncomfortable ever since they came into the tavern. He took a seat that faced the door.

Edwin shrugged. "Titles are just that. Titles."

"Not if you're king," Lyman said.

"Especially if you're king," Edwin said. He finally took a long draft of his ale.

Lucas changed the subject. "Adelaide is everything you could want in a wife. Good breeding, good looks, good—"

"You're sounding like Markus now, Luke," Artemis said with a joking leer. Lucas barked a laugh.

"But she is!" he insisted. "She's a good woman. And she was close to the queen." He smirked at John. "She'll need a big, broad shoulder to cry on, Johnny."

John felt his cheeks flush deeper. He'd hoped they wouldn't talk about Adelaide. Now all he could feel was her body pressed gently against his, her lips…

"What is all this business with Elanor of the Roses?" Artemis wondered aloud.

"Have you been living in a bush, Art?" Lucas asked.

"King Tanor's been living in hers, it seems," Artemis said quietly. Edwin shot him a fiery look, then took control of the conversation.

"It's been an oft-talked-of bit of gossip in the court as of late," he said, steepling his fingers in front of him. "All kings have their dalliances. And with his queen in confinement…unfortunately, the truth led the queen to destroy herself."

Edwin spoke so matter-of-factly of the tragic event, as though he were recounting a story that occurred hundreds of years ago, written in the annals of the ancient kings.

"Did Markus' body make it back to his village?" Artemis asked, wiping ale froth from his thick, black beard.

Lucas nodded. He wiped the sweat from his brow, then shouldered off his cloak. The room was warm, for certain—the barkeep had lit every hearth to stave off the chill of the Harvestmonth night.

"His body was delivered to his family," Lucas said. "Apparently, his betrothed had already married another man before Markus returned home. Never wrote to tell him. I suppose he was spared the grief of that."

John remembered how he found Markus, with the inside of him on the outside. He had chased after one of the serving girls for stealing from him—but John imagined Markus wanted something else from her, too. Perhaps it was also better that his once-betrothed never knew about his Northern trysts.

Lyman remained quiet, sipping his ale, but John noticed his face had gone white, and his eyes had stopped traveling around the room. They were trained on something in front of him. John followed his gaze. A patron sitting by the door stared at them with a scowl, draining the rest of his cup as he did so. John turned back to Lyman when he caught the man's eye.

"He's been staring for a bit," Lyman said quietly. He sounded terrified. War had awakened a fear in him—not one that caused him to cower in terror, but one that caused him to monitor everything at once.

"He's just drunk," Lucas shrugged. "Speaking of, let's get another."

Edwin looked thunderously across the table at him. "No. We go to the Five Oxen. Have a drink there if you'd like, after we've hunted out our pretender prince."

"Their ale tastes like piss," Artemis said. "At least it did ten years ago."

"Perhaps it's under new management," Lucas said with a flourish. He threw a few argents on the table and polished off his tankard. He was about to stand, but he stopped. His face took on the same look as Lyman's had.

John turned. The man, young and overweight, had stood up from his table and was lumbering toward them. He was unintimidating—a pasty member of the gentry wearing cheap velvet and shoes that wouldn't survive a day in the Northern snows—but he stepped toward them with half-drunk bluster. He scowled at them, his pale blond eyebrows making a naked crease on his pig-like face.

"*You,*" he snarled. "The green men." He pointed a fat finger at Lucas.

Lucas looked down and realized his mistake. His green tunic was on full display now.

"The intimidators," continued the man. "Did you come back from the war just to be the king's puppets? I thought you fought for *us.*"

"*We* fought, yes," Lucas said, staying calm. His deep voice rumbled with accusation. "Where were you? Fighting alongside us?"

"I became a man the day my father went to fight," said the man. John realized just how young he was. Maybe not much older than Markus. "People still bought and sold during the war. I kept his ledgers."

Artemis chortled. "A merchant," he said. "How brave."

"Braver than you lot, squeezing money out of us to shove into the king's weasel pockets," said the man. "Heard one of you got killed in Barnswood a few days back. Good riddance." He spat on the wood floor. The globule glistened in the firelight.

Lyman's hands tightened around his tankard. "You watch your mouth, *boy.*" John felt the ire rising in his own chest, too.

"My father gave his life," the man continued, "and I know he would've rather died than become the king's cronies, taking money from his fellow man." He peered at all of them, one by one, through his beady eyes. They landed on John.

"And *you,*" he sneered. "The king's own bastard! I suppose you'd have nothing better to do since you'll never wear the crown."

The man was drawing the attention of other patrons in the tavern. He noticed and raised his voice and address them.

"You might have seen these men a few days ago in the village," he said. "They want us to fear them. But this is all they are. Mere men, drinking in a tavern."

John remembered the day they rode out, and how Markus had accosted the man selling bread. This man must have been there that day—or at the least heard about it. Edwin's expression was steely as he looked up at the man. He chewed on the inside of his cheek, maybe out of annoyance, maybe out of anger.

"They're merely washed out soldiers, whoremongers," said the man, and he looked directly at John, "and king's bastards."

John rose out of his chair. He immediately saw the man's gumption turn into fear. He was no physical match for John, and he knew it. John enjoyed seeing the bravery melt away from men's eyes—it showed him when a man was truly a coward. And this man truly was.

He grabbed the man's shoulder without hesitation. It was soft, no muscle underneath his flesh. He lived the comfortable life of a merchant. He'd never seen a man die in front of him. He'd never been responsible for another life beyond his own.

It took everything within John's body not to squeeze the man's neck, and keep squeezing. The urge to kill him was like a bubble floating on the surface of water, ready to burst.

"Would you like to say that again?" John asked. The man seemed to have lost his words. He was working his mouth strangely, like a babe suckling at his mother's teat.

Then he spat on John. John grabbed his neck and squeezed. And kept squeezing. A red haze fell over his eyes as he stared down at the man, watching his skin turn red, his eyes bulge.

A hand landed on his shoulder and a strong voice said, "John. Stop."

Edwin's voice brought John back from the brink of rage. He let go of the man, who sunk to the ground at John's feet, sputtering. John breathed, focusing on the feeling of Edwin's hand on his shoulder.

"We need to go to the Five Oxen. Now." Edwin said firmly. "Leave this man to his drink and his poor, sorry life."

John turned away from the man with a little reluctance. Almost as though he were worried the man would spit on him when he wasn't looking. But he turned away all the same.

Until he heard a chortle from behind him. "Does he carry your sausage and potatoes in his pocket for you?" asked the man, still laying prone.

John rounded on him, but Edwin stopped him again. "To the Five Oxen," he repeated. "Now."

Blood still boiling, John joined the rest of the men as they shouldered their way through the crowd that had gathered around them. John felt another hand squeeze his shoulder—a gentler one. He turned and saw Lyman, who gave him a reassuring nod. A spark of color was returning to the older man's cheeks, but his eyes were still wide and alert.

A light drizzle hit their faces as they stepped outside. They all wrapped their cloaks around them again, even more aware of the color of their tunics now. The street was brightly lit against the gloom of the autumn night.

John knew as soon as they entered the poor quarter of the neighborhood. The street turned from cobblestone to mud. The lights dimmed. But the merriment was no quieter. In fact, it may have been more raucous. The peasants were free of their work for the day, and their pockets were full of pennies to spend on the night's drink.

The men found the Five Oxen in a disheveled alley next to a tannery along the canal, the fetid smell of drying leather filling the close air around it. A small, low-slung building, men crowded at the door, and through the windows, John could see the throng packed together inside. As they came closer, the unwashed smell of the men hit them like a damp wave in the drizzly night.

"Cover your tunics," Edwin said, looking pointedly at Lucas. "Hoods up."

The windows weren't paned, and the shutters were open to allow air into the stuffy room. Edwin led them toward the windows, following several other men who couldn't fit into the tiny building.

"Smells like a cow's ass out here," Lyman grumbled. "Johnny, do you think you could get us inside?"

"It won't smell any better in there," Lucas said.

John sighed and started plowing through the crowd. Most people were smaller than him, so he found that if he walked with purpose, people would move. He pushed past the men gathered at the door, and was immediately hit with the heat of so many bodies packed into the tavern. It smelled of bad ale and body odor, only a little better than the alleyway.

Men sat on tables and on the floor. They tucked themselves into the corners of the hearth and along the walls. There wasn't a place in the taproom that wasn't occupied by a body. Even John had difficulty navigating through the crowd without jostling someone and calling attention to the green men. The barkeep did the same, stumbling around the mess of arms and legs with a tray full of tankards. John didn't see Antony anywhere, but some men wore hoods over their faces. This was the kind of meeting not everyone wanted to be seen at.

John and the men found a corner of the taproom less occupied and crunched themselves into the small space.

"What's supposed to happen?" Artemis asked in a low voice.

Lucas shrugged. "It's a lot of talk, from what I understand," he said. "It's a lot like the court. Everyone has a lot to say, but nothing gets done."

Somehow, John had a feeling this meeting of the Men of the Lion would be different. This wasn't a room full of tacit men. There was an energy in the taproom as though lightning were about to strike. An evening at the tavern was supposed to be rowdy. But the men here, despite their number, spoke to one another in hushed tones and murmurs. The beer wasn't loosening their tongues.

Then, a man entered the taproom, and everyone's attention seemed to shift to him. He entered disheveled and damp from the autumn night, but he didn't look or seem important. He was tall and spindly, like a long-legged bird. Yellow, lank hair hung over eyes that bulged out of a small head. The first thing he did was glance around the room, an almost fearful look in his eye. His gaze landed on a man with one hip cocked against the hearth, muscular arms crossed over a powerful chest. The thin man crossed to him and spoke to him hurriedly. They both looked around the room now—as though they were looking for someone. The strong man's green eyes flickered in the firelight when they caught John staring. John quickly looked away.

The thin man turned to the taproom.

"Welcome, all," he said. His voice was hardly audible above the rumble of the room, but still everyone quieted. "We gather here because we have all been cheated by the crown. A crown that sits on the head of a pretender."

The crowd rumbled. It seemed to John that he opened every meeting this way as a sort of ritualistic reminder.

"And we've seen his Green Men in the town just this week for the Harvestmonth Tax," the man continued. "My coffers are much lighter this evening, gents. What the war didn't take, the king took anyway."

John hid his face deeper in the cowl of his cloak. He noticed the other men do the same.

"Anyone else at the Commoner's Ball?" A red-haired man stood up. "The King threw a lavish party for his court while the true commoners got bread and brown in the wet courtyard! And they still charged a halfpenny to enter." He wiped ale froth from his beard.

"We had no business fighting in the war for as long as we did," another man said. "What good did it do fighting the sick king and his bitch queen in the North?"

"His grace said the North would invade the moment we retreated," said a younger man defensively. "Until the old Northern king died and his queen surrendered the borderlands."

"Did the borderlands bring King Alfred back?" yelled a voice. "King Tanor threw a party for his court. What King does that after a costly war?"

"Perhaps to bring..." The man stammered, his eyes searching the air for an answer. "To bring good cheer? To brighten spirits?"

The room rumbled angrily. The red-haired man brayed out a laugh.

"Good cheer?" he sneered. "You think that was about good cheer, Seth? What good did it do us? Did it put a fat goose on my ma's table, or prevent my sister from selling her maidenhead on the Pleasure Road? A dinner party thrown by the King isn't going to bring me good cheer for shit."

"Saint Odette carried away his child and his wife not long after," said another voice. "There's a curse on his house."

"And Saint Aethel gave him a whore," said the red-haired man. "I pray the babe curdles in her belly."

John felt a strange sense of rage to hear them talk of Claudia and the child. *It's my father, not them, you ignorant beasts.*

"Malcolm is right," said the broad-shouldered man. "Tanor's done naught to bring 'good cheer' to us. He barely shows his face to us."

"His bastard was in Barnswood a few days back," someone blurted out, somehow thinking it would contribute to the conversation. The entire room turned to him. "He's one of the Green Men." John pulled his cowl even further over his face.

"His bastard kid?" the man called Malcolm asked. "Was *there*? What the hell was he doing there?"

"Punishing us for being good people," said the Barnswood man. "Spilling blood on our streets and raping our girls."

"At least one of them got their comeuppance," said an older man in the corner. John's blood boiled. He searched the room incessantly for anyone who looked remotely like Antony.

"And what are we to do about it, Nathan?" someone asked the thin man. "We come here to talk, and our numbers have grown, and we've avoided capture. But they are hot on our heels now with these Green Men. And all we do is sit here and complain about how bad it's been and how bad it is. What are we to do?"

Nathan's watery eyes shone in the dim light. "I have an answer for you tonight." His voice broke. "Lads, we've kept to ourselves for years. We've done as we've been told. We mourned King Alfred and his prince. We sent our sons, or even ourselves, to fight. We questioned what the king told us was true, but we didn't cause a stir. Because we wanted to be sure. But lads, we *are* sure."

The room grew quieter than it had been before.

"A pretender truly sits on the throne," Nathan continued. "It's no longer a whisper spoken among us, or a hope we hold in our hearts. The lost prince is still alive. I have it on good authority from a trusted contact who calls himself The Woodsman that Prince Adrian the First, flower of the realm, son of his majesty King Alfred the fifth and his wife Queen Catherine of Riversate, is alive. The King lives. Long live the King."

The room was unnaturally quiet. Shadows danced across Nathan's proud face in the firelight.

It wasn't possible, John reminded himself. Adrian had fallen a long way. The blow to his head had been severe.

I only killed the other boy because I couldn't find his body, he thought. If he wasn't able to find the body, then who else could have?

Unless the body got up and walked away, a smaller, more haunting voice said.

Edwin frantically whispered something to Lucas, and Lucas shuffled out of the room.

"Is it true?" asked the red-haired man.

"And how can we know for certain?" asked the strong man by the hearth. He was no longer leaning on it. He stood straight and tall, as though he were in the presence of a king. John wondered if he had ever been a soldier.

Nathan pursed his lips. "He is in Southborn, but he is not here at the Five Oxen."

"Dammit," Edwin said under his breath. "Damn all of it."

"I trust my friend The Woodsman with my life. He is an old friend of Malcolm's." Nathan gestured to the red-haired man. "The prince is alive. A prince no longer—the *king* is alive. King Adrian."

The answer filled John with a strange sort of rage. *No, he's not,* he thought. *Because he's dead. Adrian is dead, and I killed him. I killed him.*

Lucas had returned. John heard the commotion outside. And only then did he understand what he was part of. A raid.

They burst into the tavern, barreling over anyone who was in their way. Men from the city watch, a dozen of them or more. They blocked the entryway. No one was getting away.

"Make sure he doesn't escape," Edwin said, casting a look at Nathan. The room descended into chaos around them. John understood exactly what he meant. And he followed the order.

The men in the taproom had all stood up when the city watch entered. Some tried to flee by jumping out the windows. John knew there would be other watchmen outside for that purpose. Others charged for him, now that his cloak was pushed back from his tunic. He pushed them back easily, and those that he didn't were seized by the watchmen.

Nathan had seen him, and the fear in his eyes had grown. He was trying to stumble away in the mess of overturned chairs and tables and men. But

John barreled through to him without hesitation and seized him before he could go any further. He saw that fear again—the fear of a man whose gumption has been stripped away.

John hit him, and Nathan went toppling back onto the floor, landing hard on his elbows. In the fracas of the taproom, John descended on him and hit him again. He hit him, and kept hitting. He hit him until he couldn't see for the red haze over his vision. He hit Nathan until a pair of hands pulled him away.

"Saints' teeth, Johnny," said Artemis. "He has to stand trial."

Nathan's face was a bloody pulp, and he was no longer conscious. The light had left his eyes and he would remember no more.

Ellena

A day and a night passed with no sighting of Antony back at their camp. Ellena was surprised to find that her heart sank. The life that she and her Pa lived was a lonely one.

And he'd reminded her so much of him. Of *Antony*. It was uncanny, she realized. If her Antony had grown up, he would've looked a lot like *this* Antony.

Her thoughts were dark and bitter as she trudged to Barnswood. The day was overcast and cold. Harvestmonth was settling in to stay in Barnswood, threatening a cold winter. Ellena was only twenty. Winter had never been cold in the South, only mild and rainy. A cold winter could mean sickness, even famine. The townspeople seemed to understand this. Granaries were being filled, looms hung with scant cotton for warmer garments. The Harvestmonth tax had been paid, leaving the villagers wanting. Looking around, Ellena thought they all looked more drawn and world-weary. Ellena didn't want to take from them. *We're all just as poor as the other these days,* she thought as she snuck through the market bundled in her cloak.

And apart from that, there was a strange pall about the market. Maybe it was because of Markus, or the oncoming weather. Or both.

But then, Ellena saw another reason when the king's men rode into town. She had just pilfered a bit of bread when she saw their tall horses in the street. Their well-tailored cloaks stood out among the roughspun of the villagers. They looked to be the same men who collected the Harvestmonth Tax, only now without the pinch-nosed collectors and their wagon.

Ellena ducked behind a broad-shouldered man as the horsemen made

287

their rounds in the market. They seemed to be asking a question—the same one over and over again. Ellena strained to hear in the low din of the street, cowering behind the tall man that lingered near the wool merchant's stall, talking to the woman who manned it. She recognized the woman—it was Sally, one of the prettiest girls in Southborn, which wasn't saying much.

The man was talking too loudly and gruffly for Ellena to hear the men.

"Listen, Sally," he was saying, "I'd have bought you a ring if not for the Harvestmonth Tax—"

The woman, just as loudly, cut him off. "Rob the Red bought a ring for Marie with naught but two half-pennies, and they're to be wed before Hornmonth."

"Two half-pennies is just a penny," grumbled the man.

"What?"

"I said two half-pennies is one penny," he said. "You don't have to say two half-pennies. And Marie is getting fat. She'll have a red-headed babe not long after Hornmonth. Or perhaps another color. Rob's in a hurry so Marie's pa doesn't tan his hide."

"How dare you," said the woman. "After what your brother did, you can't blame anyone for anything, Carter."

Ellena flinched. *Carter.* She could only see the back of the man's head, but realized it *was* him. His younger brother Benjamin stood next to him—Benjamin, who had been in smallclothes the last time she'd seen him. Antony's brothers. The Antony *she'd* known. A strange pang hit her, a reminder of summer days spent playing in the forest without a care in the world.

The woman raised her voice, calling to the soldiers in the street. "Over here, boys! It's the killer's brother! He knows where the whelp is!"

Ellena shot a glare at Sally. So did Carter, evidently, based on the raise brow Sally gave him. Ben grimaced up at both of them, especially when Carter yanked his arm and pulled him away from the stall. When Carter fled through the crowd, Ellena followed.

The horsemen had heard Sally and seen him—he was tall enough to stand out. But Ellena followed undetected, even as Carter and Ben broke out into a run. The crowd parted behind her as the horsemen charged through.

Carter had led Ellena and the horsemen to the bowyer's house—her Uncle Bron's house. All saints, it had been years since she'd seen him.

"Not very smart, are you?" Ellena asked as she approached.

Carter was panting from the run, but Ellena had barely broken a sweat. He whirled around and looked incredulously down at her. His eyes widened. "I know you, don't I?"

"I'm your cousin, you idiot. Where's Antony? Do you know?"

"He could be suckling Saint Aethel's teat for all I know."

The horsemen trotted up behind them, led by a man with gray in his hair. He regarded them calmly. "You're the pretender's brother, are you?"

"I don't know what you're talking about," said Carter. "I don't know what a *pretender* is."

The man scoffed. "Do you know where he's gone after he killed one of our own?"

Carter's blunt face looked even more confused. "I don't."

The man narrowed his eyes. "I think you do, son," he said. "A man doesn't just disappear."

"I'm telling you I don't—"

Carter was getting red in the face when Bron stepped out of the cottage, wiping his hands on his trousers. Uncle Bron. He still had the same kind face and earnest eyes, the same powerful frame. He regarded the soldiers calmly.

The graying man swung his attention to Bron. "Bronwell Bowyer, I presume?" he asked.

"The same," Bron said. Ellena saw deep worry lines on his face, perhaps from the events of the last few days, perhaps from the last several years. "What can I help you with?"

"We are wondering where the traitor and pretender Antony Bronson has run off to," said the man. "Your son, I understand."

"He's not here," Bron replied simply.

"Where is he, then?"

Bron shrugged as though it were the most casual conversation in the world. Ellena thought she could see his hands trembling as he wiped them. "Not here," he said.

"Are you sure?" The horsemen behind the man were beginning to move, all three of them. They were different men from the ones who came to collect taxes. Except for the graying man. Ellena recognized him—Edwin was his name. He might have recognized her. She hid behind Carter as best as she could.

"We suspect you of lying to the crown and hiding a pretender, man," said Edwin. "We would like to know if you are guilty of this crime."

"He's not," shouted Carter. Ellena grabbed his arm and squeezed. He gave her an incredulous look. "Well, he's not!"

"I think he can speak for himself," Edwin said, "Where is your son?"

Bron hadn't moved. The incident was drawing a crowd. Villagers passing by had stopped to watch and listen, murmuring to themselves. Bron gave them a wary look with his keen brown eyes, then turned back to Edwin.

"You know as much as I do, my lord," he said.

Edwin chewed on the inside of his cheek, as if thinking. Then, he said, "Bronwell Bowyer, you are under arrest for harboring and aiding a pretender, murderer, and traitor to the crown. We will take you to Southborn to stand trial."

"*No!*" Carter yelled. "*Pa!*"

Ben made a break for their father, but Ellena grabbed him. He was easier to handle than Carter.

"Don't make it worse, Carter." Ellena was surprised her voice stopped the big man. The veins and tendons on his neck stood out like cords of rope.

Edwin nodded to his soldiers. They dismounted and began walking toward the house. One of them held a lantern. The other two grabbed Bron by either arm, holding him fast although he didn't resist. A strange thought passed through Ellena's mind. *He looks so much like my Pa. But Pa would've fought back.*

"Burn it," said Edwin.

The soldier threw the lamp onto the thatched roof of Bron's home. The glass shattered, the oil soaked into the straw, and the flame licked it hungrily. It wasn't long before the flames roared across the dry roof, consuming everything they could touch.

"You need to get out of here," Ellena said to Carter under the crackling of the fire.

"But my Pa," Carter said. "He can't just go with them—"

"Your Pa wants you alive," Ellena said. "Come with me."

Carter took a longing look at the house as flames continued to envelop its roof, its sturdy frame. Ellena saw him and Bron exchange a look that would've broken her heart had she not been in a hurry. Then, Carter grabbed Ben and followed Ellena into an alleyway.

Ellena stopped and caught her breath. They were well enough away from the main road now, away from any prying eyes. They weren't far away from where Antony had killed Markus, she realized. She looked down at Ben. She remembered Ben and Carter's mother—he looked so much like her.

"Those men get what they want. One way or another," she said. "It's better if he goes willingly."

"They didn't have to burn his damn house down," Carter muttered. "His pa built that house, for Aug's sake."

"They're after you, too," Ellena said. "You should come with me."

"Why should I?"

"Your brother trusted me."

"And now he's on the run, apparently."

Ellena rolled her eyes. "Is stupidity a family trait? You can't go back unless you want to meet the saints. Now come on."

"Where are you taking us?"

"Do you remember Uncle Herne?"

Antony

The incident at the Five Oxen shook the whole of Southborn. Even in the monks' dormitories in the Cathedral of the Nine, Antony could hear occasional commotion outside. He'd spent the night there after talking to Adelaide, and David had come and told him about the incident. It would be safer, he said, if Antony didn't leave until things settled down.

Only now Antony was going stir-crazy. The dormitory he was in didn't have windows. After sleeping and waking up, he had no semblance of what time it was. The room itself was bare of anything other than basic furniture—a small bed and a table with a washing basin. He tried to busy himself by staring at the silver ring he now wore on his finger, trying to make it magically conjure up more memories for him.

The way Adelaide had spoken to him the day before was strange. It felt as though she knew something he didn't. When he'd told her the story about his teeth, she'd said something strange—*the truth spoken is the truth known.* What *was* the truth?

He looked over at the bow and quiver of arrows he'd taken from Ellena. He wanted to go somewhere and shoot, fire off one arrow after another, feel the tension and release across his shoulders. Shooting was when his mind was clearest, when it was just him in a quiet forest or field.

"It's like taking a breath," his father had told him once. He thought harder and realized Bron hadn't been the one to teach him that. It was someone else.

The dappled side of a fat doe. A confident, warm hand on his shoulder. The golden light of Harvestmonth disappearing with the sun—

Antony blinked, and the image disappeared. That was where he'd shot his first deer. But it hadn't been Bron with him. It had been someone else.

He heard footsteps in the hall and willed them to stop at his door. To his surprise, they did. The door rasping against the flagstones sounded sharply in the small, quiet room. David ducked in, holding a tray of bread, a pitcher, and two cups.

"Good morning, brother," David said with a smile. "I'm sorry we don't have anything...nicer for a repast, but this bread is fresh-baked by Millon, and his hands are blessed by Saint Juniper himself."

David acted with a strange reverence around Antony—as he placed the tray down on the table, he cut the bread and poured Antony a glass of water, presenting them to him with something like a bow.

"What's it like out there?" Antony asked, then realized he'd been rude. "And—and good morning to you." He wished the water was ale.

"Not...good," said David. He squeezed his big hands together in front of him. "Almost all the men from the Five Oxen were arrested last night, specifically Nathan, who has been one of my contacts with the Men of the Lion for a long time." A shadow of fear crossed David's bright face before the jovial mask returned. "Of course, it's making people unhappy that people in the town were arrested without notice. Nathan was also beaten very badly."

Antony took a sip of water. "I wonder who did *that*," he mumbled. His black eye was still turning yellow and healing around his cheekbone from when John had punched him mercilessly.

"I'm sorry?"

"Nothing."

Antony moved over on the bed for David to sit. David poured himself some water and sat beside him. Antony saw the tin cup tremble in his hands.

"Are you all right?" Antony asked. He took a bite of bread. It was still warm. Millon was indeed blessed, he thought.

"Of—of course," David said. The tremor was in his voice now. Then, his whole bulk seemed to sag. "Many of those men are my friends. Getting arrested by the crown never bodes well."

His words sent a chill into Antony's core. "I never had a family," David continued. "The brothers have been my family, but...as you might tell, we put the Saints before each other. We're a brotherhood that serves the Great Maker, not our fellow brothers. The Men of the Lion...they're different. I can't tell you how many times they've protected me, helped me. I was just a child when King Alfred died. The other brothers didn't believe the stories, but..." David lowered his eyes as if in shame. "Perhaps it shows a weakness in my faith, that I looked so intently for hope here on earth.

"I know I'm supposed to live a life of peace as a brother, but..." David's hand squeezed around his tin cup, veins popping from his flesh. "I would fight to the death for my brothers. My *true* brothers."

Antony didn't know what to say. He forgot how young David was—just a few years older than Benjamin, really, and risking his life for a better future.

"But how do you know it's worth it?" Antony asked. "You've based everything you believe in on...on hearsay." He couldn't believe he said it, but it was true.

David's cheeks reddened, his brow furrowed. "It's more than hearsay, dammit." He turned even redder, realizing he cursed. "It's more than hearsay. One of our leaders was *there*. Herne Woodsman *saw* what happened that night."

Antony's blood nearly went cold. The man in the forest with the suspecting coal-black eyes. Herne had *been* there. Why hadn't he said something? Why hadn't Ellena said something?

But Ellena *had* said something, he realized. She was with Antony—the real Antony—that night in the forest. She'd watched him die. How did she feel to have a different man pretend to be Antony? If anyone could be mad at him for being a pretender, it was her.

"And I believe him," David said. He looked earnestly at Antony. "If anyone is to be believed, it's Herne."

Antony shook his head. Nothing was clear. He only knew one thing for certain—Bron had lied, and the real Antony had died.

"I just don't know," he said.

David seemed to become exasperated. "By Aug's beard—" he said, then reddened again at the curse. "With all due respect, how do you *not* know? How do you *not* believe? The ring in your possession, the fact that you were found in the forest the same night the prince went missing—how do you not *know?*"

"I know I should believe it," Antony said, "but I just…don't. I can't. It seems too…"

"Impossible."

"Yes. Impossible."

Before either of them could speak again, they both heard footsteps flying outside. The door burst open, and a small figure appeared, closing the door quickly behind her. Ellena. David stood up abruptly.

"Ell, how the hell did you get in here?" he said.

She raised an eyebrow at him. "How the hell did you get permission to curse in here?" she asked.

Antony rolled his eyes. "What is it?"

She was panting, and her cheeks were stained red with cold. Her red hair was strewn around her pale face. "You're not gonna like it," she said.

"Just tell me."

"Your Pa's been arrested."

Bron. Not his pa. It pained Antony that that was his first thought.

"He's going to stand trial here in Southborn," Ellena continued. "He's been accused of harboring a pretender and a murderer."

Bron may have known that Antony was not his trueborn son, but he couldn't be blamed for *hiding* Antony. Well, he could be, Antony supposed, if the crown really wanted to. But Antony had done enough to hurt Bron already. He had not been a good son, trueborn or no.

"I need to go to the palace," Antony said.

Ellena looked confused. "Y'know they'll kill you on sight, right?" she said.

"That may be," Antony said, "but if it keeps them from killing P—from killing Bron, I'll do it."

"All you Bronson boys," Ellena muttered, "as stupid as they come."

"Are you sure that's a good idea?" asked David.

"No," Antony said honestly, "but it's the only one I've got."

Silence hung in the small room. Ellena scanned the walls, avoiding Antony's face, as though trying to come up with any other solution.

"If you're going to the palace, there's something you should know," Ellena said finally, something like resignation in her voice.

"What?"

"My pa is the one who found you in the woods that night. He was out searching for me, and Bron was searching for...for Antony. My pa is your pa's brother. Bron's brother, I mean. My pa has known exactly who you are from the start. So has Bron. And he's helped Bron keep you safe."

Antony thought all of his shock had been used up when he'd overheard Bron's revelation. But he was wrong. Something deep and heavy dropped in the pit of his stomach. *From the start.* Something like anger rose right alongside it. *Why didn't they tell* me? *Why did Bron have to lie to me for so long?*

"You *are* the prince, Antony," said Ellena, clearly and confidently. "You are."

The words rang in the room. The truth was spoken. But Antony still didn't believe it. He'd been told so many lies already—how could this be any different?

"If you say so," Antony said. He gave both of them one last look, then walked out of the dormitory.

Tanor

T anor finished the dregs of wine at the bottom of his cup and filled it again. Wine had begun to have less of an effect on him, he drank it so often. He prayed for it to dull his senses and ease his mind as he gazed down at the mountain of parchment on his desk. Godfrey hunched over the desk at his side, scribbling on even more parchment in his small, neat script.

First, there were edicts to be sent out to each lordship in Southborn—dissent would no longer be tolerated. Any talk against the king was punishable. If the offense was minor, a public lashing would suffice. If it amounted to an act of treason, the lord had permission to sentence the person to death without permission from the king. The signet ring on Tanor's finger was warm from pressing his seal into so many beads of wax.

Then, there was what to do with the Men of the Lion currently rotting away in his prison. Edwin and his men had captured fifteen of them. Their talk in the Five Oxen had been just that—talk, though they talked of something that Tanor had not yet heard. That they had *found* Prince Adrian. *Found,* even though John had killed him.

Was that treason enough to kill fifteen men? Tanor wanted to. He wanted to down to his core. Not only because it was treasonous, but because it was outrageously stupid what simple men were willing to believe.

"Your grace," Godfrey said feebly, "perhaps now is not the time to mention it, but Lady Elanor has been asking persistently about a wedding date."

Tanor couldn't staunch the groan that sounded in his throat. He pressed his fingers to the bridge of his nose. Elanor. His beautiful headache. He'd not meant to get her pregnant, and she had promised him she had been tracking her monthly bleeding to prevent it. He smiled grimly. It would be just like her to do the opposite. Tanor knew her father well, and if Elanor had one ounce of the man's ambition, then she was more ambitious than half the members of his court.

"There will be no wedding, as you know, Godfrey," Tanor said, pressing his ring into another dab of wax.

"Yes, your grace," Godfrey said. "Then what shall I tell Lady Elanor?"

"Nothing," Tanor said. "Yet. We don't want to cause undue stress on the baby. We know all too well what that can do." He looked knowingly at Godfrey.

The doors of his solar were thrown open unceremoniously, and Tanor felt ire rise in his throat. He washed it down with wine. Edwin entered, followed by John and two sentries, who held a man between them. The man held his head high, though his clothes were tattered and his face bore bruises that were still healing. The man was thrown to his knees in front of Tanor's desk. Tanor saw the man flinch when his knees hit the stone.

Tanor scrutinized the man's face. He knew him. It was that Bronson boy. The archer. The murderer.

"Your grace," Edwin said. "The pretender has turned himself in."

The pretender. Tanor rose from his chair and stepped around the desk. Antony wasn't looking at him—he looked levelly at the ground, his lips still twisted in pain from being thrown to the floor.

Bronwell Bowyer had been brought in the day before. Tanor had interacted with the man only a few times—a simple, honest man. Too honest of a man, in fact. Tanor didn't trust men who were too honest, too vulnerable. Bron was a weak man. He had let everything in his life be decided for him. He'd probably never taken anything by force, by sheer will. Bron had been complicit when the soldiers brought him in—he didn't resist. He didn't fight back. Tanor had been disappointed.

"Antony Bronson," Tanor said. He stood in front of the man. Antony still hung his head.

"You have my father, your grace," he said. "I want you to let him go."

Tanor chuckled. "*Want* me? I can't let him go. The law doesn't permit it. Not until he has stood trial." He tried to peer into the man's face, but Antony's head remained lowered.

"He came here under his own volition, your grace," said Edwin, "and I have formally arrested him for the charges of murder and treason against the crown."

Antony looked up at these words, straight up at Tanor, a look of defiance in his eyes. Tanor wondered how he hadn't seen it that day in the inner ward. Perhaps he'd only needed to see Bron again, see the simplicity of the man's features to know—definitively—that this man was *not* his son. Perhaps they had the same brown hair and brown eyes, but that was where the resemblance stopped.

No, this man looked too much like another man that Tanor had known long ago—what now seemed like a lifetime ago. The man's face had faded a bit from Tanor's memory, but it became dazzlingly clear when he looked at Antony. The stern dark eyes, the sharp nose, even the way his mouth was set in that firm, hard line. He was every inch Alfred's son.

Antony grimaced at him, as though Tanor's fear and wonder were showing. He tried to cast the emotion off his face. It cast itself off when anger boiled deep within him.

Alfred's son is kneeling before me, he thought. He glanced over at John. *Which means someone didn't do his damn job.*

"Who do you think you are, boy?" Tanor asked.

"I don't know," Antony replied.

Tanor sighed. Mercifully, whatever had truly happened, the boy lost his memory. Tanor cocked his head, considering him. He twisted the signet ring on his left hand, then deftly moved it to his right. Antony was going to stand trial in front of dozens of courtiers—courtiers who had known his father well. They couldn't see what Tanor had seen.

He punched down at Antony, hitting him squarely in the face. Antony toppled back in shock as Tanor wrung out his hand.

"Very good, Lord Edwin," said Tanor. "Bring him to the dungeon. He can share a cell with his...father."

Edwin bowed neatly at the waist and led the guards out of the room, Antony now slumped between them. John turned to follow.

"Sir John," Tanor said. His voice rang sharply in the room. He saw John's shoulders flinch. "A word."

John turned slowly around, not meeting Tanor's gaze. Tanor motioned for Godfrey to leave. The little man collected his papers and shuffled quickly toward the door. A long silence hung in the air after he left.

"Who is that man?" Tanor asked. He watched John closely. Tanor could always tell when John was lying when he was a child. He would always look quickly away, his blue eyes wide with fear. John seemed collected now, calm, his hands folded in front of him.

"Antony Bronson," John replied, finally meeting his gaze. Tanor could've spat. Malicious compliance was something he could never tolerate.

"I'll ask it another way," Tanor said. "What *actually* happened on that night? The night you...*supposedly* killed the prince?"

John was silent. Tanor thought he saw his face go a shade paler. He stalked a few steps toward his bastard, barely containing his rage.

"John. What happened?"

John looked away.

"What happened?"

Tanor instantly went for John's throat. His blood was still up after hitting Antony. He could've easily squeezed the life out of John, and the bastard didn't fight back. He only gripped Tanor's forearms, trying to force him off, but nothing was going to stop Tanor from breaking him. John sputtered, blood flooding his face.

"What happened, you fucking bastard?" Tanor hissed. His hands urged him to keep squeezing, but instead he let John go and pushed him to the floor. His bastard fell to his knees, coughing and wheezing. Tanor fought the urge to kick him while he was down.

John looked up at him, his eyes bloodshot. Fear. That was what Tanor had wanted to see. After all these years, his bastard still feared him. It was better that way. John took a gulp of air and struggled to speak.

"I hit the prince over the head with a rock," he said, words spilling out of him like blood from a wound. "He fell into the Skeldergate River. By the time I reached the river, I...I couldn't find his body. But there was no way he could have survived that fall."

"It seems he might have," murmured Tanor.

"It's not possible," John said again before fighting a fit of coughing.

"Are you that stupid?" Tanor asked. "Do you not see it?"

John shook his head. "It can't be," he wheezed.

"If it wasn't Adrian's body you brought to me, whose was it?"

John pulled himself to his knees. Tanor could see his hands shaking.

"There was another boy in the forest that night," he said quietly. "A runaway. Of an age with Adrian. I...I killed him instead. Cut off his head with my training sword, threw it in the river. Stripped him of his clothes. That's who I brought to you."

Tanor worked his jaw ferociously. "You should thank your saint's star that Antony doesn't remember," he said. "And you should thank me, too. Because I should kill you, but I won't." He scoffed. "I don't know what's harder to believe—that I trusted you, or that you managed to make a mess of the one task I trusted you to do."

John stood feebly to his feet. "I was only thirteen," he rasped. "And you told me to *kill* someone."

"I'm sure you understand now how easy killing is," Tanor said. He stepped toward his son, inclining his head to meet John's eye. "I'm not going to kill you because you're still useful to me. Both Antony and Bron are to stand trial. They cannot be found innocent of their crimes. And we are going to make certain of that."

Antony

For a moment, he thought he was in the cave again. His head rested against cool, wet stone, and he was propped on a swept dirt floor. But it wasn't right. Even from behind his eyelids, he knew it was too dark. It smelled damp and vaguely of excrement. A cool cloth was held against his face, which he slowly became aware of. One eye was hard to open, and pain throbbed down one side of his head with any slight movement. His lips felt like a piece of raw meat.

The cool cloth stroked his cheek and made Antony flinch. He regretted flinching. A horrible pall of pain shuddered through his head.

"I'd advise you to be still," said a low, calm voice. "I will give you something for the pain before they take you up."

Take you up. Antony didn't know what that meant. But in his state, he couldn't very well understand anything. He tried to remember what had happened. He had been in town, in Southborn. What had he done there? He'd dodged through the crowds, face concealed, to a church. *The* church. The Cathedral of the Nine, where he'd first met David. And David had been there. So had Adelaide.

He had turned himself in. For his father's sake. For Bron's sake. His cheek pounded with pain at the memory. The guards had given him another swift beating after he'd been presented to the king. *The king.* He'd stood before the king. The king had hit him, too.

The pain caused his eyes to flicker open. His left eye opened only a crack. His face felt huge, swollen, misshapen. Close to his face was that of a middle-aged woman, her hair pulled tightly back on her head, her

302

mouth a hard line as she dabbed his wounds.

"Are you awake?" she asked. Her expression hardly changed. She didn't take her eyes off her work. He grunted an affirmative.

"Can you see me clearly? Or is your sight warped?" Antony shook his head once, lolling against the wall behind him. "Good. Perhaps there is no damage to the brain. Can you speak?"

A slurred, monstrous word came out of Antony's mouth. "Yes," said a thick voice that could've been his. His mouth felt dry, full, bloody.

"Good," said the woman. "But don't speak. You need to save your strength for the trial."

His expression must have changed. Because this time, she looked at him. Did Antony know her? She was old enough to be his mother, with fine lines all around her face, but enshrined in a stern beauty. She studied him.

"You are Antony Bronson, no?" she asked. "They say you are the one who murdered Sir Markus Huston. Not only that, but you claim to be royalty. That is a crime in and of itself."

"I'm..." Antony began. It hurt too much to speak.

The woman shushed him. "Save your words for when you need them," she said. "You needn't explain yourself to me. I am neither your judge nor your executioner. I'm only here to make sure your wounds don't kill you before they can." She sat back on her haunches and looked at him for a long time. Antony thought he saw tears in her eyes. "But you do look quite a lot like him, I must say."

She stared at him for a moment, then brushed the thought away. "You could have fooled me." She reached into a knapsack at her side and took out a small jar. "This will lessen the pain without dulling your senses. Open your mouth." She opened the jar and poured liquid down his throat. It tasted like earth and grass and dying leaves.

After she left, he closed his eyes against the dark. His head throbbed. He was in the palace prison, then, awaiting trial. For murdering a man who had tried to violate a woman, and for pretending to be someone...someone he'd never pretended to be. Someone he didn't realize he was until his father—

"How are you feeling, boy?"

The warm voice in the darkness made Antony's eyes snap open. In the corner of the small room was a shadow, barely visible in the scant light from the barred window above them. It must have been barely dawn. The voice filled Antony with a strange irritation.

He didn't answer Bron's question. "Why did you turn yourself in?" Antony asked.

Bron shuffled closer to him until the faint light illuminated the deep lines of his face. They had beaten him, Antony realized. Bron, a man who would never raise a hand to hurt anyone. They'd beaten him. The bruise under Bron's eye made Antony sick.

"I could ask the same of you," Bron replied, a wry smile on his lips.

"Because what they're saying about me isn't true," Antony said. "I'm not *pretending* to be anyone."

"And what about the boy you killed?"

"He was going to hurt someone. Someone who didn't deserve it."

Bron was quiet for a moment. He shuffled closer until he could lean against the same wall as Antony. How strange, Antony thought, that this man suddenly felt like a complete stranger to him.

"I heard you," Antony said. "I heard you the night Sir John came to the house. What you said about me."

He didn't look at Bron. He knew he would find pain in the man's eyes. Antony felt a burning anger in his throat as he thought about Bron weeping that night—feeling sorry for himself.

"Do you know what it's like to hear your Pa say that he's *not* your Pa?" Antony asked. It was difficult to speak. "That he's been pretending this whole time? That every memory you have is a lie?"

He was surprised when hot tears stung his face. Bron watched him sadly. The older man put a hand on Antony's knee.

"I find myself without excuse," he said, his voice dry. "I have taught each of you to be good men, to tell the truth, to show respect. But here I am, a liar who hasn't been worthy of your respect. And for that, I can only beg for your forgiveness…your grace."

Your grace. Those words didn't belong to him. They certainly didn't belong in Bron's mouth. The way Bron looked at him now, with strange reverence, the same way David had...

"Don't call me that," Antony said. The strength of his voice surprised him. Bron shied away, taking his hand away as though he'd been burned.

"But that's what you are," Bron said. "If I'm to have any excuse, it's because you were in danger when I found you in the forest that night. My brother risked his very reputation to keep you out of danger. He *killed* for you. Now it seems I'm risking mine. And it's worth the cost."

Hearing Bron say it made the truth all the more horrifying. Bron *wasn't* his father. The man who should have been trustworthy, who should have been the person he could lean on—*wasn't.* He didn't want it to be true. He didn't want any of it to be true.

The cell door opened and two guards shuffled in. They hoisted Antony to his feet before he could say another word. Though his pain was dulled from the poultice, Antony felt as though his brain was being rattled around in his skull.

Then, the guards threw a sack over his head.

As Antony was pushed forward, tripping on his own feet, flickers of light filtered between the fibers of the cloth. Sounds passed him, barely audible above his shuffling footsteps. The sack had obviously been used for other purposes—it stank, and with every breath Antony got a mouthful of it.

The trial. That's what the woman had called it. In Barnswood, the lord of their village or his deputy would hear grievances all the time—petty things like theft of a mule or a fight at the tavern. Punishment was rarely any more severe than an afternoon in the stocks or a small fine.

But Antony wasn't in Barnswood. And he had the feeling someone more important than a lord would try him.

A door pushed open in front of him, and a blast of cool air met him as it did. He had the feeling of being in a much larger room now—*much* larger. He heard a low murmur of voices around him, but they echoed cavernously off of walls he couldn't see. He heard their words, spoken in whispers, as he was pushed past them.

"...Murderer."

"...Killed him in cold blood on the streets. No reason at all."

"He pretends to be the lost prince."

"A monster. A madman, if ever there was one."

The guards on either side of him halted and pushed him to his knees. They pulled the sack off Antony's head and his eyes flooded with terrible light.

As the pain subsided, he saw where he was—the throne room of the palace in Southborn. The *palace.* A cold fear shuddered through him. His hands weren't bound, and he was barefoot. He wore what he was wearing when he killed Markus, he realized. He had not been home since then. *Home.* No such thing anymore. He stood as tall as he could with his bare feet and aching head.

He was as good as naked, standing in front of the king and his court. He stared up at the king, like a mite beholding a god.

The guards had put Antony on a raised, roughshod dais before the king. The lord of Barnswood used a similar one when he held court, as Antony could recall. But the king sat higher still on his own dais of stone, in the ancient throne that stretched toward the vaulted ceilings of the throne room.

Antony had sat on that throne before. And he'd been beaten for it..

Afternoon light filled the hall and cast beams across the marbled floor. King Tanor looked fit for a tapestry, wearing a richly-embroidered red tunic and cloth-of-gold mantle lined with ermine that cascaded down the chair like water awash in sunlight. Beside him on a smaller chair sat the red-haired woman he'd seen at the Commoner's Ball. Her green gown complemented the king's. She wore no crown, only her luxurious red hair tumbling around her shoulders.

Antony felt the eyes of the court on him, but did not look around him. It would hurt his head to do so anyway. He spared himself the pain.

King Tanor spoke, and the murmurs in the hall quieted.

"Esteemed members of the court," he began, "I do not often call you forth for so lofty a task. Not since the murder of King Alfred has High

306

Court been called. But today we are called to a great purpose. To judge—and judge fairly—the guilt of a man accused not only of murder but of impersonation of a member of the royal family."

The court behind Antony gasped. It felt to him as though the stone walls themselves had done so too, the sound was so complete.

"Young man," King Tanor now addressed him. "State your name clearly for the court to hear."

"Antony Bronson." His voice felt thick and muffled. Speaking made his jaw ache.

"And what crimes do you stand here accused of?" Tanor asked.

Despite what the woman had said about the poultice, Antony's head still felt muddled and heavy. All he wanted to do was lie down.

"I don't know," he said.

"I think you do, young man," Tanor said coldly.

Antony paused. "Murder and impersonation."

"Impersonation of whom?"

A nauseated feeling filled Antony's stomach. "Prince Adrian."

The court reacted even louder, almost in outrage. Tanor merely nodded, pursing his lips. The woman beside him watched impassively, almost completely disinterested.

"Impersonating a prince," Tanor said. He sounded less like a king and more like a father chastising a child. "More than that, a dead prince. I believe I speak for the entire court when I say *how dare you*, boy. You desecrate the name of an entire royal line. You bring shame to Saint Odette and the tears shed in the name of the lost prince—whose body lies in the Crypt of Kings beside his father."

Antony stared blankly up at him. His pain was too great. The King's words meant almost nothing to him.

"Now, I am willing to believe that perhaps you were fooled yourself. Fooled by the lies whispered by the Men of the Lion. Their lies are dangerous. They, too, will be tried justly for the lies they have told. However, we must first determine who you are, Antony Bronson, and how you came to believe you were the lost prince."

The King tilted his head slightly. "I must admit you at least bear a slight resemblance to King Alfred. Rather, you would under different circumstances. It seems…someone has made the task of properly identifying you a bit difficult."

Antony swore Tanor smirked a little. *You did this to me,* Antony thought.

"Well, young man," Tanor said, "consider this the beginning of your trial by oath." He looked beyond Antony at the court. "If any person of reputable nature has evidence supporting or discrediting the claim that this man is the dead Prince Adrian, please approach the Court of the King's Bench."

To Antony's surprise, the man who first approached the bench was the lord of Barnswood, a man he only saw in passing in the village. He looked red-faced and sweaty, the color of his face clashing with his straw-yellow hair. He gave Antony a sideways glance as he bowed to the King.

He held a parchment in his hand. "Your majesty," he said. "A copy of Barnswood's birth records from Hornmonth of the year 387 After-Conquest."

He presented the parchment to King Tanor. "It was copied and sealed by my own record keeper yesterday upon your request."

Tanor scrutinized the parchment. "Lord Barthow, could you please indicate on this document the name Antony Bronson?"

Lord Barthow pointed to a place in the middle of the page.

"And Lord Edwin Darkshire, can you confirm that the name Antony Bronson is written there?"

Antony hadn't noticed the small, lean figure of Lord Edwin until then, standing near Sir John on the far side of the dais. He strode to the King's side and glanced at the place where Lord Barthow pointed.

"I can confirm it, your majesty," he said clearly. "Antony Bronson, born on the 10th day of Hornmonth to Bronwell Bowyer and his wife, Maella."

"And this document, Your Majesty." Barthow produced another parchment. "This is the Barnswood census of Harvestmonth in the year 393 After-Conquest."

Tanor examined the page longer than the first. Then his eyes brightened suddenly, and he smiled. "Ah, yes, here," he said. "Lord Barthow, we men of a certain age must take care of our eyes. Tell your record keeper to write bigger next time."

The court chuckled before the King returned to business. "Lord Edwin, can you confirm this?"

Edwin leaned studiously toward the document. "In the year 393 Post-Conquest, Bronwell Bowyer reported having two sons by his wife Maella, Carter Bronson, then aged nine and Antony Bronson then aged seven."

That was the son he had, Antony thought. *The son he loved.*

"That's not right," he found himself saying. "That's not me."

The court rumbled. Edwin stifled what seemed like a laugh.

"When is your birthday, young man?" he asked.

Antony realized whenever Bron had given him a small celebration, it had always been the tenth of Hornmonth, in the dreary first few days of spring. When he didn't answer, Edwin said, "So I thought. We have it in plain writing here that you were born to your father and mother twenty-three years ago. And while Prince Adrian was born the same year, he was born on the twenty-first of Rainmonth, more than a month later. I was in his majesty King Alfred's employ at the time. I remember it well. The young prince was very late in time."

He stepped down from the dais toward Antony, hands folded neatly behind his back. His presence took command of the room immediately.

"Do you have a person of repute who can substantiate your claim that this is—how did you say it?—not right?"

King Tanor smirked. Despite his exhaustion, Antony was infuriated.

"I wasn't aware I could have one," he said.

Edwin chewed on the inside of his cheek. "You must understand, young man," he said, "your claim, to us, sounds quite ridiculous. We all know and understand Prince Adrian to be dead. His body lies in the Crypt of Kings. So for a young man, unknown to this court, to come to Southborn claiming to be a prince who is very obviously dead, it's, well—it's absurd. It is an immense courtesy that his majesty is even hearing you."

"I never claimed to be anything," Antony said. "This is just what people are saying. It's what they believe."

"'Just what people are saying?'" Edwin had an uncanny ability of making him feel like a fool. "People like Nathan, perhaps? Sir John, fetch Master Nathan, won't you?"

John disappeared behind a door near the dais. When he returned, he dragged a tall, thin man behind him. He threw the man at Edwin's feet. The man—Nathan's—face was a mess of swelling and blood. The skin was so engorged around his eyes, Antony wondered how he could see. Black, dry blood matted the man's pale hair to his forehead.

"Master Nathan, tell us where you were two nights ago," Edwin paced around Nathan, taking him gently by the shoulder and lifting him to his knees.

Nathan swallowed. Antony saw the movement in his long, crane-like neck. *They've threatened him somehow*, he thought. *He's in danger because of me. Someone he's never even met.*

"At the Five Oxen. At a meeting of the Men of the Lion." he said between swollen lips.

"And was this man there?" Edwin pointed to Antony.

Nathan looked up at Antony as best as he could. In the stranger's face, Antony saw deep pain, almost horror.

"Yes, sir." He paused and swallowed again. "He had a silver ring. A real silver ring. With King Alfred's lion sigil."

Antony searched his fingers for the ring. It was still there, heavy on the middle finger of his right hand.

"And what did he say to you?"

"He said he was the lost prince."

It was a lie. Antony's stomach dropped. He was angry, but not at this poor man. He had put himself, perhaps his family, in danger, and Tanor was using him.

"Can you show us your hand, young man?"

Antony knew what he meant. Slowly, he lifted his right hand, palm facing inward.

"Lift it higher so the court can see, young man."

The silver ring shone in the dull light.

The court murmured. Edwin looked pointedly at Antony. "So when you say it's what people believe, young man, do you really mean it's what *you* believe?"

Antony's heart pounded in his chest as he dropped his hand, the ring suddenly feeling heavier. "I don't—I never—"

Nathan looked desperately at Antony. Antony almost thought he saw the man whisper *please.*

"I don't know what I believe," was all he could say.

Edwin furrowed his brow. "How can you not know what you believe? Every man has his beliefs and knows what they are. A man should know who he is. How do you not know who you are?"

Nathan was looking at him through swollen eyes. Antony thought he saw his puffy lips mouth *I'm sorry.*

"My memory was taken from me when I was a child," Antony said.

Edwin cocked his head. "Taken from you? How can your memories be simply taken from you? You are a young man. I doubt age has affected your recognition."

Antony drew in a shuddering breath. "When I was a boy, I fell from a tree. When I fell, I struck my head on a rock. My—my father said when I woke up, I didn't know who I was or who he was."

"I've never heard of such a thing," Edwin said. He turned to King Tanor. "Have you, your majesty?"

Tanor shook his head. "I have not."

"Little boys fall from trees every day," Edwin said. "They may break an arm, or a leg, but certainly not their memories. Who here can confirm this young man fell from a tree as a boy?" Edwin extended his arms and looked around the room, then back at Antony. "You see? When we were little boys, all of us fell from trees and all manner of high places. And all of us remember doing so."

"Then perhaps he didn't fall from a tree."

It was Nathan who spoke, to everyone's surprise. Edwin flicked his head down to him, like a snake finding its prey.

311

"You will speak when spoken to, peasant," Edwin said. Antony saw a dangerous glint of anger in his eye.

Nathan rose, slowly, weakly. He was of a height with Sir John—he towered over Edwin.

"It seems you just spoke to me," he said. "Perhaps it was a fall of another kind. Or an attempt was made on his life."

"You're insinuating someone wanted to kill a peasant boy?" Edwin scoffed.

"No, I'm insinuating someone wanted to kill a prince. And when it didn't work, they had to take other measures."

Edwin's eyes glared dangerously at Nathan, willing him to stop talking, but Nathan's courage had grown. He strained through his words despite the pain.

"Saint Augustus uses many molds to cast the forms of men," he said. "Have you read your *The Saints and All Their Wonders*? Do you remember the story of Dominik and Danael? Two men as different as can be, born of different sires, but looking entirely alike. Dominik, the lowly fuller's son, was found to be a far nobler man than Danael, the River-Prince. So Danael's courtiers murdered him and replaced him with the noble Dominik, and no one was the wiser."

Nathan's head swung meaningfully to King Tanor, who was now looking disapprovingly at Edwin. Edwin's eyebrows came down like storm clouds.

"Yes, of course I have read my *The Saints and All Their Wonders*," Edwin spat. "And the Rock Monks took many liberties in their translations, creating stories out of poetry and song. But this court will have no talk of treason, Master Nathan," he said. "I have no further questions for you, besides. Take him away, Sir John."

John took him through the door they came. Edwin turned back to Antony.

"Memory, no memory, belief, no belief," Edwin said. "Your majesty, I move we adjourn for the day and give Antony Bronson some time to remember. It seems that this trial has come as such a shock to him he can't remember anything."

"I approve the motion," King Tanor said. "We will adjourn until tomorrow."

The bag went over Antony's head again, and the surrounding room became mere patterns of light through the burlap. The guards pushed him back through the palace until he was dumped back into his cell. The burlap sack came off. The barred door slammed shut. Antony was alone—he'd been placed in a different cell from Bron this time.

He wondered if he was going to die. He wondered if he deserved this after killing Markus. He wondered if he'd ever be able to convince the court he knew almost nothing about himself.

He lay there in the damp hole of a cell, his head throbbing. There was a small window just above head height. It was too narrow for a man to crawl through, and barred besides. The light from the window was thin and fading quickly. A cold, harsh wind blew through and whipped around the small room. Time passed. The light faded into complete darkness. Night fell.

Somewhere in the darkness, keys jangled and footsteps stopped at his door. In the dim torchlight from the hall, Antony made out two forms, one tall, one short. John and Edwin. Antony scurried into a sitting position.

"No need to trouble yourself, young man," Edwin said, but his voice wasn't warm. "We merely came to see if you remember anything yet."

Antony stood, realizing he'd been standing all day. His knees ached and his legs nearly collapsed under him.

"I'm not lying when I tell you I remember nothing," he said. "Memories come and go."

"You see, those are two very different things," Edwin's voice purred in the dark. "You have a brilliant way of making absolutely no sense, young man. You remember nothing, yet sometimes you remember *some* things. If you remember some things, what do you remember?"

"I don't know."

He heard footsteps approaching him. "Fetch a torch, Sir John," Edwin said. John took a torch from its sconce in the hall, closing the door behind him. "I'd like to see this young man's face. Perhaps he needs a bit of encouragement to remember what he doesn't know."

Edwin and John's faces floated in front of him, shadows dancing with every flicker of the flame. Antony imagined he looked the same to them.

"Give me the torch, Sir John," Edwin said coolly. John handed him the torch. "Now, young man, who are you?"

"I don't know."

"You have to decide. Are you the lost prince, as you told Nathan? Are you not, as you told us?"

The heat of the flame grew closer to Antony's face. Antony's eyes flicked to John, staring blankly down at him.

"Sir Markus was going to rape that girl," Antony said, a kind of appeal to the knight.

"Sir Markus was going to mete out justice that needed to be given."

"And I meted out justice for Markus."

"Sir John, hit this young man."

John did. On the same side of Antony's face as the rest of his wounds. Antony's thoughts shattered into a million shards of pain as he tumbled to the ground.

John hauled him to his knees. Antony coughed a spray of blood onto the floor. That afternoon, the pain had weakened him. Now, it was simply making him angrier.

He remembered the small boy standing in front of him, rock in hand. *I hate you,* the boy had said. Antony looked up, meeting John's eye.

"I remember you from well before the Commoner's Ball, even before we met in the tavern," Antony said. "You hated me. You still hate me. Why would you hate someone you barely know?"

"Shut up," John growled.

Antony kept talking. "You're the reason for all of this. You were supposed to kill me." Antony rose unsteadily to his feet, seeing what he thought was fear on John's face as shadows danced across it. "I'm the greatest mistake of your life. Why aren't *you* on trial, *Sir John?*"

"Shut up!" John hit him again, a blow that made Antony see a flash of light behind his eyes. The pain was unbearable. But he didn't stumble this time.

Antony spat out more blood that filled his mouth. "You want me to decide who I am?" he said, looking levelly at Edwin. "Whoever I am, I'm your enemy. And you won't get rid of me easily."

Edwin laughed as though he'd just heard a jape. "Really?" he said. He stepped in close to Antony and hissed into his year. "You do not know what we can do to you. To your family. To the people you love."

"I have no family," Antony whispered back.

"Don't you?" Edwin asked. "Not even good Bronwell Bowyer, the man who so lovingly raised you and your brothers, even as a widower? He is going to speak on your behalf tomorrow."

Antony's whole body felt as though it were sinking to the floor. *Pa.*

"We just wanted to pay a friendly visit before the trial continues," Edwin said. "And remind you that your words and deeds have consequences. Not just for you, but for the ones you care about."

John opened the cell door, and Edwin stepped out briefly. He came back in, holding something long in his hand—with something larger stuck to the end of it. He propped it in the corner across from Antony.

"You must be lonely in here," Edwin said, "so I've brought you a cellmate."

He held the torch up to the object. It was Nathan's head on a spike, his mouth open and grotesque, the tip of the spear jutting out of his skull.

Antony backed into the corner and stumbled back.

"Your words and deeds have consequences," Edwin said again. Then they both left.

Antony remained cowered in the corner for a long time, even after a jailer brought him a meager supper of moldy bread and cheese. He took a few bites, but the food immediately turned his stomach. All he had was a bucket, and he emptied himself several times before the night was through. He hardly slept. He could barely see the shadow of Nathan's head, but he felt its eyes on him.

"I'm sorry," Antony would whisper occasionally. A cold wind blew in through the window and whirled around the room, doing nothing to quell the putrid stench. A cold rain followed soon after and dripped through the bars.

Antony lay there in pain, in agony, until sleep finally took him.

Ellena

Herne sipped warm stock from a bowl across the fire from Ellena. He had been quiet ever since she'd come back to the camp with Carter and Ben. Carter had been amazed to see Herne. Then, he had done nothing but complain since they arrived, and continued to even after Herne shared the clutch of rabbits he'd hunted that day with them.

"I can call off the wedding to Sally, I suppose," he was saying. "She won't have me now. Gave me quite the tongue-lashing this afternoon."

"It's a shame," was all Herne said. "She's a good girl."

Carter scoffed at that. Beside him, Benjamin had remained quiet. Ellena had wrapped him in a fur against the chill, the poor skinny boy. Ellena remembered her aunt Maella. She thought Ben looked the most like her.

"They burned down our house. Why?" Ben asked to no one in particular. He'd been too young when Herne had to flee Barnswood—he barely remembered his uncle.

Ellena put an arm around him. "Men do stupid things when they are afraid."

Ben stood up. "We should go back," he said. "If we just explain what's actually happening—

Herne laughed sadly. "You are your father's son," he said. "I'm afraid there's no going back now. You're with us now."

"I knew Antony shouldn't have gone to pay tax," Carter said. "It should've been Pa. Antony was bound to do something stupid."

Herne stared into the fire, nodding slightly. Ellena saw lines of pain on

317

his face. The pain of a father.

"Now Pa's in this mess, too," Carter grumbled.

"Oh, Bron. There was so much I should have told him," Herne said. He put down his bowl of broth, hardly sipped. He pulled a piece of grass from the ground and played with it between his fingers. He looked wistful. His thoughts were anywhere but there, at the camp.

"Why did you leave Barnswood, uncle?" Carter asked.

Herne leaned back on his haunches. He looked meaningfully across the fire at Carter. "I think you know why," he said.

"But you just—disappeared," Carter said. "You didn't say anything to any of us."

"Because one of the king's men almost found out the truth," Herne said. "One of King Tanor's men, not King Alfred's." He squeezed the blade of grass with sudden vigor. "He was on his way to Bron's house when I found him. I made sure he was never heard from again."

"You killed him?" Ben asked quietly.

Herne said nothing. He offered the ghost of a nod.

Carter scowled. "It's *his* damn fault," he said. He threw a stick into the fire. "For all of this. I don't know why Pa bothered with him in the first place. No matter *who* he is—who he *was*—he's not that person now. He's just a man."

Silence enveloped the camp. A stiff wind blew around the fire.

"It'll be a cold one tonight," Herne grunted. "The weather's finally turning. Harvestmonth will be over before we know it. Woodmonth will be with us soon, and all of its chill. I've plenty of spare pelts to go around. They don't smell too fine, though."

Ellena met Herne's eyes across the fire. They were large and black and glowed in the heat of the flame.

"Are we going to do anything to help them, Da?" she asked. "David said they're standing trial again tomorrow."

"My brother knows how to look after himself," Herne said, "and I think we all know that Antony does, too."

Carter rolled his eyes. "Why do we keep calling him that?" he said. "We know that's not his name."

It wasn't, Ellena knew. She remembered the boy she used to play with. The boy with brown hair and brown eyes and a plain face. The one who ran away from home every other week. The one who was stabbed by a boy his own age. She'd watched as the boy had taken up a dull sword that was too heavy for him and start hacking, like a butcher with a piece of meat...her eyes stung. Her Antony. Her friend.

Herne closed his eyes for a long time—pressed them tight, willing them shut. When he opened them, their corners glistened with tears.

"Da, we can't just do *nothing*," Ellena said, her throat surprisingly full. "They'll kill him."

"It's too dangerous," Herne replied simply. "Antony and Bron will be all right. Now, we should get some rest."

Ellena ground her teeth. The life they lived was dangerous. They faced death every day—from the elements, from their fellow man. Herne had worked hard to keep them safe for years. But the time for safety was over.

I'll do something, then, she thought. *I couldn't help my Antony, but I can help this one.*

Antony

He turned feebly toward the door at the sound of footsteps. Antony did not know what time it was, only that he was cold, and it was still dark. His face felt a little better, even after being hit by John again. It felt less like raw meat and more like tanned leather—taut and rough. He'd stayed turned away from Nathan all night, but the smell was becoming too putrid to ignore.

The door opened. Antony wondered if it was the medicine woman again. A shape slid through the door, holding things in its hands. It turned behind itself and took the torch from the sconce, the same torch John had taken, now burning lower. It must have been morning.

Antony couldn't have been more surprised. The face that was illuminated was Adelaide's.

"I can't stay long," she said. "I shouldn't be here to begin with. But I convinced the guard I needed to pay penance to Saint Hogarth and provide for the needy. And you are *very* needy."

She dropped something on the floor. A bucket. "Water. As warm as I could get it. The front row of the court complained of how much you smelled yesterday."

"Were—were you there?" Antony asked her groggily. He blinked several times to ensure she wasn't a dream.

Adelaide nodded. "I was. And I was horrified," she said. "Lord Edwin is an ass." She dropped something next to the bucket. "I couldn't find any trousers. But I found you a clean shirt. You're still—you're still covered in blood, you know."

She knelt closer to him. "And this." She unwrapped something from a cloth. It was bread—not moldy or dry, but fresh. A delightful smell wafted from the loaf. "You need to eat. Has Magg been in to clean up your face?"

"Yes." Antony said. He realized she hardly looked at him. She busied herself in hastily handed him the bread. Its beautiful smell overcame him, and he tore into it. While he ate, Adelaide looked around. She gasped when she saw the head of Nathan.

"By all the saints—" she breathed. "Did Edwin do that?"

Antony nodded, his mouth full of bread.

"I'm sorry," she said earnestly. "I would move it, but—I can't."

She knelt in silence while he scarfed the bread. She still didn't look at him. He looked up at her, trying to will her to turn toward him.

"Thank you," he said. He stood up, using the wall as a support. His cold limbs unfolded gradually after being frozen in a fetal state all night. Adelaide stood with him, holding her arms out in case he had to steady himself. "For everything."

Adelaide looked at him, her eyes piercing through the dim light of the torch. Her eyes were beautiful and fierce. He didn't want her to stop looking at him.

"What are you going to do?" she asked.

He didn't know. He didn't want to answer her. The sooner he answered her, the sooner she'd leave. She was the only beautiful thing in the room.

"Some people believe one thing about me," he said, "others believe another. Edwin is running in circles around me. My *mind* is running in circles."

Adelaide took a small step toward him.

"Antony," she said, her voice low. "Whatever they say—whatever Edwin says—I believe you."

She paused, and her words nestled deep into Antony's core. She half-chuckled. "I haven't slept at all this night," she said. "After what we talked about in the crypt. After the trial yesterday. You would have to be a madman to have come here if you weren't really—" She stopped. "If it wasn't really you."

Antony's mind hummed with clarity. He didn't stop looking at her. He'd seen so many women, and he'd been with beautiful women. But none of them had been Adelaide. Adelaide with the glowing chestnut hair, with the freckles on her nose. Adelaide with the shining, spirited eyes.

"Did you tell me you're marrying Sir John?" he asked suddenly.

She immediately looked away. "Yes," she said. "Not until Wintermonth, but—"

"What if you waited?" Antony asked. Adelaide furrowed her brow. "What if you waited for me?"

Adelaide searched the ground. She didn't look at him again. *Look at me.* Antony tried to will her eyes toward his. He needed them.

Her lip trembled. "I dreamt I'd marry a prince when I was a little girl," she said. "But dreams aren't anything more than memories we've created for ourselves."

"But what if—"

"My family needs me. I'm doing it for them."

"What about your brother? Can't Landon help?"

The words left his mouth before he could even think of them. Brother. Landon. Memories raced through his head of a boy older than him. Playing together in the courtyard. Chestnut hair, the same color as his sister's.

Adelaide looked bewildered. Antony imagined his face looked the same. Then she sighed.

"No," she said. "Landon can't help." She took another step toward him. "This is how it must be. For now."

He was acutely aware of how close she was to him now. He felt the low heat of the torch on his face. He could see the freckles on her skin. Without thinking, he reached up and pushed a strand of hair out of Adelaide's eyes.

"Dreams don't have to be memories," he said. "Dreams can be...a future. And we both know John will never be a prince."

Adelaide smiled sadly. "This is how it must be," she said again.

"For now."

"For now."

She stepped away from him. "You really do stink," she said. "Wash yourself before the trial today. It begins at nine bells."

"Will you be there?" Antony asked.

"I will," Adelaide said. "Do you know what you're going to do?"

He drank in her eyes for as long as he could. So he could stare into them long after she was gone.

"I do," he said. "I've decided."

Antony scrubbed himself as clean as he could be with the water and lye soap Adelaide had left for him, and put on the clean shirt. When the guards came again to retrieve him, they didn't put the burlap sack over his head, but one of them held it in his hand—in the event of a hanging, Antony presumed. They pushed him through the palace again, and this time Antony saw it all—the steps up from the dungeon. The narrow corridor into the courtyard, the fresh cold air of morning. Past the great hall where the Commoner's Ball had been held. And into the throne room and the Court of the King's Bench.

He saw more splendor than he had the day before as he entered the room. The grand windows cast colorful light across the floor, carpeted down the middle with a deep red rug. Courtiers stood on either side, dressed their best for a trial in crushed velvet and cloth-of-gold and cloaks lined with fur. In the midst of them, Antony saw Adelaide. He knew she didn't dare look at him. She wasn't a dream. There was her long chestnut hair, now fastened behind her head in an elegant braid. There were her flashing eyes, not looking at him, but not looking away either.

At last, Antony approached the king's bench. The king was there as he had been before, with the woman seated beside him and other courtiers like Sir John and Lord Edwin nearby. Antony looked at them each in turn. Edwin looked smug, John looked sullen. Then he met the king's icy stare as Tanor glared impassively down at him.

"You will kneel before your king, boy," said one guard, who pushed Antony to his knees. Antony knelt, but he didn't break his gaze with the king until Tanor stood and addressed the court.

"After an adjournment, we have returned to try this young man, Antony Bronson, for the crimes of murder and impersonation. Any members of the court, or members of the kingdom who are of respectable repute, may approach the bench and confirm or deny the crimes of this young man." Tanor's eyes flicked back down to Antony. "Unless, of course, this young man has had time to…remember what he's forgotten."

Antony rose. "I have, your grace."

Tanor motioned to Lord Edwin. "Lord Edwin will conduct the questioning of the suspected murderer and impersonator."

"With pleasure, your grace," said Lord Edwin. He approached Antony with his hands behind his back, chewing on the inside of his cheek. "I trust, young man, that you've had time to think about the events of yesterday afternoon."

"I have."

Edwin seemed surprised by his ready answer. "Very well," he said. "Yesterday, you were unsure as to who you were and what you believed. Perhaps, with some rest, you have more clarity on this issue?"

"I didn't sleep at all, Lord Edwin," Antony said. "I don't think you slept much either, considering you and Sir John paid me a visit last night."

The crowd rumbled, and Edwin's cheeks briefly flamed red. "I ask that that statement not be recorded," Edwin muttered toward the court scribe. He straightened again. "Now, young man, who are you? Murderer? Impersonator? Simple bowyer's son?"

"Lord Edwin, do you know the story of *Vispilio*, from *The Saints and All Their Wonders*?" Antony asked.

Edwin smirked. "As we concluded yesterday, young man, yes, I have read my saints. Are you insinuating that you are *Vispilio*?"

"It was kind of his majesty the king to allow the mystery play of *Vispilio* to be performed during the Commoner's Ball," Antony continued. "It was as though he admitted even kings can be blind to the troubles of his people. And that his justice is not always just."

Edwin's brow furrowed. "You're not a mummer yourself, young man. Unless you've decided that you are one," he said. "Get to your point."

"I've seen injustice in this land that Tanor does not see," Antony said. "He either refuses to see it, or cannot see it at all. When the Harvestmonth tax was collected in my village, families gave their entire livelihoods to the crown, only to have nothing to live on the next day. My father was ready to send my young brother into servitude to pay our debt to the crown."

"As he should," Edwin said. "He's a good citizen of the crown."

"He's a *slave* to the crown," Antony said. His voice felt strong and resonant in his chest. The words came to his mouth before he could think of them. "We all are. We are paying for a war that never needed to be fought. A war fought for greed and power, not for justice."

"How *dare* you," Edwin seethed. His true anger was rising to the surface. His small frame sharpened. "The king's war protected us from any villainy that the North could have meted upon us."

"The North was innocent," Antony said.

"The North killed our king. And our prince."

"King Tanor killed the king."

The court all but roared. Antony saw Tanor's face become deathly pale, but only for a moment before he gained his composure. Edwin's eyes bulged out of his head.

"Not only are you a murderer and impersonator," he said, "but now you've branded yourself a traitor as well."

"I am no traitor," Antony said. "I'm no impersonator, either. The only accusation I may truly stand on trial for is murder—the murder of Sir Markus Huston. In that moment, I dealt justice as I saw fit, as Sir Markus was about to take the innocence of a young woman. Like *Vispilio*, I saw injustice that the king could not among his own men."

"Who are you to take justice into your own hands?" Edwin asked. "*Vispilio* was thrown from the High Saint's court for such a crime."

"Perhaps the justice of this land is mine to uphold," Antony said. "Because I am Prince Adrian, son of King Alfred and Queen Catherine. I've lived in hiding for ten years, but I won't live in hiding any longer. I've remembered who I am. I denied it yesterday, but I've known it all along."

Antony had to raise his voice against the shouting in the court. Tanor rose from the throne, his mouth hanging open. Edwin was shouting futilely for order. Antony waited, staring levelly at the king, until Edwin finally gained control of the court—and his own composure.

"Young man," he said, his voice dangerously low. "You certainly have a tongue on you, don't you? Where was such a revelation yesterday? Where was your passion?" Edwin turned to the king and half-bowed at the waist. "Your grace, I apologize on behalf of this pretender. The things he has said—the lies—are truly disturbing. They have no place in this court, especially not the Court of the King's Bench."

"No need, Lord Edwin," said Tanor. The color had come back to his face, and he looked strangely placid. He addressed Antony. "Antony Bronson, we've given you the courtesy of a hearing in front of this court, to which you've responded with slander and libel. You've made no attempt to defend yourself, only to offend the entire court. Therefore, in the name of Saint Augustus and all the high saints, the Court of the King's Bench will sentence you to death by beheading."

The court rumbled in approval. Antony tensed. Tanor had this planned from the beginning, he knew. He would never win. *But they heard me*, he thought. *I spoke, and they heard me. They've seen me. And now they're afraid.*

"And of course," Tanor began again. The rumble of the court subsided. "There is still the matter of your father." His eyes adjusted, looking at someone behind Antony.

The rush Antony felt in his head washed away immediately.

He turned and saw Bron approaching the bench, looking so ragged and shabby compared to the splendor around him. Bron was looking directly at him, his brown eyes determined. He shuffled onto the dais beside Antony.

"Pa, what are you doing?" Antony breathed. It felt like all the air had left his lungs.

Bron only gave him a slight nod before kneeling.

"Your grace," he said in a clear, loud voice, "I humbly thank you for hearing me at such a late hour. I have come to speak on behalf of my son, Antony Bronson."

"And you are welcome to, Master Bowyer," said Tanor. "Forgive me, but you should have been called to this court earlier. Your son has made quite a…spectacle of himself."

Bron looked askance at Antony, the ghost of a smile on his face. "This does not surprise me in the least, your grace." He stood. "I was just outside the door a few moments ago when he gave his testimony. And on his behalf, your grace, I apologize."

"Apologize, Master Bowyer?" Tanor asked. "For what?"

"For putting such notions in his head and letting him run wild with them," Bron said.

A whisper rushed through the court. Tanor pursed his lips. "Elaborate, Master Bowyer," he said. "You intrigue me."

Bron looked at Antony for a long time. Antony wasn't sure what the look meant. His father's eyes could be deceptive—brave though he was afraid, calm though he was manic. Before Antony could discern, Bron had turned away again and addressed the king.

"My second son Antony Bronson was born to me and my wife on the tenth of Hornmonth in the year 387 Post-Conquest. My wife died in childbed when Antony was just ten." Bron paused. "He was an angry boy. Angry at me. Angry at the world. He ran away often as a child. If his older brother punched him, he'd run away. If his younger brother kept him awake wailing half the night, he'd run away. I'd go look for him and pray to the saints I'd find him. And somehow I always did.

"One Harvestmonth night, it took me longer to find him than before. When my brother found him, the boy had fallen. He'd hit his head on a rock. By all the saints, I thought he was dead. I picked him up in my arms and brought him home. I'm a praying man, your grace. I prayed all night for my son. And by the grace of the saints, Antony came back to me."

Bron bowed his head for a moment, gaining his composure. The story unfolded in Antony's mind as his father told it. How he woke up bundled in a fur, warm and afraid and confused. Bron's face hovering just above him. *He still lost a son that night*, Antony realized.

"The fall changed my son," Bron said. "He'd run away the night Prince Adrian was killed, on Darkest Day. And in the years that followed, I'd hear whispers in the village of how the prince hadn't actually died. And—saints

327

forgive me—I spoke those whispers to my children. To my Antony." Bron looked at Antony again, his eyes somber. "Your grace, I fear I put a notion into my boy's head that he was someone different. That the boy I found in the forest wasn't the son I lost."

Tanor was nodding slowly, observing Bron as though he were some mummer's spectacle.

"All fathers want their sons to be great, Master Bowyer," the king said. "But if what you say is true, then you are guilty of treason against the crown."

"I am," Bron said, his voice trembling. "And I should have never deceived my son in such a way. It's not something a truly loving father would do. I beseech you, your grace—whatever punishment you have in place for my son, place on me instead. Let my son go free. Let him live his life free of me and free of the stories I've put in his head."

Bron looked at Antony again, and this time there were tears in his eyes. This time, Antony knew what they said. They said *I'm sorry.* They said *I love you.* Antony felt tears burning behind his own eyes.

"You would take on your son's punishment?" Tanor asked. "You swear that your testimony is true?"

"I swear it," Bron said. "I swear it on the lives of my three sons, on my sainted wife's grave, and on the heart of Saint Augustus. What I say is true. My son is not to blame. If I had told him the truth, he would not have acted so rashly with Sir Markus. If I had told him the truth, he would not have come here as a pretender."

"Pa, no—" Antony breathed, but a look from Bron told him to be still.

Tanor straightened on his throne. "Very well," he said. "Bronwell Bowyer, for the crime of treason against the crown of Southborn, you are sentenced to death by beheading."

Antony's knees buckled beneath him. His father stood tall, unwavering. He stood as he had stood in front of King Alfred, with his son by his side. Antony remembered his face, stern and fearless.

"Antony Bronson, while your father has answered for your crimes as a pretender, he has not answered for your crimes as a murderer," Tanor said.

"You will remain in custody until we can rejoin for a trial in the coming week." He rose. "The Court of the King's Bench is thus adjourned. Sir John, please escort Antony Bronson back to his cell."

Antony rushed to his father before John could reach him. He grabbed Bron's shoulders. "Pa, why did you do that?" he hissed, words spitting angrily from his mouth.

Bron was calm. "So you can live long enough for the world to know the truth." He gripped Antony's neck. His hand was trembling but strong. "I've loved you like my own, your grace. I pray I raised you well enough to be a king one day. I did my best. I love you, son."

Bron pulled him into an embrace. Antony held him tight. He realized he'd never hold his father again, never see him. He would be gone. He'd never go back to Barnswood, never go back to bowmaking. His other sons. His livelihood. Hot tears rolled down Antony's face.

"I love you, Pa."

John pulled Antony away as the court adjourned around them. The guards holding Antony seized Bron instead. Antony strained against John's grip, watching his father until he disappeared into a sea of crushed velvet and cloth-of-gold.

"When will they kill him?" Antony asked when they were in the muted corridor outside the throne room.

"Today," John said tersely, pushing him forward.

"Let me stay. Let me watch."

"Stop talking."

John pushed him down the stairs to the dungeon. Antony's head swam. What was once hidden behind frosted glass was now clear, blindingly clear. Painfully clear.

"He was lying," he said desperately. "John, you must know he was lying. He was lying because *I know you.* I know you and I know Adelaide and Adelaide's brother Landon—"

"*Stop talking.*" John said again. He shoved Antony into his cell, now familiar to him. The rank stench. The damp. It didn't matter now. He would stay, and his father would die, and it was his fault.

It was all his fault.

John

John volunteered to behead Bronwell Bowyer.

He could have spat in his father's face if it weren't treason to do so. After what had happened two nights before—after the truth that John would've taken to his grave had been revealed—he needed to. He saw the look on his father's face. Tanor had seen weakness in him. John had let his father hurt him again. His neck still ached from where Tanor had nearly throttled him. He wore a high-collared tunic to hide the bruises that were still healing. He had let fear get the better of him.

That wouldn't happen again.

Only a small crowd had gathered when it was erected that evening—a brilliantly bright and beautiful autumn day. Bron was resigned, and John barely felt as though he had to guide him through the courtyard to the scaffold. John had led innocents to their death before—the boys, the deserters in the North, had not been deserving of death. They had all bucked under John's grip, trying to run again. If he'd let go of Bron's shoulder, he was certain the man would continue walking that way. Nothing in him fought back. Nothing in him resisted.

I wonder if I will greet death that way when it meets me, John thought. *Softly. Like a friend.*

Tanor said Bron would be beheaded with a sword, not an axe. "It seems fitting, don't you think?" he had said. When John had protested, Tanor had hissed in his ear, "You can either pass the sentence with this sword or spend the rest of your life trying to move one of these pillars in the throne room. You will do what I say. So choose which one is an easier task for

331

you."

Moving an unmovable stone seemed far easier.

"Why are you trembling?" Bron asked him. The question surprised John. As he walked slightly behind the older man, he saw Bron's keen brown eyes flick back at him under thick brows. "You are only doing your duty."

"I am," John said. His voice wasn't coming easily. "But I'm sorry that I have to."

"You have nothing to be sorry for," Bron said.

If only you knew, John replied without words.

They arrived at the scaffold, where Edwin and the others waited. Edwin gave John a knowing look. He presented the sword to John, a simple, heavy longsword, probably pulled from the armory. John's stomach turned.

Godfrey read Bron's sentence from the parapet, which seemed miles away from John and Bron and the scaffold. A cold wind whipped through the beautiful sky. A harbinger of winter, of frost, even of snow. Of dead and dying things.

The last of Bron's sentence was read. Bron knelt and placed his neck on the block in front of him, then turned his head once to look at John. John almost thought the man nodded to him before resting his neck on the block, as easily as if he were nestling into a pillow.

John swung, hoping one blow would be merciful and quick.

But it's not easy cutting a man's head off with a sword. He knew that. And so did Tanor.

The first swing sent a fountain of blood heavenward, splashing warmly onto John's green tunic. The small crowd gasped. Bron choked, but the urgency in his eyes showed John he was still alive. John swung again. The sword went deeper, but still Bron breathed and blinked and suffered.

The sword was too dull.

John turned to look at this father. Tanor watched him with bright, gleeful eyes, willing the smirk to stay off his face. John bit his lip so hard it nearly bled.

He hacked at Bron's neck. From the corner of his eye, he saw onlookers turn away. Some of them retched. Still, Bron breathed and blinked and suffered. John stared at the man's eyes, praying for the light in them to go out.

John labored for what felt like an eternity, dancing with this poor man on the brink of death. To his surprise, John stifled a sob. Somewhere, he knew Adelaide was watching, too. Her husband-to-be, the monster.

He knew, he thought, willing himself not to look at Tanor. *One day, I'll tear him limb from limb.*

Finally, the sword's blade struck wood, and Bron's head fell to the basket in front of the block. From his hands to his elbows, John was streaked with the blood of an innocent man. He felt the warm droplets on his face, tasted it on his lips. He dropped the sword. His forearms were sore. He rushed from the scaffold and didn't stop until he was alone in the barracks, where he sobbed into his bloody hands.

Adelaide

The next day was the twelfth day of Harvestmonth, and Adelaide awoke with a heavy feeling in her chest.

She felt that way on that day every year. Though others had lost sight of that day, she had not. She and her family honored that day every year for the last ten years. This was her first year honoring it in Southborn.

She didn't call any servants in. She dressed herself as she looked out at the gray, overcast day. She found a dress of Queen Claudia's that was black and trimmed with lace. She always wore black on the twelfth of Harvestmonth.

The twelfth was Darkest Day, the day that King Alfred's family died.

Adelaide walked out into the cold morning alone, her cloak billowing around her, her face shrouded in mourning, the heaviness in her heart deeper than ever. Deeper because she felt she couldn't help Antony. Deeper because she felt alone. Deeper because she had watched Bron Bowyer die by the hand of her betrothed the day before, and she had been powerless to stop it. And she would still have to marry Sir John and clasp his bloody hands in hers.

She walked by herself through the quiet streets toward the Cathedral of the Nine. Many people knew what Darkest Day was, but only treated the day as a passing thought, maybe a brief prayer. A prayer for a betrayed king and his son. Laid to rest on the same day. A cruel twist of fate that left more questions than answers.

She lit two candles in the church. She knelt in front of the carved figure of Saint Odette, the saint of the dead. The legend was that after the High Saint Augustus created men, his creation grew tired and weary, not filled with the same vigor as he and his siblings were. Saint Odette was the one who took these men in her arms as they grew weary of living and gave them rest, closing their eyes and enveloping them in the earth.

Normally, Adelaide lit these candles for King Alfred and Prince Adrian, for their souls as they sought that rest. But the candles she lit that morning were for King Alfred and Bron Bowyer, two men who had died protecting a son they loved. And that morning, she prayed fervently for two people who had become one—Prince Adrian and Antony Bronson. The prince who was lost on Darkest Day, then found again.

She prayed she could help him. She prayed she would not be helpless. And she prayed for the end of the reign of King Tanor.

Adelaide reluctantly returned to the palace in the early afternoon. She kept her head down as she shuffled through the courtyard. She swore she could still smell the tang of blood. Bron's death had been so horrific she'd had a nightmare about it—only instead of Bron being cruelly murdered by John, it was Antony in his stead.

Her impending marriage lay heavy on her thoughts. When she had talked to Antony in his prison cell he'd mentioned it. It had sounded like a death sentence in Adelaide's ears. John had murdered two innocent people—Bron's trueborn son and Bron himself. She knew Antony might even be dead before her wedding. And that was a thought she couldn't bear.

She was so wrapped in her own thoughts that she ran straight into a small figure, sending the other person toppling. Adelaide stumbled back, looking down, her heart racing. The figure was a brother of the Nine—a very small brother, who desperately clung to the cowl of their robe as they fell. But Adelaide saw it before it could be hidden—a tendril of long, red hair spilling out from under the hood.

Adelaide offered her hand and a small, feminine one took it. "I don't recall the brotherhood ever allowing women into their ranks," she murmured as the small girl stood up.

335

The girl met her gaze from under the hood, fear glowing in her eyes. "You wouldn't happen to be Lady Adelaide, would you?" asked the girl cautiously. "Brother David told me about you."

"I am," Adelaide said. David's name brought a little comfort to her heart. She was not alone in her desperation. "Do you need my help?"

"Well, I didn't bind up my tits and put this stuffy robe on for nothing," said the girl. "We will not let Adrian die. I'm going to get him out of there and somewhere safe. His family is safe. Well, his brothers are."

Adrian. This woman was truly on Adelaide's side. There was hope after all.

"Tell me how I can help," Adelaide said.

Antony

A drian saw it. The dappled side of a fat doe. Each breath he took seemed thunderous in his ears amidst the silence of the Harvestmonth forest.

"Focus on your target," said the voice beside him. The voice not of Bron, but of Alfred. "Only draw when you're ready. It's like taking a breath."

Adrian drew, took a breath, and fired. The arrow arched gracefully through the chill and embedded itself with a smack just above her front legs. The animal seized and darted across the clearing, but then slowed down almost immediately as her heart pumped its life's blood out of the wound. She collapsed heavily into the underbrush, a river of red blood running down her front leg. She twitched futilely for a few moments, then expired.

Alfred laughed and slapped his son on the back. "Well done, my boy." Adrian felt his chest swell with pride. The youngest of the hunting party at thirteen, and he had shot the only kill that day. The king turned and called over his shoulder. "We've got one!"

The memories seemed cruel now, taunting. They would wake him up when he was close to sleep, arriving with stunning clarity and disappearing just as quickly. It wasn't Bron beside him in the memory anymore. Bron hadn't been there.

"My father said that wolves come out in the Hemlock after dark. Or even worse—outlaws."

"Don't be so scared, John," Adrian said. "I could shoot an outlaw from a mile away."

The other boy rolled his eyes. "Just because you shot one deer doesn't make you the champion of the hunt, Adrian."

Adrian lifted his chin. He was a year younger than John, but he prided himself on being a few inches taller than the other boy. John had always been spare and slim and timid.

"And how many have you shot, John?" Adrian asked. John stared back at him blankly. "That's what I thought."

He should have seen it that day. He should have seen how nervous John looked. How Lord Tanor seemed more watchful than ever. How Lord Edwin seemed to be everywhere that day, a great longbow slung over his back. John had been right—wolves did come out at night. But the wolves had been among them.

"Fa—" Adrian couldn't speak. His mouth felt suddenly full and dry, and he realized his hands were shaking. He couldn't feel his feet on the ground anymore.

Did he see the ghost of a smile pass across his father's lips as Adrian looked down at his bleeding body? Did his father speak? Adrian didn't know.

Adrian's hand slipped out of the one that had guided his own that day, the one that landed proudly on his shoulder after he'd killed the deer.

"The Northern men did this," someone yelled in the forest behind him. "They never wanted peace with us. They shot him in the back. Find them!" The voice barked orders to no one in particular. "I need to take him back to the palace and sound the alarm—we will find these men and kill them. Find the prince!"

Adrian continued to stare down at his father, unblinking. His legs had a little more feeling in them, his heart had slowed a little. As he stared at his father, he realized that Alfred had said something to him, something just below a whisper.

Run.

"I'm sorry," Antony whispered into the cold, empty air of his prison cell.

In his mind, he'd never gone to the Commoner's Ball. In his mind, he had never followed Sir Markus. He'd never gone back to Southborn. In his mind, he was sitting by the fire with his father, watching Bron's eyes get heavy in the evening light.

He wished he'd never remembered anything.

"You didn't deserve this," Antony said to himself. His father had tried to help, as he had always tried to do. He was a man who helped people. He thought what he was doing was right.

338

"I deserve this."

He prayed for his father. His second father, but the only one he ever truly knew, now also a memory. A sleepless night turned into another dark day in his cell. Antony had huddled in a corner and never left. He would join Bron in the stars soon. And his true father, he supposed. He wondered if he would recognize Alfred among the stars.

Then they can bury my true *body in the Crypt of Kings.*

A clanging at his cell startled him, and he wondered if it was time. But when he looked up, he didn't see the guard. He saw two figures, one in a hooded cloak. As they stepped into the dim light, Antony saw it was Ellena and Adelaide.

"By all the saints, I wish I'd come sooner," Ellena said. Antony realized her eyes were rimmed with red. "I could've helped him, too. But I'm going to help you now. And you're not going to say no." She lifted a dented helmet into the dim light. "Now put this on. We're getting you out of here."

Ellena unlocked the door and Antony shuffled stiffly out, pausing before Adelaide. To his surprise, she embraced him, throwing herself into his arms. He savored her touch, burying his face in her hair. When he left, he would go back to the outlaws. He couldn't bear the thought of never seeing Adelaide again.

"Come with us," he whispered in her ear.

"I can't," she replied. She pulled out of his embrace. "I'll fight for you here. But you need to go. You need to run."

Run.

As they made their escape—Antony disguised as a soldier and Ellena a brother of the Nine—he realized it was much darker outside than he thought. His days had all melted into one. How much time had he lost? As they passed through the courtyard, he knew what had happened there. The scaffold still stood. Even in the fading light, Antony saw dark patches in the wood. Blood.

"Who did it?" he grunted to Ellena as they passed.

Ellena didn't have to ask what he meant. "The big one," she said. "The sullen one."

As they escaped, Antony prayed. He prayed he would be strong enough. He prayed he would take back what was his. He prayed for the end of the reign of King Tanor and for the death of Sir John.

III

Part Two: Vispilio

The Traveling Lord

"These damn Southern roads," cursed Martin Sudbury as the carriage rattled.

The fact that it was the coldest Wintermonth Southborn had seen in years didn't help. The rain had frozen on the dirt Weschurch road, making every divot, every hole, every indentation unbearable.

Especially because he had to piss. And badly.

Every jostle set his teeth on edge. He crossed his legs, bracing his hands against the sides of the carriage, steadying himself futilely against the movement.

He would *not* stop in the Hemlock Forest. First of all, it was colder than Innermost Hell, and his prick would probably retreat into his body the moment it touched the cold air.

Secondly—after all the business with the Men of the Lion in Southborn two months before, the Hemlock Forest was no place for a lord to have his manhood exposed.

Caution is advised when traveling to Southborn, the king had written in his invitation. Perhaps he also meant that his dirt roads were now small mountains underneath the first chill of winter.

"Sweet mother of all *saints*—" Martin cursed again. He banged on the top of the carriage. "Stop! Stop the carriage."

The carriage shuddered to a stop. "Your bastard's wedding better be worth risking my life over, *your grace,*" Martin muttered as he clambered as quickly as he could.

He was right—it was colder than a Northwoman's teat. He could've

343

sworn his blood froze in his veins. But something else was certainly not freezing, and he unfastened his trousers as quickly as he could, far out of sight from the carriage driver.

It was the fault of that tavern keeper in Barnswood, he thought as he pissed. That man had filled him so full of ale, of *course* he'd be fit to burst. The man had wanted this to happen. Commoners loved to play those kinds of tricks.

The forest was completely silent. The bare trees revealed a vast expanse of black sky and nothing else. The commoners loved their stories of the Hemlock forest—of the trees that would come to life and dance under a full moon, or the bog witches that would emerge from the depths of the river and steal children from their beds. Martin chuckled to himself as he thought of the stories. His wife was one to tell such stories to their children, and Martin sometimes wondered if she believed them, she would tell them with such wonder.

He shook himself out and laced his breeches again, letting a sigh of relief slide out of his mouth. No outlaws, of course. And no more piss, thank all the saints. The rest of the journey would be much more comfortable.

Martin turned and his heart nearly leapt out of his chest.

A dark figure stood between him and the carriage, featureless in the dead night. Martin's scream was nothing but a yelp in his throat before he clamped a hand over his mouth. If he hadn't just pissed, he would've wet himself.

"Don't speak," said the figure. Its voice was flat, dead. Expressionless. "Unless you want an arrow down your gullet."

Martin thought he heard the creak of sinew, of a bow being pulled taut. Saints save him, he realized. It was the *Vispilio*.

His wife had already taken to telling the stories of him. Of how he stalked the forests around Southborn, as fast and as quiet as a shadow. That he was so deadly with a bow and arrow, he could split a single hair in two with one shot. That he would kidnap children who stayed up past dark.

Martin suspected Liza had added the last part as her contribution to the legend—because little Martin often never wanted to go to bed when it was time.

The stories said many things—that he could grow wings like a bird, that he had four long legs like a spider's that he walked about on, that he could slide through the crack of a door as though he were thin as parchment.

All Martin saw was the shape of a man of his own height, with broad, square shoulders. *If I survive this,* he thought, *I can't wait to tell Liza.*

"Are you going to the wedding?" asked the man.

Martin said nothing. He bit his lip. Was it a trick?

He thought he heard the man sigh. "You may speak," he said.

"I am," said Martin. "his grace invited me to the wedding of his son and the Lady Ade—"

"Shut up," snapped the man. "Are you bringing the happy couple a gift?"

Yes. Liza had picked it out—she would have joined him, but she was too close in time to birthing their fifth child.

"I have," Martin said.

"Show me."

Martin walked cautiously back to the carriage, the *Vispilio* close on his heels. Occasionally, he would hear the bowstring creak. It was still drawn, still ready.

"You all right down there, m'lord?" drawled the driver from his seat atop the carriage.

"Just fine, Jem. Just fine," Martin said. His voice came out as a weak warble from his throat.

In his traveling trunk was the gift. A pair of pewter goblets—simple, Liza had said, but useful.

"They aren't worth much," Martin said. "It's a cheap metal—"

"I have something better you can give them."

Martin didn't think he heard correctly. The *Vispilio* was going to give *him* something? He heard the bowstring relax, the shuffle of leather. Then, something heavy and cold was pressed into Martin's hand.

"That is your wedding gift to Lady Adelaide," said the *Vispilio.* "Now I'll take the goblets."

"But my wife—"

"—wants you to come home in one piece. Give me the goblets. The lady would much rather prefer the hairpin I've given you. Trust me."

Martin dropped the goblets into invisible hands.

"You should go," said the *Vispilio*. "You don't want to be late."

Martin didn't have to be told twice. He all but leapt back into his carriage. When he turned, he was surprised to see the *Vispilio* still standing there. He remembered something else Liza had said about the outlaw—nothing she had ever said to their children, but had mentioned to him.

"They say you are the ghost of Prince Adrian," Martin said.

He thought he saw the shadow cock its head, even laugh to himself. "Maybe," said the *Vispilio*. "They may be right."

John

A gush of blood poured down the man's face. He spat something
onto the ground that landed with a soft plunk. A tooth.

John's hand hurt. He knew he shouldn't have gone for the face,
but he hadn't been able to stop himself. The man—a Man of the Lion—had
said a word that didn't belong in his mouth. *Bastard.* As though it made
John so much worse than him.

Lucas' eyes were on him, questioning. The man was strung up by his
arms. Hit them in the gut to get them to talk, or whip their back. But don't
hit them in the face, Edwin had said. If you do, they won't be able to speak.

The prisoner only grinned a red grin, one tooth missing from it.

"Who is leading the Men of the Lion?" John asked again. "Who is causing
the trouble in the village tonight? Is it the *Vispilio?*"

"I'm not telling you *nothin'*, bastard," lisped the man around his missing
tooth. John didn't realize he'd wound up his fist again until Lucas grabbed
his arm.

"When was the last time you ate meat, man?" Lucas asked.

Something new glittered in the wounded man's eye. Hunger. His cheeks
were gaunt and his body hung on the chains as lean as a scarecrow.

"When was the last time your family ate anything at all?" Lucas asked.

The man pressed his swelling lips together, assessing Lucas.

"You lie," growled the man. "You all do. Promising me meat and mead
to sell out my brothers? If the *Vispilio* were on the throne, every family
would have meat and mead on their table every night of the week."

"It seems your *Vispilio* has abandoned you," John snarled. "Where is he?

Hiding in the woods while you all starve and burn down your own homes in anger? It's been well over two months since anyone has seen or heard from the false prince."

The man swallowed, as though weighing the truth in John's words. The village was burning outside. This man was one of the few Edwin and his men had captured thus far.

"You'll give me meat today," said the prisoner, "but you'll cut off my head with a dull sword tomorrow. Make me suffer."

John steeled himself. His heart was pounding in his chest, his vision was narrowing. It wouldn't take much to snap this man's neck.

"They're calling you Bloody John," said the prisoner. "I was there that day. I watched you kill the bowyer. Seems as though you always have blood on your hands, don't it?"

"We'll send you back to your home with food for your family," Lucas said. "Then you can tell your brothers when they comply with us, they will be fed."

The man spat—directly on John's face. The globule landed dangerously close to John's own mouth. He gingerly swiped the bloody mess away, still feeling its stickiness on his skin. If he looked at this man any longer, John would tear his head from its body.

Lucas seemed to understand. "I'll keep talking to him," he said. "I'll see you up on the wall."

John turned and left, grateful to be away from the stink of the prison.

High above the town on the palace walls, the frozen wind was unrelenting. The blasts made John think of long nights keeping watch in the North, scanning the bare forests for any sign of movement until his eyes crossed with exhaustion. John didn't mind the cold anymore. It was better than the searing heat of Second Summer. He scanned the village below to find the rioters. He could see the long line of torches on the main road. As the wind blew, he heard snatches of shouts and cries. A tax collector's house was on fire. John wondered if it was one of the collectors he'd traveled with.

Not long after, Lucas' short, stocky shape limped into view on the narrow parapet. He caught his breath and leaned against the wall next to John. His cheeks were bright red, a crimson shield against the bitter wind.

"All he said was it was some of those peasant boys causing a stir," he said. "It's the tax collector's house. They're coming down Highroad now, toward the palace gates."

More than I got out of him, I suppose, John thought. He squeezed his jaw. The poorer class had been growing restless, especially after the death of Queen Claudia and the execution of the bowyer. The Men of the Lion were louder than ever. Edwin had promised the crown would be lenient if they complied. John wondered if the time for lenience was over.

"Have you sent men down to help?" asked John. He squeezed the hilt of his sword. He would make them all pay if he could. Lucas shook his head.

"The captain thinks it would make them angrier," Lucas said. "I think he's right. Nothing will make them happy except King Tanor's head on a spike. Or another gift from the *Vispilio.*"

John could have rolled his eyes. It was the only name on anyone's lips lately—a made-up name from a made-up legend. John remembered governesses telling him the story when he was a child. Now it seemed to be all anyone ever talked about, ever since the common folk began receiving mysterious gifts on their doorstep.

"I'll never know how one man broke into the soldiers' food store and single-handedly bring it all to St Aethel's Row." Lucas mused, his muscular arms crossed over his chest.

"Maybe it wasn't one man," John said. "Antony has a following with the Men of the Lion. They worship him more than Augustus."

Lucas laughed. "Probably not," he said. "But it's a better story, isn't it? I grew up hearing stories about a mysterious man who lived in the forest. Maybe not even a man, but something else. A child of the saints, of Saint Augustus himself."

"It's foolish," John said. He leaned against the parapet, watching tiny villagers running and shouting, bringing buckets of water to the fire, breaking ice that was forming at the top of their wells. He watched the line of torches march down the Highroad toward the palace.

"Is it?" Lucas asked. "It's no secret that none of 'em are happy with the king. And there's nothing they can do about it. Nothing but hope for someone who can do something."

"What makes you think this man can do anything about the king?"

Lucas smirked. "Because it *starts* with one man," he said. "Remember the deserter at Semhowen? All he had to do was say something once before the other men listened to him. And you remember what happened to them."

John remembered. Their own men hanging from trees. Boys no older than he.

"But in this instance," Lucas continued, "the man doesn't have a face. And maybe he *is* more than one man. Perhaps the *Vispilio* did one good deed and others followed suit. I don't know if we'll ever know."

"They'll be at the front gate at any moment," John said. "Would you like to alert the king?"

Lucas looked at him knowingly. He knew John did his best to avoid his father whenever he could. "I will," he said. "I'll report back. I've already ensured that every entrance is sealed. Only the Brothers of the Nine are welcome in and out to do their Wintermonth penance. I imagine the king will want everyone in their rooms with the doors bolted."

"Except us."

Lucas chuckled. "Except us. G'night, Johnny."

Lucas retreated from the wall, but John remained for a moment, watching the fire continue to burn below, watching the line of torches. The tax collector lived in the wealthy quarter of town, where many of the houses were stone or brick. The revelers must have thrown pitch at the house to set it ablaze. John could smell the smoke even from his vantage point.

He pushed his hair back from his face. He had let it grow longer since he'd returned to Southborn over two months before. He hadn't paid much attention to his stubble either—it was on its way to a full beard. It made him look old, and he felt old. He would need to shave and trim before the wedding. He let the cold wind hit him for a few moments longer. If he closed his eyes, he was in the northern mountains, keeping watch next to Lucas or Artemis or Lyman. The cold wind had a song of its own, one that was different from a warm summer breeze. The cold wind sang something much more haunting, but sweeter music to John's ears than anything.

It understood him. Warm winds were changeable and soft. These icy blasts were strong, unrelenting, fearless. The South wasn't ready. But he was.

Adelaide

Adelaide's eyes snapped open at the sound of Elanor's piercing laughter. She had fallen asleep again, and no wonder. It had to have been close to midnight, and Elanor had kept her and Ilse awake late for nights on end. The baby wouldn't let her sleep, she said, to where Magg had joined them that evening to check on her pregnancy.

"It just feels so strange," Elanor said, covering her hand with her mouth as if to stifle her laughter. "The way he moves about within me."

Magg offered Elanor a cautious smile as she pressed various places on the woman's belly. "Remember, there is no way to discern whether the child is a boy or a girl, my lady," she said mildly.

"I suppose *you* might be in the family way before long, too, Adelaide," Elanor said, glancing up at her. Elanor had regarded her with caution the last few months, ever since she had revealed her secret to Queen Claudia. The secret didn't seem to matter much anymore, and Elanor knew how the court game was played. But it seemed Elanor had learned to keep Adelaide at arm's length. And Adelaide was grateful for that.

"And Magg," Elanor continued. "I'd like you to call me 'your grace.' No more of this 'my lady.' I am to be queen soon." She straightened her neck and lifted her chin, as though she were already wearing a golden crown.

Magg and Adelaide exchanged a look. All Elanor could talk about was her upcoming wedding and coronation—though there was not a date for either. She said the king was waiting for the baby to be born before he wed her. Adelaide was not about to tell her that she heard Lord Edwin speaking to the king about a marriage prospect from across the sea. Another benefit

352

of being at arm's length from a woman writing her own demise. *If Tanor is keeping this a secret from Elanor, my head would be on a chopping block if I told her.*

Ilse stood by the window, looking out. "The fire is bigger now," she said, fear in her voice. "Don't you think the crowd is getting closer? I think I can hear them."

Elanor laughed again. "You must have incredible hearing, Ilse. I haven't heard a thing," she said. "It's as though they don't exist outside our high, safe walls."

Adelaide approached Ilse at the window. The small girl didn't take her eyes off the scene on the other side of the warped glass. Far below, Adelaide could see the flames too. While Elanor's chambers were high in the walls of the castle, the flames were not far away from the palace gates. She knew Lord Edwin's men were carefully patrolling the wall and ensuring the gates were sealed, but she had to admit it was frightening to see the chaos below.

"I think I can smell the smoke, Addie," Ilse whispered. Her face was white.

Adelaide put a hand on her arm. "You are all right, Ilse," she said. "Lord Edwin's men will protect us."

"And so will Adelaide's big, strong fiance," Elanor smirked. She watched Adelaide for a reaction. She seemed to sense Adelaide's distaste for John, especially after what happened with Bron and the trial. Adelaide hoped she didn't suspect how she felt about Antony—or that she had helped him escape.

The thought of John made her feel ill. Adelaide had hardly said two words to him in the last two months, ever since Bron's execution. She'd watched him. She'd watched him hack a man's head off with a blunt sword. He spent a lot of time interrogating prisoners in the dungeon after they were captured. The prisoners had taken to calling him Bloody John. And she had to marry him in two days.

Since then, Adelaide had retreated further into herself. Elanor wanted her and Ilse to serve as ladies-in-waiting. The other ladies had been dismissed—Adelaide didn't know exactly why. She hoped it had nothing to do with the uprising that was happening in those girls's home villages, and whether their fathers were supportive of the king or not.

But it might be, she warned herself. And she had helped one of them—one who was thought to be the cause of all the trouble—escape. More than that, she missed him. Not a day went by where she didn't think of being in his arms, close enough to feel the warmth of his body. She remembered the way his eyes had glittered as they danced, like the dying embers of a fire. She found that she adored those eyes.

"The babe is healthy," Magg said. "You are perhaps seven months into your pregnancy. The child has not turned yet, but it is still many weeks before the birth. I would recommend you enter confinement within the month. I have peppermint leaves for the nausea."

Elanor was unceremoniously sprawled across her lounge chair, wearing a red, fur-lined robe over her nightgown, her red hair tossed into a braid behind her head. She was beautiful, Adelaide admitted. She could see how Tanor would fall for her charm. Her alabaster skin glowed in the firelight, and her lips tipped slightly upward as if she were perpetually amused.

Adelaide took Ilse's shoulder and guided her away from the window. "We will be all right, Ilse," she said again. "Would you like me to call for a guard to walk you back to your chamber?"

"Not John, though," Elanor said. "He belongs wholeheartedly to Addie."

Adelaide stopped herself from glaring at the woman. Elanor crossed her legs along the lounge chair. Her feet were bare, and she wiggled her toes absentmindedly.

"Perhaps rubbing my feet will take your mind off it, Ilse," Elanor said. "There's a dear."

Ilse did as she was told. Adelaide wondered if it felt strange to Ilse too, to serve a woman who was not the queen, and probably never would be.

"By the way, how are your wedding plans going?" asked Elanor. She tilted her head back as Ilse rubbed her feet. Magg had retreated to the other side of the room to retrieve the mint leaves for Elanor.

Wedding. Adelaide dreaded the day. "Good. I think." she said stiffly.

Every time Elanor smiled at her, her lips were tight around her teeth, as though she were keeping a secret.

"Wonderful," she said softly. "Interesting how quickly things change, is it not? Here we are nearing the year's end, you have returned to the palace and are to be married, and I am to be a queen and a mother." She traced an idle finger around her belly.

Adelaide could have rolled her eyes. Finally, Elanor yawned dramatically.

"Good saints, I am tired," she drawled. "Ilse, would you be a dear and help me get ready for bed? I'm sure Adelaide doesn't mind returning to her chambers on her own."

Adelaide certainly didn't mind. Magg intercepted Elanor as she stood and made a slow procession to her bedchamber door, followed closely by Ilse.

"The leaves, my l—your grace," Magg said. "Chew them as needed for your nausea, or put them in hot water for tea."

"Thank you, Magg," Elanor put a hand on her belly. "My son and I appreciate your attentive care."

Magg's shoulders heaved in a sigh after Elanor and Ilse were gone. She seemed much more relaxed as she packed her things. Adelaide watched her for a while, despite her exhaustion. She knew Magg had helped Antony when he was in prison, but she also remembered her tense conversation with the physician. If Magg had any suspicions, she kept them to herself.

"Magg," Adelaide said. Her voice sounded strange in the quiet room. The physician's head snapped up. "I want to talk to you about…something."

A shade of fear crossed Magg's face. "What is it?" she asked.

"About…my wedding night."

Magg seemed to relax again. She probably feared Adelaide would ask her about Antony. She smiled wryly. "Of course." She smoothed the front of her simple dark gown. "I am not a married woman myself, but…I suppose you may have questions."

"My mother wasn't alive long enough to…" Adelaide's cheeks grew hot.

"Come. Sit." Magg gestured to the lounge chair. Adelaide sat, and Magg sat beside her. "You do know how the…how the act is done, yes?"

"Yes." All because of a mortifying incident when she had walked in on her brother and a woman from the village—an older, married woman. It had been not long after their father died.

"Some women say that it is painful the first time," Magg said. "So it may hurt. I can give you something to help lessen the pain, a poultice you can apply on the area. Are you currently bleeding?"

"Not right now." Thankfully.

Magg nodded. She explained it all so simply, and all the while, Adelaide's heart pounded with dread in her chest at the thought of it.

"You may fall pregnant, even after your first time," Magg said. "I would expect you to be with child within the year, if you…if you and John, well…if it were to happen often."

Adelaide's stomach turned even further. Children. With John. With Bloody John. Children that could easily tear apart her womb and kill her, as John had killed so many. Childbirth was a woman's war, and one that many women didn't survive.

"You will know if you are with child or not if you have your next monthly bleeding," Magg said.

"Is it…" Adelaide didn't know how to say it. "Is it enjoyable?"

It was Magg's turn to blush. "I do not know, my lady. But there *is* a reason many babies are born, and why some are conceived outside of marriage. There is often…a passion, I am told."

A passion. When she thought of John, she did not think of passion. She thought of how his lips tasted sour when he'd pressed a kiss on her, his huge, fumbling hands on her neck. She imagined those hands pawing the whole of her body and cringed.

"Thank you, Magg," she said. She couldn't bear to hear more. She didn't want to.

She left the solar, leaving Magg to collect her things. The halls were quiet at that time of night. Most of the guards were probably down fortifying the castle gate. Adelaide didn't mind her solitary walk, especially after spending hours trying to entertain Elanor. The only problem was now she was alone with her thoughts, and they spun around her conversation with

Magg. How she would have to lay with John in two days' time, eventually bear his child…

A small figure clad in robes rounded the corner toward her, walking quickly. Relief washed over Adelaide. She glanced around even though the narrow corridor was empty. What she did always sent a thrilling fear down her spine—she could be caught. She *should* be caught, with how frequently David and Ellena entered the palace as novices paying penance.

As the figure passed her, its arm shot out and grabbed the crook of Adelaide's elbow, pulling her around the next corner. Ellena knew better than to remove her hood. Even in the shadowy corridor, Adelaide could see the delicate curve of her nose, her pointed chin.

Ellena slipped something to Adelaide from under the folds of her robe, which was much too big for her tiny body. A heavy iron key.

"Thanks for that," Ellena murmured. "We gave out all the food from the stores. Probably means your betrothed will go hungry for a few days. But I don't think you care about that."

Adelaide scoffed. "I thought David was coming tonight. You were here last night." Adelaide remembered her fearful mission the night before—stealing down to the kitchen to lift the key to the foodstore just after supper.

The cowl of Ellena's deep hood shook. "They—there was an incident. Some of the Men of the Lion were run out of town. Including David."

Adelaide's heart sank. Every time they won, they lost something. She'd done what she could for the outlaws for months—stealing food, keys, money, and delivering them through David or Ellena. *That could be all of us soon*, she thought. *The truth of what we're doing will come out. And the truth spoken is the truth known. But death would be better than marrying Sir John.*

"Any word from…from him?" Adelaide asked. She asked every time. She never said his name.

Ellena shook her head. "He's not been himself, y'know," she said. "But—" A gentle hand emerged from the folds of the robe and gripped Adelaide's arm tightly "—he does need you. We need you."

Adelaide nodded. "Tell him—" She realized she didn't know what she wanted to tell him. Everything. All of the things she'd felt the last few months. "Tell him I need him, too. I need all of you."

"Take care of yourself, you hear?" Ellena said. As soon as she'd appeared, she turned and skittered away down the corridor.

Adelaide watched her shadow disappear into the gloom of the corridor. The deep silence enveloped her again. *A friend*, Adelaide thought. The iron key felt heavy in her hand. *A friend I wish I could follow.*

She wanted to run. Every day, she wanted to run out of the palace gates and into the forest. But she heard her aunt's voice. *You have a duty. To your family and to your father.*

As though her thoughts conjured him, she turned back and nearly collided with John. He stepped back quickly. Adelaide tucked the key into her sleeve, praying he didn't see.

"My lady," he managed. He inclined his head.

"Sir John."

He stood awkwardly in front of her, uncomfortably close. It reminded Adelaide of the night he was drunk in the barracks, such little distance between them. She noticed he had his hands behind his back. Normally he crossed them in front.

"Has the threat passed?" Adelaide asked, hoping the question would remind him to return to his duties. She thought maybe the image of him up to his elbows in blood would fade from her memory, but it hadn't.

And I marry him in two days, she thought.

"It is…under control," John said. "Are you returning to your chambers?"

"Yes."

"May I escort you?"

"Yes."

It would've been rude to have denied him, she thought. She turned and started walking again, letting him fall in step behind her. He walked with his hands still behind his back.

They arrived at Adelaide's chambers. John opened the door to her dark solar. Compared to Elanor's chambers, hers were as cold as a crypt.

"Do you need anything else, my lady?" John asked.

"I didn't need anything to begin with," Adelaide replied before realizing how cold it sounded. She was surprised to see how hurt John looked by that. He lowered his head and turned to leave.

"Wait," she said. He paused and looked across the solar at her. In the moonlight, his blue eyes were almost colorless.

"What do the Men of the Lion want?" she asked.

John sighed. His hands dropped back to his sides. "Our wedding is a reason they're unhappy. The expense of it. And—and the death of the bowyer. They haven't forgotten."

Neither have I. The blood on his arms. Bron's head in a basket. The day came rushing back to Adelaide's mind.

"As far as I know, Sir Lucas was going to drive them out of the city." He stepped to the window, gazing out at the cold, quiet meadows beyond the palace.

He succeeded, Adelaide thought, remembering what Ellena told her.

Adelaide watched him for a while. He continued to stare futilely out the window, avoiding her gaze. A hint of stubble shadowed his face. His hair was unkempt, shaggy around the ears. She wondered if he would cut it for the wedding.

He dropped one of his hands onto the windowsill, bathing it in moonlight. Adelaide saw now why he'd been hiding them. They were bruised, shadowed with red. *Bloody John.*

"Addie," he still didn't look at her. "I know that with all that's going on it's been...difficult. You might...see me in a different light now, and I understand. But—" He turned to her. "I do still want to marry you. I care about you. I'll protect you."

"Why are you saying all this now?" Adelaide was tired. His words irritated her. They seemed so false.

"You've been distant from me these past few months," he said. His mouth was a rigid line. He didn't look angry about it. Just disappointed. Almost sad. Adelaide didn't care.

"You told me what you did," Adelaide said, "that night in the barracks."

She hated remembering that night, how drunk he was, how hungry his lips were. And she hated remembering the horrible secret he'd told her.

He went even whiter in the milky light of the moon. "What do you mean?" He spoke slowly, as though trying to feign innocence.

"You told me what you did to Adrian that night."

His eyes searched her face, like he was trying to remember the words he spoke to her. Adelaide's mouth burned with the words. She couldn't believe she'd actually said them. *It's not what you know or who you know, but what you know about who you know.*

"Was it all your father, or did you want to?" That was what Adelaide had wondered ever since that night. If John, a thirteen-year-old boy, had willingly killed the prince.

No response. John worked his jaw.

"You always hated bullies," she continued. "And yet when I look at you, all I see is a bully. And a murderer."

When John looked at her again, his pupils were pinpricks in his colorless eyes. To her surprise, Adelaide felt fear as he stepped toward her. She became aware again of how much bigger he was, how much stronger.

"You don't understand what it was like," he said, his voice ragged. "You had a father who loved you. You didn't have bruises where no one could see. I had to do what he said. Some part of me knew I was already becoming his weapon rather than his son."

Somehow, Adelaide knew it was true. John had never stood up for himself as a boy, and she knew Tanor was capable of cruelty. But John was a man now.

"But why keep his secret?" Adelaide asked. "If you told the truth, how he used you, you would be blameless."

Adelaide never saw John smile. The smile on his face now was tragic. He shook his head.

"A weapon does what its wielder commands."

He let the words hang between them and this time, he didn't look away. Adelaide realized he still showed no anger. If anything, he was afraid. The key burned cold in Adelaide's closed fist.

"I'm going to bed," she said. "I'll see you in two days' time."

She went through the door to her chamber and shut it, waiting for a moment on the other side. She quickly slid the key into the drawer at her bedside. She'd return it in the morning after breakfast.

She heard nothing. He didn't follow her. Relieved, she collapsed onto the bed, feeling exhaustion in every crevice of her body. The room was cold, but she fell into sleep before she could reach for the blanket.

And she opened her eyes to her cold, dark chamber, starting awake. The winter sun still hadn't risen, it seemed, but the windows were tinged with predawn gray. She sat up drowsily. Once the sun rose, she would need to bring Elanor's breakfast to her chamber and then return the key. She wasn't looking forward to seeing her mistress that morning.

Adelaide stood up and opened the door to her solar. She was surprised to see that John never left. There he lay, spreadeagled awkwardly across the sitting-sofa, his head at an uncomfortable-looking angle against the arm of the chair and his long legs splayed out to the floor. It looked as though he had had for a while before succumbing to sleep and drooping to one side. Adelaide stared at him for a long time. Her husband, in two days' time—even shorter than that now. A boy who became a murderer.

She thought of all the times he'd ever treated her as a friend and wished he never had. Wished that he had never been kind. *And yet here he is. He stood vigil all night until he could no longer stay awake. A murderer and a liar who loves you.*

Adelaide turned back into her chamber and softly closed the door behind her.

Antony

He forced himself to listen to the sound of the Skeldergate River. To most others it would've been a peaceful sound. But it kept him awake. And he didn't want to sleep.

Antony waited in the dark, perched in the bare bones of an oak tree, straddling a branch like the back of a horse. Being high off the ground was peaceful. He no longer had to be involved in the world—he just had to watch it. During the day, he'd watch a deer picking through the rotting leaves for food, her hoofs whispering through the underbrush. He'd follow the trail of a chipmunk as its tiny body tunneled through the thicket and disappear into a tree. Now that the autumn leaves had all but fallen, he could see songbirds as they flitted from branch to branch, their songs a white vapor in the air.

Nighttime was more for listening. The distant call of an owl. The creeping of a rabbit, even a mouse, if it was quiet enough. The river was wide and slow, a gentle, constant burble. Water sucked at the mossy bank far below him.

Antony hadn't slept well since his father died. He would be sluggish and doze during the day, but found himself most animated at night. Nothing seemed to compel him to wakefulness more than darkness. That was when the rest of the world slept—when Southborn slept. When he could do his work.

He toyed with one of the silver goblets, watching their dull gleam in the moonlight. He prayed the lord would give Adelaide his message and not take it straight to the king. He wanted to believe there was still some goodness in wealthy lords, that they weren't all like Tanor.

Antony would not go back to camp anytime soon, he decided. He needed to let Carter cool off. Before he'd left, Ellena was about to leave for Southborn, breathless. The Men of the Lion were getting desperate. She hadn't heard from David in weeks.

"That's not a good idea, you know," Carter had told her as she wrapped herself in the novice robes she'd stolen from the church. "Traipsing around the Weschurch Road when you have a target on your back. And at night, too."

Ellena ignored him. "There's a fire."

"Where?"

"One of the tax collector's homes in the rich quarter."

Carter had scoffed. "Serves him right."

Antony looked at him sharply from across the low fire. "Burning down a house won't change anything. You know that."

"It did for us," Carter said. "We became outlaws, remember? Or have you forgotten that, too?"

Carter had been wearing on Antony's nerves for months. He wanted to punch him, but knew he was no physical match for his older brother. And no matter how angry he was at Carter, Antony knew Carter had a reason to blame him.

Herne had been quiet until then. "A revolution is coming, whether we like it or not," he said. "A house fire is only the beginning."

"That's not what Pa would have wanted," Antony said. "He died trying to do things the right way."

"Exactly. He died," Carter said. Antony sensed Carter hid his grief over his father with anger and stubbornness. "Maybe there's more than one right way to do things."

"What do you want me to do, Carter?" Antony raised his voice. "Start a war?"

Carter shrugged. "You're the high-and-mighty *Vispilio*. You're the one with the nickname who runs around the forest stealing from the rich and giving to the poor or whatever the hell it is you do. I never asked for any of this either, y'know." He bit his lip and glared into the fire. "If Pa never picked you up from the forest, we wouldn't be here."

Antony looked darkly up at his brother. "Say that again," he said.

Carter met his eyes and didn't break from his gaze. "Hell, *Antony* would still be alive if you'd died that day like you were supposed to. Do you know how hard it was to pretend that you were the brother I'd loved for thirteen years? To act as though nothing had happened, even though there was a complete stranger in our home instead of *my brother?*"

To his surprise, Antony had never considered that. Carter had always just been his cold and distant older brother. He thought it had always been that way.

Carter blinked into the fire. "I just miss that old man," he said, wiping his nose. "I miss him. I miss Antony—" He glared at his brother. "The *real* Antony. I even miss Sally. Hell, I never thought I'd say that."

Antony said nothing. He watched a tear slide down Carter's face. Another followed it. Then another.

"Somethin' was bound to break," Herne said. "A secret like Antony doesn't stay hidden forever. And people are seeing who Tanor really is, if they didn't see it already. They're emboldened now, by the *Vispilio.*"

"Don't call him that stupid name," Carter grunted in disgust. "He's Antony. In fact, he's not even Antony. He's Adrian."

Somehow, that hurt Antony even more.

"To you, maybe," Herne said. "To others, he's a symbol. To them, he's not just one man. He's a name that's been passed down, and when Antony's gone, there will be another."

Carter looked sideways at him. "Pretty words," he said. "I still don't buy it. I'm going to bed." As he walked past Antony, he stopped and looked down at him. "Don't think it's not your fault. Because it is. All of it is."

Antony brooded on Carter's words even hours later in the oak tree. He tucked the goblet back into its bag. He nocked an arrow on his bow, resting it gently across his legs. A cold, harsh wind rocked the branches around him, whistling through them like a swansong.

I never doubted that it was my fault. He remembered when Adelaide came to him in prison. He never thought he could feel that sure of himself. He had been ready to die.

It was Pa's fault, really, he thought. *He didn't have to say what he said.*

But he did anyway, said a voice deep within him. Because he knew who you truly are.

At the end of Second Summer, Antony had been none the wiser about who he was. But now that Wintermonth was upon them, he had started a full-on rebellion.

A sound somewhere in front of him pulled him out of his thoughts. In the gloom of naked trees stretched across the darkness, Antony thought he saw movement, but not the lope of a deer or the flight of a bird. The movement was larger. The sound louder.

People. Men.

Figure after figure dissolved out of the darkness and into the silver light of the moon. Antony watched, stock-still, and counted. A dozen appeared. Two. He counted nearly thirty men, walking as a group along the river bank. The closer they got, the more Antony could hear their ragged breaths. If they came From Southborn, it had been a long walk for them.

Antony's first thought was soldiers, king's men. But these men looked too disheveled —and not dressed for the elements.

They stopped mere yards from Antony's perch. They stamped their feet against the cold. Plumes of a breath steamed from their mouths like smoke from small chimneys. One of them spoke.

"What now, Malcolm?" he said. "Did you really think they'd be easy to find?"

"Shut it. I'm thinking." A man stood looking out at the flow of the river. His broad frame was wrapped in a cloak, and his red hair shone in the moonlight like gold.

"I wish Nathan were here," said a hollow voice. "He'd know what to do."

Nathan. The name washed over Antony with regret.

"Well, Seth, you've got me," Malcolm said, crossing his arms against the chill.

Antony saw who he was talking to—Seth, a reedy, bird-like man with milky white-blond hair.

These aren't enemies, Antony thought. *They're friends.*

"I knew Herne well," Malcolm continued. "His door was always open to those who needed aid. I never said he'd be easy to find."

"I can help with that."

The men murmured in surprise and looked up at Antony. Malcolm rubbed a tired hand over his eyes.

"By Saint Aug," he exclaimed, beaming. "Is that really you up there? We feared you were dead!"

Antony slung his bow around his shoulders and swung easily down from the tree. He'd done it enough times that he had developed a rhythm, knew where every branch was. The men watched him, open-mouthed.

"*Vispilio*," he heard one of them whisper.

Malcolm clasped Antony's hand. His eyes glittered in the moonlight, almost with reverence.

"Should—should we bow?" asked Seth, making to do so.

Antony must've made a face, because Malcolm barked a laugh. "I don't think this lad is used to being bowed to just yet," he said. "But what do we call you? Antony? Adrian? *Vispilio?*"

Antony realized he hadn't thought about it. Herne, Carter, Ben, Ellena—they'd continued to call him Antony. And it felt right. It was the name of the life he knew, the life he remembered.

"Antony," he said simply.

The group of men became disrupted as someone moved forward—a big man who towered over the rest, his hair tousled over his eyes.

"Antony. Thank the saints!" The man pulled Antony into a huge bear hug, nearly lifting him off the ground. When he pulled away, Antony realized it was David, the novice from the Cathedral of the Nine. But he didn't wear his robes, and his hair wasn't neatly trimmed.

"Brother David," Antony said.

David shook his head, still gripping Antony's shoulders. "A brother no longer," he said.

"What's happened?"

Malcolm looked sideways at him. "Do you know what's been going on in Southborn, Antony?" He didn't wait for Antony to answer. "You've inspired us. All of us. We aren't bowing down to 'em anymore. Because they're all pretenders."

"I was stripped of my robes," David said bitterly. "It seems the order would rather worship Tanor than the Great Maker. They said I was a radical for believing you."

"They're afraid of us now," Malcolm said confidently, "Else they wouldn't have pushed us out into the Hemlock with naught but the shirts on our back."

"But our families, Mal," said Seth. Seth looked at Antony, almost apologetically. "We can't go back. They'll kill us all. All because Mal thought it was a good idea to set a house on fire and try to storm the castle."

Malcolm rolled his eyes. "I'm sorry, Seth, I didn't realize starting a revolution meant sitting back and twiddling our cocks while the world spins round."

The men rumbled—dissent, anger, hunger. Antony looked at their faces. They were all tired. Some of them were smeared with soot. Their eyes were sunken, their features craggy in the moonlight.

"Enough," Antony said, loud enough for everyone to hear. "You've come looking for Herne, is that right?" A murmur of assent. "You all need food and rest. We don't have much, but we'll share what we have. Come with me."

Herne

The sound of footsteps and voices sent ice through Herne's veins. He'd told Ben to get in the cave—Carter was already asleep. It was too late to douse the fire—whoever was coming had already seen. So he waited, crouched and taut like a spring, his rusty sword drawn.

He'd known this would happen eventually. Their existence there was too fragile. And as much as it helped them for Ellena to go to Southborn—to steal, to gather information—it put them all the more at risk. The outside world had finally found them.

To his surprise, the first person to come over the hill was Antony. And behind him were nearly thirty other men, streaming down the hill, glancing curiously at the cave, at the fire, at Herne himself.

And Malcolm—by the saints, Malcolm came down the hill. He locked eyes with Herne. He looked every bit Marga's brother, only now nearly twenty years older. Marga would've had the same gray streaks in her hair, the same crow's feet around her laughing eyes. Seeing her brother brought a lump to Herne's throat—the last resemblance he had of her.

"My old friend," Malcolm laughed, his chuckling choked with tears. He didn't hesitate to pull Herne into an embrace. As they did, Malcolm murmured into his ear, "You smell like shit, Herne," sending both men into peals of laughter.

"What is all this?" Herne asked as he pulled away. He still felt on edge by the surprise, but Antony looked calm—calmer than he had in months.

"They've run us to ground, Herne," Malcolm said. He was still as wild-looking as he had been as a lad. His thick brows creased in frustration.

"We've nowhere to go," said a big, dark-haired young man with sorrow in his eyes.

Herne looked around at them, throwing an arm around Mal's shoulders. "You've somewhere to go," he said. "And that's here. I'll stoke the fire. Make your own fires if need be—we've plenty of chopped wood. We don't have much to eat, but we'll all set out to hunt at first light. I'll see what I can drum up."

Soon the little valley was bright with cookfires and Herne distributed what little dried meat and vegetables he could afford to give. *More hands mean more hunters,* his father had always liked to say. Many of these men would be capable enough to find their own food. Though Mal was a healer by trade, Herne had always known the man to be good with a bow and hunting knife.

Yet it still nagged at him, the thought he had before they'd arrived. *The outside world has truly found us.* More people in their camp meant more noise, more smoke, more attention. They were easier to find now.

Antony stood apart from them, his arms crossed. He had changed in those last few months since Bron died. The shadow of a beard grew on his face, making him look more like the man he was becoming. He talked less. He was more patient when they went out hunting. He'd sit for hours alone in the forest, surrounded by the cold and dark. Herne walked up beside him and shared Antony's silence.

"You have the makings of an army, Antony," Herne said after a while. "These are men who trust you. Who would follow you anywhere."

Antony smiled ruefully. His dark eyes flickered like an ember in the firelight. "You sound like Ellena. What are you going to suggest? That we all make weapons out of sticks and storm the castle?"

"Well...not *tonight,* anyway."

Herne was pleased to see Antony laugh. He hadn't seen so much as a grin from him since Harvestmonth. The half-conscious boy he'd found outside their cave had grown on him, he found. He could be impetuous, but he was also brave.

But Herne was only half-joking. They *did* have the makings of an army.

An army that was ready and willing to fight for Antony. For Adrian.

"What am I doing, Herne?" Antony asked. "Nothing has changed. Tanor is still king. I'm still here. I've done nothing."

"I think some would say you've done something," said Herne. "Many would say so. There are people who believe in you. A good number of them are here with us now."

"But it changes nothing," Antony said. "They have a king who spends all their money on saints-know-what."

"On a wedding, I've heard," Herne said, watching Antony closely. He saw it. The flicker of pain, of regret, even of yearning. Herne hadn't been in love for a long time, but he knew the feeling. He knew a woman could change everything about a man, and someone had certainly changed Antony.

Herne put a hand on the boy's shoulder. "I don't think you're seeing it clearly," he said. "They see someone who hasn't given up on them. The bigger battles will come later."

"It seems the bigger battles have found us," Antony said, looking from man to man around their fires.

As they stood together, the dark-haired young man approached them. The man was huge, but Herne saw by his face that he was just a boy, probably only sixteen or seventeen.

Antony nodded to him. "Have you gotten what you need, David?"

"And more," David smiled. He reached out to clasp Herne's hand. This must have been Ellena's contact in Southborn, he realized. A fiery youth, just like his daughter. "Thank you. These men need their strength for what tomorrow brings."

"Tomorrow?" Antony asked.

"The big wedding," David said. "It's our chance. We'll steal robes from the cathedral, go into the palace as brothers serving penance to Saint Morgan."

"And do what?" Antony looked concerned.

"What we have to do to put you back on the throne," David said. He had the look of one awestruck, as though he were standing before Saint

Augustus himself. He added tentatively, "Your grace."

Antony looked at Herne, who probably reflected his expression of confusion. Then, he shook his head. "You can't, David," Antony said. "It's foolish. Now's not the time."

"Then when is the time, your grace?" David's expression turned from one of awe to one of disappointment. He'd made his mind up, Herne knew. He knew what disagreement could do to a young man.

He took a step closer to Antony. Antony tilted his chin to look up at the boy, but otherwise he didn't move.

"With all due respect, your grace," David said, "we've waited for you. And you've done nothing."

"You can't do it, David," Antony said. He lowered his voice. "They'll kill you. All of you. They won't hesitate. I've been in the palace. You don't have enough men to fight."

"We'd all willingly die for you," David said, his fists squeezed at his sides. He hadn't lowered his voice, and some nearby men looked their way. "We'd die for our king. Don't you know that?"

"I don't need anyone else to die for me," Antony said. He turned away. Herne was tempted to reach out to him. *No. Let him lead. Let him make the decision, however difficult.*

To his surprise, Herne saw tears glisten in the corners of David's eyes. "I joined the order to serve the Great Maker, to give my life to him and the saints," he said. "But they've rejected me. Allow me to serve you, your grace. Let me fight for you, command your armies. Let my service mean something."

And suddenly, David knelt low, grabbing Antony's hand, bowing his head. His huge shoulders shook with sobs. Antony looked wide-eyed at Herne.

Antony helped David back to his feet. "I don't need a commander, David," he said. "I just need friends. People I can trust. Storming the castle is a fool's errand."

"Then what do we do?"

Antony paused and thought for a long time. "We'll wait. We'll continue to gather men to our cause. You all need to get your strength back, anyway."

David's reverence turned to rage. A young man's anger isn't easily quelled. A storm brewed in the boy's blue eyes, flickering with the light of the fire.

"We'll *wait*?" David spat the word as though it were a curse. "The life I built for myself is over because I decided to follow you. And you tell me to *wait*?" He took another step toward Antony—this time not to implore him, but intimidate him. His strong shoulders heaved in anger. Antony didn't flinch, but Herne saw the ghost of fear in his eyes. He brushed the hilt of his hunting dagger at his side, assuring himself it was still there.

David seemed to swallow the anger growing inside him. "You're no better than Tanor," he said in parting, then turned from Antony and stormed off.

Antony's shoulders slumped. He watched David clamber off, past the cookfires, into the gloom of the forest.

"He'll walk it off," Herne said, but even he wasn't sure. A young man's anger could burn hot for days. "He loves you and he trusts you. He will come around."

"I'm not so sure," Antony said. "Am I, Herne?"

"Are you what?"

"No better than Tanor."

Herne barked a laugh, then stifled it when heads turned their way. "David has served the perfection of the Great Maker for so long that he demands perfection from you," he said. "You were naught but a bowmaker's son a few months ago, and now you're stuck in the Hemlock with me and Ellena, shitting in the woods and eating berries for supper. I'd say you're making the best of it. And you're preparing for the war that's to come."

"I never wanted to fight a war," Antony said.

"And I never wanted to shit in the woods," Herne said. "Good night, boy."

Herne tried to stifle a yawn, but it escaped from him anyway. The moon was on its way down toward the horizon already. He would talk with Antony about David in the morning. He gave Antony's shoulder a squeeze and retreated to Malcolm's fire at the far end of the camp.

Herne sat down beside his brother-in-law with a grunt.

"You sound like you're getting old, Herne," Malcolm said, a smile in his voice. The fire was low, and Herne could see the flickering crags on Malcolm's face. They were *all* getting old. Time always moved too quickly.

"And that would be unfortunately true," Herne said with a chuckle. "It seems we've found ourselves in a young man's game, all this carryin' on and starting fires."

"I were the one who started the fire," Malcolm conceded. He poked at the fire with a stick, sending a spray of ashes into the winter night.

"We need to leave a better place for them," Herne gestured with his head behind his shoulder. "For our children. Did you ever end up havin' any?"

Malcolm shook his head. "Never got 'round to it. Perhaps I was too busy playing the young man's game. But whether they want to admit it or not, they need us still. We've lived more life than they."

"Aye," Herne said. The silence of the forest fell around them for a long while.

"It's David I'm worried most about," Malcolm finally said. "He's lost everything now. And a boy who's lost everything often goes looking for trouble."

"He wants to raid the palace tomorrow," Herne said, "during the wedding."

"I know it." Malcolm shoved the stick forcefully into the embers of the fire. It crackled in response. "He is right, though. Something needs to be done."

"And Antony will do it."

Even Malcolm looked hesitant at that, but not with the same anger that had burned in David's eye.

"We really believe it, don't we?" he said. "That he's the answer to all our woes. A kid half our age. A kid who used to be a prince, no better than rich fat Tanor."

Herne shook his head. "He's not the answer," he said. "He's the spark. We're the tinder. The fire in the village isn't the only fire we'll start."

"If you say so," Malcolm said, leaning back on his hands, arching his neck to stare into the clear, starry sky. "I've missed you, Herne. Losing Marga and then losing you...it was too much for these old bones. I'm glad to be in your company again, brother."

The words warmed Herne's heart more than the fire ever could. Fireside talks with Mal—just as it used to be. Perhaps the world *had* finally found them, but the world was about to find out what they'd truly found.

Herne awoke before most of the party, though he'd only slept a few hours. Dawn crept gray and bleak over the burnt-out firepits, men wound in tattered cloaks or pieces of fur Herne could offer. But there were fewer men than the night before. Herne walked among them as they slept and saw no sign of David.

He wasn't afraid. He wasn't worried. The feeling in his chest was disappointment.

Footsteps crunched behind him. Antony emerged from the cave, rubbing his eyes and blinking against the darkness of the winter morning, making out Herne's shape in the gloom.

"Something wrong?" The disappointment must have been written on Herne's face.

"David is gone," Herne said. "So are some others." To his relief, the sleeping figure of Malcolm still lay near their burnt-out fire. He would never put it past the man to do something impetuous.

Antony's brows fell over his eyes like storm clouds.

"Shit," he said. "*Shit.*"

The world had found them. And if David or the others were caught, or killed, it would start a fire none of them could douse.

Tanor

"Did they send a portrait?"

Tanor reviewed the letter from the Duke of Lubchen. His eyes fell on the name *Isadora, Viscountess of Lacheln, youngest daughter of Duke Isadore.* He then found the sum of money the duke promised. Two of three things he needed to know.

Edwin stood before the king's desk, his feet together, arms behind his back, as though he were taking orders from his commander.

"No, your grace," he said. "I was told by the emissary that she is a great beauty. The only one in her family to have dark hair. The Lubchens have a penchant to be blond, you know. And Viscountess Isadora is only nineteen."

This was the third marriage proposal sent to Tanor in the two months since Claudia's death. The other two had included portraits, and those portraits were wanting.

"I can arrange for the viscountess to visit Southborn in the spring, if it pleases you," Edwin continued. "The snows are already nigh insurmountable in Lubchen, according to the emissary. And the seas will be rough this time of year. Isadore does not want his daughter traveling until at least Hornmonth."

"No need," Tanor said. "Send a letter of acceptance."

Edwin bowed tightly. "I will arrange it, your grace."

Viscountess Isadora, Tanor thought. *Queen* Isadora. His first wife had been a duchess, his second the daughter of a lord. But never a viscountess. He tried to imagine Isadora—youthful, slim, radiant with beauty. Naïve, perhaps. But innocent.

He was pondering Isadora when there was a knock at his door. Before he could speak, Elanor stepped in. Tanor hadn't talked to her much since Claudia's death. He thought inviting her to any further dinners or council meetings might invite suspicion. And her belly was huge now—she was near her confinement. Pregnancy made their lovemaking tiresome.

She beamed at him. Her face had grown swollen during her pregnancy, and she waddled more than walked, which Tanor found distasteful. She slowly made her way to his desk, a hand on her belly. She looked tired, her hair unkempt, a plain dress stretched taut across her growing body.

"Your grace," she said, panting slightly, as though a short walk across his solar caused her great exhaustion. "I believe I've found a suitable dress to wear for the wedding tomorrow. Seeing as no expense could be taken to make me a new one, I asked Ilse to alter one of Queen Claudia's."

Elanor looked suddenly bitter, her mouth twisted. It was true. Edwin had not allotted her any funds for this wedding. And she had become awfully quiet when Tanor tried on his new tunic from Ettelia.

"Very well," Tanor said. Claudia had always had good taste to a fault.

Elanor smiled again, but now as an afterthought. Her eyes remained cold and cautious. Tanor noticed that unlike other women, she took time to think before she spoke. He could see her working through her next words, deciding which would be the most appealing to him.

She took a few steps toward the desk and leaned forward on it. Her breasts strained against the bodice of her dress, veined and blotchy and swollen. Tanor looked away, back down at the letter from the duke.

"I promise I will be an ornament for your arm tomorrow, my king," Elanor said. She giggled mechanically. "No one will pay any heed to the bride and groom. They will only see us, sitting together in the apse—"

"You will not be sitting with me, my dear," Tanor said. He poured a blot of wax onto the letter. He felt her presence wilt above him.

She laughed again. "Why ever not, my dear?"

"*Your grace,*" Tanor corrected. He looked up at her. Her usual strength and steeliness were gone. Her face had dropped. She looked hideous.

"First of all, you should be in confinement. You are well into your seventh month, by my count. Second of all, a king in need of a new bride cannot parade about with an *ornament* on his arm, as you say."

Elanor's brow furrowed. Tanor stood up. "A new bride?" she asked. She paused. She was thinking again. "Your grace, I have drawn up plans for our wedding. In the springtime, perhaps, after the baby is born and when the weather is fine. It will be even grander than the wedding tomorrow. A *true* royal wedding."

Tanor tilted his head at her. "There will be a wedding in the spring, my dear," he said. "I have just agreed to marry the Viscountess Isadora of Lacheln. A beauty, I am told."

Elanor's entire body seemed to droop as he walked away from her toward the door to his chambers. "*Lacheln,*" she spat out the word. "That backwater town of inbreds? You told me I would be your queen, that we would rule together."

Tanor glanced back at her, briefly looking down at her belly. *One hated. One loved. One forgotten.*

"I will ensure that you want for nothing," he said. "I've secured a lovely estate for you in the Midlands. Our son will take your family name. After you are settled there, Lord Edwin will send suitors to you. You will have your pick, and a handsome dowry to offer."

And both will be forgotten soon enough.

Elanor stared at him, speechless. "I don't understand—" she sputtered. "My—your grace, you cannot do this. I am carrying your prince, another heir." Her voice strengthened. "I cannot, I *will* not be forced aside. What suitor will have a woman with a bastard child?"

"Another bastard," Tanor replied. "There are plenty to go around. Some of them are even handsome."

"This cannot happen," Elanor said. She wasn't thinking anymore. "What have I done wrong? Tell me, your grace. I will do anything to be your bride."

"You will do anything to be *queen,* Elanor."

"I love you! I love you more than *she* ever did. I never asked for anything in return."

"Until now. I'll see you at the wedding tomorrow, my dear. You may sit with me at the head table, if that is your wish—but after that, never again."

Tanor closed the door on her protestations, and soon her sobs and cries faded away when she closed the solar door behind her. His thoughts were his own again.

Viscountess Isadora of Lacheln...

Adelaide

delaide woke before dawn on the morning of her wedding, unable to sleep anymore. As she lay in the darkness, listening to her own breaths, she realized it would be a long while before she slept alone again. She would have to share John's bed until she conceived a child. And that duty would begin that night—her wedding night.

She wrapped herself in a cloak and stepped out into the hall. The palace was now full of visitors for the wedding, looking for any excuse to celebrate at the king's expense. Tanor had thrown many large events in only a matter of months, and they had come at a cost. But if he continued to invite his favored lords and ladies to the palace, they wouldn't ask questions about why taxes were so high.

The morning was cold and gray as she stepped out onto the parapet. Only one more morning in this wretched place, she thought. She hugged the fur-lined cloak tighter to her. She should have been sadder to leave. Even this courtyard had once been a happy place. But the palace of her memory seemed like an entirely different palace all together, one that disappeared ten years ago.

She turned at the sound of footsteps approaching her. Lucas, already dressed for the day in a deep blue velvet doublet, came and stood beside her, a gentle smile on his face.

"I knew I couldn't be the only early riser here," he said, leaning his elbows on the balustrade. "Are you ready for today?"

Adelaide shook her head, but said, "I don't know."

"John is a good man, you know," Lucas said, reading into her answer. "You should give him a chance. I know happy marriages are rare, but you might be surprised. He's a surprising fellow."

"Will I see you at the church?" Adelaide asked, hopeful for a familiar face.

Lucas shook his head. "I'm to stay here, guard the gates, and let the brothers in when they come to do their penance," he said. "We drove the men who tried to break it down out of the city, but Lord Edwin wants every man on guard today."

Adelaide didn't respond. She barely heard what Lucas said. Her eyes remained steady on the palace gate. She tried to will the figure of Antony to appear there, to break through the gate. To take her away.

Ilse found her and implored her to return to her chamber to get ready. Suddenly Adelaide was back in her solar, surrounded by ladies pulling petticoats over her head and cinching her dress tight to her waist. Ilse brushed out her hair and fastened it with golden pins.

Adelaide looked at herself in the mirror. In a world that had fallen into winter, her gown was spring. The threads were intertwined with shades of milky white and soft blue, like an afternoon sky. It seemed to change color with every movement she made. Her long, fluttering sleeves almost dragged along the floor with the train of her dress. Her veil flowed down her hair like a silken river, lightly concealing the cascade of golden pins that pulled her hair back from her face. Her face looked miserable. The gown was wasted on her.

Pauline entered her solar after Adelaide was dressed. When she looked at Adelaide, her eyes were wet with tears. She swept forward and gripped Adelaide's hands. Once again, Pauline wore a bodice much too tight for her generous figure. Her cleavage rippled as she shook her head brusquely.

"My dear," she said in a half-whisper. "My dear."

To Adelaide's surprise, Pauline embraced her, holding her like a daughter, her chin resting protectively on Addie's head. Then, she held Adelaide at arm's length. Her tears left streaks on her wrinkled face.

"I only wish your father were here," she said. "And your mother. I'm sorry that it is only me."

"Is Landon coming?" Adelaide hated to ask it. She yearned to see him. She yearned for anything familiar.

Pauline paused for a long time before shaking her head. Adelaide felt tears prick her own eyes. *But I'm not alone,* she thought, looking up at her aunt. She still felt it.

Antony must know, she thought. *Any moment he'll come and take me away. He won't let this happen to me.*

The townsfolk had started calling him *Vispilio* after the trial. She'd helped him raid the soldiers' foodstores to provide for them, for saints' sake. Had he forgotten all about her? *I need your help too,* Vispilio.

The carriage had arrived to take her to the Cathedral of the Nine. Pauline escorted Adelaide on her arm downstairs. They climbed into the carriage. Every moment seemed to flash past Adelaide's eyes—the shoes slipped onto her feet, the fur-lined cloak placed gingerly around her shoulders, the cold sky above them as they stepped into the carriage. She watched it all like a mummer's play, unattached, uninterested.

As they rode to the cathedral, Adelaide heard voices behind the curtained windows. She remembered the day she and Pauline arrived in Southborn. The road around them had teemed with the daily activity of the town as the carriage jostled along the cobbles.

These voices were angry.

When she stepped out of the carriage at the cathedral, Adelaide saw the faces that belonged to the voices. They watched her dourly, spitting in her direction, cursing at her.

"Another whore Tanor is marrying off?" someone said.

"A stitch of your gown could feed my son for a week," said another.

"Whore," said another.

"Bitch," said another.

Adelaide looked into their faces. *I'm with you,* she tried to say. *I'm on your side. I don't want to be here.*

She scanned the crowd—faces dirty, cheeks red with cold, brows furrowed into scowls—but her gaze stopped.

Beneath a dark cloak, she saw Antony's face. She blinked, wondering if she imagined it, but he was there. His handsome face was shadowed with stubble. He didn't scowl like the rest. He seemed to be trying to tell her something, too.

Adrian, she tried to say. *Help me. Help me, please.*

But Antony only turned, disappearing into the crowd.

Pauline coiled a protective arm around Adelaide as they walked the short distance to the doors of the cathedral. "Pay them no mind, my dear," she whispered. "You are not to blame for any of their anger."

But I am, Adelaide thought.

They walked into the cathedral.

The cool stone air enveloped her at once. Even in the quiet little narthex, Adelaide could sense the immense space beyond the wooden double doors. She could hear the hum of people, the lilt of music. She thought of Brother David. Even he wouldn't be there today.

"Dry your eyes, my dear," Pauline said. Adelaide didn't realize she'd been crying. "You are capable of this, my dear."

Adelaide's heart only beat faster as the doors opened to the sanctuary. The hum of people became louder, then immediately hushed. She heard the rustle of dresses and trousers brushing against the wooden pews as hundreds of people stood up at once and turned to look at her.

She barely knew half of the people there, but Tanor wanted a spectacle— after all, weddings meant peace and prosperity, even if it was the wedding of a bastard. Each pew was adorned with winter ivy and holly and pine. She could smell them just below the ancient scent of the sanctuary. Guests seemed to have worn their best as well, Adelaide thought as she looked across the sea of crushed velvet and cloth-of-gold.

Some faces seemed confused to see a miserable bride on her wedding day.

Reluctantly, Adelaide lifted her eyes to the apse, blinded briefly by the bright, cold light shining through the windows. Tanor had new clothes tailored for John. It was a fine garment, a dark blue velvet tunic, slashed at the wrists to reveal delicate white satin underneath. The hem and collar were embroidered with gold thread. Adelaide saw John fidgeting with the sleeves, tugging them further down his wrists. With his hair oiled back from his forehead and trimmed since the last time she saw him, he didn't look like himself. She was sure she didn't look like herself, either.

King Tanor sat at the front of the church. In the pew behind him stood Elanor, a lady-in-waiting beside her with Prince Charles on her lap. Tanor watched Adelaide smugly. His eyes slid up and down her body in a way that made her face flame with heat.

Finally, she joined John at the altar. The priest prayed the Rite of the Saints over them as they stood, then invited them to kneel and join hands. Adelaide gingerly took John's hand, not looking at him.

The priest prayed to each saint in a slow, monotonous tone. Adelaide's knees hurt. She barely heard what the priest spoke. Their hands were wrapped with a piece of winding sheet as the priest prayed the Prayer of Saint Odette.

"In life, these two are joined. In death, they join with the saints. May naught part them till they are shrouded by Saint Odette," droned the priest.

The priest blessed them again, and they rose. John presented Adelaide with a silver ring studded with a simple blue stone. He slid it onto the smallest finger of her left hand. Adelaide looked at it for a moment as it caught the light.

"In the eyes of Saint Augustus and all the saints, we now recognize John Behrens, lord of Highmoor, and Adelaide DuMont, lady of Highmoor."

John stooped and kissed her gently. Adelaide could only think of the night in the barracks, the uncomfortable closeness of his body. She thought of the night that was to come.

John and Adelaide made their way to the transept, where they would receive gifts and tokens from the guests. Adelaide looked wearily at the people queuing down the aisle of the transept. Tanor sat on a decorative chair nearby and watched them, Edwin close at hand.

She was married. Antony never came. He'd let it happen.

Women Adelaide had never met came up to her and embraced her, making her dizzy with noxious fumes of rose petal or lavender. They would press a coin into her hand, or a gem, or handkerchief. One placed a small vial into her palm and closed Adelaide's fingers around it.

"A gift just *for you*, my lady," said the older woman. She leaned in and whispered in her ear. "Put this on your nethers and you'll be sure to conceive tonight."

Other women looked at her slyly and gave her advice she didn't ask for, whispered in her ear. One woman, round-faced and pimpled, took hold of Adelaide's waist.

"Love your figure while you can," she said. "He'll fill you with sons ere long!"

A pale man approached with limp blond hair. He bowed to both of them.

"Lord Martin Sudbury, my lady," he said, his wide eyes on her. He was older, but his face was handsome, familiar. *Did he serve on the council with my father?*

"My wife sends her regrets that she could not join me," Martin said. "For you, my lady." He produced a simple wrapped piece of linen. Adelaide opened it.

It took her a moment to realize its importance. Inside the linen was an ornamental hairpin studded with glass jewels. Nothing ornate, but something that Adelaide had often worn to match her favorite blue dress...

It was *hers*. It was the hairpin the outlaws had stolen when she and Pauline traveled to Southborn. She looked at it in awe now, as though it were a sacred treasure, then back at the man, wide-eyed. She glanced around and realized that John had been pulled away, talking to Edwin in the corner of the transept.

Her eyes returned to the lord. His expression seemed to say, *Not a word about this.* He merely bowed again with a, "My lady," and left. Before John returned, Adelaide tucked the pin quickly into her hair.

This could only have come from one person, she thought. *He has not forgotten.*

When the gift-giving was complete, Adelaide felt crumpled, poked, and prodded. She took John's arm, and they walked through the throng of guests. More poking. More prodding. In the narthex, Adelaide heard the anger outside. It was louder. Now it was John with an arm around her as they rushed to the carriage. Adelaide heard cries of "Bastard!" as they passed. Neither of them spoke in the carriage on the way to the palace.

She searched the crowd. Antony was gone.

They greeted their wedding guests again while they filed into the Great Hall for festivities. The Great Hall was decorated even grander than the cathedral, with festoons of delicate cloth-of-gold arraying every table. Seasonal sprigs of holly and pine boughs adorned the columns, and the air was heavy with the scent of forest and smoke.

Finally, when all the others were seated and awaiting the meal, John and Adelaide joined them at the front of the room.

"To the happy couple, the lord and lady of Highmoor," said a voice from among the guests. The room raised their glasses of freshly poured wine and chorused, "To the happy couple!"

Adelaide looked up at John and met his eyes. It was one of the few times she'd looked directly at him that day. He was paler than usual, his eyes wide. She could've laughed. He was terrified.

"Well," said Adelaide, her voice low and husky. It was the first time she'd spoken to him beyond her vows. "Are you going to take my hand?" She lay her hand, palm upward, on the table. He clasped it gently. "For a man who doesn't shirk in the face of battle, you certainly let a small army of flabby noblemen intimidate you to the point of near fainting."

John turned red as the meal was served. The evening wore on, the light outside dimming into nothing from the early winter sunset. More candles and torches were lit, and the room grew hotter. After the meal, couples began to dance and jig merrily in the center of the room.

Slow music played—the Ballad of Saint Juniper. Adelaide knew it was customary for a bride and groom to dance to that song. She and John stood, and he took her hand. His palm was damp as he led her to the center of the room. It was a simple dance, one easily mastered, even by children, but John's arms shook. His steps were ever so slightly offbeat. Their movement was awkward and clumsy, despite Adelaide's best efforts to compensate.

"I'm out of practice," he said awkwardly as she turned about him. He had been on the periphery of her sight and mind all day—her groom. Her husband. Now there he was, unavoidable, his body close to hers again.

And looking at him then—terrified, cowardly, oafish—something in Adelaide broke. Perhaps it was the heat of the room, the exhaustion she already felt, that Antony didn't do a thing to help her. She felt the weight of the pin in her hair. This whole thing was so ridiculous—did no one see it but her?

Lucas might have thought he was a good man. Pauline might have thought he was gentle. But Adelaide truly knew.

"I blame you for everything," she said, softly so only he could hear. "You *are* to blame for everything."

The grip on her hand became stronger. Almost painful. She didn't look away from him. *This is what you wanted,* she tried to say. *Now you have me.*

"Will we ever love each other?" John asked abruptly. The question surprised Adelaide.

"Love has nothing to do with it," Adelaide answered. "There's no love in this room at all, John. Look around. Everyone in this room is putting on a show, just like us. Arranged marriages to produce male heirs. Doing whatever they want in the dark, away from the performance. Like your father and Elanor—"

"Addie—" John pulled her closer. His anger was becoming dangerous. Adelaide felt Tanor's eyes on them, watching, wondering what they were saying.

"—making amends for his wrongdoings by marrying off his whoreson heir to an orphan and sending them away. The sooner you realize that it's all a ruse, the less obviously self-conscious you will be."

"I'm not self-conscious."

Adelaide spun suddenly as the music rose and clasped his hand again. Now it was her grip was fierce. "You're trembling."

"I'm not trembling," said John stoically, but his hand was shaking badly.

"What are you afraid of?" She let her voice rise. All the other couples were too far from them to hear. As her question hung in the air, the music shuddered to an end, and for the first time that evening, Adelaide truly exhaled.

The other nobles clapped for them, their moods mellowing with wine. John took a deep draft as soon as they sat down. Adelaide desperately wanted to get drunk. But she knew she had one more duty left for that night. And it was almost time for them to depart.

Tanor stood up with a self-satisfied smile on his face, his goblet of wine in hand. The guests quieted when they saw their king rise and spoke.

"It does a father's heart good to see his child married," he said, his voice thick and saccharine. "In fact, twenty-four years ago yesterday, the Saints saw fit to make me father to this young man. Before I was a king, before I was hardly even a lord, I was his father. And that is what I hope for myself in all things—to be father to my children first, and everything else second."

Adelaide hadn't known it was John's birthday the day before. She glanced at him. He was watching his father, his mouth a firm, hard line. His guests were touched by Tanor's stirring words. His son was not.

"To my son and my new daughter, Lord and Lady Highmoor."

The festivities continued. Well-wishers came and went to Adelaide and John's table and dancers whirled around the room. Voices grew louder as full carafes of wine replaced empty. Prince Charles was ushered to bed as the hour grew later. The Brothers of the Nine entered and cleared plates from the table, paying their penance to Saint Morgan—hooded and silent, almost unseen. Adelaide was asked to dance by men young and old. More poking. More prodding.

As Adelaide watched the revelry from her chair, a voice surprised her. "Would you dance with me, my lady?"

Adelaide turned and saw Lord Edwin standing in front of her. He was a handsome man, his gray-flecked hair slicked back and his eyes keen and bright. His hand was extended to her across the table. She took it. It was strong and confident as it guided her around the table and onto the floor.

Where John was an uncoordinated dancer, Edwin was brusque and precise. They moved seamlessly together, and Edwin's eyes never left hers. He was barely taller than her, so her hand rested easily on his shoulder.

"You make a fetching bride, my lady," Edwin said, his voice low and warm. "The least you could do is smile. You've looked miserable all day."

Adelaide said nothing. She was a little breathless by the speed of the caper. Edwin seemed unfazed.

"I heard your dress was custom made in Ettelia," he continued. "In fact, I know it was. I signed the ledger myself."

"I just don't see a reason for all of this," Adelaide said. "The people outside are angry. They're hungry."

"Exactly," Edwin said. "They are *outside.*"

The caper continued. Edwin's hand came to rest on Adelaide's waist as they turned. He leaned into her, their faces inches apart. She smelled the wine, red and earthy, on his breath.

"His grace would like to give you a message," he breathed. "Lord John will bed you tonight. You will not try to escape from this. Your dowry has been paid, and lands have been secured for your brother. His grace intends to see blood on the bedsheets tomorrow morning."

Adelaide's blood turned cold. She glanced warily at Tanor.

As she did, a brown blur hissed through the air. It hummed past Adelaide's ear like an angry wasp to where she almost attempted to swat it away. But it wasn't an insect. The object flew across the room and collided with the goblet in Tanor's hand. With a clang, the goblet clattered to the floor behind him. The music petered to a halt, and the room went still.

"Your grace, your reckoning has arrived," a voice rang across the Great Hall. Adelaide turned toward the door. The crowd of now-frightened guests parted and there stood a hooded, broad-shouldered novice, with an arrow on the string of a bow. "No one move. Or an arrow is going through your king's heart."

The other brothers in the room remained hooded too, but many of them now held knives to the throats of nearby revelers, men and women alike. Adelaide scanned the crowd and saw the pale-haired man from earlier. The tip of a knife was held to his throat. *He has a wife and children*, she thought.

The room was suddenly silent, and eerily so. Adelaide didn't hear so much as a breath. The brother stalked into the room, his arrow still trained on Tanor. The king had gone white, and beside him Elanor was clutching her belly. This man had the entire room hostage.

"Why are you here?" Tanor asked. "What is the meaning of this?

"I come on behalf of Prince Adrian, son of King Alfred."

Adelaide stared at the figure. Edwin was still holding her, gripping her tighter now. The frozen crowd gasped and murmured as they scrutinized the man. Tanor didn't say a word. His face remained stolid, but Adelaide could see fear flickering in his eyes.

"That crown belongs to him, Tanor," said the man. "Now the question is, are you going to give it to me, or are we going to take it from you?"

With a flick of his head, the man pushed the hood off his face. Adelaide's breath caught in her throat. It was David, the novice from the cathedral. He looked determined, his grip strong on the bow. When Adelaide met with him in the palace, he was hooded. Adelaide saw how shaggy his hair had grown, how drawn his face had become. The ghost of stubble dotted his face. She had not seen the anguish he was in when she met with him. Now, all she saw was desperation.

"I'll do what I have to," he said. His eyes fell briefly on Adelaide, but he didn't seem to register her. "The *Vispilio* isn't the only one trying to change things. I helped start the fire in the village. Because things need to change—and fast. And it starts with *him*."

He motioned his head brusquely toward King Tanor. Beside him, Elanor fluttered a hand to her mouth.

"No one here is that stupid, your grace," David shouted. "They're just well-paid. You know very well who the *Vispilio* really is. You know very well that *you're* a pretender."

The guests gasped. Edwin's grip on Adelaide was like a vice now.

"I wonder what it felt like," David continued. He was looking at John now. He stalked past Adelaide toward John until the sharp tip of his arrow pricked the taut flesh of John's neck. David looked up only slightly to meet the taller man's eye. A small stream of blood ran down toward John's collar. "To have your head lopped off by a child."

"I didn't kill him," John said. His voice sounded strangely small.

"So you're blameless, then?" David barked. "So someone else hit the prince's head with a rock and sent him tumbling into the Skeldergate River?"

A whisper within Adelaide willed David to kill him. John's desperate eyes swung around the room, looking at Tanor, then at Adelaide.

"That's not true," John said. "That's not true."

"Your father sits on a faulty throne," David said. "And that's not right. That's not *just*. And all of that injustice started here, in this room, with all of you! And it will end here too."

Adelaide saw something in his eyes that terrified her. He was still afraid, yes, but now he was angry. It burned on his face, his brow damp with sweat. Hot tears rolled down his cheeks.

"*Men!*"

The room erupted in noise and chaos. More brothers burst through the door, pushing past the well-dressed guests, holding clubs, blunt knives, even scythes that they'd hidden in their cloaks. Edwin pushed Adelaide away from him and darted off, out of sight. Adelaide rushed away from the floor and back to her table, cowering there. The only door was blocked by these men. There was no way out.

As she watched, the men seemed rowdy, but not violent. They grabbed women by the waist, smacked lords upside the head with clubs sending them sprawling. They gobbled up the dregs of the meal before heaving tables over. They caused chaos. They didn't use their knives.

But David still had a dangerous look in his eye.

In one fluid motion, David aimed his bow toward one guest sitting near Tanor—one of his council members. He fired an arrow, and it pounded into the man's chest with a meaty smack, followed by an alarmed cry.

The cry silenced the room for a moment. Peasants and nobles alike watched the nobleman in horror. With a final wheeze, the lord toppled from his chair.

The room erupted in more screams as David pulled another arrow back. John was charging toward him as the other guests began standing up, trying to run out of the room. Before John could apprehend him, David had fired one more arrow in King Tanor's direction.

In the flurry of activity, it missed Tanor and struck Elanor in the throat. She stared wide-eyed at David, then at her lover. With a frightened gurgle, she fell out of her chair.

Just as the arrow twanged off the string, Adelaide saw John tackle David, yanking the bow from his hands. David struggled with him for a moment. He was strong enough to be a match for John, but he only flailed halfheartedly, terror still gleaming in his eyes. John gritted his teeth and punched the boy soundly in the face. Then, they were both lost in the melee of the room as guests crowded the door to escape and as the men destroyed the great hall. Edwin was with Tanor now, kneeling under the head table.

A hand grabbed Adelaide's arm and she screamed. She whipped around and saw Lucas, his face bloodied.

"Come with me," he said. "Don't look back. Just keep your head down."

She cowered into him, and he barreled through the crowd. Since he had been guarding the gate, he had his sword. He brandished it to anyone who stood in their way.

"Are you all right, Addie?"

"Yes," Adelaide said breathlessly. Though her heart was racing from the events that had just occurred, her mind remained numb. She was still trying to understand what had just happened. Moments flashed before her eyes. The arrow in the lord's chest. The one in Elanor's throat. Edwin's terrified eyes. As they rushed down the corridor, Lucas yelled at every guard and soldier they passed to go to the Great Hall, and to *hurry.*

"They'll be apprehended soon enough," Lucas panted. "They've only a few men. What a foolhardy lot they are."

Adelaide could hardly hear him above her pounding heart, the blood rushing through her ears. She realized she was shaking from the energy, shivering though the corridor was warm. In the back of her mind, she knew what would happen to David. She knew what would happen to every single one of those men.

But in the front of her mind, a single thought remained. *Perhaps I won't get bedded tonight after all.*

Lucas led Adelaide back to her own solar and stood in the doorway. "Do you need anything, my lady?" he asked. He was more composed now. His hair was a mess and his face was still bruised and bloodied, but he stood at attention before her.

Shut the door and don't let anyone come in. Anyone. "No. Thank you, Lucas," Adelaide said.

Lucas nodded, then suddenly gripped her arm. "I promise you are safe, Addie," he said, looking at her earnestly. "I'll be outside this door until John comes—if he is able. I'll stay there all night if need be."

Until John comes. Bile rose in her throat. Her heart set to pounding again.

Lucas closed the door, and the silence of the room crashed around Adelaide. It made her more aware of the ringing in her ears, the pounding of her heart. A servant had started a fresh fire in her solar, knowing she would be back soon. She stood as close to it as she could bear, still shivering though not cold. Her hands trembled as she tried to unfasten her own gown from the back. She tugged and pulled, worming her shoulders out through the bodice so she could pull it down her body. She left it in a pile on the floor.

Adelaide paused when she heard the cathedral bells ringing frantically. The night was already thick in the winter evening outside. That sort of toll usually meant an early curfew, that villagers were to go home and bolt their doors. It was the kind of toll used in wartime. It was the toll she heard the night King Alfred died.

She sat on the sofa for a while in her dressing gown, collecting herself. John could walk in at any moment. For a long time, she didn't hear any footsteps, only the occasional shuffle or reassuring cough from Lucas outside her door.

Perhaps he won't come, she thought, twisting the ring on her little finger. It felt so strange and heavy there. *There was a fight, after all. They'll need him to apprehend the men, bring them down to the dungeons. The guards will need to discuss what happened and clear the Great Hall, and calm the guests—whatever guests are still left in the palace.*

She laid back on the sofa. The day passed behind her closed eyes in brief moments. That was all the day would ever be for her, now. Moments. Flickers in time.

As the fire warmed her, Adelaide wondered where Antony was. If he had sent David to the palace. He wouldn't have. Antony would've known that was stupid. She remembered him in the dungeon, how defeated he looked. Then at court, and how strong he became. How could anyone deny it? He was the picture of King Alfred.

Then, as her thoughts became addled with exhaustion, she remembered them dancing. The closeness of him. The strength of his arms. The warmth of his smile. The moment she looked up at his face and knew. The way he looked down at her, his lips open and his head tilted, as though ready to—

The door flew open, and Adelaide's eyelids snapped up. John's figure filled the doorway. Lucas was gone. He and Adelaide immediately locked eyes and Adelaide's stomach sank. His tunic was crushed and torn. There was a smear of blood on one satin sleeve. Adelaide didn't want to know whose it was.

And she was suddenly aware of how loose her dressing gown was, how it was unfastened at the front. She bunched the collar together in her fist.

Husband and wife shared a long silence.

"Are you all right?" John asked.

"Yes. Are you?" Adelaide noticed the dried line of black blood on his neck.

"Yes."

He closed the door and stood there awkwardly, staring at her. His breaths came heavy, and his eyes looked tired. "They've all been arrested," he said. "Other than Lord Wistenbroek and...and Lady Elanor, no one is harmed."

"That's good," Adelaide said. She found her hands were trembling again.

"I..." John stammered. "I need to wash my...self."

Adelaide nodded. "There's a bowl of water over in the corner, by the mirror." She indicated the direction with a wave of her hand, every

393

movement feeling awkward and rehearsed.

He started off in that direction, then stopped as though realizing something. "This tunic, it—it fastens in the back. Can you—"

She had already stood up and walked over to him. She couldn't bear him being so awkward and uncomfortable. The tunic was fastened to him tightly with a crisscross of leather string. She pulled the tie loose and made her way up his back, pulling the string loose until he could pull it over his head. The loose satin tunic came off next. Adelaide had not seen him so bare before. She watched as he bent over the bowl of water and splashed his face. He was corded with strength, finely honed after a decade of fighting. Everywhere—his arms, his back, his chest—had scars of some kind, some deep and craggy, others raised and pink. Some were shaped like the slash of a sword, others like the bite of an arrowhead. Then there was the one on his cheek, shaped like a gemstone.

He rose, wiping the excess water from his face with his hands. He looked at her again, as though the sight of her was the anchor of his eyes.

"Are you sure you want to..." He trailed off, turning red in the face. "I mean, after tonight, don't you want to rest? We don't have to..."

Adelaide remembered what Edwin had said. "We should." She saw fear in his eyes. "We wouldn't want your father to ask questions, would we?"

John did not respond. Instead, he stepped forward and closed the distance between them. She saw a small scar, a gash at her eye level, just below his collarbone. She stared at it. She felt the warmth radiating off him. His breaths were slow and even, but she could see the vein in his neck pulsing fast and frantic.

"Look at me," John whispered. "Look at me, please."

He reached out and tilted her chin upward. *He won't harm you,* Pauline had told her. *He loves you.* Their bodies were touching now. He bent down and kissed her gingerly. She didn't reciprocate. She tugged her dressing down from her shoulders and let it slide down her body. She was suddenly vulnerable, on display for John to see. The room was warm, but she shivered, aware of every angle and curve and flaw of her body. John's face only turned redder and his eyes searched her face, afraid to look anywhere else as he unfastened his belt.

Adelaide closed her eyes.

Tanor

He watched the white winding sheet as it descended over the body of Elanor, lying prone in the infirmary. Magg stood across from him, watching the same motion. She was always stoic, but Tanor could see emotion pulling at the sides of her eyes. Magg's attendants had moved Elanor from where she'd lain after the chaos of the night, where her blood had flowed down her neck and around her head. Her beautiful red hair was tangled in black, coagulated mats. Magg had put her in a clean, white gown.

The baby could not be saved in time, Magg had told the king. The baby was a boy. He had already been wrapped for burial.

One hated. One beloved. One forgotten. But this one was not the forgotten one, nor was Claudia's daughter. Only three seeds would take root, the milky-eyed woman had said. This seed had been choked out.

"Send her and the boy back to the Roses." Tanor instructed her. "The weather will hold. Her father can bury them."

Magg said nothing. She was as white as the sheet that her attendants now wound around the woman. Lord Wistenbroek had already been wrapped. A man who was alive and sitting near Tanor mere hours before.

So had Elanor. Her eyes were open and staring upward in his direction. Cold. Almost accusatory. She had wanted to be by his side. She had paid the price.

Sir Lucas came panting up to the king and bowed. He made to speak, but then paused when he saw the winding sheets. He cleared his throat.

"They've all been apprehended, your grace," he said. "They all await your judgment in the dungeons. Shall we schedule the Court of the King's Bench?"

Tanor looked down at Elanor's empty eyes. He could've had another son. Charles could've been in Elanor's lap when the arrow flew through the air. The arrow could just as easily hit Tanor himself. His mind raged with unending thoughts.

We are no longer safe.

"No need for a trial," Tanor said. "Hang them all except for their leader at first light. He'll set a different kind of example."

Adelaide

She lay awake in the early hours of the dawn, watching John sleep beside her. Her body felt poked and prodded. Adelaide now knew him, and that knowledge gave her a sick feeling in her stomach. The feeling that she would have to know him again, and again, until they produced a child. Perhaps she had already conceived, and there was already a quickening in her womb. She still felt the stickiness of his seed between her legs.

The pale moonlight turned into the first rays of a gray winter dawn, silhouetting John's broad shoulders as he breathed deeply in sleep. In that first light of day, his form was colorless. As the light continued to rise, he became a translucent pale, before he finally became something of substance. Her husband.

John stirred and turned onto his back. She wondered what he dreamt of. He knew her now, too. Later that morning, they would ride out to Highmoor and live the rest of their days there. John would cease to be a knight and instead be a lord. She couldn't imagine him idle, doing the dull work of a nobleman. He seemed like a man destined for the battlefield. But their fates were both sealed.

The events of the night before seemed so distant. Adelaide had almost forgotten the chaos. Before she and John went to bed, she closed her mind off so she wouldn't have to think, so she wouldn't have to feel the discomfort, the awkwardness, John's clumsy fingers searching her body. When they had finished, Adelaide saw it on the bedsheets. A small bloom of blood. She had done her duty.

She must have fallen asleep again, a deep and consuming sleep, for she awoke bleary-eyed from a knock at her door.

"Come in," Adelaide murmured, her speech slurred and drowsy.

Ilse peered in cautiously, then stepped into the room. Adelaide realized John was gone. That made Ilse much more at ease. Adelaide was still naked under the bedclothes.

"Good morning, my lady," Ilse said with a curtsy. Adelaide noticed a sly look in her eye. "Would you like me to draw a bath for you?"

"Yes, please," Adelaide replied, still aware of the stickiness between her legs. "What time is it?"

"A little after nine bells, my lady," Ilse replied.

"Do you know where...my husband is?" The words felt strange in her mouth. Ilse smirked again.

"He went to the hanging this morning," Ilse said, as though it were the most obvious thing in the world. She prepared a white sheet over the wooden tub in Adelaide's chamber.

"Hanging?"

"The perpetrators last night. They were all hanged at dawn. Their bodies are hanging on the castle wall now. They're a warning, I guess."

Adelaide felt a little pang in her heart as Ilse left the room. That meant that David was dead. She remembered his innocence, his sweetness. He had been so kind to her without hardly knowing her. *A warning.*

Servants brought steaming hot bathwater into her chamber, and Ilse helped her ease into the tub. She brushed out Adelaide's hair as she soaked. The water was too hot. It pricked her skin. Adelaide liked it.

"Tell me everything, Addie," Ilse leaned in conspiratorially. "I've never seen a man's...well, I've never seen one before. What's it like?"

"Hairy," Adelaide replied, the memory twisting her stomach. "And ugly."

Ilse burst into giggles. "Did it hurt?"

"A little."

"Did you bleed?"

"A little."

"Was he pleased?"

"Ilse, please."

Ilse sighed in disappointment. "I want to *know*," she whined. "Do you think you're pregnant?"

"There's no way to know so early," Adelaide said. Her stomach turned again. Feeling nauseated could be a sign of pregnancy. Maybe she was.

"My mum said there's a way to tell after—the day afterward," Ilse said. "All you have to do is stick a finger up your—"

The door flew open, and John appeared. Adelaide had never been more thankful to see him. She did not want to talk to Ilse about her wedding night. John's face was pale, but his cheeks were red with cold. His eyes immediately fell on Adelaide, cautiously observing her body under the water.

"Er—" he stammered. "My lady."

Oh, by all the saints, we're married now. Don't be such a prude, Adelaide thought bitterly.

"His grace would like you in the courtyard as soon as you are able," John said.

Ilse huffed. "We've only just drawn a bath," she said.

John ignored her. "I'll wait outside," he said.

"You can wait *inside* if you want," Ilse murmured, out of his earshot. Adelaide splashed water on her.

Adelaide dried and dressed quickly. She found a maroon dress that was one of her many wedding gifts from the court and fastened a thick black riding cloak over it. Ilse braided her hair down her back. Adelaide slid her cheap hairpin into her hair, as though a little piece of Antony would go with her.

When Adelaide saw herself in the mirror, she looked tired, still flushed from the bath. She looked as though she'd aged years overnight. The dress felt a little tight. *Could Ilse be right? Could I know if I am with child already?* Her belly looked flat in the mirror, no more prominent than it usually was. Magg had said nothing about how soon it could happen, just that it could happen.

She hesitated before opening the door. She remembered the riot the night before. *Whatever this is, it won't be pleasant.* There had been hangings in the courtyard that morning, Ilse said. Was she on her way to witness more?

She met John outside, and he offered her his arm. He was dressed simpler than the day before, merely a dun-colored tunic and a roughspun cloak. His hair was no longer lacquered back on his head. It hung around his eyes and forehead in unkempt strands.

Adelaide didn't say a word to him. They passed their entire walk to the courtyard as quiet as a tomb. Adelaide felt John would make to say something—by an intake of breath or turning his head toward her—but never did. *A lifetime of silence ahead of me,* Adelaide thought.

The late morning was cold down to the bones, but the bright sky was piercingly blue. In the center of the parapet stood King Tanor, crown still perched upon his head. He turned at the sound of their footsteps. He looked as though he hadn't slept at all. His eyes were bloodshot and his face speckled with unkempt stubble. He did his best to look happy to see Adelaide.

"My beloved daughter-in-law," he said. As she approached, he leaned toward her and kissed her cheek. She smelled wine on his lips. "I am so sorry that your celebration came to such a state last night."

"I am sorry as well, but not for my sake," Adelaide said. "I am sorry for the loss of Lady Elanor, your grace."

Tanor's face did not change. "As am I," he said. "As am I." He gave John one dismissive glance, then turned toward the courtyard. "But justice shall be served."

"*Shall* be?" asked Adelaide. "Weren't all the perpetrators hanged this morning?"

Tanor ignored her. "Nothing short of insurrection," he continued. "We are not safe anymore. We're not safe from *them.* They disguised themselves as brothers, for Saints' sake." He gestured to the closed gate. "They want to kill us. All of us. We're surrounded by murderers."

The scaffolds were still erected in the middle of the courtyard, but they were empty. The ropes had been cut down. Two guards heaved a bent figure toward them.

"Not all the perpetrators were hanged this morning," Tanor said. "See for yourself."

The guards brought the figure onto the scaffold and yanked his head back by his hair. David. His shirt was tattered, bloody. He had been beaten. Instead of his right eye, all Adelaide saw was a deep purple gash, swollen and malformed, oozing blood and pus. His face was unreadable.

. "I apologize if this sight upsets you, my lady," Tanor said. "But he needed to be punished. And he must be punished further. Isn't that right, whelp?"

He raised his voice for David to hear. David didn't move.

David, Adelaide thought. *Was this your plan all along?*

"My only regret," called David between swollen lips, "was that *you* didn't die last night, *your grace.*"

"Shut up!" One guard punched David across the mouth. David sputtered and spit out a tooth.

"I pray that the Saints will continue the work that I have done," David lisped, fresh blood pouring out of his mouth. "That they will ignite the heart of Southborn against you!"

The guard struck him again. David fell face-forward. The guard heaved him up again, this time holding him in place so he wouldn't fall again.

"How old is this boy? Eighteen?" Tanor breathed. "A life wasted. I was making a name for myself at his age. I didn't take anyone's pity—or charity. I worked long and hard to become the man I am." His eyes flashed bright in the light of the clear blue sky, mimicking its pale color.

"John," Tanor said mildly. "Go join them on the scaffold. Show me there's at least one person I can trust. Beat him for as long as you see fit."

John hesitated until Tanor pointed his icy eyes at him. Though he towered over his father, John seemed to shrink like a child from a reproachful parent. Adelaide saw it—the need to please his unpleasable father. Tanor had broken his will. *He was right. He was only ever his father's weapon.*

Adelaide remembered David's cutting words to John the night before—

he announced John's secret to the entire court. Adelaide wondered if the court would believe him. She'd known the secret already. It could just as easily have been her on that scaffold, awaiting punishment.

The guards handed John a whip as he approached. Adelaide tried to read him, her stomach turning at every passing moment. David would die, just like Bron did, at her husband's hand.

The whip found its mark across David's shoulders. He flinched, but made no sound. Again, the whip came down. The guards held him upright. He shuddered a bit when the whip descended again. He was like a horse under the rod of his master—huge and capable of ending his captor, but unable to do so.

David's one good eye met Adelaide's. His gaze was so placid, as if he were in no pain at all. She stared back at him until tears flooded from her eyes. He was so young. She somehow felt responsible for him.

John's strikes were becoming more frequent and forceful. He barely paid attention to the mangled, bloody back. He simply swung, and swung, each swing bringing a splatter of blood across his hands and tunic. Adelaide caught the dangerous anger in his eyes—a look she'd seen so often when they were children, when John was so often slighted and bullied.

Then she watched as David's eye flickered, sometimes alight, sometimes glazed over. *Go be with the Saints,* she willed him. *Let Saint Odette embrace you and bring you peace.*

Suddenly David collapsed completely, prostrate on the scaffold. John dropped the whip, panting. His entire front—face, tunic, hands—was speckled with blood, like a macabre painting. He didn't look the same as when he'd executed Bron—he'd looked almost ashamed, then, embarrassed. Now, he looked triumphant, as though he would gladly beat a dozen more men.

Immediately he stepped down from the scaffold and back up the parapet, brushing past them both and disappearing into the palace. Tanor lingered, looking down at the broken boy, paying no heed to Adelaide.

"When he dies, dump the body in the Skeldergate," Tanor called to the guards as he glided away. The guards gave the rumpled body one last kick and left the courtyard.

When they were gone, Adelaide walked numbly down the stairs toward the scaffold. David was still alive, wheezing, motionless. She smelled hot blood as she got closer. His eye was barely open, and didn't seem to see anything. Suddenly his low, gravelly voice wheezed.

"My lady, I'm sorry."

"You have nothing to be sorry for." She could barely speak. She put a hand on his matted hair and started to cry. She didn't know what else to do other than stroke his hair.

"Do—" she said. "Do you have any family? Anyone I should tell?"

A small smile played on David's swollen, bloody lips. "No," he whispered. "Tell the order, maybe. The brothers might say a prayer for me. And tell the outlaws. Tell them I'm sorry."

Warm tears drifted down Adelaide's cold face.

"You are the only good thing left here, my lady," David said.

He stared into nothingness, unblinking. A few moments passed before Adelaide realized he wasn't breathing. Her hand glided downward, and she gently closed his eye, his skin still warm under her fingers.

She slowly realized, as David's soul flew from his broken body, far away from her, that she was alone. He had been a connection to Antony, a connection to hope. He'd said Antony was in the Hemlock Forest. But what had he been doing all this time?

The air suddenly felt close. She smelled David's rank blood and corruption around his eye and wanted to retch.

There's nowhere to go now. I'm not going with John. No safety. I won't win this. Everyone who could've helped me is gone.

"Addie."

When she turned she saw John. All she could see were the smears of blood on his arms. Everything else about him faded away. Bloody John.

He had once been her friend, a kindness in her life. But now he was a monster.

It was all she could see.

"Addie," he said when he saw her distress. But his eyes were still bright with that violent light, the need for more bloodshed. "I'm sorry. I didn't know you knew him."

"Leave me alone." Adelaide was trembling. She could barely hear herself through her pounding ears. Her vision became blotched, and she tried to blink it away.

The front gate was opening. A carriage was arriving to fetch one of the wedding guests, she assumed.

"Adelaide—"

"Leave me alone!"

Adelaide bolted. She tried to block everything out of her mind—David's swollen eye, blood spattered on John's sleeves, Tanor's look of madness. She had to find the outlaws. The air was brisk and stung her face.

She knew there were eyes on her as she rushed down the street, stumbling in front of carts or running into passersby. She wrapped her cloak tightly around her ornate dress and pulled the hood up against the cold. She didn't care who or what she toppled over. She stepped on feet and rammed into shoulders. The anger around her was still palpable. She needed to find somewhere safe.

The Cathedral of the Nine loomed above her. The place of her wedding. But also the place of safety. Where she had found Antony. Where they had found each other.

She heaved open the great oaken door. She ducked into the enveloping coolness, so much more inviting than the day before. Her aunt had stood with her there in the transept yesterday. Her aunt. *I'm sorry, Aunt Pauline,* she thought. Pauline would leave soon anyway. She had her own children and grandchildren to nurture.

Adelaide slid down the stairs to the crypt, the plainchant of the brothers ringing in her ears. *I have to tell them,* she thought. *David said I have to tell them.* Fresh tears welled in her eyes. The cold darkness of the crypt sucked her in. She knew where Adrian's tomb was. She raced right toward it and collapsed.

The silence in the crypt was total. No plainchant. No mice scurrying among the tombs. No bustle of the streets above. Adelaide wasn't sure she could hear her own heartbeat either. Even her sobs came quietly. They racked her body but made no sound. When she put her hand to her face, she realized it was wet. Wet with David's blood. It only deepened her tears.

"All saints," she prayed frantically, angrily, her voice a breath. "Bring David's soul into the stars and let him dwell with you. He did nothing wrong. He only thought he did your bidding. Let me do your bidding now. And all saints, I pray that if there is a quickening in my belly that you curdle it where it grows!"

Her words were hot, an anguished scream. She breathed. Her tears dried on her face, taut and itchy. Her eyes felt swollen. She became aware of a deep pain in her belly and wondered if the saints had heard her prayer. That there was a baby inside her, and they were killing it for her.

But she felt a familiar warmth between her legs, a slow seeping that followed the discomfort. Her monthly bleed. She sighed shakily. She was not pregnant. She did not carry a monster's seed.

Antony

The air only grew colder as the sun fell. The dusky sky was clear above Southborn. As Antony had approached the day before, the city seemed peaceful—warm yellow light in the tight-quartered homes, blanketed by a purple sky. But as he drew closer, he smelled its rank. Closer still, and he heard the cries.

He stayed in the city for the rest of the night, finding quiet corners of busy taverns where he wouldn't be seen. The bastard's wedding seemed to be all that the commoners could talk about.

That was when the curfew bells had started ringing and the commoners were forced out of the tavern, spilling out onto the cold streets in confusion. Antony hid in an alleyway until morning, not sleeping, wrapping his cloak around him against the cold.

Southborn erupted again the next morning. A clear, tepid blue sky hung over the town, and throngs of people jostled in the narrow streets. There seemed to be unrest everywhere now. First, it had started in the wealthier quarter of town, with peasants marching up the clean streets to start fires or break in doors. Now it didn't seem to matter to anyone what house started on fire, what shop was looted. Shop doors hung open, swinging loosely from broken hinges. Carts of vegetables were overturned and rotting.

Antony shouldered through a tight crowd gathered near the entrance of a tavern. They were watching something. Antony heard it before he saw it. Feet scraping against the cobbles, the grunts of a fight. He craned his neck. A man in a green tunic was raining blows down on a dirty-faced young man.

"You deserve as much as the blokes on the rampart and worse, pigfucker!" panted the man in green. He stopped punching the boy when the prone figure started convulsing unnaturally. White froth burbled from his open mouth, and his eyes glazed over.

"You killed him, you monster!" screamed a woman in the crowd. The crowd surged forward as one around Antony, who resisted their pull. They fell upon the man in green mercilessly. As Antony peeled himself away from the crowd, he heard the tearing of clothes and breaking of bones, and a sickening gurgle from the green man.

His heart pounded for a different reason now. Somehow, Southborn had become far worse overnight. How had it happened so fast?

The cathedral seemed to be the only place untouched in the village. It loomed above the chaos like a judge who had not yet made his ruling, silent and calculating. The surrounding cobbles seemed quieter too, as though shielded from the noise and confusion. Antony heaved open the door to find it even quieter inside.

The sanctuary was alight with the gentle glow of hundreds of candles—some lit in remembrance of loved ones, others in honor of each saint.

Antony took a moment to breathe in their waxy, burnt smell, mingled with the cool stone of the cathedral. What was happening? Had he caused all of this?

Out of the gloom walked a brother, draped in a dark robe, his face gray and downcast.

"Brother," Antony called softly out to him. His voice felt thunderous in the huge, silent space.

The brother looked up at him. He was middle-aged, his eyes deeply sunken into his face, colorless in the faint light.

"I heard someone outside talking about men on the ramparts, and that they deserve to be there," Antony said. "What's happened?"

The brother grimaced. "Do you not know?" he asked flatly. "Some men disguised as members of our order raided the palace yesterday evening. They killed a lord—and his grace's mistress."

Oh no, Antony wanted to say. He remembered David and his determination. He had been successful.

"And all the perpetrators have been…?"

"Hanged. Yes."

Antony felt a tightness in his chest. *David, you fool,* was all he could think. *You absolute and total fool.*

The brother took a step toward him, his grimace deepening. "You're…" He lifted a pointed finger. "It's you."

Antony raised a finger to his lips. "I was never here," he said. "And I had nothing to do with what happened at the palace. I'd like to visit the crypt, if I may."

The brother allowed Antony into the crypt. It felt so familiar to him now. He walked along the lines of tombs, some worn, some centuries old, until he came to King Alfred's. The marble was newer, more freshly carved. Queen Catherine lay beside him, and finally his own childhood likeness. He saw it so clearly now in the boyish features.

He walked around the family of tombs, around to the place he slept that first night in Southborn—and saw a dark shadow cowering away from him.

A woman's voice came from the shadow.

"Antony?"

The shadow launched itself at him, clinging to his waist in a tight embrace. Antony knew her by her smell, the tendrils of thick hair tickling his chin. Adelaide.

He realized she was sobbing into his chest, so he saved his questions. He wrapped his arms around her instead, relieved. He never thought he'd be able to hold her like this. She was closer to him than she'd ever been now. The thought filled him with warmth.

Adelaide's breath came in shallow gasps when she pulled away to look up at him. "I didn't even try," she said. "I've done nothing. I've done nothing to help anyone. The people in the streets yesterday—they hated me. They *hated* me. And I hate myself."

She collapsed into his chest again. "I watched him die," she mumbled into the fabric of his tunic. "I watched his soul leave his eyes." Her voice faded away into more tears.

I've seen that happen, too. Antony thought of Markus.

Adelaide pulled away to look up at him again. In the dim light, Antony could see her beautiful features, marred by streaks of tears. Gingerly, he lifted a hand and wiped some away with his thumb. His finger brushed her wet eyelash, so delicate.

"Are you really here?" she asked. Antony nodded. "I never thought I'd see you again."

"Neither did I."

The words hung between them for a long time.

"It's my fault," Antony said quietly. "David came to our camp a few nights ago. He told me about his plan. I should've done more to stop him."

Adelaide placed her hands gently on his arms. He was silent for a long time. He examined every part of her face that he could make out in the darkness. The chestnut hair he wanted to bury his fingers in. The eyes he wanted to gaze into. The lips he wanted to…

"We met when we were children," he blurted. "Your father brought you to stay with us and be introduced to court. I thought you were a prude for the longest time. But then I became jealous of John because you would spend so much time with him."

A smile played on Adelaide's mouth. That was before they realized how terrible the world could be, Antony realized. Before his father and mother died. Before Adrian was ripped from his family, like flesh from a bone.

But the world was still terrible, he thought. He looked down at her, a strange prickling feeling in the corners of his eyes.

"You're married to him now, aren't you?"

More tears flowed down her face.

"Yes," she said, her voice barely a whisper. Another wave of sobs took her, and she cried. As she did, Antony slowly wrapped his arms around her, pulling her into his chest, resting his chin on the top of her head. He gripped her firmly, never wanting to release her. She was safe there with him. He could protect her.

"You're so strong, Addie," he said. "Stronger than I could ever be."

"I'm not," her voice bubbled out of her throat, her face a wet mess on his tunic. He held her tighter.

"We used to dance, didn't we?" he asked sheepishly.

Adelaide nodded, looking up at him. "You loved to dance."

"When I danced with you in the Great Hall," Antony said, "at the Commoner's Ball. That was the last time I think I felt truly happy."

Adelaide looked up at him. "Me too." He reached up and brushed the tear tracks off her cheeks.

"Addie, I'm sorry."

"For what?"

"I'm...s—"

Before he could say it again, Adelaide kissed him. She pulled his face down to hers with desperate hands, pressed her lips firmly into his. He yielded to her, and they melted into one another for one sweet moment, a moment lost long ago when they were innocent children. Antony held on for as long as he could. He laced his hands into her hair and pulled her in. He wanted her closer, as close as she could be to him. He wanted to unfasten the cloak around her neck, pull down the sleeves of her gown, and—

He pulled away suddenly. "You're married," he said. He felt guilt wash over him.

"I don't care," she said firmly. Her voice rang in the silence of the crypt. "I'm married to a murderer."

"I'm a murderer, too."

She shook her head but said nothing. She leaned against him again, nuzzling into his neck. Antony felt her warm breath on his skin, still shallow, still urgent, but growing calmer the longer they held each other.

"They're probably wondering where you are," Antony said after a while. John *is probably wondering where you are,* he thought.

"I don't care," Adelaide said again. "I don't care about any of them anymore. I want to run away with you."

"What?"

411

Adelaide looked up at him, passion in her eyes. "Take me back with you. Take me to your camp. Let me fight alongside you."

"Addie, you can't be serious—"

"I am. I can't go back there. Don't make me go back there."

Antony looked at her, fiery, beautiful. Of course he wanted her with him. But she had a duty—to her family, to her husband. But Antony remembered she hadn't any family, only a drunkard brother. And he didn't give a damn about her duty to John.

"Alright," he said. And he kissed her again.

The door to the crypt creaked open above them, and footsteps descended.

"He went down here. I showed him the way. You'll have him trapped."

John

He'd expected to see Antony cowering before him when he and the guards reached the crypt, led by a sullen-faced brother.

He'd not expected to see his wife there with him.

They had pulled away from each other, but John had already seen. Antony's hands had been on Adelaide's arms. His lips had been on hers. The way she looked up at him was never how she looked up at John.

Time stood still as they all stared at each other, the silence of the crypt engulfing them. A plume of fire hissed on a torch the brother carried in one hand, making their shadows dance grotesquely against the walls. John watched the shadows flicker across Adelaide's face. She looked shocked, frightened. And yet, the way the light played on her face, she could have just as easily been laughing at him.

"Sir?" asked the brother. "Is this not the pretender?"

John had completely forgotten about Antony. But now that he did, he wanted nothing more than to break every bone in Antony's body, starting with his fingers. Antony wore an expressionless mask—no flicker of the light gave him away. A sneer, perhaps. His lip curled in defiance.

They stood in front of the crypt of King Alfred, with darkness stretching out behind them into the far reaches of the room. They were trapped.

"It is," John muttered.

Antony stepped in front of Adelaide, shoulders square. His face danced in the flickering torchlight, looking so much like the face of someone else.

"I never realized," Antony said, "how much your father hurt you when you were a child."

413

John's jaw tensed, but he said nothing.

"And I never made it better for you," Antony continued. "I was an ass. And I'm sorry for that."

John didn't let himself flinch. His cold heart didn't hear the words. All he saw was Adelaide, his wife, standing behind the man he hated.

"I may not have killed you when I should have," John said, "but your days are numbered, *your grace.*"

Antony turned and quickly whispered something in Adelaide's ear. He gripped her hand tightly. John wanted to break his fingers even more.

But before any of the men could act, Antony had pulled his bow from his shoulders and drawn an arrow across the string in one fluid motion.

He shot, one after another, hitting the guards around John. Then, an arrow bit deeply into John's cheek. His head jerked as though he'd been slapped, and he lost his balance.

As soon as he'd gained his footing again, Antony was already gone. It was no use trying to chase after him, John realized. He would disappear into a crowd of townspeople who hated John. He would be torn apart if he ran after him.

"I'll alert the other sentries, sir," said the brother. Antony had not shot him. The brother had grabbed Adelaide's arm, but she made no move to escape. The other men were only wounded.

John rubbed at the blood pouring down the side of his face. He turned and closed the distance between himself and Adelaide. She swallowed and looked down, avoiding his eyes.

"Please," she said in a small voice. "Please, John. How could you not have known—"

"That my wife was a whore? I wouldn't have known," John spat. A fire raged deep within him, one that surpassed any anger he'd ever felt before. It tasted like bile in the back of his throat. It sounded like Adrian's taunts. It felt like blow after bloody blow he'd taken from the older boys in the North. Until he was able to show them true strength.

"John…" she began, slowly starting to look up at him. "It's not what you think—"

"What *do* I think, Addie?" He towered over her. "Tell me what I should think."

"Please, John, I know you love me—"

John could've strangled her. He felt the hot rage behind his eyes.

"Not anymore," he said, his voice strangely quiet. "Maybe never at all."

She flinched when he seized her arm. She didn't struggle. He yanked her toward him and grabbed her other arm, winding both arms behind her.

"What did he say to you? Before he ran?"

"Nothing."

"What did he say?"

He could've sworn Adelaide smirked. "He called you a worthless bastard. He said you're no better than your father."

John's arm had lifted before he realized what he wanted to do. He wanted to hit her. Even in his rage, the thought terrified him. Somehow, he knew that's not what Antony had said. It was what Adelaide wanted to say.

His grip on her tightened as he led her out of the crypt, into the sanctuary, and back through the streets to the palace. The chaos still erupted around them as he pushed them through crowds and riots. He still felt the need to protect her as he shouldered through groups of rowdy men, to shield her with his body. *Ungrateful bitch.* He hated himself for thinking it. Voices taunted them as they passed, perhaps some who recognized them from the wedding.

"How did a murderer's prick feel inside you, my lady?"

"She running around on you already, big man?"

"You know what they say about big lads, they're always makin' up for something!"

He brought her through the gates and past the scaffold, still standing from that morning. When he glanced at it as they passed, he felt the flash of rage from that morning. He'd beaten men to death before. One had been a Northern soldier, the other a deserter. The man he'd beaten that morning had been a traitor and a murderer. Justice had been served.

John pushed Adelaide into Tanor's chamber uninvited. Tanor sat in a large chair by the hearth, legs crossed serenely, shuffling through some documents. He looked up at them as they entered, almost unsurprised. He looked between the both of them with raised eyebrows.

"What's going on?" Tanor asked, slowly rising from his chair. His eyes landed severely on John. "Adelaide, where have you been?"

"I found her in the Cathedral of the Nine," John said, "with Antony."

The fire in the hearth glinted across Tanor's face. "Did you catch him?" John shook his head, and Tanor's face dropped. He stood slowly, his gaze sliding down to look at Adelaide. She wasn't fighting against John's grip. She wasn't doing anything.

"His name is Adrian," she said, her voice deep and desperate in her throat. "You know as well as I do who he is. You know what he means to you."

A smile grew slowly on Tanor's face, like a vine along a wall. "You've been listening to too much talk, my dear," he said. He added mildly, "Let go of her, John. You're hurting her."

John didn't realize how tightly he'd been gripping her arm. The joints of his hand were stiff as he released her.

"I think you've seen what you wanted to see, my lady," Tanor said. "I know how much you loved Prince Adrian. I loved him, too. You desperately wish he could come back from the dead, as do all those people out there. As if his resurrection would solve all our problems."

Tanor suddenly snatched her throat, and she stopped cold. He looked at her, his eyes almost blank, his mouth making out the right scathing words to say.

"Do you think I'm afraid of him? Of you?" he asked blandly. He was past madness, John realized. But Tanor knew he was mad and wore it like sanity. His lucid eyes stared deep into Adelaide's.

"I'm not afraid of anyone," he continued. "Least of all you. I do wish all of this had come to light before the wedding, though. Such a wasted expense. A hanging would've been much cheaper."

Tanor let go of her throat and promptly back-handed her across the face.

"Whore," he said plainly. To his surprise, John flinched when Tanor's hand connected with Adelaide's face. Then he remembered how badly he'd wanted to do the same thing. *No better than your father.*

Adelaide splayed across the floor in front of him. Before Adelaide could crawl away, Tanor lifted her by the jaw and forced her against the table, cramming her face against the wood.

"You know what whores are good for, Adelaide?" Tanor leaned harshly against her back. His other hand slunk from his side, hiked up her skirt, and began snaking up her thigh.

John didn't have to think. He reached forward and grabbed Tanor by the shoulders, throwing his body against the hearth and pinning him into place. Tanor winced as his back hit the stone wall.

"Don't you dare touch her again," John hissed in his father's ear. He could barely keep himself from strangling Tanor then and there. "She's still my wife." He looked into his father's eyes and saw fear.

"You'd best let go of me, *boy*," Tanor said. A shower of spittle landed on John's face with the last word. John reluctantly released him.

Tanor brusquely adjusted his tunic and looked coolly up at his son. John's face felt hot. His breaths came fast. Tanor's eyes flicked to Adelaide and John's followed. Tears were spilling out of her eyes.

"I'll take her upstairs," said John, his voice quiet and strained. John moved heavily toward Adelaide and seized both her arms. Without another look back, he steered her out the door.

He would take her to her chambers, he decided. To *their* chambers. To the place where they'd consummated their union the night before. Even now, the image of her danced in John's head. Unclothed, on the bed. The taste of her. He could almost understand Markus' hunger now. He craved her, he *wanted* her, even now. It infuriated him. She infuriated him.

He took her to their chamber and threw her none too gently onto the bed and stood over her for a moment, trembling with anger, uncertain of what to do next. She turned and looked up at him fiercely. He realized he could do whatever he wanted to her. It made him sick to think about it. She seemed to realize the same thing. She looked so small, so vulnerable, her body taut and alert. Her breaths came fast. John could see her heartbeat fluttering in her neck.

"I am not yours," Adelaide said simply. "I never will be."

John's face contorted and his fists clenched. "No. You won't."

He turned to leave, but her voice stopped him.

"Wait," she said. *Save yourself,* he willed. *Confess. Apologize. Make me hate you less, please.*

But he only saw defiance in her gaze. "When you cut off my head, make sure your sword is sharp, Bloody John."

John squeezed his jaw. Without a word, he turned and left the room with a slam of the door.

When John returned to the barracks, he nearly retched. He spent a long time bent double on the floor, trembling with a myriad of sickening emotions. He shuddered at the thoughts that ran through his head as he stood over Adelaide—thinking about the things he could do to her. About what his father almost did to her. Only a day before, they had been married. They should have been on their way to Highmoor. Instead, his wife was a prisoner.

And a traitor.

The barracks felt warmly familiar to him now, although they were cold and empty. He was grateful no one was around. If Markus were alive, he would've laughed in John's face and called him a cuckold. The thought angered him.

Finally, he stood up and looked out the window. The afternoon was already dimming, the light trickling away in the pale blue sky. It would be another cold night.

The light was dim enough that he could see his face reflected in the window. His brow was set in a deep crag of anger, his mouth a frown. He had just turned four-and-twenty. He had just been married. He had just been betrayed.

As he took off his tunic to change it, the door to the barracks opened. John expected to see Lucas or Artemis, but instead the small figure of Edwin appeared. He didn't seem surprised to see John back in the barracks. Then again, he never seemed surprised at anything. The cold evening light suited him. He seemed to absorb it, become part of it, as he walked into the room, his hands neatly behind his back.

"I hope you're putting your armor on," Edwin said. "Is it still here?"

"In the livery, yes."

"Good. You're needed in the town again. The situation is getting…rather out of hand."

John pulled a simple brown tunic over his head and began fastening the leather thong on its front. He hadn't realized until then that his hands were trembling violently. His fingers fumbled at the string. Edwin strode to him and caught the strings in his fingers. With pursed lips, he gazed down his nose at the strings and tied them together neatly.

"Do you remember what I asked you on the night Prince Adrian was killed?" John asked. That night suddenly felt so close again, days ago instead of years.

"You asked if it's a sin to murder if someone tells you to do it," Edwin replied, straightening the shoulders of John's tunic and turning to find his leather jerkin. "Do you remember my answer?"

"That I would have to answer to the Nine for what I've done."

Edwin's eyebrows shot up as he picked up the jerkin. "I would be more worried about answering to your father after all this mess," he said. "None of this would have happened if you'd done as you were told."

John's hand grabbed Edwin's throat before he realized what was happening. "Maybe I'm done with doing as I'm told. I've done what I was told and now I'm married to a wife who hates me."

"Calm down," Edwin said. He reached daintily for John's hand, prying each finger off his throat. John let it happen. "I could tell on your wedding day that she wouldn't last long. I was betrothed once, you know. But never married. I know the look of a woman who isn't in love. Or wasn't in love with *me*, anyway."

John's heart sank further. He didn't know what he'd expected. He'd expected a carriage ride of icy silence to their new home in Highmoor, where they'd spend their days growing old together in a cold, drafty manor house.

"His grace told me what I needed to know," Edwin said. He looked up at John, blinking slowly like a cat. "When men have been put in situations like yours, they either need to fuck or fight. Which do you need?"

John didn't have to think about it. "Fight," he said.

Antony

Adrian felt a sudden wave of exhaustion after the excitement of the hunt. The chilly air wasn't enough to keep him awake anymore. In fact, it drove deeper into his bones, irritating him further. He was cold and tired and his backside hurt from riding and chasing wild game. And he had made his father proud. He could go home now, back to the palace with the doe he'd shot.

Lord Edwin met them at the bottom of the hill and ordered a broad-shouldered attendant to retrieve the deer.

"My son got that one. He's a regular marksman," Alfred said to the small hunting party in his booming voice. "That doe will feed us for a fortnight at the least."

"It's getting dark, Your Majesty. We should return to the castle," said Sir Edwin. The man glanced at the prince and regarded him with something like amusement. The man had always unsettled Adrian. Maybe it was his large pupils or unblinking eyes. Maybe it was the way he looked at everyone like a hawk looking at prey.

The attendant came down from the hill, the dead animal bouncing on his shoulders as he stepped heavily on the steep ground. Alfred smiled at the sight and ran a hand through his thick chestnut hair. He was nearing middle age but still full of vitality, and Adrian took after him in bearing and appearance. At thirteen, the prince was growing fast, tall for his age, and handsome.

"Of course, Sir Edwin." Alfred put a hand on Adrian's shoulder. He turned to the rough, bearded men who had joined the hunt—the Northerners from Greyridge. "Gentlemen, tonight you'll get an excellent taste of southern venison.

421

It pairs excellently with the vintage Rose Red you seem to have a liking for."

The men muttered among themselves, eyeing the prince with respectful caution. Four of them had come on behalf of the Northern king as a gesture of peace and, hopefully, unity. They seemed perpetually sad, and Adrian didn't know why.

The night before, the largest of them had drunk his fill of ale and sung a melancholy tune in his deep, baritone voice—something about a maid with flaxen hair. The song had been stuck in Adrian's head all day, but with the wrong lyrics—the maid with the ass of a mare. He had found it deliciously funny, but John had not.

"You could start a war if you sang that loud enough," he had hissed to Adrian earlier in the day. John was watching him now, probably waiting for him to say something stupid. His friendship with John was only one of convenience—he was the son of his father's advisor, and he was small enough to beat when they sparred with wooden swords.

As the hunting party prepared their horses and weapons to return to the palace, John hovered over to Adrian once again as the prince shoved his bow into his squat pony's saddlebag.

"My father said that wolves come out in the Hemlock after dark. Or even worse—outlaws."

"Don't be so scared, John," Adrian said. "I could shoot an outlaw from a mile away."

John rolled his eyes. "Just because you killed one deer doesn't make you the champion of the hunt, Adrian."

Adrian lifted his chin. He was younger than John but he prided himself on being a few inches taller. John had always been spare and slim and timid.

"And how many have you shot, John?" Adrian asked. John stared back at him blankly. "That's what I thought."

"Be kind, Adrian."

Adrian turned and looked up at his father and saw the stern look of chastisement in the king's face—one he was used to. "I know it's late, but remember you're being watched."

The prince looked sideways at the four rugged men standing a few yards away from them—the Northern men. They were used to the cold climes of Greyridge in the north, so even a cool autumn day in the South was sweltering for them. In the early afternoon, they had stripped off all the fine clothes they'd worn that morning and now only wore white linen tunics. Even then sweat had gathered in their underarms and down their backs. Through their tunics Adrian could see the thick black hair on their chests—they seemed to be covered with it from head to foot.

"They're so big," John said as Alfred walked away, following Adrian's gaze. "And they smell. They're like bears."

"They hardly speak our language," the prince replied. He could hear their guttural tones from where they stood. They seemed especially quiet now, avoiding meeting anyone's eyes.

John pulled his own pony alongside Adrian's. "I heard the snow gets shoulder-deep to a horse in Greyridge," he said. "How do they hunt?"

"In the dead of winter, the richer folk will eat the peasants when they run out of food," Adrian said.

John looked at him, wide-eyed. "That's disgusting, Adrian."

"They are a curious lot, are they not?" Lord Tanor came up alongside them. As he approached, Adrian noticed John's body tense and his eyes stare intently at the ground. Tanor looked down at the two boys with a smile. It was a wonder John was so afraid of him, Adrian thought. Tanor was always so agreeable, and a good friend to his father.

"Men of the North are good people," Tanor continued as the ambassadors walked their horses out of earshot. "They just live differently than we do. But they don't eat their own. They are experts in hunting mountain goats and elk. You would know that if you paid attention in your studies, John."

John stared at the ground, jaw set, and mounted his pony to ride alongside Lord Tanor. Adrian turned back to his own father.

"Can we go home now?" groaned the prince, heaving a dramatic sigh. "I'm hungry."

King Alfred gave him a sharp look. "Not yet." Adrian turned away. He must always put on airs for these people. Adrian resolved that he would not do that when he was king.

"Be patient," Alfred continued. "Our friends, the northerners, believe they saw *a wild boar near here while we were hunting the doe."*

Adrian's ears pricked, his exhaustion suddenly gone. Wild boar were rare in the forest. He'd shot a doe, yes, but if he were to shoot and kill a wild boar all on his own, people would write songs about him.

"Where is it?" he asked, swinging onto his pony and reaching for his bow.

"You are not to come with us, Adrian. Neither is John," Alfred said firmly. Adrian immediately deflated. "It's far too dangerous. A doe is one thing, but a wild boar could gore you quicker than you could fly an arrow."

"You don't know that, Father," Adrian said. "You saw me shoot the—"

"I do know, Adrian." Alfred had a look in his eyes that told Adrian he wouldn't change his mind. "You'll stay here with Sir Edwin. The both of you."

A hunting horn blared, louder and longer this time. The boar. The hunting party flurried around them, and Tanor laughed as Alfred quickly mounted his horse and joined them. The galloping hooves and blaring horns quickly died away, and Adrian was left with John and Sir Edwin in the gloom, their horses nickering and pawing the ground.

Adrian threw back his head and groaned. Whoever killed the boar would get all the praise now, and all he would have was a stupid doe. He heard a snort next to him and flicked his head to John.

"What are you snickering at?" he asked.

"You're being a brat, Adrian," John replied, just loud enough for the prince, but not Edwin, to hear. Edwin was facing away from them, scanning the forest. "You just want to go home and see Adelaide."

Adrian felt his cheeks flame red. "No, I don't. I'm just tired."

"Do you dream of kissing Adelaide, Adrian? Mwa, mwa, mwa." John made ridiculous kissing noises into the air.

"Shut up, John. I see you looking at her all the time. You're always following her around the castle like a poor lost puppy."

"I saw you kiss her one time in the gallery—"

John couldn't even finish. Adrian grabbed him from his saddle and pulled him to the ground. He had John pinned under his knee, but John was grabbing at his neck, trying to push him off. Adrian was about to throw a punch at John until a strong hand pulled Adrian off the boy.

Edwin was small, but he was by no means weak. He set the prince on his feet. In his hot rage, Adrian looked up at the man.

"Don't touch me again," he snapped.

Edwin's face was calm, his eyes, as always, unblinking. "I didn't want you to harm the boy, your grace. He's smaller than you." Edwin's voice was like deep water, chilling to the bone.

"It was none of your business." Adrian straightened the front of his tunic. He looked over at John, who had dirt on his face. In the dimming light, Adrian saw tears welling at the corners of his blue eyes. John rubbed his throat emphatically.

"He started it," Adrian continued. "He needs to learn to fight if he's going to say things like that."

"I don't need to learn anything," John replied.

"They've been gone a long time," Edwin said. He swung the longbow from his shoulders. "I'll go see if there's any trouble. John, I trust you to look after the prince."

Edwin disappeared. Adrian wondered if he was just tired of looking after the both of them. The light faded faster, and the moon rose above the naked trees. The forest was eerily quiet. Adrian grumbled to himself. His legs and buttocks were sore and chafed and they complained no matter how he stood or sat. He was tired, hungry, and fuming. Why did they have to chase after that boar anyway? What did his father have to prove?

And what did John have to prove? Maybe Adrian's heart did beat a little faster when Adelaide was around. In the last few years, as they'd grown up together, he'd become fond of her. And now there was something about the way she laughed, the funny things she said, the way she teased him, that made him feel something strange, a feeling that he was told would come as he grew older. John feels that way about her too.

"I'm going to go find them, too," Adrian said. "Maybe they need my help."

Even in the dim light, he saw John roll his eyes.

"Hold onto my horse, will you?"

And then he had run off. And he'd found his father's body, nearly lifeless. And his father had told him to run.

He came to the edge of a steep ridge that plummeted down to a raging river

425

below, swollen by the autumn rains. The Skeldergate River. For decades it had cut into the edge of that hill and turned it into an almost sheer cliff. A fall from it could be fatal.

Adrian turned and saw someone following behind him—John. No sign of Tanor. John's cheeks bloomed red on his pale face.

Adrian took a cautious step back. His father's word rang in his head. But why? John was hardly a threat to him.

John drew his small training sword. Adrian had left all his weapons with his pony.

"Where are you going to go now, Adrian?" John had him cornered.

Adrian lunged. He grabbed John by the collar and threw him to the ground. John's training sword flew out of his hand. The other boy floundered on the ground for a moment, then regained composure and stood back up.

"I hate you, Adrian," John said. Adrian knew he meant it. He ran at John again, kicking and punching. He started to panic. John wouldn't stop until he won. Using all the strength his exhausted body had left, he pushed John off him.

"Let me go," Adrian said. "Please. Why are you doing this?"

While he spoke, John found a stone on the ground, and suddenly it met Adrian's forehead. A bright, blurry light flashed in the corners of his eyes. His head buzzed. His eyes struggled to stay open, but it was a losing battle. They closed of their own accord and he found himself falling.

He hit the water below and fell below the current, but felt no pain. By then, he was fast asleep.

The memory was clearer than it had ever been.

As Antony ran until his legs nearly gave out, weaving through the angry townspeople and finally breaking free of the city, he remembered exactly how that day had happened—the last day of his old life. The night that had cost him so much, and he had awakened the next day none the wiser.

His lungs burned with cold air. The air even *smelled* cold. He stopped by the Skeldergate River to catch his breath, gasping through the pain. Antony had grown used to pain. Not just being hit in the face, but the gnawing hunger of living in the forest. The aching loss of the ones he loved. Pain didn't seem to matter anymore.

He prayed his plan would work. He prayed to the Great Maker—he didn't care how much of a grievance it was to pray directly to Him.

This wasn't supposed to happen. None of this was ever supposed to happen.

He could have stayed in Barnswood forever. He could've forgotten about the ring, ignored what David had said about it, and melted it down to pay the Harvestmonth tax. Even now, the ring was on his hand. His finger had formed and calloused around it so it stayed in place.

Antony squeezed his eyes shut against the pain and tried to will his old life back into existence. He willed himself to believe that when he opened his eyes, he would be sitting across the hearth from Bron, whose eyes were growing heavy with sleep. Benjamin sitting on the floor, whittling at a small piece of wood. He willed the smell of woodsmoke into his nostrils, the sound of a sleepy summer evening into his ears.

He opened his eyes, and nothing had changed.

Antony would never go back to that life again. He lost it the day he lost Bron. Long before that, even. He realized that his life had never been his to begin with. It had been stolen from someone else, from another Antony. What he'd been living was false. And then the truth had been spoken.

He kept running. He ran as the light of day died, and any other traveler would've lost his way in the woods. Antony knew the way by heart, even as a deep gray settled into the trees.

He ran until he saw the glow of cookfires from their camp, and even then he didn't stop until he was at the mouth of their cave. Herne sat next to Malcolm at a nearby fire, sharpening the iron tip of an arrow. Both men looked up when Antony panted toward them.

"Good saints, boy," Herne shot up. "What's happened?"

Antony took a moment to catch his breath. Each gasp came like a wheeze in his lungs. He swallowed cold saliva.

"David and the others are dead," he said. "They stormed the palace. They killed people. They're all dead. And now Adelaide is—"

He fell to his knees. Herne rushed to his side.

"Slow down, boy," he said. "Where is Adelaide?"

"She's at the palace. And I've made her part of this."

Herne took Antony by the elbows and helped him stand. Antony's heart had slowed, but the world around him was still dizzy. Herne's face spun in front of him.

"She's *been* part of this, lad," Herne said, "because she's with us. You didn't *make* her part of this. Because if I'm not mistaken, she's always been a part of *you.*"

The kiss. The warmth of her so close to him. He wanted her. He *needed* her.

She can do this. She's brave. Braver than I ever could be.

"The plan is in motion, Herne," Antony said, straightening his back. "We need to get ready. It's time to fight."

Adelaide

A ntony had told her what to do. But as she waited in her chamber, she found herself trembling.

Adelaide had no semblance of the passage of time in her room. She merely sat, staring but not seeing, thinking, pondering. She imagined herself tossed by the waves of the sea, her father watching on the black sands of the beach. She felt the cold water buffeting her body, refreshing her, invigorating her. She was once again innocent. She was at peace. Anything to take her away from her stale, cold room and the thought of death.

She barely heard the footsteps as they approached the door, but she started when the door began to unlock. She tensed, expecting to see John fill the doorway. Instead, she saw the fearful face of Godfrey peer in. Her shoulders relaxed with relief.

"Thank the saints you made it here," she said. "I was worried you'd—"

"So was I." Godfrey's face looked paler than normal. "It's a wonder you and I have stayed alive this long, my lady."

"Why didn't you ever tell me that you were—that you're one of them?" Adelaide asked. Fear still hid behind her relief.

Godfrey raised a manicured eyebrow. "How was I supposed to know *you* were one of them, my lady?"

They stared at each other, both equally terrified, both wondering who was listening, both wondering if anyone else knew. Finally, Adelaide spoke.

"You are to tell the king you received an urgent message from the Lord of Barnswood. That his men captured the *Vispilio* while he was trying to escape on the Weschurch Road. They are holding him in Barnswood. Antony will—"

Godfrey held up a hand. "No. I do not need to hear any more. I do not want to *know* any more. The less I know, the safer he is."

"Am I safe?"

Godfrey seemed surprised by her question. He pursed his lips.

"His grace would like to see you. He asked that I...bind you."

Adelaide bit her lip fiercely. She was truly a prisoner now. "Is this my death sentence?"

"No, no, my lady," Godfrey said, and she believed him. "I promise you, it is not. May I?"

"Yes. Where is John?"

"He...did not wish to see you."

Adelaide was silent as Godfrey's cold, delicate hands tied her wrists in front of her. His hands were papery, the hands of an old man though Godfrey was not much past middle age. They shook, not with nervousness, it seemed, but rather the constant tremble of a palsy. The knots were so loose the ropes could have fallen off. Adelaide had never realized that she was taller than Godfrey. Poor man, she realized, living in the shadow of kings for so long that he's become a shadow himself.

She looked into his eyes one last time before they left the room. She knew he was sincere. He barely touched her arm as he began to lead her out of her room and down the hall.

Godfrey took her to the throne room, where Tanor was pacing impatiently. His crown was cocked at an odd angle on his head, and the matted fur mantle he wore made him look like a bear. Adelaide thought briefly of the Northern king from her father's stories, the king who communed with half beasts. Tanor seemed more beast than human, pacing like a dog, his eyes wild. He turned when he saw them enter.

"Kneel," he said, staring at Adelaide as they approached. Adelaide didn't want to, but she submitted. Godfrey remained behind her, an assuring presence. He cleared his throat.

"Your grace," he said. "An urgent message has come from Lord Barthow.

He caught the traitor on the Weschurch Road and is holding him in Barnswood."

Tanor raised an eyebrow. The silence in the room was thick, impenetrable. Adelaide's heart beat so loudly she wondered if the whole room could hear. Tanor stepped down wordlessly from the dais and approached them slowly.

"It seems the outlaw travels fast," he said. "I wonder why Lord Barthow didn't think to bring the traitor here."

He lunged at Godfrey, nearly bowling Adelaide over. With his hands on the small man's throat, Tanor squeezed. Adelaide only watched for a moment, then turned away when Godfrey began to sputter and turn purple. If her hands weren't bound, she would have covered her ears against the sound of his choking. The room echoed with each agonizing cough until finally Tanor threw Godfrey's lifeless body to the ground.

A hand grabbed Adelaide's face. A hand that had just murdered. Tanor pulled her face close to his, so close that spittle flew onto her cheeks.

"Did you really think I'd be that stupid, you whore?" he roared. Adelaide was paralyzed by his wild eyes, raging like a stormy sea.

The door to the throne room opened behind them and Tanor dropped her, smoothing the front of his tunic and flexing his hands. Adelaide could still feel his hand, the strength of it, on her jaw, ready to squeeze the life out of her, too.

Behind them, Edwin stepped into the room, followed by John. He was dressed in armor. Adelaide realized she'd never seen him in armor. It made his broad shoulders look broader, his whole figure more monstrous. He didn't look at her. Neither of them acknowledged the body lying prone on the floor.

"Just in time," Tanor said. "It seems the outlaws have an ambush planned for you on the Weschurch Road. How many men do you have, Lord Edwin?"

"Enough," Edwin said. "Lord John will lead the cavalry into the forest."

Tanor scoffed. "If John still doesn't have the balls to kill Antony himself, do it for him, Edwin. And then kill *him*."

John didn't flinch, even when Tanor pointed to him. Then, he dismissed them both with a hand. Adelaide was left alone with Tanor and the body of the friend she had just made.

"Why?" Adelaide asked Tanor, her voice cutting the air. "Why are you doing this?"

Tanor didn't respond for a long time. "I decided a long time ago that I would not be overpowered again. By anyone," he said. "That I would remove everything in my path, by whatever means necessary. You, my dear, are in my way. And so is the *Vispilio*."

Ellena

Novice robes wouldn't work again.

The thought was bitter, but true. The bodies hanging from the palace walls were naked, but Ellena—and everyone else— had heard what David had done. It seemed to be the only thing anyone could talk about in the backwater tavern Ellena often found herself in. The Hobbled Horse lived in the shadow of the castle walls. It always smelled of piss, had the worst beer, and was impossibly loud no matter the hour. Ellena loved it. No one cared who anyone was, and most were too drunk to care.

Find Adelaide, Antony had told her with guilt in his eyes. Guilt and love. He loved Adelaide. Ellena could tell when a boy was in love. Her Antony had been in love with her.

The remaining Men of the Lion back at the camp were outraged. They had been sharpening sticks or dull dagger blades against makeshift whetstones. Antony had planned an ambush. Ellena hid her bow and quiver of arrows under her cloak. Even Carter quietly hewed a large piece of wood into a fearsome quarterstaff.

"Can I help?" Benjamin had asked him as he worked.

"You can help by staying hidden," Carter had growled. "I ain't losing you, too."

Ellena watched the boy as he stormed into the cave. She knew how it felt to be helpless, to watch someone die while she was powerless to stop it.

The memory of that night was so close to her that night as she sat in the squalor of the Hobbled Horse. She couldn't remember what game she and her Antony had been playing. Only that it got dark without either of them realizing. It must have been some kind of hiding game, because she couldn't find her Antony. She didn't find him until she saw him with the other boy.

Even in the moonlight, she saw the other boy had nice clothes, the clothes of a noble. Her Antony looked ragged next to him. And scared, even though her Antony was bigger than the other boy. Ellena saw the silver glint—the boy had a sword.

When the boy plunged the sword into Antony's chest, it hadn't seemed real. Ellena had felt like she was in a dream, and when she blinked she would wake up. Maybe that was why she didn't scream, didn't give herself away.

The only time she'd wanted to scream was when the boy started hacking at her Antony's neck. The color was dim in the moonlight, but she knew the boy was covered in blood before her Antony's head was completely off.

She had to run away before she screamed. She didn't vomit until she told her father what happened. Herne held her hair back while she did. He held her all night. Neither of them slept. Their cottage in Barnswood had felt so strangely safe that night, even though terror was so near to them.

Ellena didn't go back to the forest until she and Herne were forced there.

As she sat in the gloom of the darkest corner of the dim tavern, tears swam unbidden in her eyes. *Why did it happen? Saint Aug, why?*

Through the wetness of her eyes, she caught sight of a bright blue dress shimmering in the scant light. It gave her pause, even in her sadness. A few tables from her, closest to the hearth, sat a mouse-haired girl in a fine dress and a man in roughspun. By the looks of it, the girl was very drunk, and the man seemed to encourage it. He pushed a clay cup on the table closer to her. Her voice had gotten loud, slurring high above the din of the tavern.

"Stephen, it's so cold," she whined. "Hold me. Keep me warm." She leaned close to him. The man put an arm around her. Ellena couldn't help but notice his hand slide down slowly, past the girl's hips.

Before long, the girl's shoulders started to shake. "I've no friends left but you," she said, still loud enough for Ellena to hear. "Lady Elanor is gone, the other girls were dismissed, and Adelaide is—well, you know."

The man shushed her and glanced around. Ellena kept her eyes averted but listened as closely as she could. *You poor drunk fool,* she thought. *You might be my way into the palace tonight.*

"Poor little Ilse," said the man. Ellena saw the dangerous glint in his eye. He knew when a boy was in love, but she knew when he felt something very unlike love, too. "You don't look very good. Come on."

He stood up, and the girl wobbled to her feet. The man took her shoulders and began steering her through the crowd. Ellena sighed and stood up, sliding through the throng after them.

The Hobbled Horse had plenty of dark corners and rooms that patrons used for their own purposes. Ellena followed the man into a storeroom. The girl mumbled incoherently.

"I'm tired," she said. In the gloom, Ellena made out her shape. The girl tumbled back onto a sack of flour, and the man got on his knees in front of her, sliding his body along hers. Ellena heard the rustle of silk as he pawed at her dress, the smack of greedy lips against skin.

Ellena drew her dagger and grabbed the man's shoulder. Spinning him around, she stabbed him once in the leg, in and out. Before he could scream, she smacked her other hand on his mouth.

"Put *that* in her, and I'll put this in you again," she hissed. She said a quick prayer and hit him over the head with the hilt of her dagger. She sighed with relief when she heard the limp thud of his body. *I hope he doesn't make it through the night. I hope he suffers.*

She wiped her dagger on her cloak and grabbed the girl. "I'm sorry, love," she said, "but I need your dress."

Switching clothes with the girl proved tiresome. The girl was completely limp with drink. Ellena shimmied her out of her dress like a giant ragdoll. Finally, the dress was off. Ellena's ragged gown fit the skinny girl passing well. The blue dress was a little long, but Ellena cinched the belt as tightly as she could, hiding the misshapen clothes and her bow under the girl's lovely fur-lined cloak.

She bolted the storeroom door behind her. The girl had money in a purse at her side. Ellena used it to pay for a room at the Hobbled Horse. The innkeeper gave her a sideways glance as Ellena half-dragged the girl up the stairs after her and sprawled her out on the small cot in the room. It would be the safest place for the girl that night.

Then, Ellena made her way to the palace gate, just a few hundred paces away from the door of the Hobbled Horse. She hid her face and hair in the deep hood of the cloak and added a slight sway to her step. She knew the Men of the Lion hung on the walls just above her. She didn't stop to look.

"Open up," she called to the gatekeeper. She added a hiccup. "It's…" She paused to remember the girl's name. "It's Elsa."

A shadowy figure appeared at the other side of the gate, big-bellied and slow-moving. He grumbled something under his breath, then the portcullis groaned open.

"Be quick about it, you little wench," he said. And Ellena certainly was. She quickly skirted past him, almost forgetting to keep up her drunken ruse. She was in the walls.

As she walked through the courtyard, a stiff wind blew into her face and something cold hit her cheek. She looked up at the darkening sky. It was a slate of gray above her, growing ever dimmer as each second passed. Snow fell. The first snow in Southborn in years, even decades. Ellena dropped her head and hurried up the parapet and through the palace doors.

She knew where Adelaide's chamber was—she had met her there to get the key to the food stores. She turned left and hurried up a flight of stairs, keeping her head lowered. The cold was a good excuse to keep the hood over her face. Even with in the palace, the air was drafty.

On her way up the stairs, she collided with someone.

A low voice apologized and a hand reached out to steady her. Ellena stumbled back, holding her hood in place and cautiously looking up. She recognized the man—brown-blond hair, a handsome face. She had seen him around the palace before. He walked with a limp.

"I'm sorry, sir," Ellena said as quietly as she could.

"The fault is mine," he said. "And where are you headed? I'm sorry—I have to ask. I have to ask everyone after—you know…"

"I know," Ellena said. She wished she could push past him and not say another word, but that would only cause him to chase after her. "I'm going up to check on Lady Adelaide."

The man tried to peer under her cloak. "You're one of Elanor's ladies, are you not?"

"I am."

"What is your name?"

"Elsa."

The man nodded. His eyes seemed gentle, almost sad. *Remember, he might have been the one to kill David*, she thought with a flare of anger. *No one in this castle is your friend except for Adelaide.*

"Why don't I escort you up to Adelaide's room?" asked the man. Alarm bells rang in Ellena's head. She was glad her face was concealed. Her eyes were probably wide as silver coins.

"There's no need, sir," she said. "In fact, the men down at the gate said they needed help. It's getting bad out there. I was just out in the village."

The man's shoulders slumped. "Will it ever end?" he said under his breath. "Very well. Perhaps I can help them better than I did…last time. Good evening, lady."

Ellena curtsied as he limped past her. She allowed herself to pity him for a moment. He'd been powerless to stop what David had done. She knew what it felt like to be powerless. She continued up the stairs.

Her blood turned to ice in the royal wing of the palace. She was well aware that she could run into the king at any moment. But the corridor was quiet. The royals were probably advised to stay in their rooms.

Adelaide's room was the second to last on the left. Ellena had chanted that to herself the first time she'd made her way into the royal wing, terrified of knocking on the wrong door. Even as she knocked on Adelaide's door, she worried.

No response. Ellena leaned her ear to the door. Nothing. She tried the door. Locked.

"Adelaide," she hissed, glancing again to make sure no one was around. "Addie."

Finally, a shuffling from the other side of the door. Then, Adelaide's muffled voice.

"Ellena? Is that you?" it asked.

"Yes. The door's locked."

"I know. Godfrey is dead."

Ellena grimaced. She didn't know a Godfrey. He hadn't been one of their contacts in the palace, only David and a few others. She shook the thought away.

"How am I supposed to unlock this door?" Ellena asked. "Do you have something like a hairpin, Addie?"

Shuffling from the other side of the door, then something metal slid under the door. It was a small metal hairpin with cheap glass decorations. It looked somewhat strangely familiar to Ellena.

Her hands shook. She cursed at herself as she tried to get the pin in the keyhole time and again. She kept waiting to hear footsteps behind her. The footsteps of the king. Or the man. Or an executioner.

Ellena's entire being sank into the gentle click as the hairpin found its mark. The door slid open, and Ellena was surprised when Adelaide flew into her arms.

"Thank all the saints, Ellena," she said. "Thank you. You are brilliant."

"I know," Ellena shrugged. She pulled away from the embrace. "We need to get you out of here. Now. I'm sure the soldiers are already on their way."

"They are," Adelaide said. "Tanor sent them out before locking me in my chamber again."

Ellena clasped Adelaide's hand and realized it was trembling. "Do you have a cloak you can wear? It's getting cold."

Adelaide returned not long after with a deep-hooded cloak, and they made their way together back down the stairs, arm in arm. This time, they both agreed, if anyone tried to stop them, they would run. Ellena had her knife clutched in one hand. She prayed they didn't see the short soldier again. She didn't want to kill him.

Ellena knew one of the stable boys. Getting a horse was easy. She noticed Adelaide looking around as they walked along the rows, passing sleeping horses and numerous empty stalls.

"A lot of horses are gone," Adelaide said. Ellena heard the edge of fear in her voice.

Ellena opened the stall door of a long-necked palfrey, wide awake and watching them with a shake of its mane. "We are prepared, Addie," she said. "We're prepared for anything." She flicked back her cloak to show Adelaide the bow resting across her shoulders.

They mounted the palfrey and rode out into the courtyard. As they approached, the gate opened, but when they drew closer, the fat guard Ellena had encountered earlier stood in their way, arms crossed over his belly.

"*Elsa*, is it?" he growled. His face was an ugly sneer. "I knew something wasn't right 'bout that name. 'Twas *Ilse* who walked out of these gates an hour or so ago."

Sitting behind her, Adelaide squeezed Ellena's arm. "*Shit*," Ellena hissed to herself. She wheeled the horse so it stood lengthwise to the man, and with a downward punch stabbed him in the eye. The man immediately started screaming—so did Adelaide.

Ellena shushed her and slapped the horse's reins. "What the hell did you do that for?" she asked. "You'll alert the whole palace."

"You could've killed him," Adelaide said, her voice strained.

"I hope I did," Ellena said. If Adelaide spoke again, Ellena couldn't hear her over the clatter of the palfrey's hooves against the cobblestone street. Snow drove into their faces.

The Hemlock Forest

Snow hit John's face in fat flakes as he led the men in a steady gallop down the dark road. He could've easily been back in the North had the terrain been rockier and treeless. The cold that bit into his cheeks was the same bitter cold he'd faced time and again when charging toward the enemy.

But his enemy was different this time.

The wind made his eyes water but he forced them to stay open. He willed his eyes to stay keen, to watch for any movement on either side of the road, a shadow jumping out at them from the side or the front or even above. But all he saw in the torchlight were white flakes whipping past them, hissing in the flames. The wind had extinguished all but a handful of their torches, including his own.

He wasn't the one to see it. A voice on his left cried out, "Up there! Halt!"

"Halt!" John echoed, though he still couldn't see it. He yanked his horse's reins and the big animal skidded to a stop on the slippery road. He felt the press of the men behind him as they did the same, reining in next to him. Steam curled from his horse's flanks and nostrils. He peered out into the darkness in front of them, just outside of their small halo of light.

"I don't see them," he growled. He looked to the man on his left, who still had his eyes trained in front of them. The man pointed.

"There."

And John saw him.

A solitary figure stood on the road in front of them, rising out of the ground like a shadow without a maker. John rode out ahead of the rest of the men until the figure became clearer. He knew exactly who the man was.

"Surrender," John called, his voice echoing in the empty trees, "or burn."

The figure did nothing. It didn't move. John threw his dead torch to the ground and drew his sword.

"My lord," said a voice behind him. "Wait. Look."

John looked cautiously to one side. Other shadows seemed to dissolve out of the darkness of the forest, just outside of the torchlight. They wavered like ghosts in the gloom and snow, but they were real. They held weapons in their fists—stolen swords, bows, clubs.

There were more of them than there were of John's men. Fear ate at his stomach, but John swallowed it back. He'd faced worse odds before. They still had horses and armor and steel on their side.

"Kill them all!" John roared. He charged, and his soldiers followed suit.

* * *

Innermost Hell broke out around Antony and his men, but they stood their ground.

As John came charging toward him, Antony quickly drew an arrow back on his bow, breathed, and fired. The arrow glanced the side of his horse's flank. The big animal kept charging.

"Scatter!" Antony cried. The soldiers knew the Weschurch Road well, but they didn't know the forest. The snow was a surprise. Antony's clothes were too thin, and the wicked wind bit into his flesh.

The horse was still charging toward him, but was surpassed by a gray blur—another horse and rider. The rider extended her hand down to him, and Antony grabbed it without question. He swung onto the saddle behind her

"What the hell are you doing here?" Antony asked, still bewildered at the sight of her.

"I'm helping you," Adelaide said. "I'll steer. You shoot."

John had circled back after missing his mark. When he saw Adelaide, a new kind of rage burned in his eyes.

Antony looked around them. He saw Herne and Carter and even Benjamin scattering into the forest, chased by the burning light of torches.

"You'll all die," he said.

"We'll die for you," Ellena replied.

Antony pulled back an arrow on the string and started firing.

Like taking a breath, his father's voice said to him, and his trembling hands became steadier. In one fluid motion, he drew the arrow back to his cheek and fired at one of the horsemen. It hit him between the shoulder blades, and the man toppled off his horse, his torch flailing out of his hand.

A crossbow bolt came flying out of the gloom and glanced Antony's arm with a sting. He nearly fell off the back of the horse. Within seconds of the arrow being fired, Antony pivoted and aimed directly at the crossbowman, firing back. The archer let out a gurgling cry. He'd been hit in the throat.

"Antony, look out!"

Adelaide had been looking behind them, but it was too late. John had swung back toward them, and as he did, he grabbed not Antony, but Adelaide, yanking her into the saddle with him. He rode off into the darkness of the forest.

* * *

Adelaide squirmed in John's tight grasp around her waist. The darkness consumed them instantly, and Adelaide worried they would run right into a tree.

"Let me go!" she screamed.

John said nothing. He reined in the horse, swerving to look behind them. Adelaide looked down at his bare hand, holding the leather reins in front of him.

Adelaide took hold of John's wounded hand in her teeth. Her mouth filled with warm blood. John barked a cry of pain and withdrew his hand

442

from the reins. The horse screamed and reeled under them. John lost his grip on Adelaide, and she slid from the saddle.

She landed hard on her hip but ignored the pain, skirting away from the frantic horse's hooves as quickly as she could. She scrambled away from him, moving into the snowy darkness.

The snowy ground bit into the thin soles of her shoes, but she ran. She followed the dim line of torches. Before Ellena had dismounted, she'd given Adelaide her hunting knife, still tinged with blood from her kill. Adelaide had to swallow her disgust—the gatekeeper wouldn't be the only death that night.

As she approached the road again, she found Antony.

He hadn't made it far. Someone must have apprehended him, because Antony squirmed on the ground under the grip of a small man. The soldier held a knife to Antony's throat, and Antony was pushing him away.

Adelaide didn't think. She charged forward with her knife and drove it into the man's back. She hated the way it sank in so easily, through flesh and muscle. The man made a strange grunting sound, arching his back and falling away from Antony. Adelaide retracted the knife and let the man fall.

It was Edwin. His ember eyes glinted up at her in the pale firelight. He smiled up at her with bloody lips, then died.

She grabbed Antony's elbows and helped him up. When he was on his feet, he didn't let go.

"They have the advantage," Adelaide said. They looked around together. Torches danced in the dark forest. Bodies lay strewn on the road—bodies of soldiers, and bodies of their own. Adelaide looked up at Antony. His arm was bleeding.

Ellena came panting up to them, her eyes wide, blood on her face. Her eyes traveled down Adelaide's arm to the knife. "Glad you were able to make use of that," she said.

Antony pulled Adelaide into a quick kiss, and she savored it. They were no longer strangers, and they were no longer afraid. She wrapped her arms around his waist, dreading what would happen next.

"You need to get out of here," Antony said. *You.* Not *we.* Adelaide's heart dropped.

"There's too many of 'em," Ellena said. "I'll bring you to our camp."

But Adelaide didn't let go of Antony. "I'm not going without you," she said.

Antony pushed the bow into her hand and unslung the quiver of arrows from his back. "Take these. I have to find John."

Before she could protest, Antony was gone.

"Come on," Ellena said. "We'll go to camp and wait there. There may be some wounded."

Adelaide started following her as Ellena's small figure darted into the forest in the opposite direction that Antony had gone. Ellena deftly drew an arrow and shot it into a soldier ambling toward them. The smack of the shaft into flesh made Adelaide's stomach turn. It seemed to hit something deep in her core, something that brought the chill deeper into her bones.

She turned away from Ellena and ran the opposite direction, pulling the bow from around her shoulders.

* * *

As Antony ran, he watched the dancing shadows in the distance—outlaws fighting soldiers in the dim torchlight. How many were there? Antony hadn't counted. Edwin was dead. If Antony could get to John, the soldiers would be without their leader.

He was well aware he didn't have a weapon. He was intent on not needing one.

Then, he heard hoofbeats behind him.

The horseman appeared out of the snowy darkness, surrounded by swirling, icy flakes.

Antony ran faster than he ever had, hardly able to breathe for the frozen wind lashing his face. He felt his legs failing him and cursed. His muscles cramped and screamed. The hoofbeats came faster and harder behind him.

They'd arrived at a ridge overlooking the Skeldergate River. Antony had nowhere else to go.

From the corner of his eye he saw the horseman appear, followed by a blinding flash of light behind his eyes.

The world stopped when Antony collapsed to the ground. He felt suddenly warm, peaceful even. Then the pain of the blow swelled into his mind. As he lay there, time standing still, he vaguely remembered when the rock made contact with his forehead, and when he fell and kept falling toward the riverbed. He pawed the ground around him. He prayed to whatever saint was responsible for creating rocks.

Under his fingers numb with cold, he found one. A stone, hard and freezing like a block of ice. He gripped it.

A hand gripped him by the collar and yanked him up. Antony dangled in the grip, completely limp.

"Get up," a voice spat from inside the helmet. "Get up and fight me."

Another hand grabbed Antony's shoulder and heaved his body up, shoving it against the trunk of a wide oak tree. Antony's senses slowly returned to him—warm blood trickling from the back of his head, cold snow landing on his skin. A dark, frigid sky behind the outline of the horseman looming above him. *Wake up,* he willed himself. For a moment, he thought he'd be sick.

John let go of Antony. Antony fell limply back onto the tree. He felt as though he'd drunk a whole barrel of ale. His vision swam and he pitched and reeled as he tried to stand up.

John didn't wait for him. He kicked Antony in the side before Antony could stand again.

"Get up," John's voice was ragged. "Fight me."

As the dizziness subsided, Antony moved to his feet and hurled himself at John. He lifted the rock above his head and swung madly at John. It flew out of his hands. It missed.

John glared down at the rock as it fell. He kicked it angrily away and rose to his full height. Size was not on Antony's side, but he was still fast and strong.

"You won't humiliate me again," John said. "*Ever* again."

John hurtled toward him. Antony thought he would break his back with the impact on the tree. John pinned Antony there for a moment, his hot breaths steaming in the cold air.

I'm not going to win this, said a small voice in the back of Antony's mind. John's blow to his head had weakened him, and John was far too strong.

John threw him down to the ground and kicked him in the chest. Antony heard the hiss of steel on leather.

"You have no right to your throne," he hissed. "You have no right to anything. You have no right to live."

Antony coughed, trying to pull breath into his lungs. "You're a monster," he said.

"I know."

John skewered Antony in the chest. Antony rolled over, letting out a gasp. John kicked him for good measure.

Antony gazed up at the sky. Snow fell on him, cool on his warm skin. His breaths felt strange, incomplete. The front of his tunic felt wet. But the world felt strangely calm, even as John appeared above him, looming, holding his sword aloft to pierce Antony in the heart.

A dark object hissed through the air and struck the sword with a clang, knocking it out of John's hand. Another landed with a thud in John's middle. A last arrow hit him in the shoulder. John staggered back, surprised. Antony couldn't see what he was looking at, but his pale eyes were wide with shock and rage.

He looked steadily in front of him as he backed away, clutching his stomach. He toppled over the side of the ridge and landed with a thud somewhere far below.

＊ ＊ ＊

John was going to kill Antony. Adelaide had seen it in his eyes. And she had

446

seen that look before—when John had seen Antony in the throne room. When Tanor had reached up Adelaide's skirt. John's rage was terrifying.

Adelaide had watched as Antony fought back feebly, hurling John back with dead weight. He didn't have much of an advantage for long. John seized him and threw him to the ground. He drew his sword.

"...You have no right to live," Adelaide heard him say, his voice far away, carried by the wind. She stifled a scream when John pierced Antony in the chest.

Adelaide gripped the bow in her hand fiercely. Her hands were shaking. John wasn't that far away from her. She had a clean shot.

She took a breath. She thought of Bron. Of David. She thought of her wedding day. Her wedding night. She thought of the past, its bleakness. Its death. She remembered lips that tasted like strawberries. She remembered the happiness she had. She remembered who took it away.

She drew the arrow back with all her might, her arm tense and straining to pull back farther, and farther still. The last time she'd fired an arrow was in the courtyard with Antony. She remembered how it felt, the strain of pain across her shoulders. She fought through it, steadied herself.

The arrow flew off the string and clanged against John's sword, knocking it out of his hand. He looked up in surprise, but didn't see her.

She drew again. This time she didn't care where she hit. Her arm burned. Her grip almost slipped on the handle of the bow.

The arrow flew through the darkness and hit John somewhere in his middle. He stumbled back from the impact.

She rose from her hiding place and saw his cool eyes meet hers. This time, she didn't look away. She had one more arrow. She pulled it back, her arm protesting as the string became tighter and tighter. She fired again.

She had hoped the arrow would find John's heart. It found his shoulder. That terrifying rage in his eyes—she didn't look away. He clutched the arrow in his stomach and backed away, looking almost drunk as he reeled and toppled over the side of the ridge.

Adelaide turned to Antony and realized she was trembling. She saw stars

in the corner of her eyes as blood rushed through her ears. She dropped
the bow and ran toward him, kneeling on the snowy ground beside him.

"Ah," Antony breathed when he saw her. He managed a smile. "It was
you." He reached up and touched her face. His thumb found her lips. He
grimaced. "What's this?"

Adelaide realized she must've looked a sight—she still had blood on her
mouth. She tasted it on her teeth. "I bit John," she said.

Antony spurted a laugh that soon turned into a wheezing cough. "Of
course you did," he said. "Adelaide."

"What?"

"I love you."

Adelaide felt hot tears in the corners of her eyes. She gingerly touched
the wound in Antony's chest, a small hole underneath his ribcage.

"Put your hand here," she said. She grabbed his hand and placed it on
his wound. "Hold it tight."

"All right," he mumbled. Snowflakes fell on his dark eyelashes. There
was blood inside his mouth.

"Let's get you back to camp," Adelaide said. "Do you know the way?"

"Yes, I do." His voice sounded far away, quiet.

Adelaide helped him to his feet. His movements seemed halfhearted,
reluctant. She knew he was in a lot of pain. He leaned heavily on her
as she wrapped an arm around his back, and swung his arm around her
shoulders.

They made their way through the snowy forest, listening as the distant
shouts began to die. Either the soldiers gave up after their leaders fell, or
they were all dead. Antony moved painfully slow, and his breaths came in
short wheezes with every step.

"It's so cold," he said. "I've never felt this cold before."

The forest enveloped them. In between Antony's jagged breaths,
Adelaide heard nothing. Soft snow blanketed their footsteps, muffled
all sounds. The snow seeped into Adelaide's soft shoes.

"*Augh*, my back," Antony stopped and stretched in pain. "Your husband
is really big, you know."

She didn't want to think about John. She never wanted to think about John again. "Come on. Which way do we go now?"

"I—I can't—"

Antony collapsed. His whole weight tumbled onto her and she tried to catch him as he fell. His body was fully limp, she realized. She eased him down onto the ground, being careful of his head.

She looked down at him. His face was pale, his lips purple and blood-stained. She was reminded vaguely of Prince Adrian's crypt in the Cathedral—the soft, boyish face carved into the marble. Peaceful. Dead.

"I don't think I'm going to make it, Addie," Antony whispered.

Fresh tears tumbled down Adelaide's face. His words were true, but she wouldn't believe them.

"I'm not going to lose you now," she said, her voice thick. "I have a whole life to live with you yet."

Antony swallowed. "But you're married," he said.

"Not anymore."

Antony smiled. "What will our life be like?" he asked.

Adelaide rubbed his hands in her own. They were as cold as the falling snow. "You'll be crowned king," she said. "And I will be your queen. If not of Southborn, then we'll be king and queen of the outlaws."

"The outlaws," Antony chuckled weakly. "I like that."

"Stay with me," Adelaide said. She kissed his hands and tasted blood.

"I want to."

The snow fell around them for a long time. It buried everything. It brought death.

"Addie?"

"What is it?"

"Do your lips still taste like strawberries?"

Adelaide leaned down and kissed Antony deeply, helplessly. All she tasted was blood, but she savored the softness of his lips, the brush of his stubble against her nose and chin.

When she pulled away, his eyes were closed, but still he breathed, a weak wheeze. Adelaide squinted into the darkness behind her, trying to make out their footprints as they disappeared in the dark and snow. Then she looked back down at Antony. He didn't have long. But if she could find the outlaws, they could get him to the camp. They could help him.

Adelaide realized then just how cold she was. She rose slowly, stiffly, rubbing her arms. Her fingers were tinged with dark blue. She panicked and shoved them in her armpits.

She looked around. There was an alarming amount of blood in the snow. She could hardly feel her feet as she walked. She needed to find the outlaws.

Antony

delaide.

When he'd fallen unconscious, she'd been there. Her warmth had been all around him. But now he awoke in the all-consuming dark and cold and wondered if he had arrived in Inner Hell.

Plump flakes of snow still landed on his face. He looked down at his chest. It had been oozing a lot of blood, and with each breath he took, he heard a strange whistling sound coming from the wound.

He tried to stand up, but immediately collapsed onto his stomach, a wave of pain jarring through his chest. He coughed. A dark bloom appeared in the snow when he did—freckles of red in the fresh whiteness. He used his elbows to crawl forward, but after a few moments his hands stung from the biting cold. Every breath he took didn't feel complete, as if he couldn't fill his lungs all the way.

His body went slack, prone on the ground in the middle of the forest. *I've been here before. Just like this.* The strange thought entered his head, then disappeared. He rested his cheek in the snow like a pillow, feeling suddenly warm, even though he was shivering. As his eyes closed, he thought he saw figures in the forest beyond coming toward him—walking at first, then running. Maybe it was his father. Maybe it was the king.

"Antony!"

The voices, the footsteps sounded far away. In another world. As they picked him up, he felt as though he were floating on nothing at all—a current of water buffeting him to some unseen shore.

He closed his eyes, soothed by the sudden comfort, feeling his body slip away.

John

He was surprised when his eyes opened. He didn't think they'd open again. For so long, he'd been enveloped in dreamless darkness. As he awoke, he wanted to go back. He wasn't in Inner Hell, but he might as well have been.

He shivered as snowflakes fell upon his prostrate body. The Skeldergate River rushed nearby. All of his strength, which he had been lauded for on the battlefield, was gone. He was finally going to die. With every breath, his heartbeat got slower.

He stared up at the sky, and with every breath the arrow in his belly and shoulder trembled. He snapped the shafts where they met his flesh, one after the other. He knew it would be futile trying to pull out the barbed tips. He watched the small snowflakes drift closer, grow larger in his vision, fall on his face.

You failed, he told himself. *You didn't fail your father, but you failed yourself. You failed yourself when you started listening to him, when you believed a man like him was capable of loving anyone.*

He thought of Adelaide. His rage was gone now. He was too tired to be angry. He'd gotten what he'd deserved.

He heard movement nearby and wearily turned his head. A small shape dissolved out of the darkness, walking slowly. John saw that it was limping. The boy realized that John was moving and tried to scurry away.

John held out a shaking hand. "W-wait," he said hoarsely. "I'm not going to hurt you." *I couldn't if I tried,* he added in his head.

The boy stood still for a moment, then crumpled, unable to stand on his wounded leg. Slowly, John dragged himself to the boy's side, seeing his features more clearly. It was a yellow-haired boy, one he had seen among the outlaws that night. The boy looked to be about the age that John had started to fight.

"Can you walk?" John asked. The boy shook his head, then shifted his leg to show John. A broken arrow was lodged deep into the muscle. It looked as though the boy had tried to pull it out, but was unsuccessful.

"They—" The boy started, staring at him. "They got me." He seemed to realize that *they* meant John and his men, and he tried to shuffle back.

You'll die no matter what you do. Do this and redeem yourself. He stared at the boy. *If you stay here, he will die too. If you return him to the outlaws, at least he'll live.*

He straightened onto his knees. Every movement took great strength and effort. Carefully, he slid both arms underneath the boy's limp body and lifted him. Though the boy would weigh scarcely nothing to him, it seemed as if his weak arms were lifting a grown man twice his own size.

"Do you know the way to your camp?" John's words came out as though he were drunk.

"We use the signs of the saints," the boy said, his voice small. "We mark the trees."

Slowly but with determination, John rose to his feet, holding the boy like an infant in his arms and trying to keep him from growing too cold.

John looked into the snowy night. He knew the outlaws wouldn't be too far away. He could find them fairly easily, with the boy's help. It was just a matter of getting there alive.

Adelaide

Dawn was near, and she was lost.

Adelaide had walked back the way she thought was toward the Weschurch Road—but hers and Antony's tracks were lost in the quickly falling snow. By the time the snow stopped, the tracks were gone. Her heart pounded in her chest.

She was going to die.

Now she just walked to keep warm. Any feeling in her feet was gone. They felt misshapen in her shoes, stinging with each step. She imagined Antony somewhere in the forest behind her, somewhere with no track to get back to him, dying. Soon, she would be dead too.

I killed John. The cold air stung her cheeks. She'd never seen snow in Hemlock Forest. On any other day, it would have been beautiful and otherworldly. She barely noticed it.

I killed John. I killed my husband.

If she survived, she wouldn't be safe. If she stayed with the outlaws, they'd be in danger. She was a murderer. And in Tanor's eyes, she was a traitor, too. She put Antony in more danger if she stayed.

Cold tears streamed down her cheeks. Tears for Antony. For David. For Bron. One of them might've even been for John.

No more death on my account.

She saw a clearing. Wheel tracks down a road. The Weschurch Road. And a carriage was clattering toward her, crunching through the snow.

Herne

Herne started a fire as soon as they returned to the camp, wrapping Antony in his cloak in the meantime. His wound looked mortal, but Malcolm immediately began tending to it. He quickly got to work, tearing Antony's tunic off to clean the wound.

"I'll need something to close the wound," Malcolm said. "There's a hole in his lung. Do you have a coin? A half-argent, perhaps?" When Herne had known him, Malcolm had been a barber-surgeon.

"Do we look like the kind of folk who carry half-argents?" Herne said. Malcolm smiled ruefully as he knelt by Antony. He lifted Antony's arm, revealing the lion ring on his finger. He ran his fingers over it, testing the metal.

"This is real silver, ain't it?" Malcolm asked. "This was King Alfred's."

Herne nodded. It had been clutched in the boy's hand when Bron found him all those years ago. "Far as I know, yes."

Malcolm puzzled over the ring while Herne took stock of the other wounded men. No wound was as serious as Antony's, but two of their men had died. The eastern sky began to glow with morning light. The horizon was gray, promising sunrise. The ground was now covered with snow and the forest lay quietly in its depths, buried in silent white tombs.

Footsteps crunched in the snow and stop near him. It was Carter. His quarterstaff was smeared with blood. He leaned against a tree, out of breath.

"I can't find Ben," His voice was strained with worry.

"He's a tough lad," Herne said. "He'll come back. Just wait."

Carter shook his head. "The more I wait, the more worried I get."

More footsteps approached them. Herne and Carter looked at each other, Herne reaching for his sword. They looked around, but could see nothing.

In the growing light, a large man appeared near the ridge. In his arms he held a small boy.

"Who the hell's that?" Carter breathed.

As he came to the top of the ridge, the tall man fell to his knees, still doing his utmost to support the child in his arms. Herne hurriedly ran up the ridge to keep the man upright.

"It's Benjamin," he called down breathlessly. "Carter. He's all right."

Carter was distracted by the other man. He peered into the soldier's face as he clambered up the hill behind Herne.

"Is that who I think it is?" he breathed hotly. He rushed forward and lifted the man's face to him. Herne vaguely remembered the young man's face from months before, when he and Ellena had found him searching the forest.

"You!" Carter roared. "You *murderer!*" He spat on him and shoved him to the ground. The man groaned but did nothing to protect himself. Herne saw the stub of an arrow sticking out of his shoulder. "You've done nothing but destroy our lives. You've spilled innocent blood—for nothing!" He spat on him again.

"Carter," Herne said firmly. "Leave him be. He needs a physician."

"Bloody John," Carter spat, kicking John's limp body. John did not move.

"Carter!" Ellena appeared and pulled him away from John with her good arm. "Now ain't the time for this. He very well might have saved your brother's life. He doesn't deserve this right now."

Carter's tense muscles relaxed, but he still looked contemptuously down at the wounded man. He brushed Ellena's hand off him.

"I will need your help," Herne said. "I'm going to take this man back to Southborn. He is too heavy for me alone."

Carter shook his head. Herne saw in his eyes that he had endured enough that night, and he was not about to save one of his enemies.

"What is another death in all of this?" Carter asked. He lifted his quarterstaff. Ellena held him back, looking ridiculously small as she pushed back Carter's bulk.

"I will not be responsible for another death. Your father's death is not on his head, even if he delivered the sentence. But your brother's life is."

"Antony's death is on his hands." Carter glared back at Antony. "My true brother. Not the pretender."

Carter took Benjamin from Herne's arms and walked away, with Ellena following. Benjamin clung to Carter helplessly. Herne saw tears glistening in the boy's eyes as Carter walked away.

Without hesitation, Herne used his last reserves of strength and painfully lifted John's arm over his shoulder and wrapped his own arm around John's waist. The man was barely breathing.

"Can you walk, boy?" Herne asked.

Weak streams of breath came from the man's mouth. He was so young, Herne realized, only Antony's age. His head lolled down toward his chest, but he nodded weakly.

"I don't want to die," the man said huskily.

"And you'd better not. I'll see to it."

Herne walked slowly, careful not to put the young man in more pain. Still, he felt a sense of urgency to get him back to Southborn. He had deep wounds in his shoulder and stomach, both from arrows that still jutted from his flesh. His skin was pale and bloodless.

To Herne's surprise, the man spoke as they limped along.

"Will I go to hell for what I've done? I don't want to go to hell."

Yes. You and your ilk should and will burn in Innermost Hell for the misery you've caused, Herne thought bitterly. But even thinking those words made him tired. He remembered something his wife had always used to say when a young mother died.

"We all deserve the wrath of the Innermost Hell for the cruelty we cause," he said. "But it is the Great Maker that grants us mercy when we turn from the things that have made us cruel."

As dawn rose, the outlaw stumbled through the forest with his burden.

458

The remaining snow fell, concealing the dripping trail of blood he left in his wake.

Lucas

"Any sign of Sir John?"

Lucas was exhausted, and his leg ached. Sir Lyman stood beside him, dancing on the balls of his feet to keep warm. The fight had lasted long into the night and dawn was upon them. A few soldiers had limped into the palace gates just before dawn, including Sir Lyman. He'd given Lucas the report—Edwin was dead, so were five others. No word on John.

All Lucas was able to do was watch. He had stood on the rampart all night, and he was tired of standing out in the cold. He felt empty and sick. He wanted to leave, to get away from that place and sleep and forget what happened.

As he looked out into the brightening dawn, he saw movement in the village. It was too early for villagers to be out and about. The streets below were beds of untouched white snow—the first snow in Southborn in decades, Lucas was told.

A shapeless form melted out from between the houses and along the cobbles. Labored plumes of breath billowed from the form's mouth. As it came closer, he saw that it was not one man, but two, one supporting the other.

As the man approached, Lucas saw the raggedness of the man's clothes and the unkemptness of his hair and beard. He was not a knight. When the soldiers realized he was an outlaw, they drew their swords. The man was only a few yards away from the palace gates. He stopped when he saw the swords outstretched toward him.

"Don't come nearer," warned Lucas. "What do you want?"

Lyman put a hand on his arm. "Wait, Luke, look—it's John."

As soon as Lucas heard John's name, he careened down the steps of the wall as fast as his leg would let him and hobbled straight through the palace gates.

"Put your swords down," Lucas said to the men. They didn't move.

The outlaw carefully slid John's weight off his shoulders and onto Lucas'. Lucas braced John with one arm. The weight was unbearable on his sore leg. Lyman appeared by his side to help him.

They held John's sagging body between them.

"I said put your swords down!" Lucas said again, louder.

"What does he want?" asked a soldier, cautiously lowering his sword.

The outlaw put his hands up. He was ragged and dirty, his face smeared with blood. "I don't want nothing," said the outlaw. "I just want that boy to live. He's too young to die."

"They always want something in return," said the soldier to Lucas in a low voice. "There's probably five more lying in wait for us, coming up behind him."

The outlaw said nothing. He only shook his head.

Lucas was aware of how labored John's breathing was. He had to get him inside. He gave the outlaw one more glance. "Thank you," he said. "I'd suggest you get out of here before the sun gets any higher."

The outlaw was silent. He slowly backed away, nodding to Lucas once and then disappearing back into the village.

Tanor

T anor tapped the table impatiently. No sleep, no rest all night. Lucas had cordoned him and Charles in Tanor's chambers, barring the door and placing guards everywhere. All night he had paced, he had wandered, he had thought, he had planned. His mind was ragged. He had carefully thought of each possible outcome. Now, he was exhausted. He wandered in and out of his bedroom, watching Charles sleep, tousling his hair. At all costs, he would need to be protected.

He slouched onto his bed early in the morning beside his son. The candle that burned on the table was burning low and shadows threw themselves chaotically around the room. Tanor caught rosy whiffs of Elanor's perfume on the pillow. He thought of her dead eyes staring up at him.

Morning crept slowly through the windows and Tanor heaved a sigh. He heard the small grunts of his son waking up beside him. Charles awoke at the break of dawn every day, and today was no different. He peered up at his father with sleepy eyes, stretching his small arms as high as he could.

"Good morning, Papa," he said, squinting his face into a tired smile.

"Good morning, my boy," Tanor said. He pulled the boy toward him. Charles snuggled into his father's chest. "Did you have any bad dreams?"

"No," murmured Charles. In a few moments, he was dozing again. Tanor played absentmindedly with the boy's hair, twisting the curls between his fingers.

"I'm sending you away, Charles," he said. The sleeping boy didn't hear him. "It's not safe for you here anymore. I must send you away—I've put it off for far too long. I will send you to Baronskeep—it's beautiful there, and always warm. No snow like this. You'll live there. You'll be taken care of. You'll be taught."

His voice quavered as he looked down at the tiny body, its little chest rising and falling. "I love you, my boy," he said. "You're my only son and heir. You're all I have left. I must keep you safe from savages like them."

Tanor's moment with his son was interrupted by shuffling footsteps through the corridor. He turned toward the chamber door, waiting for a figure to occupy it. He heard shouting, but no audible words, interspersed with urgent murmurs. It was the silence before a summer thunderstorm, the unperturbed grass waiting to bend and blow in chaos. Tanor anxiously twisted his ring around his finger, chafing the skin to bleeding.

Finally, Sir Lucas limped through the doorway. His face was ashen. Something dark was smeared across the front of his green tunic.

"Your Majesty." He bowed his head quickly. "Our men returned early this morning. Five of our men are dead, and some are seriously wounded. The most serious of them is...well, it's your son, your grace."

"Are the outlaws dead?" Tanor asked quickly. "Is Antony dead?"

"Sir Lyman reported at least two were killed," Lucas said. "They scattered back to their camp."

Tanor sighed. The news was better than nothing. "Take John to the infirmary and fetch Magg to look at him. She will do what she can."

Lucas nodded and left. Suddenly exhausted, Tanor sat down on the bed, swaddled his son in a blanket next to him, and lay down into a heavy sleep.

Lucas

L ucas arrived at the infirmary as John's body was being laid on a bed in an inner room, set apart from the wide hall lined with cots. John had moved very little since returning to the palace. Lying on the white sheet, he looked like a corpse already. Magg, the court physician, stood by, examining the patient from afar while she mixed a poultice. She had a dozen attendants swarming around her, weaving in and out of the halls of the infirmary. Their long white smocks made them look like ghosts in the dim halls as Lucas had passed. They were all young women—Women of the Veil, they were called. Their sisterhood lived apart from Southborn in a convent near Dark Harbor. Magg must have summoned them at the first sign of violence.

Magg worked quickly, her long fingers carefully selecting each herb and mixing it with a mortar-and-pestle. An attendant stood by her elbow, waiting for instruction. When Magg was called out of the room to tend to other patients in the infirmary—of which there were many—the young woman took over for her. Magg instructed her with a firm voice, ordering her to fetch water and wine and bandages. She would return to John's room panting and exhausted. Her brow was deeply furrowed as she looked John up and down.

"I do not know how he's still alive," Magg said, leaning down to feel his breath on her hand. She turned to her attendant. "Bring some warm water, and wine for the pain." She nodded to the draft on the table. "This will put him in a deep sleep. Don't give him too much, or he'll be put into a sleep like death."

John's armor and clothing were wet and frozen and his body was no better. His breaths came in long intervals, each one a huge, meditated effort. Magg put her fingers on John's neck and shook her head. Magg was a kind woman, but precise and terse. She brought the draught to his lips and forced him to swallow it. After a time, his breaths became more even and his head lolled back.

The attendant returned with the instruments. Lucas helped take off John's armor. John had been wounded before in the North, but none as bad as these. Lucas cringed as he worked the plates of armor around the arrows studding his body. Magg tore open John's tunic with a sharp knife and pulled it off his chest and shoulders. The arrow wounds were deep and crimson. She used a small scalpel to remove the arrow tips. Even in sleep, John writhed, even when Lucas brought more wine to his lips.

"Hold him steady," Magg said. "He's moving too much."

Lucas pushed down on John's shoulders. Every breath from John brought a new rivulet of blood flowing down his skin out of the open wounds. *How are you still alive, my friend? And why? Why not just leave this pain and go to the saints?*

"This arrow narrowly missed his left lung." Magg gingerly opened the flesh and smeared some of the poultice inside the deep gash. Her long fingers were now covered in blood, as was her white smock. She looked up at Lucas. "You knew him well?"

"He was my squire before he became a knight," Lucas murmured. "It was one of the bloodiest things I've ever seen, our war in the North."

John groaned lightly at the sting of the poultice. Magg rummaged through her tools and prepared a blunt needle and thread. The attendant returned with more water and wine. Magg took a seat by the bed as she began washing John's wound.

"If he cries out, give him some wine." Magg said. "Even with the sleeping draft, this will hurt."

Lucas nodded and knelt by John's head. He didn't watch the physician at her work. Though he was a seasoned fighter, he could never stand the sight of open wounds. The wound on his own leg had made him faint more than once.

John flinched occasionally as Magg stitched, but his face remained expressionless. Lucas suddenly found tears springing to his eyes as he looked down at his friend. John was the strongest man Lucas knew. This couldn't be how he died.

"Are you all right, sir?" asked Magg, who had looked up briefly from her work.

Lucas sniffled, embarrassed. "Yes," he said. "I just hope you're doing everything you can."

"I am."

Magg continued to work quickly, her thin fingers sliding the needle through flesh. Her face was stoic, concentrated, even as she spoke.

"I treated him many times when he was a boy. He was often sick, as you know. And he often had...strange injuries, as if he'd been beaten. He said the bigger boys would hurt him, but I never fully believed that." Magg paused. "I saw how terrified of his father he was."

"He wouldn't have let the bigger boys beat him." Lucas laughed. "*I* wouldn't have. When I was wounded on the battlefield, he ran back and pulled me out even after we'd retreated. He was only seventeen. I knighted him that day, though he was so young. I have four older brothers, but John has been more like a brother to me than any of them."

The final stitch was set. Magg leaned back in her chair, craning her neck in an exhausted stretch.

"It's done," she said with a heavy sigh. She wiped her hands on her smock. "I will bandage his wounds and let him rest."

"When do you think he'll wake up?"

Magg shook her head. "I don't know," she said. Concern crossed her face. "Young man, get some rest. If you're like any of the guards, you've been up all night. Sleep."

Exhaustion hit Lucas all at once as she said the words. He'd been tense as he'd held John down, waited for Magg to finish stitching. He realized how tired he truly was. If he went back to the barracks, it wouldn't be quiet enough to sleep—or it would be too quiet. And if he closed his eyes, he still wouldn't sleep. Even though his mind was tired, his body was ready. Ready for the outlaws to attack or the Men of the Lion to storm the palace. Ready to be given orders. He headed for the courtyard to see if there was anything else to be done.

It had stopped snowing sometime that morning, but the sky remained a pall of clouds. Drifts of snow crowded every corner of the courtyard. Muddy, slushy footprints tracked chaotically everywhere else. More sentries lined the walls. The portcullis was shut. One of the gatekeepers had been killed in the night. Lucas knew that had something to do with Adelaide's escape, but couldn't imagine Adelaide herself killing him.

Lucas drew a shuddering breath. Edwin was dead. They had thrown his body on the cart with all the others and sent it off to saints-knew-where. It wouldn't be the last cart to leave Southborn either. The last directive Edwin had received was to kill all Men of the Lion. Who would pass that sentence now, Lucas wondered. Was it up to *him,* as a former commander of the king's armies? And with what men? Many of them were wounded or exhausted, including himself.

A shout rang out from the top of the wall, and the portcullis creaked open. A carriage clattered up the cobblestones, rolling as fast as its horse could pull it. The big animal's nostrils flared, its breath steaming white, its mouth foaming. It had been ridden hard to get there.

Lucas thought the carriage looked familiar, but didn't place it until the large woman emerged from inside of it. It was Lady Pauline, Adelaide's aunt. Lucas had never seen her move faster. Her driver came down from his seat and helped her move a small bundle from the carriage. Whatever the bundle was, it was wrapped tightly in blankets and cloaks. A braid of chestnut hair slipped loose from the bundle. A pale, almost white face appeared among the blankets.

Though his leg roared in pain, Lucas limped down the stairs as quickly as he could toward Lady Pauline. The woman's face was stern, her mouth a straight line. Determined.

"My lady," Lucas said as he approached. "Is she alright?"

Pauline didn't hesitate. "She's very cold. Too cold," she said. "I fear his grace will not like her presence here in the palace."

"To Innermost Hell with what his grace thinks," Lucas said. He took Adelaide from Pauline. She was indeed cold. Lucas felt her trembling, even while unconscious. "Let's get her warm."

Antony

Antony opened his eyes to darkness. Wherever he was, it was completely silent, unlike his violent dreams. They had all been about Adelaide.

His chest was in immense pain. He wasn't as cold—he was wrapped in furs—but he could barely breathe for the stinging deep in his lungs.

He sensed someone near him and tried to crane his neck to see if there was another person with him. In the darkness he made out the faint outline of a man's face. He still did not know where he was. It was cool and smelled of earth; he imagined it was a cave.

"Who's there?" he asked, his voice barely a whisper.

"Carter," replied the man in a broken voice. He had been crying.

"You found me," Antony said.

"You found *us*," Carter said. "It was some kind of miracle. We were on our way to camp, and...well, there you were."

Antony's eyes began to adjust and he saw a dim gray light behind Carter's figure. He felt the ground beneath him. He was laying near the stone wall of the cavern, a cloak drawn over him. He tried to sit up, but a strong hand gently pushed him back down.

"Stay still for a while," Carter said. "I'm not going to lie to you, brother. You're in bad shape."

"You don't have to tell me that," Antony said. He chuckled once, realizing it hurt too much. "Carter?"

Carter sniffed and wiped his nose. "Yeah?" he asked brusquely.

"I'm sorry," he said. "I'm sorry for everything."

Carter nodded. He was quiet for a long time.

"You should be," he said, and nothing more.

Another shadow entered the cave, just past Carter's shoulder. "How is he?" asked the voice. It was Malcolm.

"I'm awake," Antony said.

Malcolm rushed to his side. "If you breathe another word, boy, I'll put a hole in your other lung. You need to rest." He began adjusting Antony's bandages. Each movement sent a stinging pain down Antony's skin. "This is going to hurt. I need to make sure your lung hasn't collapsed. Your breathing makes it sound like it has."

Antony was silent. He realized his breaths were coming shallow. He could barely fill his lungs. He leaned his head back, overcome with exhaustion. As he breathed, he realized guiltily that it would be easy to die at that moment—he was just so *tired*. But a thought sprung into his head.

"Where's Adelaide?"

Adelaide

She woke up feeling surprisingly warm, almost hot. A heavy weight on her chest and body—blankets. Their fabric scratched her skin, all of her skin. She was naked under them. When she opened her eyes, she saw a dark room and smelled smoke. She heard the crackling of a fire. Was she home? Was this her manor by the sea?

"Adelaide?" asked a woman's voice. For one delirious moment, Adelaide wondered if she'd arrived in First Heaven, if her mother was there somewhere beside her. But when she turned, she saw the formidable figure of Aunt Pauline at the bedside.

"Adelaide, thank all the saints," Pauline said. Adelaide saw tears glistening in her firelit eyes. "It was some miracle of heaven that I found you out there in that storm on my way back to Easthempton. His grace had told me I couldn't see you before I left."

Adelaide couldn't say anything. She became aware of the weight on her little finger, her wedding ring. Lady Adelaide Highmoor. Was she a lady anymore? And where was she? And where was Antony?

She lifted her hands. When she was in the forest, they had begun to turn blue. They were wrapped in cloth bandages now, and felt raw and chapped underneath. In the darkness, Pauline reached out and took one of them, placing it gently back on her lap.

"My dear girl," Pauline said. To Adelaide's surprise, she began to weep. "My dear girl."

They remained that way for a long time, Pauline holding Adelaide's hand, Adelaide laying in the darkness with her mind full of questions. Her eyes

471

explored the room further. A familiar chamber, a familiar hearth—they were in Southborn. In the palace.

"Why are we here?" Adelaide asked.

Pauline must have heard the fear in her voice. "Don't worry, my dear." She squeezed Adelaide's hand. "I have spoken with the king—one of many conversations, I am sure." She sniffled away the rest of her tears, sat up a little straighter. "I have pleaded with him for you to keep your lands and titles provided that you no longer...fraternize with the Men of the Lion." She looked at Adelaide pointedly at this. "You and your husband may go on your way to Highmoor, once Lord John has recovered."

"Recovered?" Adelaide grimaced. That couldn't be true. *My husband is dead,* she thought. *I killed him.*

Pauline shook her head. "He is in the infirmary as we speak," she said. "It may be many months before he recovers. He may never be the same."

Adelaide said nothing for a moment. The arrows. The wounds. How easily they had pierced his flesh—how easily *she* had shot him.

"It was me. I shot the arrows. I watched him...watched him fall."

Pauline's eyes grew wide as she studied Adelaide's face with intensity. "Say nothing of it. Never again," she said. She glanced toward the door with a flicker of fear.

"But John—when he wakes up...he saw me. He knows it was me."

Pauline patted Adelaide's hand. The firelight glinted off her face, highlighting the crags and wrinkles on her skin. Adelaide never realized how gentle her aunt's eyes were. They were the same color as her father's.

"...Perhaps Lord John may never wake up."

Tanor

Tanor was just as shocked as Lady Pauline when he entered the inner room of the infirmary. Her shock brought her to her feet with a curtsy, but she maintained her composure as she always had. None of the events of the last few days had seemed to shake her. She was still immaculately dressed in one of her voluminous gowns, not a single hair out of place on her head.

"Your grace," she said hastily. "I beg your pardon. I was merely seeing how my new nephew was getting along. He looks well."

Tanor glanced down at John's body. He was pale. His face looked like a skull in the dim light.

"From what I understand, it may be a few days before he wakes up," Tanor said. "And it may be several weeks or even months before he and Lady Adelaide can depart for Highmoor."

Pauline seemed to relax a bit. "So I take it, your grace, that my payment was sufficient enough for Lady Adelaide's freedom?"

Tanor turned slightly toward her with a slight smile. "For now, yes," he said. It delighted him to see her flinch at his words. *For now.* Easthempton was a profitable lordship. Having Pauline under his thumb would prove lucrative, and she seemed to know it, too. She would do anything for her niece, it seemed, to keep her from ruin. Lady Pauline's only weakness was her love for her family.

Pauline cleared her throat. "The physician—I don't recall her name—"

"Magg."

"Yes, her. She told me to give him more of the sleeping draft if he begins

473

to stir."

Tanor nodded slowly. John lay still like a dead man on the sheets. "You may go, my lady. I would like some time alone with my son."

"Are you sure, your grace?" Lady Pauline made no move for the door. "It is no trouble to sit with him. I'm sure you've gotten very little sleep, and—"

"Thank you, my lady," Tanor said, giving her a sharp look. She withered again, but only slightly. She glanced once at John, then at the lone bottle on the table by his bed. The sleeping draft, Tanor presumed.

"Your grace," Pauline curtsied deeply, her skirts ballooning around her like the bloom of a great flower. "I am eternally grateful to you and your... benevolence." She left without another word.

The winter sky grew dark outside. New snow pattered on the window-panes, each landing with a soft, heavy thud. The only light offered to Tanor was the small candle on the stand by the bed. They cast grim, craggy shadows on John's sleeping face. It was a simple room, whitewashed and swept clean, with only the bed, table, and chairs for furniture.

Tanor watched John's chest rise and fall, listened to his deep, heavy breaths, examined every detail of his face. His eyes fell on a faint scar on John's cheek, still visible after a decade. It was fairly small, the size of a gemstone. Tanor looked down at the jeweled ring on the little finger of his left hand. Tanor had forgotten why he had struck John. It hadn't been the first or the last time, but somehow that scar remained.

John was the only one who truly knew now. Edwin was dead—the only other witness. Tanor's lords still believed what he told them. The lie was still intact, but barely. As far as he knew, Antony—Adrian—was still alive. One word from John, one word claiming that what Antony said at his trial was true, and all the vile things he had done would be exposed.

A dead man could carry a secret to his grave. A buried boy has no story to tell.

John looked like a ghost, as if the shadow of death were already cast over his face. Tanor's hands trembled, but he knew there was strength in them yet. *I could sentence him to death when he is recovered. I could find some reason to have him killed. Someone else could do it. There's always someone else to do it.*

Where had this hesitation been when he'd killed Claudia? He cursed himself. *They would never accuse me of murder, and if they did, they could be easily gotten rid of.* He eyed John's neck. Tanor's heart beat heavily in his chest.

You don't need him anymore. You don't love him, he convinced himself. *You never wanted a child like him. He'll be weak from now on, anyway. Weak like he was as a boy. Bury him.*

He rested his hands on John's neck. The flesh was warm, the pulse strong. *Press down. Squeeze. Do it. End it.*

Tanor felt a strong grip on his arm. John drew in a deeper breath, breaking the rhythm of sleep. The movement had roused him, and his soldier's reflexes grabbed Tanor's wrist before it could move.

Tanor immediately withdrew his hands as John began to stir. Tanor quickly settled back in the chair beside the bed, waiting, breathing slowly to calm his beating heart.

"John?" Tanor murmured quietly. He touched John's arm and shook it slightly. His hands still trembled. "John?"

John's eyes opened, wandering in the darkness until they found Tanor's grim outline, the hand resting on his arm. He attempted to turn his head toward Tanor. The effort was strenuous for his weak body.

"What are you—" His voice was dry and cracked. Tanor could hardly hear him.

"Save your strength, son," Tanor said innocently, trying to sound compassionate.

John sighed heavily, glancing down at the bandages on his chest. "I'm alive," he said simply.

"Thank all the saints," Tanor replied.

"You—" John paused, as though remembering what had awakened him. He put a hand on his throat as though remembering something there. His eyes returned to Tanor's face, searching. *My eyes,* Tanor thought. *As blue and clear as sea glass.*

Tanor stood suddenly. He cleared his throat and tried not to break apart under John's accusing stare. *Now I'm the one withering,* he thought, and hated himself for it.

"What are you doing here?" John asked, his voice slightly sharper, stronger.

"I merely wanted to see how you were faring." Tanor said. He knew John didn't believe him and he was afraid. "How are you feeling?"

"Tired." John replied curtly.

"Of course," Tanor saw an opportunity to escape. "You should rest. You have a long road of healing ahead of you."

John's eyes glowed with anger in the dim candlelight. "Whatever you came here to do, you should have done it when you had the chance. I'd rather be in Innermost Hell than here with you."

"John—"

"You should go."

Tanor breathed an inward sigh of relief. He made his way to the door without seeming hurried. As his hand landed on the doorknob, John's voice stopped him again.

"I did all of this for you." There was a strong energy in his voice now. "You caused this. You caused *all* of this."

Tanor turned and saw that he was slowly, laboriously trying to get up, propping himself on one elbow and rising to a sitting position as he spoke. He was stronger than Tanor thought. He could see every muscle working, pulsing with strength. No wonder he survived the North, Tanor realized. He tore his way out of it.

"You would rather Adrian be on the throne? And Adelaide his queen?" Tanor felt his own ire rising. John was strong, but he was still an idiot. "Is that what you want? I gave you every opportunity to have what you wanted, and you destroyed it all. You failed every time I asked you to do something. By all the saints, you couldn't even kill him yourself."

John was silent for a moment. He leaned against his elbows, breathing slowly. He gazed steadily down at the bandages on his body, wrapped around him as though he were already a corpse.

"I didn't want to become your pawn in your plot to destroy the throne," he said. "Did you ever think for a moment that maybe I've always done what you've asked because—"

His voice broke, and he stopped. He was sitting up now, his bare feet on the floor. A cold hand clutched at Tanor's heart as his bastard looked up at him.

"Tell me," John said quietly. "Is there anything I could've done that would've made you love me?"

Tanor didn't respond. He stared at John, speechless, frozen. Because he knew the answer and didn't want to say it.

Slowly John stood, wincing slightly as he bent forward to rise. He handled his right arm gingerly, mindful of the wound. "There's no chance of that now. You've made me a murderer."

A whisper of fear rose in Tanor's chest. *He's got nothing to lose now.* He knew that even a wound wouldn't stop John from tearing his father limb from limb. But he was still malleable, Tanor thought. He craved something that he couldn't have.

"You followed along willingly," Tanor seethed. "That was all your own doing. You blindly followed me. Even then, you couldn't follow it through. You're too soft. What was I supposed to do? Soften you further by gorging you with love?"

He could see the anger rising. John trudged painfully toward him. Tanor saw the power in his eyes, barely concealing his rage.

"I didn't ask to be born," he said, his voice low. "I didn't ask to be your son. The least you could have done was be my father."

Tanor fumbled for words but none came. He was frightened as John backed him toward the wall.

"Instead of being your son, I was your weapon," he said. A tear snaked down his cheek. "After everything I've done for you..."

Tanor found that fear choked his words back—fear he'd never felt before.

"J—John, please, it was never like that. It was never—"

"Then what was it?" John roared. Veins popped in his neck. "What was it, if not hatred? Admit it. All you know how to do is hate. *Admit it!*"

Tanor squinted and looked past John. To his horror, someone else was in the room with them. She hadn't been there before. And she shouldn't have been there.

Her face terrified him more than John's did.

"Claudia?"

John grimaced and looked behind him. "What are you talking about? Claudia is—" He grunted suddenly and winced in pain.

Tanor looked to the corner. Claudia was gone.

Blood seeped through John's bandages and he bent double. As he backed away from Tanor, the door opened and Lady Pauline appeared again.

"What's going on? I heard shouting and—" She saw John and immediately rushed to his side, supporting him as she led him back to the bed. "Good saints—what are you doing—he should not be out of bed. I'll give him his draught immediately." S

She gently guided the big man back to the bed, where John collapsed gratefully. Tanor had already left the room.

Antony

A utumn was his favorite time of year. Not the dusky, gray, pre-winter days, but the days that were still vibrant, alive and sunny, even as the leaves died. Golden light illuminated leaves that seemed to be made of sunlight, warming his face. They fluttered in a gentle breeze, almost sparkling with joy. He could almost smell the cool ripeness of the ground, feel the leaves crackle at his feet. The forest in autumn was more beautiful than any cathedral or castle.

He stood at the riverbed below the ridge. The water looked welcoming and serene, gently swirling around rocks and carrying dead leaves like tiny boats. The wet season had not come yet, when the river would be swollen and raging. It burbled against the shore, whispering to the branches and pebbles and soil.

It felt real. But he knew it wasn't. Even in his dreams he felt the sting of pain every time he breathed from the wound John gave him. But he wanted it to be real. He could have stood there forever. Perhaps he would. Perhaps this was First Heaven.

Someone stood on the opposite side of the river. A handsome, bearded man with dark hair and regal clothes. A face so familiar but so foreign to him, but still Adrian knew. It was his father. He wore what he'd been wearing on the day he died—a brilliant tunic with the device of their house emblazoned on it—a proud lion. The man's face broke into a smile. There was no crown on his head.

Slowly, Alfred walked toward him, stepping into the river shallows. The water reached his knees as he crossed toward Adrian. His long velvet cloak dragged in the water.

Adrian walked toward him through the peaceful shallows of the river and met *him in the middle. Alfred watched him fondly.*

"You've grown," Alfred said. "You're a man now. And I'm proud of you. I've watched you all these years. I've called your name while you slept. Your mother and I have not forgotten you, even here in the stars. You've made a path for yourself—you've become your own man. You've chosen for yourself who you are going to be."

"I've made a mess," Adrian said. "So many people have died because of me."

Alfred shook his head. "People die for what they believe in," he said. "And they believe in you. You've become more than I could have ever hoped for you."

"An outlaw," Adrian said.

"A legend," Alfred said.

"But not a king."

"Not yet. I was born a king. So were you, I suppose. But now, you must be made a king. Do what Tanor has not done—earn the trust of your people. Give them something to fight for."

Adrian wanted to go with him. He was so tired. He wanted to talk with his father for hours, but he already felt Alfred pulling away.

"I love you," Alfred said, his voice strong. "I wish I'd had more time."

Adrian blinked and his father was walking away up the steep slope on the other side of the river. He disappeared into the radiant light of the midday sun as quickly as he appeared. What was he supposed to do now? He longed to follow Alfred up that steep slope, but his legs wouldn't move. He tried calling out to his father, but he couldn't speak.

"Adrian," said a voice behind him.

Adrian turned. There stood Adelaide, her face radiant in the autumn light. She was robed in a milk-white dress, her chestnut hair framing her beaming face. In her hands, she held a crown—the crown his father wore, the crown Tanor now wore. His crown.

"We need you here," she said. "I need you here. Fight for me. Fight for us. Kneel."

Awestruck by her, Adrian knelt into the cool water. Adelaide placed the crown on his head.

Everything I need is still here.

"Rise, King Adrian," Adelaide said, her voice low and proud. Adrian stood and beheld her again. He couldn't believe she was there. She leaned forward and kissed him, cradling his face in her hands. He held her as tightly as he could, feeling the realness of her under his fingers, the warmth of her lips. Lips that tasted of strawberries.

I will love her while I have time...

Antony stirred, feeling the sharp pain near his ribs once again. He breathed shallowly to avoid the sting. He opened his eyes and looked around. It was cold. It had snowed in the South.

But he could breathe.

"Antony?" A voice whispered nearby. Antony saw Ellena's shape hovering near him in the dark. "Thank the saints. How do you feel?"

Antony grunted in response. He tried to sit up more, but movement only made the searing pain worse. A gentle hand landed on his shoulder.

"Try not to move too much," Ellena said. "It will take a long time for you to heal. Malcolm did his best. Your ring—the lion sigil. Antony, he had to melt it down. It's covering your wound. Your lung was tore wide open."

"Where's..." Antony whispered. "Where's Adelaide?"

"We don't know," she said slowly.

Antony lay back again. All of the air was knocked out of his body. *She was* here, he thought. *She was just here. I was just holding her.*

"And Carter is gone, too," Ellena continued. "He said he...he just can't do this anymore.. He was very angry. I don't know where he went. It's just you, me, Pa, Ben—and whoever's left from the Men of the Lion."

He didn't respond. He sighed heavily, thinking of his strange dream. Of course it was only a dream. From the beginning, his task had been impossible.

"What are we going to do now?" Ellena asked, looking around the cave.

You will be made a king, his father had said. How could he be made a king with so little? His own brother had abandoned him. So many who had fought for him were dead. Even Adelaide was gone.

Ellena looked at him expectantly. Agonizing pain shot through his body as he sat up.

"Antony, what are you doing—"

"Help me."

Ellena hesitated, but then sighed and grabbed his arms. It seemed like an eternity before he was on his feet. His body felt old and heavy, not his own. He gingerly touched his chest, felt the ring—what had once been his ring—covering the wound, keeping him alive.

He shuffled out of the cave, bent double like an old man, while Ellena held onto his arm. They walked together into the searing winter light. The sun had come out and bathed the bare trees and white ground with light, light that made the world too bright. As Antony blinked away the shock, he looked around their camp.

There were more than before, not less.

He looked around and saw Men of the Lion who had joined them days before, but he saw families, too. Malcolm knelt in front of a small girl, feeling her forehead and offering her a steaming bowl of broth. Herne spoke to an older man and woman nearby. The couple looked haggard and scared.

Herne's eye caught Antony's. The older man all but sprinted to his side. "Aug's beard, boy," he said, coming up to Antony's other side to keep him upright. "What are you doing back from the dead?"

"Who are these people?" Antony said. He realized he must have looked a sight. The cold air burned the bare skin of his chest and arms.

"The king has not stopped his attacks on the Men of the Lion," Herne said. "Families have found their way here for safety."

The little girl was staring at Antony, her eyes wide and unblinking. She stood up and pushed past Malcolm, running up to where Antony, Herne, and Ellena stood.

"Is it you?" she asked. "Are you the prince that was lost?"

The crowd of strangers around Antony were looking at him now, too— some with shock, some with fear, some with joy. He looked at each of them.

"You're the spitting image of him, your grace," said the man who had been talking to Herne. "How did we not see it before?"

Antony desperately wanted to retreat into the darkness of the cave, the warmth of the blankets. Every inch of him hurt.

But this is how you are made a king, he thought.

"I was the prince that was lost," he said. "And then I was Antony Bronson. Some call me the *Vispilio*—the thief by night. Many people have died for me. They died for me when I was a prince. They died for me when I was a pretender. Both of the men that I called father died for me. Men of the Lion have died in the name of Prince Adrian. They believed he would come back and take the crown once again, to bring justice to an unjust world.

"I've failed to do that." He lowered his eyes to the white earth. His bare feet burned in the icy snow. "I don't want anyone else to die for me. I want you to *live*. Live here. Live freely. I vow on the lives of King Alfred and Bronwell Bowyer that I will serve you, protect you, and, if need be, die for you. I will be your king if you will have me—until we are strong enough to return to where we belong. But for now, we build our kingdom here. I won't ask you to go where I follow. But I'll do my best to lead you somewhere worth following."

Winter silence pierced the air. A blue sky peered out from the white clouds above. The snow glittered with the daylight. Looking out at the ragged throng in front of him, spread out across the white blanket of earth, Antony felt as though he were looking upon something holy. Something new.

A man that Antony didn't know bowed, burying his knee in the cold deep. The woman beside him did the same. Like a great sea wave, others bowed alongside them. The wave continued until everyone, including Herne and Ellena, were on their knees. Despite his pain, Antony felt sudden energy rush through him as Herne's earnest dark eyes looked up to meet his.

"We will follow where you lead, your grace."

Tanor

Tanor's heart raced as he returned to his chamber and slumped in a chair in front of the fire. He quickly poured and downed a goblet of wine, staring steadily at the flames so he didn't have to look anywhere else in the room.

It wasn't his encounter with John that so disturbed him. It was when he looked away from John and saw someone standing in the corner of the room. She stood there, as real as he was, staring at him. Claudia. She wore her white nightgown over her sumptuous figure, but her swan-like neck was etched with bruises. Despite that, she stared at him placidly, and he almost thought he saw a smile playing at the corners of her lips.

He downed another goblet of wine. He knew she couldn't have actually been there. It wasn't possible. She was in some churchyard, cold and buried. He would have to consult the physician in the morning. Magg would probably give him some sort of medicine, tell him he was under too much stress and needed to rest.

Tanor's eyes became heavy. He leaned back in his chair and closed them, letting the wine and warmth of the fire dull his senses toward sleep. When was the last time he'd fully slept? He couldn't remember. He barely remembered seeing Claudia in the corner of the room…had she said something to him?

You did this to me.

He opened his eyes with a start, feeling the drowsiness of sleep but not remembering having fallen asleep. The fire was all but burnt out, and the room was cold. He must have slept well into the night and not realized it.

Yes, he must have, he thought, feeling the stiffness in his neck.

He leaned back to doze again when an icy hand grabbed his shoulder. He sat bolt upright and clung to his chair. Turning his head cautiously, he watched a tall figure come around his chair and face him. Tanor looked up until he met the empty stare of his own flesh and blood.

John's face was a pallid white, apart from his gray, sunken eye sockets. On his tunic was a bloodstain from his torn stitches.

Suddenly, John's cold hand seized Tanor's throat and pulled him out of his chair. Tanor was still trying to determine if he was dreaming or not. The pressure around his neck felt real. He couldn't breathe.

"You did this to me," John whispered, his face remaining expressionless. *"You did this to me."*

Tanor bolted awake. Light crept through the windows, and he blinked into the brightness. A servant was drawing back the curtains, humming a small tune to herself. She turned and noticed him.

"Good morning, your grace," she said with a curtsy. "Sir Lucas is outside in the hall. May I let him in?"

"Certainly," Tanor said groggily, straightening in his chair. He felt sore as he turned and saw Lucas limping into the room. It appeared the last three days had aged Lucas significantly. He probably had gotten little sleep either.

"Your Majesty," he said. "I've come to tell you that…your son died in the night."

Tanor sat ramrod-straight. "Charles?" he asked.

"No, your grace. Sir John. It was after his stitches reopened. The Lady Pauline gave him a tincture that Magg said would help, but…it didn't seem to do anything."

Tanor didn't react, but he felt Lucas' words deep inside of him. They terrified him, but also strangely relieved him. John was gone. And Tanor didn't have to do it himself.

"Very well," he said quietly. "Bury the body as you see fit. I know he was a good friend to you."

"Yes, your grace."

Lucas left without another word

Tanor leaned back and closed his eyes, unsure of what to do with the information that was delivered to him. Tanor wondered where John's mother was—she hadn't died, as he'd told John, and she hadn't been a whore. She'd been a highborn lady, young and inexperienced. He'd been young too, he supposed, and far too idle and bored. He had intended it as one night of half-drunk passion—a night they both seemed to enjoy. He had already been married to another woman for over a year. His wife hanged herself in their bedroom not long after John was born and left at their manor house—as though she couldn't bear to raise a child who wasn't her own.

He opened his eyes.

Once again, as clear as day, John stood in front of him, dripping with blood. Tanor bolted out of his chair and blinked.

John was gone.

"Lucas?" he called. Silence. "Lucas!"

He ran out of the room, darting around the castle, looking for the young man. Anyone who saw the king running about the castle barefoot and screaming would have thought he'd gone mad.

He found Lucas in the inner room of the infirmary. There was a litter on the floor, and Lucas and an attendant were preparing to lift a long, prostrate body wrapped in cloth off the bed. Lucas turned at the sound of his name.

"Your grace." He looked surprised to see Tanor there. "We are taking him to the brotherhood in Dallen with the rest—"

"Let me see his face." Tanor blurted.

"Your grace—"

"Show me his damn face!"

Lucas cowered back in shock, then knelt and pulled the cloth back.

There was John. Pale face, sunken eyes, their lids closed. Tanor swallowed back vomit. John's face seemed strangely peaceful. He stared at the face until Lucas replaced the shroud.

Why am I now seeing the dead?

Seeing that Tanor had nothing else to say, Lucas and his men lifted the litter and carried John to his rest.

Tanor spent the rest of the day in his chamber, brooding. Magg came in and examined him.

"You've been dealt a heavy blow, Your Majesty," she said. "It is not uncommon for lack of sleep to lead to hallucinations. Drink less wine before bed and you may sleep more peacefully."

Tanor downed several goblets of wine after Magg left—anything to dull his racing thoughts. Magg didn't understand. These weren't dreams or hallucinations. *I'm going mad. No one can know.* He paced constantly, sometimes sitting, then bolting upright again.

As the day darkened, Tanor realized how tired he truly was—a deep exhaustion in his bones. He sat on the edge of his bed. Maybe it was the wine, maybe the warmth of the room, but he felt suddenly at peace. He took a deep breath and laid back, acutely aware of how soft the bed was.

When he opened his eyes again, he felt somewhat more rested. More like himself. The idea of having seen Claudia, even of having seen John, seemed laughable. Just strange, waking dreams, borne out of exhaustion. He stretched and sat up.

He had dreamed again, he realized as his mind became more awake. It had been a long time since he'd dreamt of the monster in the forest.

You are not the only Unburied Boy. Those same words. The words of the blind woman. Unburied Boy. Because Adrian had not died that night. Had not been buried. John had failed in that task. Someone had found Adrian instead and hidden him away for ten years.

Tanor bolted upright. The monster had been there that night—but it hadn't been a monster at all. Someone had *watched* him that night.

He made to get out of bed, but stopped cold when he saw the king.

Alfred stood in front of him, as alive as he was on his last day. Wearing the same clothes he'd worn. A deep, bloody hole in his chest that he didn't seem to notice.

"Where's my son, Tanor?" he asked. It was him. It was his voice. Tanor blinked, but Alfred remained. "You promised me you'd take care of him should anything happen to me."

Tanor was mute with terror. He stared up at his old friend, who smiled down at him. Antony *did* look like him—alarmingly so.

"Be wary of your deeds done in the dark, Your Majesty." Alfred's voice suddenly changed. "For they may all too soon be brought to light."

"I don't know what you mean."

Alfred shook his head and laughed. "You do," he said. "And soon everyone else will too. It's only a matter of time. Secrets rot, just like corpses. And then, they start to reek."

Tanor was quickly becoming angry. *The audacity of him. What right has he to—*

"There is blood on your hands, your grace. Not only your son's, but your first queen's, and her child's. Your wife's. Your lover's. All the men you sent to battle in the North—that was your doing, wasn't it? And there's one more, isn't there?"

Alfred pressed a hand on his wound and turned the palm toward Tanor. It glistened with fresh, dark blood.

"Your grace, you have an army of death behind you. I doubt you can hide from them for long."

"Have you come to kill me?" Tanor asked.

Alfred shook his head. "No," he said. "Adrian will come for you soon enough."

Tanor swallowed. Somehow, he knew Alfred wasn't really there, but it didn't seem to matter. The more he stared, the more real he became.

"You made one fatal mistake, Tanor," Alfred said. "You know that, and you'll die for it. You know full well that Antony is my son—the only one who got away from you that night. He's the only man on this earth with a legitimate claim to the throne. And I swear by all the saints, he will have it."

Tanor blinked, and Alfred was gone.

TANOR

IV

Epilogue

The Grave Digger

I f he hummed to himself, the cart seemed less heavy. His mind seemed less heavy.

He'd dug graves since he was a lad of fifteen, and the bodies had become like husks to him—nothing left of them but rotting meat. No different than an animal strung up in a butcher's window, his Pa always told him.

But tonight, in the bitter cold of the fading light, something felt different.

He pulled the cart down the dirt road to Dallen, to the brotherhood that lived there. The country out there was hilly and the cart was heavy with bodies from the skirmish that had happened in the Hemlock just a few days before, but he was strong. His hot breath pushed against the cold in deep plumes. Coldest winter in at least twenty years, he realized. The last time he'd seen snow, it had been the day before his wedding.

This cold held on. He wondered if the ground would be soft enough to put the boys to rest. He had three of them—two lords and a knight. One of them had been married recently too, the knight with the limp had told him. The grave digger said a prayer to Saint Aethel for the poor widow.

The monastery came into view as he crested another hill. The snowy slopes around the small church were purple and blue with the fading light of day, the bare trees of the Hemlock beyond. He liked Dallen. It had an aching beauty to it in every season. The people there kept to themselves, kept the beauty of their land a secret. The grave digger liked the brothers at the Monastery of Saint Morgan the best. They never looked down on him for touching the dead—something they would never do as holy men.

They invited him in for warm stew when his work was done.

The grave digger dropped the cart with a sigh when he reached the churchyard. Three bodies. Three holes. Cold ground. He took his spade out of the cart and started to dig. He never stopped humming.

The purple world became deep blue, then black, then silver as the moon rose and illuminated the grave digger's work. He buried the smallest body first, whispering a prayer to Saint Morgan as he did.

"For your fight, may you be honored. For the blood you spilled, may you be praised. May Saint Morgan welcome you to his hall where you will tell the stories of your victories forever. Let it be so."

The night wore on, and his shoulders ached. When he returned to Southborn, he hoped to sleep long into the day. But the city had been uneasy the last few weeks. A lot of bodies to bury. Friends of his dead or missing—one day his neighbor, the next a stranger. He said a prayer for himself—that he would be able to rest.

The third body was heavy, but the grave digger was strong. He dragged the husk to the hole he'd dug. In the darkness, the white of the winding-sheet was no different than the white of the snow around it. Just rotting meat, thought the grave digger. But he suddenly felt...not alone as he dragged the body. He never felt as though the husks watched him. He always felt alone.

He heaved the body into the hole. He never flinched when it landed at the bottom with a dead thud. This time he did. He stared down at the white mound of sheets at the bottom of the pit. He never did that. He usually buried them like a farmer sows seeds; without another thought of what he'd put in the ground. But he stared at this one.

The feeling of un-aloneness subsided after a while, and the familiar loneliness returned, warm and quiet. The grave digger hummed. He lifted a spadeful of cold earth and threw it down onto the winding sheets.

The husk at the bottom of the grave screamed in response.

Roderick

Somehow, over the din of the roaring squall that had blown in from the sea, Roderick Castell heard a knock at the front door of the manor.

Strange, he thought. Who would be out in this storm? Wintermonth was a notoriously stormy month at Highmoor, with winter winds blowing across the cliffs and bringing snow and ice that battered down on all their heads.

Roderick stood up from his comfortable place by the fire. He had expected the new lord and lady of Highmoor days before. Had they finally arrived? He'd heard from traveling merchants that the weather was also ill in Southborn—snow for the first time in decades.

He opened and shut the door quickly, allowing the visitor a few seconds to dart in from the cold before he bolted it shut again. A blast of icy air hit his face and he shivered.

"Saints, what a storm," he said to himself. He looked at the visitor. It was a small figure, wrapped in a cloak that was drenched in cold rain and ice. "Who are you, then?"

The visitor took off her cloak and revealed a young, freckled face with a long braid of chestnut hair. "My name is Lady Adelaide DuMont," she said. "My husband has died. I am the lady of this manor."

The Hunting Party

Lucas Widlowe relished the green smell of wet earth. He hadn't been on a true boar hunt in ten years, ever since he left for the North. The North—where the sun warmed nothing and the cold touched everything. Rainmonth in the South meant a warm, wet spring, lush with green.

Winter had been bad, the coldest Southborn had seen in years. It made many fear that spring would come cold as well. But as soon as Rainmonth dawned, it brought sunny days and blossoming carpets of wildflowers.

New buds grew heavy on the trees in the Hemlock Forest on the day of the hunt. The hounds were inconsolable—they had caught the scent of a boar somewhere near the Skeldergate River, just off the Weschurch Road. His grace seemed in good spirits, Lucas thought. Some had noticed the king seemed reclusive throughout the winter, and emerged thinner and more haggard, but his cheeks were red with merriment that day, and he had no problem swinging onto his great black horse and riding out with the hunting party. His new queen was due to arrive before First Summer. She was a beauty, according to the king. With her marriage brought a sizable dowry—one that the king promised would ease the Harvestmonth tax that year. After the wedding, Lucas would leave with Prince Charles to Baronskeep. That was his new assignment—he would be Charles' warden. His future seemed just as bright as the spring day.

The dogs charged through the underbrush, hot on the scent. This time of year, they probably found a sow in heat. Soon, the hunting party heard the snorts and squeals somewhere deep in the brush, and Lucas and some of his men charged after it while the rest of the party waited behind.

They came to a clearing where the dogs circled and sniffed upturned earth. A boar had been there, to be sure, and had rooted in the ground for truffles and moles. Lucas deflated. His spear had been ready. Hunting was something he could still do, even with his bad leg. He dismounted his horse and limped to the bank of the Skeldergate River, his heart still racing. Sunlight danced on the forest floor, warming the new green shoots and brambles that grew.

Lucas couldn't help but feel he was being watched in such a huge forest.

He knelt down to wash his face in the shallows of the river. One of the lean hounds joined him, lapping thirstily beside him. As Lucas rubbed water into his face, he heard the dog whine. It let out a frightened bark and skittered away through the brush.

Lucas wiped his eyes. In the rippling reflection of the water, he saw a form behind him, long and dark.

Before he could turn, he felt a prick like a bee sting on his neck. When he looked askance, he could see the shaft of an arrow, a strong fist gripping the handle of a bow.

"What are you doing here?" asked a low, flat voice.

Lucas turned cautiously and looked up. A hooded figure looked down at him, two coal-dark eyes staring from underneath a cowl. The face was determined, stubbled with a scant brown beard.

"Hunting." Lucas was surprised by how small his voice was.

"Is this a royal hunting party?" asked the outlaw.

Lucas thought it was a strange question to ask. "Yes," he replied.

The outlaw was silent for a long time, but didn't move the arrow from Lucas' neck.

"The king is with you, then," said the outlaw.

"Yes."

Another long pause. The river, swollen with melted snow and ice, burbled on. Robins chirped impatiently as they scouted the ground for worms. Somewhere beyond, the hounds bayed, on the scent again.

"Give King Tanor a message for me," said the *Vispilio*. "That the Hemlock

497

Forest is my kingdom, and I am its king. If he will not give me the crown I am owed, then I will build a kingdom of my own. And once it's built, he will have nowhere to turn."

Lucas reached for the hilt of his hunting dagger, but before he could draw it, the butt of the bow came down on his forehead.

When he came to, the outlaw was gone.

About the Author

Audrey D. DeBoer is a Grand Rapids, Michigan native and has been writing for as long as she could read. *Vispilio* is her debut novel. When she's not writing fiction, she's a marketing copywriter. DeBoer and her husband Jerry live in GR with their beloved cats, Scout and Mina.

You can connect with me on:

🌐 https://www.audreyddeboer.com